The Irish Short Story

A CRITICAL HISTORY

TWAYNE'S CRITICAL HISTORY OF THE SHORT STORY

William Peden, General Editor
University of Missouri-Columbia

The American Short Story, 1850—1900
> Donald Crowley, University of Missouri-Columbia

The American Short Story, 1900—1945
> Philip Stevick, Temple University

The American Short Story, 1945—1980
> Gordon Weaver, Oklahoma State University

The British Short Story, 1890—1945
> Joseph M. Flora, University of North Carolina-Chapel Hill

The British Short Story, 1945—1980
> Dennis Vannatta, University of Arkansas-Little Rock

The Irish Short Story
> James F. Kilroy, Vanderbilt University

The Latin American Short Story
> Margaret Sayers Peden, University of Missouri-Columbia

The Irish Short Story

A CRITICAL HISTORY

James F. Kilroy, Editor
Vanderbilt University

Twayne Publishers

The Irish Short Story
A Critical History

Copyright © 1984 by G. K. Hall & Company

All Rights Reserved

Published in 1984 by Twayne Publishers
A Division of G. K. Hall & Company
70 Lincoln Street, Boston, Massachusetts 02111

Printed on permanent/durable
acid-free paper and bound in
the United States of America

First Printing

Book production by Marne Sultz
Book design by Barbara Anderson

Typeset in 11 pt. Perpetua
by Compset, Inc. of Beverly, MA

Library of Congress Cataloging in Publication Data

Main entry under title:

The Irish short story.

Bibliography: p. 225
Includes index.
Contents: Chronology ; Introduction / James F.
Kilroy—Tales from big house and cabin / Gregory A.
Schirmer—In quest of a new impulse / James F.
Carens—[etc.]
1. Short stories, English—Irish authors—History
and criticism.   2. Ireland in literature.   I. Kilroy,
James F.
PR8804.I74   1984   823'.01'099415   84-670
ISBN 0-8057-9354-2

Contents

Chronology

1883 Birth of Padraic O'Conaire.

1891 Death of Parnell.

1893 Gaelic League founded by Douglas Hyde and Eoin MacNeill.

1895 *Celibates* by George Moore.

1895–1923 *The Irish Homestead* edited by George Russell (AE).

1896 Birth of Liam O'Flaherty.

1899 Irish Literary Theatre founded. Arthur Griffith founds *The United Irishman. Some Experiences of an Irish R. M.* by Edith Somerville and Martin Ross. Birth of Elizabeth Bowen.

1900 Birth of John Whelan (Sean O'Faolain). Birth of Paul Vincent Carroll.

1903 James Joyce's first stories appear in the *Irish Homestead. The Untilled Field* by George Moore. Birth of Michael O'Donovan (Frank O'Connor).

1904 June 16: Bloomsday.

1905 Birth of Patrick Boyle.

1906 *By the Stream of Killmeen* by Seumas O'Kelly. Birth of Samuel Beckett.

1907 Abbey Theatre riots at first production of Synge's *The Playboy of the Western World.* Birth of Michael McLaverty. Birth of Mairtin O'Cadhain.

1908 *Further Experiences of an Irish R. M.* by Edith Somerville and Martin Ross.

1909 Birth of Bryan MacMahon.

1911–1914 *The Irish Review* edited successively by David Houston, Padraic Colum, and Joseph Mary Plunkett.

1911 Birth of Brian O'Nolan (Flann O'Brien).

1912 Birth of Mary Lavin.

1913 *Here Are Ladies* by James Stephens.

1914–1918 World War I.

1914 Government of Ireland Act suspended. *Dubliners* by James Joyce.

1956 *The Patriot Son and Other Stories* by Mary Lavin.

1957 *Domestic Relations* by Frank O'Connor. Death of Lord Dunsany.

1958 *The Stories of Sean O'Faolain.*

1959 *Stories* by Elizabeth Bowen. *Selected Stories* by Mary Lavin.

1961 *The Great Wave and Other Stories* by Mary Lavin. *I Remember! I Remember!* by Sean O'Faolain.

1962 *The Lonely Voice* by Frank O'Connor.

1963 *A Journey to the Seven Streams* by Benedict Kiely.

1964 *The Stories of Mary Lavin,* volume 1. *Collection Two* by Frank O'Connor. Death of Brendan Behan. Death of Daniel Corkery.

1965 *A Day in the Dark and Other Stories* by Elizabeth Bowen.

1966 *The Heat of the Sun* by Sean O'Faolain. Death of Frank O'Connor. Death of Brian O'Nolan (Flann O'Brien).

1967 Civil rights movement formed in Belfast. *In the Middle of the Fields* by Mary Lavin. Death of Walter Macken.

1968 Death of Paul Vincent Carroll.

1969 British troops called into Northern Ireland. *Happiness and Other Stories* by Mary Lavin. *Collection Three* by Frank O'Connor.

1970 *New Irish Writing: 1,* edited by David Marcus. *Winter's Tales from Ireland: One,* edited by Augustine Martin. Death of Máirtín O'Cadhain.

1971 *Collected Stories* by Mary Lavin. *The Talking Trees and Other Stories* by Sean O'Faolain.

1972 *A Memory and Other Stories* by Mary Lavin. *Winter's Tales from Ireland: Two,* edited by Kevin Casey.

1973 Ireland enters the European Economic Community. *A Ball of Malt and Madame Butterfly: A Dozen Stories* by Benedict Kiely. Death of Elizabeth Bowen.

1974 *The Stories of Mary Lavin,* Volume 2.

1975 Death of Eamonn de Valera.

1976 *The Road to the Shore and Other Stories* by Michael McLaverty. *The End of the World and Other Stories* by Bryan MacMahon. *Foreign Affairs and Other Stories* by Sean O'Faolain. *The Pedlar's Revenge and Other Stories* by Liam O'Flaherty. *Best Irish Short Stories: 1*, edited by David Marcus. David Marcus founds Poolbeg Press.

1977 *The Shrine and Other Stories* by Mary Lavin. *Best Irish Short Stories: 2*, edited by David Marcus.

1978 *Collected Short Stories* by Michael McLaverty. *Best Irish Short Stories: 3*, edited by David Marcus.

1979 *Body and Soul*, edited by David Marcus.

1980 *The State of Ireland: A Novella and Seventeen Stories* by Benedict Kiely. *The Bodley Head Book of Irish Short Stories*, edited by David Marcus.

1981 *The Collected Stories of Elizabeth Bowen. The Coronet Player Who Betrayed Ireland* by Frank O'Connor. *Collected Stories* by Frank O'Connor. *Modern Irish Short Stories*, edited by Ben Forkner. *The Penguin Book of Irish Short Stories* edited by Benedict Kiely.

Introduction

The splendor of Irish culture has been frequently and deservedly proclaimed. The intricate designs of the Book of Kells and the Ardagh Chalice, the simple power of the high crosses and round towers, and the more ornate vestiges of the Romanesque cathedrals at Cashel and Clonfert testify to the artistic achievements of Ireland in the medieval period. Its literary history in the centuries that followed earned further acclaim for those writers who were born or resided there: Edmund Spenser, Edmund Burke, Jonathan Swift, Oliver Goldsmith, Richard Brinsley Sheridan, and others. But for nearly two centuries now, a distinct and impressive culture has developed in Ireland, one indebted to the glorious past but linked to contemporary history and influenced by intellectual thought of a new era. Among its finest products has been literature of such quality that in various genres modern Irish writers are unexcelled. The poetry of William Butler Yeats, the plays of John Millington Synge, Sean O'Casey, and Samuel Beckett, and the novels of James Joyce are superior examples of the new Irish literature. But in the genre of the short story, itself a creation of the past two centuries, an even greater level of artistic achievement has been reached. The excellence of James Joyce, Sean O'Faolain, Frank O'Connor, and Elizabeth Bowen is probably indisputable, and the merits of at least a dozen others are comparable, validating V. S. Pritchett's estimate that the short story is the form "in which Irish writers have traditionally excelled."[1]

Georgian Ireland was notable for its sophistication and artistic achievements, particularly in its capital city. Dublin's elegant squares and dignified public buildings still testify to its former splendor, while the record of illustrious playwrights, actresses, and actors centered in Smock Alley reveals its vitality. Beyond the Pale, the civilized English-speaking area, there were a dozen or more towns that achieved a level of economic prosperity and cultural sophistication. But modern Ireland was born when much of this elegant style departed from the island with the political union of Ireland with England and Scotland, the Act of Union which took effect on 1 January 1801. A nation's culture is conveyed by, and largely contained in, its language, and Irish had been the language of the great majority of the populace. But after the Act of Union, in the nineteenth century, that language was nearly eradicated, and a new English-speaking culture was formulated, one that was not provincial English but genuinely and expressively Irish.

Much of the stimulus in forming the new culture came from renewed interest in the ancient past, for in Ireland's years of political and artistic prosperity a certain national pride had developed. Such institutions as the Royal Irish Academy, founded in 1785, drew attention to the country's ancient culture and encouraged the careful study of antiquities, a subject that fascinated educated members of the gentry. This was, in England and in Ireland, the early phase of the romantic movement in which the antique and the primitive claimed intense attention. The immense popularity of Macpherson's Ossian reveals the popular fascination with what purported to be authentic ancient lore; inaccurate as it is, that book impelled others to examine the heroic Celtic past.

Modern Irish literature began, then, in the heyday of romantic fervor, and it exhibits the dominant characteristics of that literary movement for at least its first hundred years. In the verses of Thomas Moore and James Clarence Mangan, the best Irish poets of the nineteenth century, qualities of the romantic lyric are evident; immediate experience and the products of pure imagination are presented vividly in a tone of exaltation as the emanations of gifted, inspired genius. Such verse favors the most compact, organic forms and a tone of intensity rather than rational calm. Thus the romantic lyric is typically short, sometimes even fragmentary.

In this same period, a distinctive kind of abbreviated prose narrative first began to appear, and these early short stories resembled the romantic lyric in technique and tonal qualities. Like the romantic poets, their writers emphasized primitive experience and immediate sense impressions, and called attention to the art of narration. In fact, some stories contain specific features of the romantic lyric, such as extended and precise natural descriptions, a tendency toward circular structures, and a sustained meditative tone. Sean O'Faolain's "Fugue," published in 1932, more than a century after the first short stories, clearly exemplifies the short story as lyric. Descriptions of the dawn open and close the narrative, in which a determinate speaker comes to experience profound loss and recognize the futility of warfare. His meditations on his own experience lead to a sense of merging with nature and finally to an annihilation of self. From observing nature, the narrator proceeds to intimacy and integration with it, and then draws back to observation and a final overwhelming sense of alienation.

Coinciding with the extension of a reading public receptive to short fiction, the late eighteenth and early nineteenth centuries' interest in folktales, a taste for rural subjects, and a fascination with fear and other sublime effects nurtured the growth of the new genre of the short story. In fact, such elements are seen in the works that various critics have proposed as the first true short stories— the tales of Sir Walter Scott, Nathaniel Hawthorne, and Edgar Allan Poe. Without entering the critical controversy over which author wrote the very first short story, we can note familiar and distinguishing ingredients of the new literary form in various narratives written in Ireland during the nineteenth century. In the many stories of William Carleton may be found extended descriptions of rural scenery, reproductions of dialect, and a fascination with discord and revolution; in James Clarence Mangan's few tales, a Poe-like obsession with exotic settings and mysterious events; and in the Gothic tales of Joseph Sheridan Le Fanu and Charles Robert Maturin, even more vivid expressions of mystery and terror.

But most distinctive of all the romantic elements seen in these short stories is the prominence given to the artist, poet, narrator, or writer. Mimetic and didactic considerations are made subsidiary to the expressive force of the storyteller. For this reason, Maria Edgeworth's *Castle Rackrent* may be regarded as the very first Irish short story; what distinguishes it from the score of moral tales she later wrote is its vivid presentation of a sharply defined narrating figure. Through Thady Quirk, a limited, biased reporter, Edgeworth presents her convictions on such issues as the need to reform a property system that allowed irresponsibility in absentee landlords. At the same time, Quirk's failure to interpret and assess what he narrates makes the reader aware of Edgeworth's superior insight. Yet flawed as he is, Thady is not merely a mouthpiece but a narrator who evokes a human response. In this regard he resembles the narrators of numerous Irish short stories that followed. Somerville and Ross's Irish Resident Magistrate and Frank O'Connor's personified narrators, variously named Larry or Michael John, are representative; but even the less distinguishable narrators of certain stories by James Joyce, Edna O'Brien, and Mary Lavin command a reader's attention. Their narrative voices typically manifest conviction and confidence: they have *authority,* investing their narratives with such importance that they demand of the reader a careful, respectful response even when the narration turns out to be biased. Authority, in this sense, is revealed in both the control of tone and the narrative structure. Particularly in a story's opening and concluding sections, but also in the manipulation and balance of details, the force of authority which controls the reader's expectations and responses may be detected. Because of the constraints of the short story, authority is revealed more by withheld information than by what is recorded. But in Irish short stories the most evocative and ironic effects come from the maneuvers of narrators or of implied authorial presences. There are few narrators as explicit in their interpretations as Thady Quirk; typically they more subtly color the narrative accounts. The youthful reporter of Joyce's "Araby," for example, determines the reader's response and forces on him a single, powerful interpretation even through indirect expression and implication. The manipulation of imagery and selection of episodes impose religious significance upon a simple story of childish infatuation, with the result that the last, emphatic statement becomes philosophically and psychologically profound. The boy who finally sees himself "as a creature driven and derided by vanity" has been disillusioned by more than the girl next door. A taste for such a forceful interpreting sensibility, for a clearly established narrative authority—Yeat's poet with "a sword upstairs"—has distinguished Irish short stories from their English and American counterparts.

Irish readers have been prepared by history and tradition to recognize and admire such authority in a writer, for in the earliest Irish civilization the poet, or *fili,* was afforded a very high position in society and wielded considerable temporal power. Descended from the continental Celtic *vatis* rather than the *bardus,* he had powers of the seer, those of prophecy, rather than the functions of a historian. The fili was an aristocrat, usually born into his profession and thoroughly trained in his craft. To master the intricate meters of Gaelic verse, formal training for six or seven years in bardic schools was required; such schools continued up to the early seventeenth century. In time, two functions of the fili were assigned to separate classes of poets: the *seanchaí* preserved and recited history, genealogies, and short, local tales, including ghost and fairy stories; the *sgéalaí,* on the other hand, told more complicated hero tales and stories of wonder, narratives classified by folklorists as *märchen.*[2]

The tales told by the seanchaí, or *shanachie* as it is later spelled, were often spoken in the first person, as though actually observed; the sgéalaí, on the other hand, favored impersonal narration, as though to present in an objective manner what would otherwise seem unlikely fantasies. Both enjoyed high regard in their communities and do so at the present time, particularly in the Gaeltacht, the Irish-speaking regions, where a few shanachies may still be found, although the tellers of the more elaborate, complex tales have almost disappeared. Some writers of short stories appropriated the techniques of oral storytelling; William Carleton made use of certain oral formulae, and even George Moore and Frank O'Connor occasionally employ the circuitous, self-reflecting, amusing locutions common to the folk storytellers. However, the influence of the oral tradition is neither wide nor deep.

After the nineteenth century, few writers consciously adapt oral techniques to narrative forms, and none of those discussed in this volume does so throughout his or her career. One of the undisputed masters of the Irish language short story, Padraic O'Conaire, who knew the tradition of the shanachie intimately, said he had to turn to literary models such as Chekhov and Conrad in learning to write prose fiction.[3]

At this point, claims of the distinctiveness of the short story must be recognized, particularly as its forms differ from those of oral tales. The modern short story typically dispenses with the most familiar formulae of spoken tales; whatever resemblances to fairy tales we discover, for instance, there is in the modern form no equivalent to the "Once upon a time" opening or the closing that settles all by reporting that the most worthy parties lived happily ever after. Likewise, the short story must be considered as different in kind from the anecdote, in which an amusing plot is presented, and equally distinct from the sketch, in which plot is omitted or underplayed so that a static impression of a person or place may be conveyed. There are, on the other hand, admirable modern short stories that so stress moral instruction they could be termed parables or fables, just as there are modern versions of older forms such as the chronicle, which records historical events, and the *geasta,* which boasts of heroic actions.

A major endeavor of literary criticism is defining genres. In attempting to describe the essential structure, typical techniques, and intentions of the short story, critics have, predictably, disagreed. The standard on which concurrence among critics may be expected has to do with length: most would agree that a story longer than fifty pages should properly be called a novel, novella, or novelette. Several of the writers discussed in this volume offer such definitions of the short story, and two, Frank O'Connor and Sean O'Faolain, have written perceptive books analyzing the literary form. Inherent in all definitions is some degree of recognition of the limitations, adjustments, and intensifications required by the fact that so much less can be told in this genre than in a novel. Presentation of character and action must be achieved in the most economical manner, so that great significance is vested in gesture and casual speech, for instance. In the most succinct and most plausible claim on the short story's distinctiveness of effect, V. S. Pritchett, himself one of the indisputable masters of the form, calls it one of "seeing through." The few incidents presented, like the few characters and limited indications of time and place, must be so clear that the reader can see other planes of meaning beyond them.

The broader sphere entered through responses to the incidents narrated is necessarily one in which fundamental human concerns dominate: the common themes of time, human mortality, love. But because these are perceived by the reader and are in all likelihood previously recognized by the author, a search for themes is not the best way analytically to approach short fiction; to do so is to begin with effects before tracing complex causes. The true themes of literature, the most evocative, puzzling, or emotionally moving issues with which human beings concern themselves, are universal ones, not subject to cultural distinctions. Sean O'Faolain claims that a concern for such universal matters as "the permanent relationships between people, their variety, their expectedness, and their unexpectedness" distinguishes the artistic short story from the subliterary anecdote.[4] Elizabeth Bowen points out that those basic themes are few, but "their recurrence is proof of their immortality."[5] However, while recurrent concerns and issues, the specific subjects of the Irish short story as an entire corpus may be described, the underlying universal themes will be considered only later, in the discussions of individual authors.

Among the subjects treated in almost every short story is the individual's relationship to society. Because humans are by nature gregarious, or perhaps because a man or woman's definition of self requires the verification of others, or even more tentatively, because the individual is shaped by a community, social concerns appear in nearly every narrative. In the novel, a defined society is likely to appear as a major force, that against which individual efforts are directed or that which assesses the individual's worth. In *The Lonely Voice,* Frank O'Connor argues that the short story dispenses with any notion of a normal society, substituting for it a minority social unit, "a submerged population group." Such intimate social units, the village or parish in some stories, a family in others, appear in many short stories, largely because smaller groups are easier to establish in a few lines or pages than a complex society such as a nation would be. Furthermore, ethical and moral considerations are felt more forcefully in a small group than in a large, impersonal society. The sense of belonging to a minority group also conveys a feeling of mutual confidence and intimacy which can foster a bond between narrator and reader.

To the extent that Ireland regarded itself as a minority in the British Isles, such feelings of solidarity had a coalescent effect. Ireland's impression of disjunction with most European nations because it was not developing technologically would have drawn such bonds even tighter and made Irish society even more cohesive. A writer in such a closed society may expect more immediate understanding and agreement from his or her audience, so that a more intimate tone and greater subtely can be achieved. The reader can be counted upon to interpret innuendo, recognize disaccommodations to social norms, and accept slang or jargon. However, O'Connor's claim that such a small society is the essential atmosphere in which a short story must be set is surely debatable. The plots of many stories by estimable writers are set in what seems to be mainstream, but vaguely described societies. At any rate, O'Connor's sociological term raises so many questions that it does not serve literary critics well. What, for example, is a social group? Who determines whether it is submerged?

One discrimination among short stories should be acknowledged, since several Irish authors have employed it in describing their own works and in tracing the development of the genre; that is the distinction made primarily on the basis of scope, between the *conte* and the *nouvelle*. Frank O'Connor employs the terms in his discussion of Turgenev's stories and then proceeds to describe the main characteristics of the first with some precision: its action is concentrated into a single episode, so that a powerful effect is suggested by the compression of diction, imagery, tone, character, and action. The nouvelle, on the other hand, encompasses more extensive action and fuller examination of character, accompanied by more varied imagery and changing perspectives. This second form O'Faolain refers to as a tale. Merely counting the number of words will not lead one to determine whether a prose fiction is one or the other, because of variations of literary style. Nevertheless, the varying breadth of stories may be easily determined, so that equally meritorious short stories may be classified as belonging to one of two groups. Most critical attention has been directed at the first group, with its sharp focus and emphasis on economy of effects; this is the short story as Edgar Allan Poe described it and as the European masters Maupassant and Chekhov developed it. The second type of story requires a different critical approach, for economy and concentration are not essential to it; Turgenev's longer "sketches," Tolstoy's "The Death of Ivan Ilyich," Thomas Mann's "Disorder and Early Sorrow," and many of the stories of O'Connor and O'Faolain range more broadly, more comprehensively examining complete societies, presenting strings of related ideas, and employing multiple perspectives. Although the nouvelle need not be much longer than the conte, it does allow for greater changes within characters, more varied actions, and a looser narrative pattern. In fact, exercises in determining whether a story fits one category or the other are less advisable than recognition that the single, most familiar notion of a short story, with its emphasis on sparseness, organic form, and highly focused revelatory scenes, describes only one of a pair of structural patterns.

Both types of short story developed steadily through the nineteenth century, reflecting changing fashions and social concerns and adapting to some extent to an expanding readership. Thus varieties of humorous sketches, ghost tales, detective stories, and contrivances with surprise endings achieved great popularity. But much more slowly a distinctive literary form was emerging, and critical standards were being formulated to account for its artistry. By the end of the nineteenth century, three continental writers—Maupassant, Chekhov, and Turgenev—had been established as masters of a distinctive genre of short fiction. The economy and narrative force of Maupassant's heavily plotted short stories attracted a broad audience, but his technical skill and graphic realism provoked imitation of fellow writers. Chekhov was an even more challenging literary influence. His intention to provide in art "absolute and honest truth" required, he assumed, economical descriptions, utterly clear, undecorated expression, and the avoidance of subjective commentary. He dispensed, wherever possible, with extended passages of exposition. Yet Chekhov's stories evoke intense concern for human beings; they have a clinical precision that reveals their author's training and practice as a doctor. Their muted, understated expression evokes emotion while being unemotional itself. Dialogue in the stories is startling in its familiarity and authenticity. Unlike figures in less artistic stories, Chekhov's characters do not provide convenient background information or honestly reveal their feelings. They are likely to lie, refrain from comment, or ignore each other; as a result, they seem much more lifelike. To most of his stories, Chekhov provides strong conclusions, "bashing the reader in the snout," as he described the effect, but even the surprise endings do not seem contrived or artificially imposed. What would seem to be trivial incidents out of the narrative context acquire profound meaning when conveyed so vividly and simply.

However, for Irish short story writers, a more widespread literary influence has been Ivan Turgenev. His *Sportsman's Sketches* (1872) may have had a special appeal to Irish writers because in that book he so vividly depicts and dissects rural society, or because the relations between serfs and masters which he there describes resemble the unhealthy relations between tenants and landlords in nineteenth-century Ireland. George Bernard Shaw's mot, "The English never remember, the Irish never forget," calls attention to the Irish love of history, genealogy, and folklore, but it also implies both their resentment and their nostalgia. And in his savoring of the past, sometimes with an air of resentment at social injustices, Turgenev was, to the Irish, a sympathetic artist. He mastered both the most pointed, compact kind of short story and the broader, more discursive nouvelle, and he made extensive use of a clearly established narrator. The sportsman whose accounts constitute that notebook grows in understanding and sympathy as his series of sketches develops. In some cases, he clearly does not comprehend the meaning of what he recounts; in other cases he refrains from expressing painful responses. In "Kasyan from the Beautiful Lands," for instance, the narrator juxtaposes a dispassionate account of a hunting trip against haunting and poetic comments on the immorality of "killing God's own wee birds and spilling innocent blood," comments only loosely integrated into the plot. At the story's end, touching details about Kasyan, the title character, are given, but the narrator seems unmoved; he simply concludes his account of the return journey.

Turgenev's sympathy for the peasants is presented with equal obliquity but even more forcefully in "Two Landowners," in which a pair of character sketches of unappealing landlords are thematically linked by reference to the social system that allows the mistreatment of servants in order to protect its pretentions of nobility. Although an implication of social injustice seems inherent in the accounts presented, the narrator concludes with a noncommittal cliché: "Well that's old-style Russia for you!"

Turgenev's stories rarely allow for heroism. In fact, the title of one of his short novels, *The Superfluous Man,* provides the term for his typical main character, a person sensitive and sufficiently educated to recognize injustice and be upset by it, but ineffectual, alienated, and even trivial. In some cases, extreme sensitivity becomes a form of acutely observed psychological imbalance. But typically, Turgenev establishes character by exterior means, rather than by reporting how people feel. George Moore cited the Russian's ability to fuse physical details with mental impressions, a technique he tried to imitate in *The Untilled Field.*[6]

The objectivity of the narrator in describing his encounters with peasants and others reflects an attitude of the author himself. Turgenev regarded the *Sketches* as curiously impersonal. He told a correspondent, "I can indeed assure you that it sometimes seems to me as if this book had been written by someone other than myself, so far removed do I feel from it."[7] Striving for unalloyed accuracy, he presents dialogue and visual impressions, particularly natural details, with exceptional clarity. He seems to savor scenes of the quiet countryside and lingers over minute descriptions. Yet the same natural settings always serve to advance some more profound subject, either as a contrasting element or as a vehicle to expand meaning; through the commentary of a narrator the stories express emotional responses of fear, regret, love, and wonder.

The balance achieved by Turgenev between visual accuracy and emotional evocation has been emulated directly or obliquely by many Irish short story writers. In their stories, natural scenes, folk customs, and alienated individuals are described vividly and sympathetically, often through the use of a narrator somewhat removed from the action. The most appealing descriptions of rural tranquillity are counterbalanced by disclosures of social inequities, ironic commentary, and even satire. Such similarities have led a few critics to assert direct influence of Maria Edgeworth on the Russian (an unlikely claim) and have brought others to note precise technical similarities in George Moore's stories (a verifiable claim). For writers of the thirties and forties, Turgenev's deemphasis of plot had particular appeal; Frank O'Connor praised the Russian for making "episodic interest" (plot) subsidiary to a dominant tone or subsuming theme in his stories and thus achieving "the static quality of an essay or poem." In "Bezhin Lea," for example, he praised the skill by which the ghost stories of a group of boys are thematically linked both to the stillness of the meadow that surrounds them and to overarching fears of death and the unknown.

The subtle effects of Turgenev's sketches and the best Irish short stories are not gained at the expense of accuracy, for just as visual art of the late nineteenth century was drawn to more realistic portrayal by the new art of photography, prose fiction aspired to greater realism. Detailed visual descriptions, transcriptions of actual speech, and a calculated rejection of what had been regarded as appropriate subjects of prose narratives in favor of working- and middle-class subjects characterize the new fiction, although the taste for rural subjects, particularly picturesque settings such as the West of Ireland, continued to exercise strong appeal. By the time George Moore's *The Untilled Field* appeared, a new audience had been developed, one that might be expected to know of recent French achievements in fiction. Moore's stories and the even more influential *Dubliners* by James Joyce reshaped the new literary form, setting a standard so high that whether or not subsequent writers attempted to employ the techniques they had perfected, the new genre was established as a serious, challenging art form. The following decades were to bring the Irish short story to such a level of excellence that it would rival the achievement of any English-speaking nation or indeed that of any nation in the world.

A stimulation for the energetic production of short stories over the past two centuries has been the development of periodicals featuring them. In the early years of the period in which the short story emerged, an audience had been established for the books of short fiction by Maria Edgeworth. Regional tales of Ireland drew strong interest from English audiences. Later, such collections of folklore as Thomas Crofton Croker's *Fairy Tales and Legends of the South of Ireland* (1825–28) and Samuel Lover's *Legends and Stories of Ireland* (1831–34) fostered in Irish audiences a taste for fiction on native subjects which was satisfied by the popular sketches of Mrs. S. C. Hall, the Banim brothers, and Gerald Griffin, and which received more artistic expression in the stories of William Carleton. After the demise of Dublin as a capital city, book and periodical publication declined, but in a few generations scores of short stories began to appear in new magazines aimed at a middle-class audience. Of periodicals of the nineteenth century, the *Dublin University Magazine* (1833–77) was foremost in importance. A conservative journal, it opposed the nationalist cause, but it included stories by Carleton and others which were later regarded as models of indigenous Irish narratives; Joseph Sheridan Le Fanu was its editor from 1861 to 1869. Less prestigious periodicals such as the *Dublin Penny Journal* (1832–36) and the *Irish Penny Journal* (1840–41), in their brief phases, often featured stories of literary quality. Of the provincial periodicals, the *Cork Magazine* (1847–48) deserves mention for publishing stories by Fitz-James O'Brien. Such newspapers as the *Comet* (1831–33) and, of course, the *Nation* (1842–92), contained some short fiction, particularly that with a patriotic tendency. However, the short story of the nineteenth century did not often serve as a vehicle for nationalist expression.

In the last decade of that century, with the appearance of the writers who were to lead Irish literature to a renaissance, several periodicals appeared which included among their offerings short stories. George Russell's the *Irish Homestead* (1895–1923) occasionally published short fiction, most notably Joyce's first stories; when it merged with the *Irish Statesman* (1919–30) in 1923, Russell (AE) continued as editor. Standish O'Grady's *All-Ireland Review* (1900–1907) published a good deal of short fiction; although it lasted a very short time, the *Shanachie* (1906–7), a Maunsel and Company publication, published many of the best writers of the period. Alice Milligan and Ethna Carbery, supporting the nationalist cause, promoted the best of the Northern writers in the *Shan Van Vocht* (1896–99). The most influential of the journals of the literary renaissance was the *Irish Review* (1911–14), edited in turn by David Houston, Padraic Colum, and Joseph Mary Plunkett. Because it lasted much longer. the *Irish Monthly* (1873–1954) published the greatest variety of worthwhile fiction of the literary revival, although only a few outstanding stories appeared in it. There were, in addition, various immensely popular weeklies and monthlies such as the *Shamrock* and *Ireland's Own*; packed with anecdotes and comic sketches, they were immensely popular, but not likely to contain fiction of literary merit—the sort of tabloids to which Leopold Bloom considered submitting a story.

In more recent times, three periodicals deserve special recognition as landmarks in the history of the Irish short story. The *Bell* (1940–54), edited by Sean O'Faolain up to 1946 and by Peadar O'Donnell for the remaining years, published most of the best writers of the period, as well as representing the voice of liberal protest against the dominant political and religious conservatism of the time. Seumas O'Sullivan's *Dublin Magazine* (1923–58) was nearly as distinguished and much longer-lived; for the thirty-five years of its existence, it served as the showplace for Irish art of all forms. Finally, personal credit is due to David Marcus, whose magazine, *Irish Writing* (1946–57), followed by his editorship of the weekly New Irish Writing page in the *Irish Press,* continues to discover and publish the best of recent short stories. His publishing house, Poolbeg Press, has reissued valuable collections by earlier masters and published much of the most interesting new short fiction.

In the two centuries in which they have appeared, Irish short stories have been inspired by those political events that would otherwise be regarded as defeats or national disasters. Because such historic events may be unfamiliar to some readers, the most provocative of them should be briefly mentioned.

On 1 January 1801, the union of Ireland with Great Britain took effect, forming the United Kingdom and combining the Church of Ireland with the Church of England. By this means, it was hoped, the revolutionary fervor of certain Irish separatist groups would be extinguished. Although there was another, smaller rebellion in 1803, led by Robert Emmet, the actions of the English and Irish Parliaments depriving the Irish of political power were effective; nationalist passions were quieted, and with the transfer of the most active cultural life from Dublin to London, original publication and intense literary activity in Ireland declined. Although nationalist convictions were not absolutely obliterated, the cultural inheritance was severely threatened as the English language began to replace the native Irish language and as formal education of the Irish people declined. In the 1820s, Daniel O'Connell revived the cause of Catholic emancipation, and in 1840, he formed the National Repeal Association, seeking the dissolution of the Union. His support was more widespread than that of anyone who preceded him; he grew in political influence until 1843 when he submitted to a government ban on one of his mass meetings, with the result that his reform movement started its decline. Nevertheless, his personality provoked strong reactions at the time and continues to do so; Sean O'Faolain's biography, *King of the Beggars* (1938), views O'Connell as an appropriate model, an effective political leader who had a realistic view of Ireland's need to adapt to modern conditions. Despite the apparent failure of the Great Liberator's scheme, the literate public had been stirred to national self-awareness. Encouraged by the work of such scholars as Eugene O'Curry, George Petrie, and John O'Donovan, whose efforts on the Ordnance Survey in the 1830s led to the discovery of rich manuscript materials of ancient and early Christian Irish culture, writers began to look to ancient times for inspiration. The leaders of the Young Ireland movement, poets and writers of the *Nation* such as Thomas Davis, looked to Irish history, particularly the ancient past, for noble literary models.

The revolution of 1848 planned by Davis's Young Ireland followers failed, as did efforts by the Fenians in the following twenty years. But their effects on nineteenth-century Irish history were overshadowed by a much more devastating event: the Great Famine, 1845 to 1849, which reduced the population by nearly 2 million, one-fourth of Ireland's total, by death and emigration. The mass suffering is nearly inconceivable, and resentment against the English who, it was felt, had ignored the dying Irish was intense. No single fact of Irish history evokes such strong feeling and impassioned expression as the Famine, for its effects on life, livelihood, and morale are still seen in Ireland. As a result of the Famine, emigration to America increased greatly; in time this led to firmer links with the New World and stimulated efforts to secure American financial support for the old country. Small benefit as it may have been, national identity was strengthened by this devastation: rather than utterly breaking the spirit of the people, it seemed to embolden them and attract sympathy and support from other nations.

A generation later, efforts at land reform were begun with the goal of transferring ownership to those who worked the land; Michael Davitt established the Land League in 1879, and new techniques of tenant protection, such as boycotting, were introduced. Encouraged by success of such reforms, nationalist leaders revived efforts to secure political independence or at least a greater measure of autonomy. Gladstone announced his mission to pacify Ireland and made several concessions to the most discontented sections of the populace by supporting the disestablishment of the Church of Ireland and even passing a land act that provided some protection for tenants. But dissatisfaction with his policies developed, and the tenuous alliance between the Irish and English liberals in Parliament did not last; the movement toward Home Rule, which had been formulated by Isaac Butt, attracted increased support.

The greatest advances toward national independence, however, resulted from political maneuvers rather than mass movements. Members of Parliament elected from Irish districts formed a parliamentary party which acquired political strength by refusing regular affiliation with the existing parties. In 1880, Charles Stewart Parnell became its head, and the parliamentary group began to exert influence, largely because of his skillful leadership. Despite minor setbacks along the way, he maintained control for several years and came close to realizing the long-standing hope of reestablishing an Irish parliament, thus securing Home Rule. However, in the debate on a Home Rule bill in 1886, old antagonisms were raised between the population of the predominantly Protestant counties in the north of Ireland and the Catholic majority in the rest of the country. Yet more destructive to the cause of nationalism was the personal fall from power of Parnell when, in 1890, he was convicted as correspondent in the divorce case of his long-time mistress, Kitty O'Shea. His death in the following year deprived Ireland of its most skillful political leader, but his leadership had, at least for a while, unified the nation and made it realize its potential political power. In 1893, the second Home Rule bill was defeated, and the rift between Ulster and the rest of Ireland grew wider. But by then a consciousness of purely Irish culture had developed, a result of the awareness of political differences with England.

In 1893, the Gaelic League was founded with an intention of reviving the ancient culture, including the Irish language. In part it attracted support because it opposed what were considered by some religious and political leaders to be dangerous modern and secular influences from England and the Continent. But the Gaelic League and similar groups fostered the Irish cultural cause in immeasurable ways, even in encouraging Gaelic sports, dress, and customs, for such organized efforts raised awareness of the importance of the arts as manifestations of culture. New journals emerged in support of the nationalist cause, and these in turn promoted the creation of new forms of literature; fiction, like poetry and drama, came to be seen as a potential weapon in the nationalist cause. The most notable literary product of the intensified cultural consciousness was the national theater, started in 1899 as the Irish Literary Theatre, later becoming the Irish National Theatre Society, and after 1904 popularly known as the Abbey Theatre. The artistic success of this dramatic movement and the international literary reputation of its moving force, William Butler Yeats, surely encouraged the development of all writers. Publishers such as Maunsel and Company, and the Dun Emer/ Cuala Press disseminated works of the emerging group, and an audience for the new Irish literature was formed. Such cultural events were more influential in the development of Irish literature than the strictly political ones, such as the formation of Sinn Fein in 1905.

The greatest symbolic event in twentieth-century Irish history was the Easter Rising of 1916, which was in fact no more than another unsuccessful attempt at revolution. It had originally been planned as a nationwide action, to follow the arrival of an arms shipment from Germany. But when the German ship was intercepted, the military plans became confused, and on Easter Monday only about a thousand insurgents took over several government buildings in central Dublin. A proclamation of independence was declared, but after five days the nationalist forces surrendered. Initially, public support for the revolution, even in Ireland, was weak; but after fifteen of the leaders were executed, including all those who had signed the proclamation of a republic, international support grew rapidly. Although Lloyd George, who became prime minister of England in December 1916, made attempts to placate the Irish by releasing convicted revolutionaries, Irish resentment intensified and the political organization, Sinn Fein, grew in power. When, in

1918, Lloyd George attempted conscription in Ireland, reaction was fierce and finally overwhelming. An Irish parliament, *Dail Eireann,* met in 1919, and Eamonn de Valera was elected its president. Declaring English military occupancy of the country illegal, the Irish army, the I.R.A., began warfare with British soldiers. This period of military strife, referred to by the Irish as "the Troubles," was particularly gruesome, involving atrocities and widespread destruction of those symbols of British control, the "big houses" of Ascendancy families.

In 1920, the British Parliament passed the Act for the Better Government of Ireland, proposing the establishment of two legislatures, one for six counties in Northern Ireland in Belfast and one for Southern Ireland in Dublin. Although the majority party, Sinn Fein, did not recognize the established legislature in the South, the partition between the six and the twenty-six counties was formulated and provided for in a treaty negotiated in 1921. As a result of the treaty, Southern Ireland became the Irish Free State with dominion status in the British Commonwealth.

However, the partition was opposed from the start by a minority faction led by Eamonn de Valera. Soon that group combined with the Irish Republican Army to oppose with force the newly established government, which had formed its own army. The Catholic hierarchy sided with the Free State government, and attempted to prevent renewed military hostility; nevertheless the Civil War began. It lasted only a year, ending in 1923 when the Free State government declared a military victory over the I.R.A., but the dissension continued, dividing the country for generations. The Civil War and the continuing discord it caused proved to be an even greater event in the minds of Irish writers than the Easter Rising or the many attempted revolutions that preceded it. Several of the short story writers fought in it—on the Republican side—but they soon were disillusioned by it, and in their stories Sean O'Faolain and Frank O'Connor denounce the violence and hatred the Civil War engendered. Although Eamonn de Valera and his Fianna Fail party took control of the Dail, the Irish parliament, in 1932 and held power for almost the entire next forty years, dissent within the nation has been vocal, and writers such as O'Faolain and O'Connor have been leading spokesmen against that government's policies.

As so often before, dissent today feeds the growth of literature. Since 1967, when the civil rights movement took shape in Belfast, and throughout the period of violent contention between the revived Irish Republican Army and various paramilitary forces on the Unionist side, a revived debate and critical self-examination have been under way, in which both writers of Northern Ireland and their colleagues in the Republic were bound to participate. Every public political or military act from peaceful demonstrations to hunger strikes to bombings stimulates renewed discussion of national identity and provokes questions of what principles one is willing to die for or possibly even kill for. Ireland's entry into the European Economic Community has accelerated social changes, particularly the adaptation to Continental and American ways which had already been advancing. But even that has provoked the kind of artistic counter efforts seen in a renewed interest in Irish folk music and in the publishing of literature with a distinctively Irish character, including new journals for the publication of short stories.

In even such a brief survey of Irish history of the last two centuries, certain recurring cultural and social concerns may be discerned, and these are inevitably reflected in the literature. In fact, certain attitudes, reactions to political frustration, and expressions of economic suffering may even distinguish the Irish short story from the form as it appears in other English-speaking nations.

By standards relative to the other Western nations, Ireland has been and is poor. In many respects, the rural areas never recovered from the Great Famine of the 1840s, and the cities have not been much more prosperous. The slums of Dublin in the early twentieth century may have been the worst in Europe; and the one-room tenements of that city were matched by the single-room cabins of Connaught. To this day, derelict houses abandoned a century ago may still be found in the rural areas. Even the proliferation of modern houses in the West and the suburban expansion in the cities throughout the nation have not obliterated the signs of widespread poverty which the nation suffered for so long. As a result, the land, infertile as much of it is, has been regarded as precious, and possession of even the smallest farm is considered an achievement of great importance. Only a hundred years have passed since massive political efforts were mounted to secure rights for tenants, and average landholdings are still quite small. In predominantly agricultural regions of any country, concern for land ownership and recognition of the perils of farm life are common, but in Ireland where available land is scarce relative to the size of the population, these issues become desperate problems, matters of life and death. As a result, such subjects as working the land, possessing it, or hoping to do so are recurrent and pressing concerns, reflected in the literature.

The shortage of land has clear effects on the social system, particularly in delaying the age for marriage and in producing greater numbers of those who never marry. The loneliness and social alienation of mature single persons is explored in a good number of Irish stories. Maria in James Joyce's "Clay" represents a type who appears in stories by Edna O'Brien, Frank O'Connor, and William Trevor; equally pathetic is her male equivalent, seen in stories by Joyce, Elizabeth Bowen, and James Plunkett. Their loneliness and awareness of social disaccommodation produce pathetic and sometimes even tragic impressions. In some accounts, the sexual restrictions of Irish society are attacked as contributing to human suffering, and indeed that fundamental subject of art is presented as a submerged but nonetheless powerful drive. But, typically, sexual passion, rather than pleasurable physical attraction, is treated in fiction, and it is a serious matter, a brooding concern. Economic more than physical facts of life account for this peculiar attitude, for natural as sexual attraction is, it can only add to one's misery if marriage is out of the question and if one adheres to a strict religious code forbidding promiscuity.

That recognition leads to another equally dominant cultural trait reflected in the short fiction: its Roman Catholic nature. Holy Ireland it is and has been, with a population fervid in its devotions; it is a nation in which early Christian culture is regarded as the richest inheritance and the most valuable contribution to Western civilization. After debate in the nineteenth century over the issue of Ultramontanism, the Irish church emerged as a strictly hierarchical and powerful authority, and at times its power has rivaled that of civil law. However, the inability of church authorities to quell the Civil War and, in recent times, the failure of their efforts to control or destroy militaristic groups point up the powerlessness of the clergy on the most consequential matters. Yet the clergy are prominent and, in small and backward communities, influential; and for that reason they are common satiric targets in literature. The priests in George Moore's stories serve as types, exposing the tyranny of absolute rulers; similar cruel or venal clergymen appear in O'Faolain's and O'Flaherty's fiction. The imposition of strict censorship laws in the twentieth century exacerbated a certain amount of inevitable hostility between writers and church authorities. So severe were the actions of the five-person Censorship Board established by the government in 1930 that thousands of books were banned, including works by most of the writers discussed in this book. Several leading short story writers, particularly Sean O'Faolain, vocally and effectively opposed such extreme censorship, which had the open support of church authorities. Since Vatican II, the Irish church has not escaped the changes in attitude and the adaptation to secular society experienced throughout the Catholic church, and some breakdown in the church's authority is evidenced. But the country's population is still 90 percent Roman Catholic, and issues of religious faith, devotion, and teaching are still matters of widespread concern, likely to be covered in daily newspapers. As a result, such matters are also frequent subjects of fiction.

The scarcity of land and the widespread poverty of the last half of the nineteenth century set in progress a still existing pattern of emigration to industrially developed nations. During the Great Famine, as many as a quarter million people emigrated in a single year; since then, continuing economic deprivation has forced great numbers to leave. The youngest children of a family, those who would not inherit the small farm, have had little choice but to leave; for city dwellers, opportunities for employment or training were usually the attractions for moving on. Naturally, English cities drew great numbers; some now estimate that there are more Irish speakers in certain industrial towns in England than in all of Ireland. But many traveled farther, to the United States, Canada or Australia, and these exiles provoked the popular imagination even more deeply, for the young men or women would probably never return to their parents and families. The family is the social unit on which Irish fiction tends to center, and other small social units, the parish or village, resemble it in their structures. Parental authority is firmly established, and the family tends to close itself off, since it is regarded as separate from, perhaps even opposed to, the larger social organizations. In short stories, the closed society manifests itself in assumptions about the secrecy of family affairs—the habit of keeping bad news "within the family." Relations among parents and children, or between siblings, are recurrent subjects of Irish short stories. Emigration, particularly when it involves enforced separation from a family given such emotional and symbolic importance, appears as an especially powerful and possibly tragic subject. In turn the exile, separated from the people and places he or she has loved, tends to exaggerate the beauty and appeal of what is lost; the suffering of the wanderer, deracinated and unadapted to an alien land, is a classic theme of art and a familiar one in Irish short fiction. Tales of emigrants returning to the old country provide a common narrative pattern. To some, the land they had come to regard as Edenic now seems corrupted by modern civilization; to others, the still undeveloped rural society contrasts with the efficiency of the New World. George Moore's "Home Sickness" provides a prototype for such a returned native, George Bryden, who discovers on his return to his village the tyranny of the parish priest, the pathos of the lives of his victims, and the "weakness and incompetence" of the natives.

Despite the rapid modernization of Ireland since Moore's time and the recent changes in attitudes and perceptions caused by films and television, the separation between the Old and New Worlds seems no less vast. The enormous changes wrought by developing technology in the nineteenth century, which transformed Europe, had little impact on Ireland except in a few cities, and other changes have affected it a generation or two later than in the more progressive nations. National cultures are revealed in their images, those natural scenes or other visual representations of the country. The perception of Ireland fostered by its short stories is of a remote, undeveloped, and austere land. The postcard scene of a single cottage in a hilly place near the rough sea captures the image well. No television antenna, no automobile, no sign of commerce with the modern world mars the scene. It is, of course, an extreme fiction, for the great majority of the Irish public live in modernized houses in towns and cities. But the perception of Ireland as an anachronistic culture nevertheless dominates the popular imagination as revealed in the short stories. As a result, the typical landscape, described in unusual detail, is rough and desolate, Connemara more often than the fertile land of County Kildare. It is not the kind of natural scene that would inspire romantic impulses of communion, but rather one that imposes feelings of separation and loneliness. Mountains and bogs have special evocative power as mysterious and threatening places, and the sea is most often seen as a destroyer. Such ominous natural settings serve to amplify those common themes of literature—the fear of death, the loneliness of old age, and the uncertainties of love. The theme of self-discovery, one of the fundamental concerns of literature, is treated in a somewhat unusual fashion, since verification of one's identity or maturity is not as often provided in Irish fiction by an established society as achieved through some inner struggle. The conflict leading up to self-realization tends to be internal, rather than resulting from contention with social forces.

Inevitably the most challenging concerns of contemporary international fiction, such as the self-reflecting aspect of literature itself, have provoked treatment by certain short story writers in Ireland, and there is a healthy amount of experimentation with technique among such artists. The survey of such writers in the last chapter in this volume reveals how varied the fiction of contemporary Ireland is, thus reminding us how hazardous the generalizations in this introduction have been. But if a single impression of the world as portrayed by the short stories of the best authors discussed in these essays may be derived from such a diverse body of literary works, it is that of a desolate place, anachronistic to its contemporary society, and uncongenial to the individual man or woman. For the expression of such an austere concept, the compact form of the short story seems particularly suitable.

James F. Kilroy

Vanderbilt University

TALES FROM BIG HOUSE AND CABIN:
THE NINETEENTH CENTURY

Gregory A. Schirmer

In the introduction to his *Tales of the Munster Festivals,* Gerald Griffin tells of being stranded by the tide one day while waiting to cross the Shannon in a remote part of County Clare. The boatman's wife invited him in for tea, and there he found himself in the company of a rather sour-looking elderly gentleman. After a few awkward attempts at small talk, the conversation turned to literature, and Griffin began arguing ardently that tales such as he was then writing had great political and social value. The old man, however, was not impressed. "I am one of those who think," he said, "that a ruined people stand in need of a more potent restorative than an old wife's story."

This anecdote suggests more than the usual rivalry between the Irish man of letters and his nationalistic counterpart. The claims that Griffin makes to the old man are somewhat exaggerated, but the connection that he insists on between the emergence of Irish fiction at the beginning of the nineteenth century and the political and social changes that Ireland was experiencing at the time has considerable validity. The first decades of the nineteenth century witnessed the rise to political consciousness of the Irish peasant and the Catholic middle class, and this threat to the established order, manifested chiefly in Daniel O'Connell's campaigns for Emancipation and Repeal, created a sudden demand in England for information concerning the manners, values, and attitudes of the race that it had been governing, largely in ignorance, for so long. The tales and sketches praised by Griffin in his conversation with his skeptical listener went a long way toward meeting that need. Irish writers from backgrounds as different as Maria Edgeworth's Big House in County Longford and William Carleton's thatched cabin in County Tyrone were committed to describing Irish life as accurately as possible, and English publishers and readers were more than ready to listen. And so, although the ruined people that were the focus of much Irish writing in this

period ultimately needed more than an old wife's story to make their dreams of
political independence come true, Irish fiction in the nineteenth century became, as Thomas Flanagan has said, "a kind of advocacy before the bar of English
public opinion."[1]

But it also became a distinctive and significant body of literature, and this is
as true of the short narrative as it is of the novel. The Irish short story is usually
considered to be a singularly modern art form, but the tales and sketches of
nineteenth-century Irish writers cannot be ignored in any study of this genre.
Few of these often bulky and digressive stories exemplify what Frank O'Connor
calls "the absolute purity of the short story,"[2] and few could live up to Edgar
Allan Poe's definition of the short story as a piece of fiction in which "there
should be no word written of which the tendency, direct or indirect, is not to
the one pre-established design."[3] Nonetheless, these tales and sketches of Irish
life, written largely for export to England, do constitute an emerging literary
form, demonstrating considerable accomplishment in the art of narrative and
clearly pointing the way to the development of the Irish short story in the
twentieth century.

"I note very distinctly in all Irish literature two different accents," W. B. Yeats
said in an introduction to a collection of nineteenth-century stories, "the accent
of the gentry, and the less polished accent of the peasantry and those near
them."[4] As Yeats suggests, there are two distinct strands of fiction in nineteenth-
century Ireland, that of Anglo-Irish Protestants and that of native Irish Catho-
lics, and they offer two distinct ways of looking at the Ireland that was beginning
to force its way into the political consciousness of the English at the beginning
of the century. Each of these traditions also had its advantages and disadvantages
in terms of the development of the tale or sketch as a literary form.

The Anglo-Irish tradition may be said to begin with Maria Edgeworth's *Castle
Rackrent,* a narrative that usually is considered in evaluations of the Irish novel,
but that just as easily qualifies for examination in a study of Irish short fiction.
Published in 1800, *Castle Rackrent* marks the first flowering of the short Irish
narrative written in English. It also represents, in many ways, the high point of
Anglo-Irish fiction in the nineteenth century; its depth of characterization, subtle ironies, and use of an unreliable narrator are unmatched by fiction writers
later in the century. The Irish sketches of Mrs. S. C. Hall, appearing a generation
after *Castle Rackrent,* constitute a less innovative but nonetheless significant addition to the Anglo-Irish tradition, as do the Gothic tales of Charles Robert
Maturin and Joseph Sheridan Le Fanu. The best stories of Le Fanu also anticipate not only the formal purity of the modern short story, but also, in their
exploration of psychological reality, many of the concerns of twentieth-century
fiction. The Anglo-Irish tradition comes to a belated close in the stories of Edith

Somerville and Martin Ross. Their celebration of the life of a resident magistrate in the wilds of West Cork represents the last gasp of the nineteenth century; by the time the last of the three volumes of their stories about Major Yeates was published in 1915, James Joyce's *Dubliners* had already pointed the way to a radically different kind of short fiction and to a radically different vision of Ireland.

The native tradition, on the other hand, was remarkably short-lived. It begins with the appearance in the 1820s of the tales of John and Michael Banim and Gerald Griffin. These writers, Ireland's first Catholic fiction writers in English, offered their reader on the other side of the Irish Sea a faithful account of rural Ireland that drew on the broad sense of humor characteristic of cabin society, but that also recognized the cruelty and violence that existed side by side with it.

The major figure in the native tradition of the nineteenth century is William Carleton, a man who was always quick to claim his status as an insider. When told once that his stories were more accurate than the sketches of Mrs. Hall, he replied: "Why, of course, they are! Did she ever live with the people as I did? Did she ever dance and fight with them as I did? Did she ever get drunk with them as I did?"[5] Carleton's record of the years that he spent growing up in rural County Tyrone stands as the most realistic account of Irish peasant life that the nineteenth century produced. His stories also exhibit the sure hand of a literary artist, especially in their use of regional dialogue to develop character and express, through humor, an ironic vision.

Carleton's was not only the most powerful voice of realism in the nineteenth century's native tradition, it was also the last. A momentous silence descends on Catholic fiction in Ireland after the Great Famine of the late 1840s, a silence all but unbroken until the appearance of Joyce's *Dubliners* more than half a century later. Carleton was keenly and painfully aware of this. "Banim and Griffin are gone," he said late in his life, "and I will soon follow them . . . and after that will come a lull, an obscurity perhaps of half a century, when a new condition of civil society and a new phase of manners and habits among the people—for this is a *transition* state—may introduce new fields and new tastes for other writers."[6]

One of Maria Edgeworth's most famous admirers, and certainly the most indebted, was Sir Walter Scott. "Without being so presumptuous as to hope to emulate the rich humour, pathetic tenderness, and admirable tact, which pervades the works of my accomplished friend," Scott wrote in his preface to *The Waverley Novels* in 1829, "I felt that something might be attempted for my own country, of the same kind with that which Miss Edgeworth so fortunately achieved for Ireland."[7] Part of Miss Edgeworth's achievement has to do with her "admirable tact"; especially in *Castle Rackrent,* she proved herself a master of irony, and the economy of this tale, which spans four generations of Irish land-lords in fewer than a hundred pages, makes it an important predecessor of the modern short story. But, as Scott recognized, Miss Edgeworth is to be remem-bered also as the first Irish fiction writer to make the English aware of the country they governed. With characteristic irony, she expresses her commit-ment to this aim in the author's description, voiced by the supposed editor of *Castle Rackrent,* of that book's intentions: "He lays it before the English reader as a specimen of manners and characters which are perhaps unknown in England. Indeed, the domestic habits of no nation in Europe were less known to the English than those of their sister country, till within these few years."

Miss Edgeworth's qualifications for doing this were many. The daughter of an influential Anglo-Irishman who sat in Grattan's Parliament, Richard Lovell Edgeworth, she lived all her adult life in rural Ireland, and spent much of her time managing her father's estate in County Longford. Her father, a humane and enterprising Ascendancy gentleman, exercised a strong, if not always aes-thetically happy, influence on Miss Edgeworth's writing. From her father's rela-tively progressive views, Miss Edgeworth shaped her own attitudes toward the troubled relationship between Protestant landlords and Catholic tenants—atti-tudes embodied most plainly in two of her novels on Irish life, *Ennui* (1804) and *The Absentee* (1812). Asked by the narrator of *Ennui* how he has managed to make his estate so peaceful and prosperous, the sober-minded agent Mr. McLeod counsels improving the lot of tenants gradually through example and education, concluding, "We took time and had patience."

But Miss Edgeworth was also acutely aware of the injustices committed by Protestant landlords, and she never spares her English reader from seeing them. Indeed, *Castle Rackrent* is, as Thomas Flanagan has said, "as final and damning a judgment as English fiction has ever passed on the abuse of power and the failure of responsibility."[8] Miss Edgeworth also realized the precar-ious position of the Anglo-Irish at the beginning of the nineteenth century, and the ruin of this powerful class is clearly prophesied in the closing pages of *Castle Rackrent.* "Better luck, anyhow, Thady," Judy M'Quirk tells the sto-ry's eccentric narrator near the end of his tale, "than to be like some folk, following the fortunes of them that have none left."

Castle Rackrent is easily the best of Miss Edgeworth's work and the most important for a study of Irish short fiction. (It is also the only one of her books in which the utilitarian hand of Richard Lovell Edgeworth is not visi-ble.) The memoir form of the tale is not, in itself, innovative, being familiar to English readers as far back as *Robinson Crusoe*. But what distinguishes *Castle Rackrent* from other works of fiction in this mode is Miss Edgeworth's choice of a narrator who is not the central character, and who is, moreover, extremely unreliable, although by no means unlikeable. Sir Walter Scott was among the first readers of *Castle Rackrent* to call attention to the significance of this choice: "And what would be the most interesting, and affecting, as well as the most comic passages of *Castle Rackrent,* if narrated by one who had a less regard for the family than the immortal Thady, who, while he sees that none of the dynasty which he celebrates were perfectly right, has never been able to puzzle out wherein they were certainly wrong."[9] Throughout the narrative, the gap between Thady's gallous story and the Rackrents' dirty deeds must be closed by the reader, and this makes Miss Edgeworth's satire all the more effective.

But the irony of *Castle Rackrent* is more complex than this. Thady's is not the only unreliable voice in the story; his tale is packaged and presented to the reader by an editor, who supplies a preface, a brief conclusion, copious footnotes, and an extensive glossary—all, presumably, for the edification of the ignorant English reader. This editor speaks in the polished, elegant voice of the English Enlightenment, and his discourse is infused with the rational optimism of that age. Unfortunately for the reader in search of a reliable guide through the tangle of Thady's narrative, this thoroughly eighteenth-century sensibility proves to be as unreliable as Thady is. The editor gives himself away near the end of the preface when he confidently assures his readers that what Thady is about to describe is decidedly a part of the past, and that "the race of the Rackrents has long since been extinct in Ireland; and the drunken Sir Patrick, the litigious Sir Murtagh, the fighting Sir Kit, and the slovenly Sir Condy, are characters which could no more be met with at present in Ireland, than Squire Western or Parson Trulliber in England."

Even the humane optimism of Richard Lovell Edgeworth could not extend to such a blindly favorable view of Ireland at the time of the Union; indeed, as Irish fiction was to demonstrate throughout the coming century, the race of the Rackrents was still very much alive in Ireland. Thus, the reader's vision of the truth of *Castle Rackrent* is the product of two blindnesses, Thady's misguided loyalty to the family and the editor's naive optimism.

The complexity of that truth can be seen partly in the contrast between Thady's two "families"—the Rackrents and his own flesh-and-blood family, represented by his aggressive, materialistic son Jason. Thady has to choose between the two, and his decision in favor of Sir Condy strongly suggests that the Rack-

rents, despite all the injustice that they are responsible for, are to be preferred
to the avaricious class that is threatening to replace them. Sir Condy's generosity
is contrasted sharply with Jason's greed throughout the closing pages of the
narrative, and the story's lament for the loss of the magnanimity that Yeats so
admired in the Protestant Ascendancy is expressed most forcefully in Sir Condy's final words and Thady's accompanying comment: "'Where are all the
friends?—where's Judy? Gone, hey? Ay, Sir Condy has been a fool all his days,'
said he; and there was the last word he spoke, and died. He had but a very poor
funeral after all."

Maria Edgeworth tried her hand at the memoir form one more time in
writing about the Irish—in *Ennui,* published four years after *Castle Rackrent.*
But the narrator of this story is also the relatively reliable central character,
and so the ironic possibilities realized in *Castle Rackrent* are largely absent.
After *The Absentee* (1812) and *Ormond* (1817), Miss Edgeworth stopped writing about the Irish altogether, although she continued to write up until her
death in 1849. Her decision seems to have owed something to the political
and social turmoil of Ireland in the age of O'Connell; the cool distance and
detachment that characterizes the best of her Irish fiction may have seemed
impossible in the midst of the turbulent rise to power of the forces that
would eventually make her prophecy in *Castle Rackrent* come true. When one
of her brothers inquired, late in her life, why she had not written about
Ireland after *Ormond,* she replied in a letter: "It is impossible to draw Ireland
as she now is in the book of fiction—realities are too strong, party passions
too violent, to bear to see, or care to look at their faces in a looking glass.
The people would only break the glass, and curse the fool who held the
mirror up to nature—distorted nature, in a fever."[10]

Any attempt to trace Anglo-Irish short fiction from Maria Edgeworth at
the beginning of the nineteenth century to Somerville and Ross at the end
must include some notice of an extremely prolific Anglo-Irishwoman, Mrs.
S. C. Hall. Born Anna Maria Fielding in the year that *Castle Rackrent* was
published, Mrs. Hall spent most of her adult life in England, where her husband founded a number of journals to which she contributed frequently. But
the best of her writing looks back to the first fifteen years of her life in the
coastal village of Bannow, in County Wexford, and provides a notable example of regional fiction in Ireland.

Of all her voluminous writings (it has been estimated that she published
more than five hundred books during her lifetime), the most important for
a study of Irish short fiction are the two series of *Sketches of Irish Character,*
published in 1829 and 1831. All the stories in these two volumes deal with

Bannow, and, although written from an Anglo-Irish point of view, they explore all aspects of that provincial world. Indeed, some of Mrs. Hall's best-drawn characters are those at the bottom of the social scale—most notably, a local gossip known as Peggy the Fisher in an otherwise unremarkable story entitled "Lilly O'Brien," and a delightfully articulate beggar named Daddy Denny in "Mary Ryan's Daughter." A number of Mrs. Hall's stories turn on the knowledge or action of these low-life characters living on the fringe of the community.

Mrs. Hall's ear for dialect, although by no means the equal of that of her contemporary, William Carleton, is also at its sharpest when she lets these characters speak. In a scene in "Mary Ryan's Daughter," old Daddy Denny climbs up to a cold and leaky loft, where Mary Ryan and her daughter Peggy have been more or less stowed away during the wake of Mary's husband. Her husband, a wealthy man and of a higher social station than Mary's, had thrown Mary and her daughter out and married another woman. In this scene, Daddy has been freely enjoying the benefits of the wake, and is a bit wobbly in the head as well as on his feet when he struggles up a ladder to the loft to assure Peggy that her mother's lawful claim on her husband's property will be recognized—as it is by the end of the story:

"Peg—Peggy, avourneen," puffed a well-known voice, "don't be frightened, darlin'—it's me, a'coushla machree—ould Daddy Denny—wait till I catch my breath, which is flying from me like widgeon from a gun—och, hone!—I'm too ould for climbing, and couldn't have reached you at all, but for the tough bames of the stable, and a ladder, dear, that Peter Mullowny's houlding. I've got the girl of the house, dear, to forget where yez are—and so keep quiet till ye're wanted, jewel . . . but, faix, dear, my head's bothered somehow, and the moon's turning round on me, so the Lord be wid yez—I needn't bid ye take care of yer mother—for sure it's Mary Ryan's daughter ye are—and pray for yer sinful soul—I mean my—hould hard and fast, Peter, dear—for somehow both myself and the ladder's mighty unsteady."

The generous spirit that clearly shines through the alcoholic haze of this speech eventually manifests itself in Daddy's successful efforts to establish Mary Ryan's rights as a widow. Many of Mrs. Hall's low-life characters embody this quality and so express, without didacticism, Mrs. Hall's intention, stated in her introduction to *Sketches of Irish Character,* "to do justice to the many estimable qualities of the Irish peasantry."

Although many of Mrs. Hall's stories are concerned with bringing those virtues before the eye of the English reading public, some of the best of her short fiction deals with her own class. And like Maria Edgeworth, Mrs. Hall often takes a highly critical view of the Anglo-Irish. "The Last of the Line," for example, affords some striking parallels with *Castle Rackrent,* including a confrontation between a conniving agent and the proprietor of a Big House, which echoes the scene in Miss Edgeworth's narrative between Jason Quirk and Sir Condy:

"The simple fact is," continued Sir John, rising from his seat, "the simple fact is, money I want, and money I must have." . . .

"It's easy say money," retorted the agent; "will you sell, Sir John?"

"What?" interrogated the baronet.

"There's the Corner estate, that long strip, close by Ballyraggan; your cousin Corney of the hill has long had an eye to it, and would lay down something handsome."

"You poor, pitiful scoundrel!" exclaimed Sir John, "do you think it's come to *that,* for me to sell *land,* like a huckster!"

The scene is not, however, as subtle as the corresponding scene in *Castle Rackrent,* partly because it lacks the ironic voice of Thady and partly because the character of the Anglo-Irish landlord is drawn without the complex mix of satire and admiration that characterizes Miss Edgeworth's treatment of Sir Condy. In general, Mrs. Hall's stories lack the moral depth of the work of her more famous predecessor and the ability to probe deeply into the political and social complexities of provincial Ireland in the nineteenth century. Nonetheless, her commitment to regional fiction and her ability to present accurately and honestly many aspects of her province should win for her tales and sketches considerably more notice than they have received to date.

Four years before the publication of Mrs. Hall's first series of *Sketches of Irish Character,* a three-volume collection of stories entitled *Tales by the O'Hara Family* appeared. This collection, the collaborative effort of John and Michael Banim, sons of a prosperous Catholic farmer and merchant in Kilkenny, marks the beginning of the native, Catholic strand in nineteenth-century Irish fiction. In these stories is heard a strikingly different voice from that sounded in the work of Maria Edgeworth or Mrs. Hall—a cruder and less accomplished voice, but one that revealed aspects of Irish rural life unknown to Anglo-Irish writing. The tales and sketches of the Banim brothers brought to the English reader's attention for the first time the singular mixture of broad humor and lawlessness that characterized Irish cabin life at the beginning of the nineteenth century. And so these stories provide a transition of sorts between the Big-House fiction of Maria Edgeworth and the view from the cabin embodied in the work of William Carleton.

In strictly formal terms, many of the stories that accomplished this are failures. The Banim brothers' writing is frequently marred by annoying authorial intrusions and a weakness for sentimentality and melodrama, and their style has little of the polish of the work of Miss Edgeworth and less of her subtle sense of irony. Their tales do, however, describe Irish rural life with realistic conviction and occasionally with considerable moral depth. In "The Stolen Sheep" (written by John), a father who has witnessed his son dressing out a sheep that he has stolen during a period of famine is called to testify against his son. The story's courtroom scene borders on the melodramatic in places, but on the whole portrays convincingly a man torn between family feeling and a sense of social responsibility rendered somewhat ambiguous by Ireland's master-servant relationship with England. The barrister tells the father:

"Stand up; take the crier's rod, and if you see Michael Carroll in the court, lay it on his head."

"*Och, musha, musha,* sir, don't ax me to do that!" pleaded Peery, rising, wringing his hands, and, for the first time, weeping. "Och, don't, my lord, don't, and may your own judgment be favorable the last day."

"I am sorry to command you to do it, witness; but you must take the rod," answered the judge, bending close to his notes, to hide his own tears. . . .

"Michaul, *avich*! Michaul, *a corra-ma-machree*!" exclaimed Peery, when at length he took the rod, and faced round to his son. "Is id your father they made to do it, *ma-bouchal?*"

John Banim deserves to be remembered for one exceptionally well-constructed short narrative, if for nothing else. "The Roman Merchant" tells with remarkable economy and effect the story of the mysterious murder of a stranger in a provincial Irish town. The stranger, known as "the Roman merchant" because of his apparently Italian origins, arrives one day, sets up a shop, and proceeds to lead, for the next five years, a life of almost total seclusion. One day he is missing, and sometime later his body is discovered in the local cemetery. The tale ends with a letter, found on the merchant's body and addressed to his apparent killer, a long-time enemy who seems to have pursued the merchant across Europe, seeking revenge for a wrong done to his daughter. The story's plot is unfolded and the merchant's character developed through a few revelatory incidents and the final letter. The story also anticipates Le Fanu's tales about characters haunted by guilt for some past action and looks ahead to Frank O'Connor's examination, more than a century later, of the closed nature of life in a small town in Ireland.

The connection between "The Roman Merchant" and Le Fanu is of more than passing significance. The Banim brothers were fascinated with the supernatural, and in some ways their contribution to Irish fiction in the nineteenth century might be weighed in the Gothic tradition as much as in the realistic one. Maturin's *Melmoth the Wanderer* had appeared five years before the first series of *Tales by the O'Hara Family,* and the Banim brothers' stories of murders and mysterious disappearances, their use of local legends about ghosts and witches, and the ruined castles and moonlit cemeteries that provide the setting for many of their tales clearly owe something to Maturin's work. Nonetheless, the Banims are important to the development of Irish fiction chiefly because they provided the first realistic insiders' account of Irish peasant life in the nineteenth century. In a note to one of his tales, the Banims' contemporary, Gerald Griffin, summarizes the nature and importance of this contribution:

They were the first who painted the Irish peasant sternly from the life; they placed him before the world in all his ragged energy and cloudy loftiness of spirit, they painted him as he is, goaded by the sense of national and personal wrong, and venting his long pent up agony in the savage cruelty of his actions, in the powerful idiomatic eloquence of his language, in the wild truth and unregulated generosity of his sentiments, in the scalding vehemence of his reproaches, and the shrewd and biting satire of his jests.

Griffin served a brief literary apprenticeship with John Banim. Born into a large Catholic farming family in Limerick in 1803, Griffin went to London at the age of twenty, where he met Banim, then making his literary way with the help of a coterie of expatriate Tory Irish journalists. But although Griffin always acknowledged his debt to the Banims, he had his own vision of Ireland, and of the art of prose fiction. When Banim asked him to contribute a story to the second series of *Tales by the O'Hara Family,* Griffin declined, and soon thereafter published the first series of his own Irish tales, *Holland-Tide; or, Munster Popular Tales* (1827), a book that earned him sudden and considerable fame.

In his comment praising the Banims, Griffin also tried to distinguish his work from theirs: "We have endeavored in most instances, where pictures of Irish cottage life have been introduced, to furnish a softening corollary to the more exciting moral chronicles of our predecessors, to bring forward the sorrows and the affections more frequently than the violent and fearful passions of the people." To a large extent, this statement is a manifestly inaccurate description of Griffin's fiction. Some of Griffin's best work—including his well-known novel, *The Collegians* (1829)—explores the darker side of Irish life in no less reserved terms than do the tales of the Banim brothers.

But there are some notable differences between Griffin and the Banims. Griffin's style is much more self-consciously literary; as Frank O'Connor once said, Griffin was, in his writing, "a civilized and intelligent man."[11] Griffin's lofty diction, complex syntax, and frequent literary allusions do not, however, always work in his favor. The fictional framework of his *Tales of the Munster Festivals* (1827) is that of a group of peasants and small merchants swapping hearthside stories, but the narrative voice in all the stories is that of a literate, educated gentleman, extremely conscious of his English reader. What Griffin misses in relying exclusively on this voice becomes evident a few years later when Carleton uses a similar framework for the first few tales of his *Traits and Stories of the Irish Peasantry*; Carleton's stories exploit admirably the full range of ironies made possible by the tension between markedly various narrative voices and the tales that they tell. Griffin's stories also differ from those of the Banim brothers in their concern with the stratum of Irish society that Griffin knew best, the Catholic middle class, and in their focus on the landscape of Griffin's youth, the area around the Shannon. These qualities tend somewhat to temper his stories, especially when compared to the occasionally savage nature of the Banim brothers' accounts of peasant life in the politically and socially inflammable counties of Kilkenny and Tipperary.

Griffin's claim of providing a "softening corollary" to the fiction of the Banim brothers is, however, difficult to accept. His stories and novels have more than their fair share of murders and dark crimes, as well as passages and descriptions that clearly sound the Gothic note. One of his most successful short tales, "The Hand and Word," concerns the murder of a young man at the hands of a violent, primitive fisherman named Yamon Dhuv ("Black Ned"). The story ends at the wake of the victim, at which Yamon is discovered to be the murderer; he then, in a fit of rage, kills the young man's lover and himself. The story tends to be melodramatic, but is told economically, and in its characterization of Yamon Dhuv brings to light the powerful passions of violence and brutality that lurk below the surface of rural Irish life.

Griffin's fiction also provides a view of Maria Edgeworth's Protestant Ascendancy as it appeared to a middle-class Irish Catholic. On the one hand, the aspiring literary gentleman in Griffin was quick to acknowledge that a comparison of Anglo-Irish culture with that of his own upbringing almost always favored the Ascendancy. In a tale entitled "The Aylmers of Bally-Aylmer," this attitude is revealed through the thoughts of young Robert Aylmer when he first catches sight of his family's house after spending several years amid the Georgian elegance of Dublin: "Accustomed, as he had been during his absence, to the splendours of metropolitan architecture, he could not avoid feeling a momentary sense of humiliation, when he perceived the utter poverty and tastelessness of an establishment which in his childhood he had been used to look upon as the perfection of elegance." On the other hand, Griffin could also be—perhaps partly because of this feeling of inferiority—vicious in his attacks on the Big House. And he often uses the point of view of the governed to satirize those that govern. In "Half-Sir," a long tale centering on the fortunes of Eugene Hamond, a socially ambiguous figure reared in an Ascendancy family but of humble birth, Griffin levels his criticism of Anglo-Irish values through the voice of a peasant trying to explain why Hamond does not deserve the honor and atten- tion that a full gentleman would receive:

"Castle Hamond! What's Castle Hamond to me, as long as the master wouldn't conduct himself proper! A man that wouldn't go to a hunt, nor a race-course, nor a cock-fight, nor a hurlen-match, nor a dance, nor a fencen-bout, nor any one born thing. Sure that's no gentleman! A man that gives no parties, nor was never known yet to be drunk in his own house. . . . A man that was never be any mains *overtaken in liquor* himself, nor the cause of anybody else being so, either. Sure such a man as that has no heart?"

If this passage carries more than a faint echo of Thady Quirk's ironic praise for Sir Patrick Rackrent's festive character, Griffin himself handsomely acknowl- edges the debt a little later in the story, when he describes Maria Edgeworth as the first Irish writer "to put the sickle into the burthened field of Irish manners," and himself, humbly enough, as a follower in her footsteps, "casting our eyes around to gather in the scattered ears which may remain after the richness of the harvest."

One need only turn from the pages of Griffin or the Banim brothers to the work of William Carleton to realize how much remained to be harvested by a writer in the nineteenth century's native tradition. Carleton is, without doubt, the most significant figure in that tradition, if not in all of nineteenth-century Irish fiction. He is certainly the first major Irish Catholic writer in English, and the first Irish writer in English who seems to be writing for the Irish as well as for the English. "No one who does not know what he tells," said Young Ireland's leading poet, Thomas Davis, "knows Ireland. . . . he has given to all time the inside and the outside of the heart and home and country of the Irish peasant."[12] Several decades later, W. B. Yeats, who agreed with Davis about little else, praised Carleton as "the historian of his class," and said of his work: "The true peasant was at last speaking, stammering, illogically, bitterly, but nonetheless with the deep and mournful accent of the people. . . . Beside Miss Edgeworth's well-finished four-square house of the intelligence, Carleton raised his rough clay 'rath' of humour and passion."[13] Moreover, Carleton's contributions to the emerging genre of the Irish tale or sketch are numerous and significant. His unfailing ear for rural speech gives his stories a richness of characterization un- matched by any other writer of his century; his control of irony and humor create a complexity and subtlety unknown in the work of the native Catholic writers that preceded him; his handling of narrative voice marks a significant advance in the development of the tale; and, finally, his ability to describe, with accuracy and authority, the landscape of the rural Irish peasant has not been surpassed in Irish writing to this day.

That someone who grew up as a poor, bare-footed boy in a large peasant family, with only the ragged learning of an Irish hedge school to his credit, could accomplish all this is something of a mystery. But, as Carleton never hesitated to point out, his roots in the Irish peasantry gave him a decided advantage over other writers trying to understand and record the life and culture of pre-Famine rural Ireland. "There never was any man of letters who had an opportunity of knowing and describing the manners of the Irish people so thoroughly as I had," he said in his *Autobiography*. "I was one of themselves, and mingled in all those sports and pastimes in which their characters are most clearly developed. Talking simply of the peasantry, there is scarcely a phase of their life with which I was not intimate."[14] Like the great Irish Catholic fiction writer of the twentieth century, James Joyce, Carleton also owed much to his father, and in his introduction to *Traits and Stories of the Irish Peasantry,* he acknowledges this:

My father possessed a memory not merely great or surprising, but absolutely astonishing. He could repeat nearly the whole of the Old and New Testament by heart, and was, besides, a living index to almost every chapter and verse you might wish to find in it. In all other respects, too, his memory was equally amazing. My native place is a spot rife with old legends, tales, traditions, customs, and superstitions; so that in my early youth, even beyond the walls of my own humble roof, they met me in every direction. It was at home, however, and from my father's lips in particular, that they were perpetually sounding in my ears.

As this passage indicates, his father was responsible, at least in part, for the important influence that the Gaelic storytelling tradition had on Carleton's imagination, a tradition that is only of marginal importance for most other writers of the period.

Under the eccentric tutelage of a hedge schoolmaster (remembered in his autobiographical story, "The Hedge School"), Carleton developed a strong appetite for learning and decided that the best way to satisfy it (and probably the only way for someone in Carleton's position) was to become a priest. He eventually gave up his vocation, however, and Irish Catholicism as well. In Dublin, he came under the influence of Caesar Otway, who published some of Carleton's first sketches in his *Christian Examiner,* an anti-Catholic journal. He also conformed to the Church of Ireland and deliberately fashioned himself, as Thomas Flanagan has said, into Mr. William Carleton of Dublin.[15] But just as Joyce, in his exile, wrote insistently about the Ireland that he had left behind him, so Carleton expended most of his literary energies on one subject—the world of the County Tyrone peasant that he had known as a boy and a young man.

As the "historian of his class," Carleton saw himself as working against the "stage-Irish" stereotype of the English theater. Perhaps his most effective

means of countering that damaging caricature—and certainly his most important contribution to the realistic tradition of Irish fiction in the nineteenth century—is his facility for rendering the speech of the Irish peasant.
From Maria Edgeworth's decision to let Thady tell his story in his own
tongue to the efforts of the Banim brothers and Gerald Griffin to reproduce
peasant dialect in their stories, Irish writers committed to describing their
country accurately for English readers had recognized the importance of
mastering the speech of a people whose English was strongly influenced by
the Gaelic language. No writer of the century was more gifted at doing this
than was Carleton, nor was any other writer better able to use dialogue as a
means of characterization. Indeed, Carleton's characters are almost always
developed by what they say and how they say it, rather than by what they
do.

How much Carleton is able to accomplish through dialogue can be seen
in one of his best-known stories, "Going to Maynooth." The story's success
depends largely on Carleton's ability to keep the reader on the side of his
hero, Denis O'Shaughnessy, while at the same time condemning Denis's an-
tisocial and priggish attitudes, and Carleton manages to do this largely
through dialogue; the reader can always see, in Denis's conversation with
others, not only how much the community is to blame for Denis's exaggerated views of himself, but also how pathetically ill-equipped Denis is for
fulfilling his ambition of going to Maynooth. This ironic perspective on Denis's comedy of language is nowhere more painfully evident than in his conversation with Susan Connor, the girl whom he gives up for the priesthood.
Denis's attempts to respond to Susan's simple speech and honest affection
are certainly comic; but the very humor in his discourse suggests that he is
making a sacrifice for which he will not be rewarded:

"Denis," replied the innocent girl, "you sometimes speak that I can undherstand
you; but you oftener spake in a way that I can hardly make out what you say. If it's
a thing that my love for you, or the solemn promise that passed between us, would
stand in your light, or prevint you from higher things as a priest, I am willing to—
to—to give you up, whatever I may suffer." . . .

Susan," he replied, "to tell the blessed truth, I am fairly dilemma'd. My heart is
in your favour; but—but—hem—you don't know the prospect that is open to me.
You don't know the sin of keeping back such a—a—a—galaxy as I am from the
church. I say, you don't know the *sin* of it. *That's* the difficulty. If it was a common
case it would be nothing! but to keep back a person like me—a *rara avis in terris*—
from the priesthood, is a sin that requires a great dale of interest with the Pope to
have absolved."

Denis's speech here reveals not only his extreme moral discomfort in having to go back on his promise to Susan, but also, in its comically pathetic irregularities, the unhappy truth, unperceived by Denis, that the grand prospect that he envisions stretching before him is an illusion.

The comic strain in Carleton—and he is primarily a comic writer—is frequently colored by this kind of ironic vision of the hopeless position of the Irish peasant. "It has been said," Carleton wrote in the introduction to *Traits and Stories of the Irish Peasantry,* "that the Irish, notwithstanding a deep susceptibility of sorrow, are a light-hearted people; and this is strictly true. What, however, is the one fact but a natural consequence of the other? No man for instance ever possessed a higher order of humour, whose temperament was not naturally melancholy, and no country in the world more clearly establishes that point then Ireland." A number of Carleton's stories are thinly veiled autobiographical accounts of his own youth, when he, like Denis O'Shaughnessy, was fired with high ambitions to fly by the nets of his upbringing. And the self-reflexive irony with which Carleton views Denis O'Shaughnessy is not unlike the ironic vision of Stephen Dedalus that informs Joyce's *A Portrait of the Artist as a Young Man.* James Joyce of Trieste and Mr. William Carleton of Dublin both wrote out of an essentially comic vision, but both also understood—and exploited in their art—the strength of those nets surrounding the very different Irelands they knew so well.

The sophistication of Carleton's short fiction is also evident, on occasion, in his handling of narrative voice. The first five stories in *Traits and Stories of the Irish Peasantry* are organized around a storytelling framework similar to that used by Griffin in *Tales of the Munster Festivals.* But whereas Griffin narrates all his tales in the same distanced third-person voice, Carleton lets his characters tell their stories in their own voices. By doing this, he avoids Griffin's failing of using a highly educated and literate voice—essentially an English voice—to describe and interpret material that tends to resist it. Carleton's technique also makes room for various kinds of irony. "The Battle of the Factions," one of the most violent of all Carleton's stories, is narrated by Pat Frayne, the local hedge schoolmaster. The story recounts a long-standing feud between two Irish families, ending in a bloodbath in which the heroine, on seeing her betrothed killed with a scythe, beats the murderer to death with a rock, only to discover that he is her brother. The lofty and erratically learned narration of the schoolmaster creates a sizable gap between the narrative voice and what it describes, and so works ironically to undermine the narrator's credibility. Thus, when the schoolmaster recommends faction fighting (battles between native Irish families) as a healthy example of Irish spirit (in contrast to religious and political violence, known as party fighting), the reader sees through the narrator to the story's under-lying criticism of violence in general. Carleton gave up this fictional frame-work after "The Battle of the Factions," arguing that it would "ultimately narrow the sphere of his work, and perhaps fatigue the reader by a superflu-ity of Irish dialogue and its peculiarities of phraseology." He may have been right, especially considering how large a work *Traits and Stories of the Irish Peasantry* turned out to be, but his handling of narrative voice in these early stories clearly marks a significant advance in the development of short fiction in nineteenth-century Ireland.

Thomas Flanagan said that Carleton was "the richest talent in nineteenth-century Ireland and the most prodigally wasted."[16] The second half of this statement cannot be disputed. For all his genius, Carleton wrote remarkably uneven stories and, most of the time, with an apparently total disregard for aesthetic form. No doubt his defective education, the financial need that forced him to write under great pressure, and his rather utilitarian views of literature account for much of this, but, whatever the reason, the result is often regrettable. "The Hedge School," for example, contains within its way-ward bounds an almost perfect short story—the account of the abduction of a schoolmaster—but it is buried in a long, wandering tale that includes several lengthy tracts on peasant education and the virtues and failings of hedge schoolmasters. "The Poor Scholar," an autobiographical story, is marred by a strain of sentimentality that makes the worst writing of his Victorian contemporary, Charles Dickens, seem tepid by comparison. And Carleton's political and religious views, especially the fierce anticlericalism that came to obsess him, frequently intrude annoyingly on his art.

Nonetheless, Carleton was capable, at times, of a striking formal perfec-tion. "Wildgoose Lodge" is one of the most admirably controlled and con-structed stories written in Ireland in the nineteenth century. It is somewhat uncharacteristic of Carleton in that it has no trace of comedy, but it is told with all the finesse of a master of the modern short story. Based on a histor-ical event, the story tells of the burning of a house and family by a group of Ribbonmen. These radicals had earlier broken into the house to steal guns; the owner, although a Catholic, had prosecuted, and some of the thieves were convicted. Part of the force of the story depends on its narrative point of view; the first-person narrator is someone who joins the expedition reluc-tantly and does not take an active part in it. Because he is an outsider, neither he nor the reader discovers exactly how the revenge of the Ribbonmen will be exacted until the house is set on fire. Carleton's powers of characteriza-tion and imagery also contribute significantly to the story's effectiveness. The leader of the Ribbonmen appears to be a cold, calculating man, but occasionally this mask slips just enough to let the narrator see the demonic urge for cruelty and violence lurking beneath the surface. This Satanic imagery is carefully worked through the story, culminating in the description of the flooded lands around the burning house:

The hills and country about us appeared with an alarming distinctness; but the most picturesque part of it was the effect of reflection of the blaze on the floods that spread over the surrounding plains. These, in fact, appeared to be one broad mass of liquid copper, for the motion of the breaking waters caught from the blaze of the high waving column, as reflected in them, a glaring light, which eddied, and rose, and fluctuated, as if the flood itself had been a lake of molten fire.

In 1853, a few years after the Great Famine, a reviewer writing in the *Edinburgh Review* praised Carleton's work in these terms: "It is in his pages and in his alone that future generations must look for the truest and fullest, though still far from complete, picture of those who ere long will have passed away from that troubled land, from the records of history, and the memory of man forever."[17] *Traits and Stories of the Irish Peasantry* was published in two series, the first in 1830 and the second in 1833. Although they earned him a high reputation in Irish as well as English circles, after 1833 Carleton devoted more and more of his literary energies to the novel. One of the best of these, *The Black Prophet,* was published in 1847 in the midst of the Famine, and the book is a painful record of the suffering and misery endured by Irish peasants in that particularly black period of their history. Carleton continued to write after the Famine—tales and sketches as well as novels—but the best of his work was clearly behind him. His comic genius had found a sympathetic subject in the world of pre-Famine peasant life that he knew from the inside out, and the forces that swept away that world, in waves of starvation and emigration, seemed also to have taken its most convincing and accomplished spokesman with them.

The Gothic dimension noticed in the work of the Banim brothers and Griffin can also be found in the stories of Carleton. But the full flowering of the Gothic tradition in nineteenth-century Irish fiction occurs, significantly, not in the work of a native Irish writer, but in that of a man who belonged to the class responsible, in large part, for the oppression of the native Irish. Joseph Sheridan Le Fanu enjoyed the diminishing but still definite advantages of his Protestant birth at a time when the Ascendancy, partly because of the Famine that had all but silenced the native tradition, was increasingly conscious of this responsibility. Le Fanu's ghost stories owe much to the Gothic tradition of English fiction, but in the best of his work, that tradition takes on a decidedly Irish coloring: behind the ruined castle of Gothic convention stands the declining Big House of the

Protestant Ascendancy, and behind the ghosts and mysteries of Gothic romance lurks the shadow of racial guilt.

Le Fanu had one important Anglo-Irish predecessor, a man whose writings left their mark on the Banims, Griffin, and Carleton—Charles Robert Maturin. An eccentric man, educated at Trinity College and ordained a minister, Maturin wrote one highly influential novel, *Melmoth the Wanderer,* published in 1820. Maturin once said that he wanted his readers to "sit down by my magic Cauldron, mix my dark ingredients, see the bubbles work, and the spirits rise."[18] And indeed all the excesses of the Gothic novel are to be found in the pages of *Melmoth the Wanderer,* a long, digressive, and indulgent book made up of five distinct tales inside an outer narrative frame. But Maturin is, at times, capable of a striking psychological realism not unlike that of Le Fanu's best work. An example occurs in "The Tale of the Spaniard," a story told by a man of noble but illegitimate birth who is forced by his family to become a monk. At one point, the monk, who has been tortured for his hostile attitude, is called to a meeting with the superior of the monastery, and his reflections reveal, with remarkable realism, his disturbed psychological state:

I went, but not as at former times, with a mixture of supplication and remonstrance on my lips,—with hope and fear in my heart,—in a fever of excitement or of terror,—I went sullen, squalid, listless, reckless; my physical strength, borne down by fatigue and want of sleep; my mental, by persecution, incessant and insupportable. I went no longer shrinking from, and deprecating *their worst,* but defying, almost desiring it, in the terrible and indefinite curiosity of despair.

Like Maturin, Le Fanu attended Trinity College, but he gave up a career in law for journalism. He was the editor and proprietor of a Dublin newspaper and, between 1861 and 1869, editor of the *Dublin University Magazine,* the single most important outlet for Irish fiction writers in the nineteenth century. His commitment to the cause of the troubled Ascendancy is evident in his journalistic work, which argues for a literary nationalism that would leave the Union undisturbed.

As V. S. Pritchett has argued, Le Fanu's Anglo-Irishness has more than a little to do with the style of his stories, which preserve the elegance and polish of eighteenth-century English prose. "The curious thing is that Le Fanu wrote this story ["Green Tea"] in 1872," Pritchett says in an introduction to Le Fanu's best collection of stories, *In a Glass Darkly,* "when the English ghost industry was turning out its stuff like Birmingham trays; his immunity is due to the fact that he wrote in Dublin, always a hundred years behind the time."[19] Le Fanu's Ascendancy roots are also evident in the vein of social criticism, directed largely at Anglo-Irish society, that runs through his stories, extending the work of Maria

Edgeworth and anticipating that of another Anglo-Irish writer interested in the supernatural, Elizabeth Bowen.

But it is in his exploration of guilt that Le Fanu's Anglo-Irish origins work their way most powerfully into his fiction. In expressing the sense of guilt and insecurity that haunted his own class, Le Fanu created stories that ultimately transcend not just the Gothic tradition to which they owe so much, but also the Anglo-Irish sensibility that lies behind them. Le Fanu's examination of the dark side of human nature runs against the grain of Victorian optimism, and anticipates the post-Freudian psychological despair of so much twentieth-century literature. As Pritchett says, guilt is the ghost in Le Fanu's writing, and, in the end, "It is we who are the ghosts."[20]

These ghosts take a number of forms in Le Fanu's stories—the mysterious small man who dogs the footsteps of Captain Barton in "The Familiar" until he meets his death in a manner that is never explained; the monkey that appears to the Rev. Mr. Jennings in "Green Tea" and that is clearly associated with Jennings's guilt-ridden feelings of religious doubt; and the figures and scenes that haunt the protagonist of "Mr. Justice Harbottle," a corrupt judge. The connection between ghosts and guilt is especially marked in the last of these stories. Harbottle is a well-known hanging judge, and one of the people that he has unjustly condemned to death is a man named Lewis Pyneweck, whose wife has run off to live with Harbottle. Harbottle's first brush with a guilty conscience occurs when he sees in court—after Pyneweck has been executed—a figure who looks alarmingly like Pyneweck. Next, he receives a letter from a mysterious "High Court of Appeals" announcing his own trial for Pyneweck's murder. This is followed by what seems to be a dream, in which Harbottle is tried by a judge very like himself and sentenced to die in a month. Exactly one month later, the judge is found by Pyneweck's wife hanged from the bannister of his house in a scene that strikingly parallels Harbottle's earlier dream vision of a set of three gallows topped by Pyneweck's figure.

The difficulty of deciding what is real and what is imagined in this story is deliberately compounded by its complex form. Like all the stories in *In a Glass Darkly,* "Mr. Justice Harbottle" is set within a fictional framework of an editor's presentation of the papers of a German physician, Dr. Martin Hesselius, interested in psychic matters. Dr. Hesselius offers one interpretation of the events of Harbottle's life, based on a pseudoscientific theory of how the human mind works, but the story subtly undermines this rational hypothesis, both in the appearance of the letter, the reality of which suggests some kind of revenge plot, and in its narrative-within-narrative structure. Among Dr. Hesselius's papers is one written by a Mr. Harmon, who tells of an elderly man who reportedly saw two ghosts, one carrying a hangman's noose, in his nearly deserted house one night. Harmon, on hearing this story, wrote to a friend interested in such matters, and this friend, in a letter, tells the story, originally heard from his father, of Mr. Justice Harbottle. This complex structure enhances the ambiguity of the story—and of Dr. Hesselius's interpretation of it—by insisting on its secondhand nature. All that is clear by the end of the story is that the forces that eventually cause the protagonist's death are, in part at least, the product of guilt.

Le Fanu's mastery over the form of the short story is also evident in his handling of narrative voice. Part of the success of *In a Glass Darkly* depends on the variety of voices used to tell the tales. Dr. Hesselius's voice, as it is heard in the narration of "Green Tea," is marked by the cold skepticism of his profession. Describing the collapse of Mr. Jennings, he says: "When Mr. Jennings breaks down quite, and beats a retreat from the vicarage, and returns to London, where, in a dark street off Piccadillly, he inhabits a very narrow house, Lady Mary says that he is always perfectly well. I have my own opinion about that. There are degrees, of course. We shall see." The first-person narrator of "Carmilla," a young woman victimized by a vampire, tells her story in a voice marked by naiveté and innocence. "My father is English," she says in the opening paragraph, "and I bear an English name, although I never saw England. But here, in this lonely and primitive place, where everything is so marvellously cheap, I really don't see how ever so much more money would at all materially add to our comforts, or even luxuries."

"Carmilla" is, at the very least, a masterful vampire story, and probably the inspiration for Bram Stoker's better-known *Dracula*. But it is also a story about sexual passion and loss of innocence. The narrator's realization that the strange young woman whom she has taken into her house and confidence is, in fact, Mircalla, countess of Karnstein, supposedly dead for 150 years, develops suspensefully and gradually; it also is paralleled by the narrator's uncertain coming to sexual awareness. The shocking parallel between vampirism and sexual passion is deliberately drawn, and the story stands as a warning against total submission to that powerful drive. Although Carmilla is eventually discovered and destroyed, her memory—and the passion that she represents—cannot be so easily erased, as the end of the story insists: "To this hour the image of Carmilla returns to memory with ambiguous alternations—sometimes the playful, languid, beautiful girl; sometimes the writhing fiend I saw in the ruined church; and often from a reverie I have started, fancying I heard the light step of Carmilla at the drawing-room door."

If Le Fanu's stories of guilt and sexuality anticipate the twentieth century, those of Edith Somerville and Martin Ross represent the last cry of the nineteenth century. The fiction of these two Anglo-Irish cousins celebrates a world of Protestant landlords and Catholic tenants that, even as they wrote, was fast disappearing. And yet the formal perfection of many of their stories stands as a significant landmark on the road from the unwieldy tales of the first half of the nineteenth century to the accomplished art of the modern Irish short story. Moreover, although they looked out at that vanishing world through the rose-colored windows of the Big House, this final view of rural Irish life in the nineteenth century is often surprisingly broad-minded, remarkably sympathetic to the class that would, before the twentieth century was too far advanced, put an end to Anglo-Irish rule in Ireland.

Edith Somerville and her second cousin, Violet Martin (who took the pseudonym Martin Ross), came from similar backgrounds. Miss Somerville was born into an Anglo-Irish family from Castlehaven in West Cork, the setting for many of the stories that she wrote with her cousin. She met her cousin, whose family was from Ross, County Galway, in 1886. It was, as it turned out, a happy moment for Irish literature, and Miss Somerville has remembered it in these terms: "It is trite, not to say stupid, to expatiate upon that January Sunday when I first met her; yet it has proved the hinge of my life, the place where my fate, and hers, turned over, and new and unforeseen things began to happen to us."[21]

By the time this meeting took place, the world that would come to life in the stories of these two Anglo-Irish women was already seriously threatened. And in the next few years, a whole series of political and social changes—most notably the land acts that gradually transferred ownership of the land from landlord to tenant—were to change radically the landscape of rural Ireland. Somerville and Ross were quite aware of these changes and by no means neutral about them. In "The Finger of Mrs. Knox," a story from their last volume of stories about Major Yeates (*In Mr. Knox's Country*), the woman who represents the old Ascendancy in all these stories, Mrs. Knox, is appealed to by one of her former tenants for help in settling a dispute with a notorious moneylender. The peasant rests his plea on his faith that Mrs. Knox would never stand by and see one of her own wronged:

"I have no tenants," replied Mrs. Knox tartly; "the Government is your landlord now, and I wish you joy of each other!"

"Then I wish to God it was yourself we had in it again!" lamented Stephen Casey; "it was better for us when the gentry was managing their own business. They'd *give* patience, and they'd *have* patience."

The creators of Mrs. Knox and Mr. Casey would be quick to agree.

Somerville and Ross have been accused of making literary capital out of the stage-Irish stereotype that earlier, Catholic writers like Griffin and Carleton had tried to eradicate. But the charge will not hold up. The humor in their stories is rarely enjoyed at the expense of the native Irish, and indeed they reserve their sharpest satire, in stories like "Lisheen Races, Second-hand" and "The Last Day of Shraft," for the English, whom they portray as hopelessly naive about the country they govern. Moreover, many of their stories turn on a comic reversal of the master-servant relationship, in which Major Yeates is outwitted by the people whom he presumes to sit in official judgment of.

Somerville and Ross's three volumes detailing the experiences of Major Yeates—*Some Experiences of an Irish R. M.* (1899), *Further Experiences of an Irish R. M.* (1908), and *In Mr. Knox's Country* (1915)—are held together by the narrative voice of Yeates. All the events of the stories are filtered through his consciousness, and although he is likeable and articulate, he is, for the most part, an uninformed narrator. The stories tend to move from relatively quiet openings to a bewildering series of fast-paced events that leave the major in the dark until the very end. But when he finally understands what has happened, Yeates usually ends up admiring the native Irish whom his adventures bring him into contact with—particularly the imagination, cunning, and wit that he comes to see as necessary survival techniques for an oppressed race.

These stories also work to win admiration for the governed rather than those who govern by expressing both sides of Yeates's Anglo-Irish character. The Irishman in Yeates frequently responds warmly to the very qualities that outrage his English side; in "Lisheen Races, Second-hand," for instance, he takes considerable pleasure in showing the visiting Englishman Leigh Kelway some of the decidedly un-English qualities of Irish life. On the other hand, the common-sensical, English side of his character permits him, in "The Last Day of Shraft," to view his wife's romantic enthusiasm for Celtic lore with reasonable skepticism:

During the previous winter she had had five lessons and a half in the Irish language from the National Schoolmaster, and believed herself to be one of the props of the Celtic movement. My own attitude with regard to the Celtic movement was sympathetic, but a brief inspection of the grammar convinced me that my sympathies would not survive the strain of triphthongs, eclipsed consonants, and synthetic verbs, and that I should do well to refrain from embittering my declining years by an impotent and humiliating pursuit of the most elusive of pronunciations.

This passage also demonstrates how Somerville and Ross manipulate narrative voice to control the attitudes of their English readers. Like much of

Yeates's narration, it embodies an attitude and tone of voice that the English reader can readily identify with, and because of this narrative credibility, when Yeates expresses views that are sympathetic to the Irish, his English reader, consciously or unconsciously, finds it deceptively easy to agree.

Quite apart from their effective use of narrative voice and irony, the stories of Somerville and Ross also merit acclaim because of their economy. "Poison d'Avril," one of their better-known stories, runs to just ten pages, and yet, through careful selection of incident and narrative interpretation, it manages to convey a wide range of Irish life—from the major's somewhat bewildered faith in what he calls the "personal element," to the sarcastic merriment of the peasant women on the train when they discover how much the major paid for the salmon that he is carrying back to his wife in England, to the crafty obsequiousness of the Irish hotel manager who winds up with the salmon. Somerville and Ross's ear for dialect is also evident in this story, especially in the conversation between the peasant women crowded into Yeates's compartment on the train:

> "Move west a small piece, Mary Jack, if you please," said a voluminous matron in the corner, "I declare we're as throng as three in a bed this minute!"
> "Why then, Julia Casey, there's little throubling yourself," grumbled the woman under the flap. "Look at the way meself is! I wonder is it to be putting humps on themselves the gentry has them things down on top o' them! I'd sooner be carrying a basket of turnips on me back than to be scrooged this way!"

Yet for all their humor and realism, these stories come up conspicuously short in some important areas. The tales that Major Yeates spins deal with the surface of social manners and customs; characterization is not developed significantly beyond caricature, and there is little exploration of the inner life of human passion. After listening to Yeates's voice through three volumes of stories, the reader realizes that he still does not know the man intimately. And yet if, as Frank O'Connor once said, these accounts of the bizarre experiences of a resident magistrate in the wilds of West Cork are, finally, "yarns, pure and simple,"[22] that is, perhaps, praise enough.

In the "Telemachus" episode of Joyce's *Ulysses,* Stephen Dedalus says of the mirror in which Buck Mulligan is shaving: "It is a symbol of Irish art. The cracked looking-glass of a servant." This remark was supposedly made on a June day only four years into this century. And indeed, from the perspective of 1904, the description seems apt. Certainly the mirror of Irish short fiction in the nineteenth century was cracked—marred, at its worst, by annoying didacticism, purple prose, weak characterization, uncertain narrative line, and a general disregard for aesthetic form. It was also the literature of a servant; whether in the hands of the oppressed or the oppressors, it was written not for the Irish themselves but for export to their curious or not-so-curious rulers across the Irish Sea. These two points are vitally connected. The issue raised by Gerald Griffin's sour skeptic in the introduction to *Tales of the Munster Festivals*—that "a ruined people stand in need of a more potent restorative than an old wife's story"—cuts both ways; perhaps an old wife's story, if it is to be more than an old wife's story, stands in need of concerns more subtle and far-reaching than the political struggles of a ruined people.

Nonetheless, the achievement of Irish short fiction in the nineteenth century is substantial. If the looking-glass that it held up to the changing world of the Big House and the cabin was cracked, it was still capable of teaching its readers something not only about Irish life but about the art of fiction as well—still capable of the subtle ironies of Thady Quirk's tale, of the strikingly realistic dialogue of Denis O'Shaugnessy, of the convincing psychological characterization of the guilt-ridden Mr. Justice Harbottle, and of the ironic humor of the bemused and befuddled Major Yeates. And if that cracked looking-glass belonged to a servant, always eager to catch the master's ear, it still managed to bring to the world's attention many corners of Irish life and culture that had lain hidden in darkness for centuries. As it develops through the nineteenth century, the tale of Irish fiction is neither plain nor unvarnished—no more so than Thady Quirk's tale turns out to be. And it does succeed, as does Thady's story, in achieving its overriding ambition, one referred to in Thady's final remarks: "As for all I have here set down from memory and hearsay of the family, there's nothing but truth in it from beginning to end."

IN QUEST OF A NEW IMPULSE:
GEORGE MOORE'S THE UNTILLED FIELD
AND JAMES JOYCE'S DUBLINERS

James F. Carens

When John Eglinton remembered the time immediately following George Moore's return to Ireland in 1901, he recalled that "often at night when the library closed . . . [Moore] would wait for me, and I would join him in long walks, as about the same period I walked with a strange young man whose importance I was then far from divining, James Joyce."[1] Eglinton's recollection perhaps exaggerated the degree of his intimacy with the strange young man, though not the extent of his exchanges and perambulations with Moore. In any case, it was early in 1904 that Eglinton rejected for publication in *Dana,* the new journal he was editing, that strange young man's strange brief prose work, "A Portrait of the Artist"—not quite an essay, not quite a short story, not quite an autobiography, not quite a prose poem, but a little of each. Toward the close of that year, another Dublin editor, the generous A. E. (George W. Russell, mystic, poet, and painter) encouraged Joyce to write some short stories for the *Irish Homestead* and published three of them. Much revised, they were to appear in *Dubliners,* most of which Joyce had completed by the end of 1905.[2] The vagueness of Eglinton's time reference—"about the same period"—may indicate only that he was straining to drop a name. More generously, we might conclude that as he wrote about Moore and *The Untilled Field,* he inevitably associated James Joyce and *Dubliners* with the period. And, indeed, the years between the spring of 1901 and the winter of 1905–6 were the ones during which Moore and Joyce each produced an unforgettable short story collection.

The literary moment of which *The Untilled Field* and *Dubliners* are products was one in which unusual changes were taking place, both in the drift of the Irish literary renaissance and in the sensibility and artistry of the two writers. Even William Butler Yeats, who was at the heart of the literary movement, was relinquishing the mistiness of the Celtic Twilight and plunging into theater work. This activity would contribute to the transformation of his poetic style and alter his attitudes toward his public, Ireland, Irish myth, and the nature of reality.

By the time he began the stories of *The Untilled Field,* Moore's relations with Yeats were strained, and he was detaching himself from the theatrical movement. He had lost his first hectic enthusiasm for the revival of Gaelic and for the literary movement that had brought him to Ireland; he had persuaded himself that the Catholic church, in particular its clergy, was the enemy of a healthy national spirit.[3] Moreover, this writer, who had already, in *A Mummer's Wife* (1885), introduced the naturalism of Zola into the English novel and produced a tour de force of ironic tone in the autobiographical *Confessions of a Young Man* (1888) and a masterly novel in the realistic mode, *Esther Waters* (1894), was in search of new material and new modes of expression. He was as much in the process of transition as Yeats.

The young Joyce, who had already declared his independence of the literary revival, its attitudes, and its themes, was testing his own skills, attempting to move beyond his collection of brief prose epiphanies to fully articulated works of fiction. His autobiographical novel, *Stephen Hero,* which he began after the rejection of "A Portrait of the Artist," was ultimately to be abandoned as unsuccessful and to be reworked into *A Portrait of the Artist as a Young Man.* In the short stories he began to write for A. E., Joyce found the form best suited to his emerging talent, and in the course of working on these stories, he found certain of the skills and much of the control he was to need for his mature works. Thus, each in his own way, Yeats, Moore, and Joyce, in the years following 1900, brought a searching and ironic criticism to bear on contemporary Irish society; but whereas Yeats did so obliquely by contrasting the present with a heroic past, Moore and Joyce attended to the particulars of the present.

It was John Eglinton who put into Moore's mind the notion of producing a collection of stories. "We talked always of his books, of Ireland—not as a field of controversy but as a subject for literature; and I remember once saying to him that he ought to write a series of stories on the model more or less of Turgenev's 'Sketches of a Sportsman.'"[4] Surely for a writer who had already achieved the self-deflating ironies of *Confessions of a Young Man* and the sympathetic detachment of *Esther Waters,* the green fields of Ireland could not become a field of controversy? But Moore had also written *Parnell and His Island* (1887), in which he paid more attention to the mud cabins of his native land than to its green fields; in that series of sketches, he had given full vent to his detestation of what seemed to him Ireland's backwardness and barbarism. And by the time Eglinton suggested a collection of stories on Ireland, Moore was already persuaded that he must be Ireland's savior, releasing his native land from the repressive puritanism of the clergy. Characteristically, he could not be swayed from a quixotic and self-defeating course of increasingly public anti-Catholicism. Whereas Joyce's Stephen Dedalus, when asked if, having left the church, he intended to become a Protestant, replied that he "had lost the faith . . . but not . . . self-respect," George Moore, who was surely an agnostic, insisted upon publishing a letter in the *Irish Times* in which he announced that he had been accepted into the Protestant Church of Ireland.[5] Moore's correspondence of the period is filled with evidence of the intensity of his feeling. When he sent his friend Edouard Dujardin a copy of *The Untilled Field* (June 1903), he averred, "I have absolutely renounced all my Celtic hopes. Of the race there is now nothing but an end left over, a tattered rag, with plenty of fleas in it, I mean priests."[6] Although somewhat more restrained than Joyce's Simon Dedalus who describes the Irish clergy as "rats in a sewer" and "lowlived dogs," Moore was, even after the publication of his book, still considerably exercised about the influence of Catholicism on Irish life. In such circumstances, could *The Untilled Field* escape the polemical qualities of *Parnell and His Island,* even after Eglinton's recommendation of aesthetic purity?

In his study of this period of Moore's life, *George Moore in Transition,* Helmut Gerber has drawn attention to Moore's essay on Turgenev and its relevance to *The Untilled Field.* Though the essay was written more than a decade before the Irish short stories, it reveals Moore's consciousness of a central artistic problem: "Whether the writer should intrude his idea on the reader, or hide it away and leave it latent in the work." Moore concludes that either alternative "is a question of method; and all methods are good." But while he seems to come down on the side of relativism and far from Eglinton's aesthetic purism, Moore also indicates that he distinguishes between idea and ideology, for he says of Turgenev that "had he not been the marvelous artist he was, his pursuit of his idea would have lured him into all disaster, and he would have been overwhelmed and lost in the shoaling waters and quicksands of instruction and purpose."[7]

"Purpose" seems never to have been far from Moore's mind as the notion of a group of stories grew in his imagination. His first and most preposterous notion was that his stories, translated into Irish, would make a contribution to the development of a modern literature in that language and would be suitable "for the use of nuns and convent schools."[8] Soon, however, a saner, deeper, and more urgent impulse motivated him. "The ordinary short (story) is about nothing," he wrote his publisher, but these stories of his are "stories illustrating the depopulation of the country (in a 100 years there will be no more people in Ireland)."[9] Months later he was rejecting *The Untilled Field* as a title, considering *The Passing of the Gael* more "attractive."[10] At the end of his life, still reflecting on the title of the volume, he asserted that "the title of the book should have been *A Portrait of Ireland,* but that seemed too flagrant and I chose another title *The Untilled Field,* which seemed to me sufficiently suggestive of the intention of the book."[11] The intention of which he speaks is manifest not only in his declared aim but in the stories themselves, wherever and whenever it is suggested that clerical puritanism is destroying the population of the island. The title for which Moore settled implies both the economic state of the country and the rejection of sexual opportunity.

But Moore was an artist who was constantly bringing his fantasies to the threshold of action, constantly playing roles and adopting perverse attitudes designed to provoke and outrage others. He could, in his essay on Turgenev, insist that "life plus the artist" is preferable to what is "merely life" and go on to declare that "the impersonality of the artist is the vainest of illusions."[12] Yet in his preface to a new edition of the *Field* (1914), he could claim that it was "a book written in the beginning out of no desire of self-expression." Only attention to the stories themselves permits us to determine whether, despite his *idée fixe,* Moore's art was sufficient to evade the quicksands of instruction.

In the first English edition of the *Field* (1903), but not in the earlier Gaelic version, the Tauchnitz edition of 1903, or the revised English edition, Moore included two stories, "In the Clay" and "The Way Back," which framed the entire collection. One of Moore's recent interpreters has regretted the removal of these stories from the revised editions, holding that " 'In the Clay' in particular is a very fine story equal to any in the book." Anthony Farrow also develops the ingenious notion that the sculptor Rodney is to be identified with the youthful Moore who excoriated Ireland in *Parnell and His Island* and that the character Harding is to be identified with the Moore of 1902, qualified in his support for the Revival but not yet as disenchanted as he was to become.[13] One has to acknowledge that the stories, viewed as evidences of the development of Moore's attitudes, are interesting. Yet Moore, who was always inclined to indulge in hyperbolical praise of his most recent book, was also apt to be shrewd in the second thoughts that led to revisions and rejections from his canon. Furthermore, there is ample evidence that by the time Moore completed his work on the stories of *The Untilled Field,* he no longer believed that Ireland would experience a cultural rebirth. The Moore who, in June of 1902, considered that *The Passing of the Gael* would be a more appropriate title for his book and asserted that all but one of the stories "tells how this country is going to pieces"[14] is not very different from the Rodney who exclaims that he does not "believe in their resurrections or in their renaissance, or their anything" and insists that "The Gael has had his day. The Gael is passing." In addition, while "In the Clay" is a stronger story than "The Way Back," it is also a story in which "instruction and purpose" overwhelm both narrative and character. Rodney's protest against the repressiveness and puritanism of Irish society—which would deny him a beautiful nude model—and his northerner's celebration of the "pagan life" of Italy, where "beautiful nakedness abounds," is insistent and crude. No real dramatic irony qualifies his role as the author's mouthpiece. The villain of "In the Clay" is Father McCabe, who complains to the parents of Rodney's beautiful model that she has posed in the nude. When Rodney's studio is vandalized and his finest work, still "in the clay" is destroyed, he blames the priest—"Iconoclast and peasant!"—and launches into a diatribe against him: "It is he who blasphemes. They blaspheme against life. . . . My God, what a vile thing is the religious mind." In fact, not Father McCabe but Lucy's younger brothers were responsible for the destruction of the statue, and this vandalism is a consequence of their curiosity, clumsiness, and devotion to the priest. Both Lucy, the unconventional model, and Rodney, the artist, are driven into exile. The repressive values of the clergy, transmitted to a naive and uncomprehending public, lead to the ignorant destruction of beauty. But Moore's fable—which was surely not far off the mark as a comment on Irish society at the turn of the century—is so close to the surface of the story that it fails to convince us, and it so dominates the action of the story that the fictional details also fail to convince. Rodney's attack is not only on the clergy but on the literary revival and on the cultural backwardness of Ireland. The inclusiveness of his attack is irrational; its tone is shrill and snobbish: "This is no place for a sculptor to live in. It is no country for an educated man. It won't be fit for a man to live in for another hundred years. It is an unwashed country."

Of "The Way Back," far less can be said in commendation. Rodney and Harding meet by chance in London, just as Harding is about to depart for Ireland and Rodney for Italy. We learn that Harding has encountered Lucy on the street accidentally and that he has made a halfhearted attempt to seduce her—though filled with fatuous timidities about being seen with her. Following his unsuccessful effort to get her onto the stage, Lucy departed for America to marry a mathematical instrument maker, a Mr. Wainscott from Chicago. Not even Moore's sense of verisimilitudinous social detail is operative in this contrived plot, which is followed by a conversation among Rodney, Harding, and Carmady, who has joined them on the eve of his departure for South Africa. These three merely amplify criticisms of Ireland that have been made throughout the two stories. The only passage of the story that is touched by life is the concluding speech of Harding in which he describes the "pathetic beauty in the country itself," the wistfulness of its country people, the interest of "what Paddy Durkin and Father Pat will say to me on the roadside." Reading those lines, one sees just how badly Moore's framing stories failed to create any palpable life and bogged down (if the pun may be forgiven) in discursive abuse. His decision to exclude them from subsequent editions, though it sacrificed a formal element that, executed rather differently, might have been aesthetically pleasing, was the right one for him to make.

As he worked on his Irish stories, Moore was convinced that there was a fundamental unity in his conception of them. By the time he had completed ten of the original English edition's thirteen, he was declaring that his book was no "mere collection of short stories" but rather "a book about Ireland which came to me in the form of short stories;"[15] less than a month later, when he had completed twelve, he described the book as "a perfect unity" and hoped that it would "not be reviewed as a collection of short stories."[16] Within another month's time, he offered as an appropriate subtitle "A Novel in Thirteen Episodes."[17] Given this attitude, his decision to reject "In the Clay" and "The Way Back"—his prologue and epilogue—suggests that he had come to see them as so inferior to the rest of the collection that he must sacrifice the unity of the whole. Even at the close of his life, Moore was persuaded that, after a year and a half of residence in Ireland, he had begun "to see Ireland as a portrait and the form in which he chose to draw her portrait was the scene of a dozen short stories."[18] In 1902, when he spoke of the unity of his book, he had said that in twelve of the stories "there is a priest and Ireland is represented as a sort of modern Tibet."[19]

When Turgenev's *A Sportsman's Notebook* was published in the middle of the century, it had a profound impact in Russia on attitudes toward serfdom—an impact all the more intense because Turgenev allowed his audience to draw its own conclusions from the scrupulous ironic detachment with which he handled his materials. George Moore's stories certainly never had the impact on Irish public opinion he hoped they would have. That the anticlerical impulse was close to the center of his imagination as he worked on *The Untilled Field* is undeniable; and certainly an insistent motif throughout the individual stories is that his country is being depopulated by the oppressive influence of a joyless clergy. We have to ask then whether Moore's art was sufficiently strong to contain the violence of his emotions. Did he produce a portrait or a caricature? Certainly "the shoaling waters and quicksands of instruction and purpose" were swirling around him as he worked.

However much unity Moore ascribed to the *Field,* both technically and generically there is considerable diversity in the work. A comparison with Turgenev is again instructive. Though the individual pieces in *A Sportsman's Notebook* range from "the sketch with a documentary slant" to the short story and the final piece is an encomiastic personal essay on the pleasures of hunting,[20] for all the heterogeneity of his subjects and concerns, Turgenev's pieces both in length and point of view seem more unified than do those of Moore. This is so, to some significant extent, because Turgenev's narrative persona is the same throughout the collection. One of Moore's pieces, "Almsgiving," is a personal essay dominated by a narrative persona identifiable with the author, but all the rest of the pieces are "stories," all but two of which are unmediated by a persona-narrrator. In consequence, "Almsgiving," ninth in the sequence of the 1903 edition, stands apart from the other pieces in the *Field* and does not participate in the unifying theme about which Moore had so much to say. (On the other hand, "Almsgiving" has the quirky flavor Moore could well achieve and, dwelling, through its description of the persona's encounters with a blind beggar, on the superiority of instinct over reason, mercifully makes no reference to priests.)

Although it has been argued that the modern short story and Joyce's *Dubliners* in particular derive from Moore, it has been more plausibly argued that Moore's short stories are rarely of the characteristic modern "single incident" type and that Moore's preferred form was the old-fashioned tale.[21] In fact, Moore did not use the term *short story* in a particularly precise way. For him the collection entitled *Celibate Lives* (1927) was "a volume of distinguished short stories";[22] yet, given the length and treatment of these works, it would make more sense to describe it as a grouping of three short stories and two short novels, nouvelles, or novelettes, with common psychological interests. Moore sometimes seemed reluctant to let the single short story have an autonomous life of its own. As we have seen, he made a determined effort to regard *The Untilled Field* as a novel. He was perhaps at his happiest in such a work as *A Story Teller's Holiday* (1918), in which he adopts the style of the shanachie, or storyteller, and makes a belated contribution to the literary revival. To make distinctions of genre, this book is actually a collection of five short stories, two short novels, and a novel in a dialogue framework from which the individual elements can scarcely be extricated. Of two of the stories later included in the *Field,* Moore wrote his publisher, "You have published two little, little briefs. The book contains long substantial stories."[23] The two "little, little briefs" were the stories "The Golden Apples," later retitled "Julia Cahill's Curse," and "The Wedding Gown," one of the finest short stories in the collection. Doubtless Moore would have regarded as "long substantial stories" "Some Parishioners" and "The Wild Goose." The latter is a short novel; and the former, which was an episodic short novel as it first appeared, became in the revised editions a group of four linked and related stories—"Some Parishioners," "Patchwork," "The Wedding Feast," and "The Window."

In the 1903 English edition, "The Exile" and "Home Sickness" followed "Some Parishioners"; but when Moore prepared his revised edition (1914), these two stories opened the collection, and opened it strongly. The epony-mous exile of the first story is James Phelan who leaves his native land and the family farm for America; thwarted in his love for Catherine, he con-cludes that he must leave her and the farm to his brother, Peter. In the second of the two stories, James Bryden returns from an exile in America to the village of Duncannon, where he was born and then suffering from home sickness for America goes into exile once again. The stories thus perfectly embody a central aspect of the history of modern Ireland and of the Irish people. There is no priest in "The Exile," except by allusion, though both Catherine and Peter embrace vocations and then abandon them; and while Duncannon's priest interferes with the villagers' dancing and drinking and thus contributes to Bryden's return to America, these details of the story are an aspect of its verisimilitude. In neither of the stories is the power of Moore's observation vitiated by "purpose."

Neither indulgent nor sentimental in the way he treats his characters, Moore is not censorious either about their petty and material concerns. Here (from the revised edition of 1914, which will be cited henceforth) is how he renders the concerns and the consciousness of the aging head of the house-hold in "The Exile":

> It was while eating the fried eggs that Pat gave Peter his orders. He would meet him about mid-day at the cross-roads. And he was there waiting for his son sure enough about eleven o'clock, his pigs having gone from him sooner then he had expected, the buyers being at him the moment they had cast their eyes over the pigs. "Just the kind of pig we do be wanting for the Liverpool market." He had caught the words out of the mouth of one jobber whispering in the ear of his mate. Michael was right; they were fine pigs. And, sitting on the stile waiting, he had begun to turn it over in his mind that if he had gotten five shillings more than he had expected, it was reasonable to suppose that Peter might be getting fourteen pounds a head for the bullocks, they being better value than the pigs. Well, if he did, it would be a great day for them all, and if he got no more than thirteen pounds ten shillings it would be a great day all the same. And so did he go on dreaming.

As mundane as Pat's dreaming is, Moore is satisfied, without exaggeration or contempt, to render the facts of experience with which such folk must live.

Nor was Moore evading the ways in which those facts of experience limited and circumscribed his characters. What Pat Phelan finally sees, as he sits rapt in his fantasy of success, is that Peter has returned from the market without having sold a bullock. Sensitive, a little delicate despite his sturdy frame, unsuited to farming, Peter has only two alternative careers to which he may aspire: "the cassock or the belt," the priesthood or the police. But when Peter turns to

Maynooth and the priesthood so that James will have a chance with Catherine, she enters a convent, believing that she can never have Peter. Touching as a picture of crossed fidelities, Moore's story also comments on the motives that lead people to religious institutions. His irony is such that it recognizes psychological motivation as an influence on the institutions, and his social perception is such that he recognizes the tormented interplay between human motives and the social circumstances that delimit them.

One of the saddest moments of "The Exile" occurs when Pat Phelan pauses to look out over the landscape he has known, conscious of how many have abandoned it:

The poor country was very beautiful in the still autumn weather, only it was empty. He passed two or three fine houses that the gentry had left to caretakers long ago. The fences were gone, cattle strayed through the woods, the drains were choked with weeds, the stagnant water was spreading out into the fields, and Pat Phelan noticed these things, for he remembered what this country was forty years ago. The devil a bit of lonesomeness there was in it then.

And yet while "The Exile" closes with the sad departure of James and "hundreds . . . going away in the same ship," it does not end without hope, nor does it end without affirmation of a distinctly Irish characteristic. At the climactic moment in the story, when Pat has come to the convent to advise Catherine that Peter has left Maynooth, she herself has determined that she must not take her vows. She has had her "call" and it has come to her both as vision and vocation:

I remembered Mr. Phelan, and James, who wanted to marry me, but whom I would not marry; and it seemed to me that I saw him leaving his father—it seemed to me that I saw him going away to America. I don't know how it was—you won't believe me, dear mother—but I saw the ship that is to take him away lying in the harbour. And then I thought of the old man sitting at home with no one to look after him, and it came over me suddenly that my duty was not here, but there.

Reluctant as she is to lose a young woman who has turned the convent farm into a successful and profitable operation, the Reverend Mother is so moved by the terms of Catherine's appeal that she is persuaded "that her mission was perhaps to look after this hapless young man." Were Moore working in the manner of his rejected prologue and epilogue, all this emotionally convincing detail might have been developed as a discursive diatribe against the wastefulness of conventual life; as it is, gently and obliquely, through the character of Catherine, he shows that the most ordinary of experiences may transcend the material world and that a commitment to ordinary life may be touched by the sacred.

"Home Sickness" continues Moore's account of the emptying of Ireland by the persisting emigration, exploring the theme of exile with a complex irony. Toward the close of "The Exile," Catherine assured James that he would one day return to his home; in "Home Sickness" Moore examines the experience of return. Bryden, who has established himself in New York as a bartender, returns to Duncannon, though he eventually departs again.

In this story, too, landscape plays a central role in establishing mood. As he sights the village he had once known, Bryden is conscious of its desolation even though the evening is fine. Later that night he visualizes the landscape: "He seemed to realize suddenly how lonely the country was, and he foresaw mile after mile of scanty fields stretching all round the lake with one little town in the far corner." From the peasants who had gathered in his host's cottage earlier in the evening, he had heard only such melancholy anecdotes as reinforced his sense of the emptiness of Irish life. "These peasants were all agreed that they could make nothing out of their farms. Their regret was that they had not gone to America when they were young." In the night, Bryden dreams of these men as "spectres." And yet Bryden has returned to Duncannon to restore the health he has lost working in a slum saloon in the Bowery, and Mike Scully, with whom he lodges, notices that he is "thin in the cheeks, and . . . very sallow," too. Bryden cannot help but contrast Ireland with the United States, sensing the "weakness and incompetence" of the people around him but noting too "the modern restlessness and cold energy of the people" in America. And the Irish landscape has its special charms, despite the wounds inflicted by poverty and emigration. Responding to its charms, Bryden feels health returning to him: "the morning passed pleasantly by the lake shore—a delicious breeze rustled in the trees, and the reeds were talking together, and the ducks were talking in the reeds."

By the time he introduces Margaret Dirken into the story, Moore has thus established a series of ambivalences in Bryden, both about the America he has left in search of health and about the Ireland to which he has returned. A herdsman's daughter who lives in a cottage near the Big House, Margaret also has an Irish charm that Bryden cannot dismiss: "Her cheeks were bright and her teeth small, white and beautifully even; and a woman's soul looked at Bryden out of her soft Irish eyes." As his health returns and his affection for Margaret grows, Bryden envisages a happy future for himself in Ireland. At this point in the story—which follows on Bryden's conclusion that the villagers are primitives who have made a pathetic submission to religious authority in the person of their priest—Moore seems to be leading us toward a conventional romantic resolution. But when Bryden receives a chance letter from an American friend, his senses are assailed by the "smell of the Bowery slum," and a "great longing" overwhelms him; he is homesick for the saloon in New York City. When his eyes fall again on the Duncannon landscape, he sees only "the little fields divided by blank walls"; persuaded that it is the repressive influence of the priest rather than the possibility of financial success in America that accounts for his longing for the Bowery, Bryden determines to abandon Duncannon and Margaret—despite his promise to return to her.

"Home Sickness" thus seems to be touched by Moore's anticlericalism, unless we conclude that Bryden blames the priest for his departure as a rationalization of his longing for the urban scape of the Bowery. Indeed, "Home Sickness" is most compelling in its final passage, which startlingly foreshortens most of Bryden's life following his return to America. Puzzled that "the smell of the bar seemed more natural than the smell of the fields," Bryden purchases the bar. "He took a wife, she bore him sons and daughters, the bar-room prospered, property came and went; he grew old, his wife died, he retired from business." An old man whose children have married, Bryden in his loneliness drifts into tender reveries of Ireland and of Margaret's soft eyes; he longs to see her, "to be buried in the village where he was born." Moore's conclusion transposes the theme of exile and return onto a level of powerful emotional suggestiveness. Bryden's "sickness" caused first by the Bowery and then by Ireland is the obverse of his longing first for Ireland, then for New York. The images with which the story closes are Bryden's memories of the Irish landscape—"the green hillside, and the bog lake and the rushes about it, and the greater lake in the distance, and behind it the blue line of the wandering hills"—but they are also universal images of longing for an ideal state. These images suddenly elevate the entire story to a level of feeling for which all its details have been a preparation.

"Some Parishioners" (originally the first chapter of the short novel of the same name) serves in Moore's revised edition to bring the focus of the collection upon the priest himself, hitherto only a threatening background figure. While it is possible to regard "Some Parishioners," "Patchwork," "The Wedding Feast," and "The Window" as a sequence, it is rather difficult to regard them as autonomous stories. Characters and themes are so interwoven that aspects of the later "stories" make little sense without reference to the earlier ones. Indeed, despite his extensive revisions between editions of the stories, Moore leaves untouched certain details that reveal the original conception. Still, whether taken as a short novel or as a linked short story sequence, the group is impressive. Registering Father Maguire's efforts to dominate the courting rites of his parishioners, arrange their marriages, and build a new church for his dying parish, Moore gets closer to the actual life of the ordinary peasant than in any of the other parts of the *Field*. Though his emphasis at this point in his career was far less on external detail than on psychological response, he brings us close to courting practices, to social distinctions, and to the festivities of the peasants.

The first episode depicts a clash between the puritanic Father Maguire, who is obsessed with rule and observance, and his uncle, Father Stafford, a far more tolerant and understanding priest, who cannot persuade Father Tom that "The greatest saints . . . have been kind, and have found excuses for the sins of others." This clash between bigoted repressiveness and a tolerant understanding is reflected in a series of oppositions and unions that dominate the "Parishioners" episodes. When Father Tom refuses to accept their inadequate donation, Ned Kavanagh and Mary Byrne consummate their love without his benefit. Kate Kavanagh, who is attracted to Pat Connex (as he is to her), first submits to Father Tom's insistence that she marry Peter McShane and then, refusing to consummate the marriage, flees the parish, apparently to America. Mrs. Connex and Mrs. McShane clash over the wedding, each revealing to what extent their values are shaped by their circumstances in life. In her sense of superiority and disdain for social inferiors, Mrs. Connex reveals that her petty social snobbery is but a reflection of the mean-spirited orthodoxy of Father Maguire. Biddy McHale and Father Maguire engage in a battle of wills and wits, and withholds her donation, until she is assured that Biddy's life savings will purchase for the new church a stained-glass window on which she has set her heart's desire.

Indeed, it is Biddy who dominates the conclusion of the "Parishioners" episodes; and, as at the conclusion of "Home Sickness," suddenly Moore startles us by a brilliance of insight and rendition that transcends everything that has gone before. As Biddy grows more obsessed with her window, she abandons her farm and the chickens that have won the savings needed to purchase it; her clothing falls to shreds, and she wanders the countryside visiting churches. In his conception of Biddy, Moore shaped a stunning portrait of religious mania. Once her window is in place, Biddy is hardly ever out of the church; she achieves the condition of ecstasy and exaltation; she *enters* her window and hears exquisite music within it:

The saints struck their harps, and after playing for some time the music grew white like snow and remote as star-fire, and yet Biddy heard it more clearly than she had heard anything before, and she saw Our Lord more clearly than she had ever seen anybody else. She saw Him look up when He had placed the crown on His mother's head; she heard him sing a few notes, and then the saints began to sing. Biddy was lifted into their heavenly life, and among them she was beautiful and clad in shining garments.

Utterly degraded physically, living in an outhouse on bits of bread, Biddy achieves a fame that attracts further money to Father Maguire's church; he depends upon her, thinking of "the many things he wanted and that he could get them through Biddy." At the conclusion of the episode, Father Maguire and a young man observe Biddy's ecstasy, little doubting that she sees visions, though Father Maguire finds her interruptions of his services "inconvenient." Moore's irony goes far beyond this exposure of Maguire's narrowness and materialism. He leaves us no doubt that Biddy is deranged and yet makes entirely real the validity of her aesthetic and visionary experience. Only two characters escape the dualities at war with each other throughout the "Parishioners": Kate Kavanagh, the rebel who flees a society that refuses to satisfy her human nature, and Biddy McHale, who believes in a way her parish priest cannot and who transcends, through dementia, all human demands. Father Maguire tries "vainly to imagine what her happiness might be."

The priest of "A Letter to Rome" and "A Play-House in the Waste" is a very different man from Father Maguire. Father MacTurnan, who has abandoned reading for knitting, is a comic figure, grown eccentric from years of isolation in a waste district. He is also, in his pathetic and inept way, a profoundly good and decent man—and sure evidence that the artist in George Moore could not remain for long a prisoner of his anticlericalism.

The action of "A Letter to Rome" is precipitated by Father MacTurnan's concern that James Murdoch will not be able to marry Catherine Mulhare until he has earned the price of a pig. Feeling that only those who, like Murdoch, cannot find the means to take passage for America are being left behind, Father MacTurnan concludes that Catholic Ireland will pass away unless a terrible sacrifice is made by the Irish clergy. Celibacy must be abandoned: priests, as "the flower of the nation," might produce such sons and daughters as would redeem the land. In the grip of this comic obsession, Father MacTurnan struggles with his Latin dictionary and produces a letter to the pope outlining his modest proposal, a proposal that elicits no response from Rome but a summons from his Bishop. That something more is going on in poor MacTurnan's psyche is revealed when, passing Norah Flynn, he blushes deeply and spends a troubled night, awakened by horrid dreams. Yet his declaration to the Bishop, as he flushes again at the latter's queries, that celibacy has been for him "a gratification rather than a sacrifice," is as sincere as the confused impulses that rise from the deeps of his unconscious—and which the Bishop seems to comprehend better than his simpler brother. Although MacTurnan has almost forgotten the original cause of his concern and blushes again when the Bishop reminds him, he accepts with gratitude the five pounds the Bishop offers; he returns to his parish, rejoicing that James Murdoch can buy two pigs and have Norah and a calf from Mike Mulhare.

"A Letter to Rome" perhaps represents the fruition of Moore's impulse to produce a volume like Turgenev's. Obliquely the story is a protest against the political administration of Ireland and its consequences in the lives of the poor; it is also, in its gently comic and understated way, a sympathetic psychological exploration of the effects of celibacy and loneliness. In its closure, which technically resembles the closures of most of these stories, "A Letter to Rome" eschews all heightening and dramatic effects. "He could not see Norah Mulhare that night; but he drove down to the famine road, and he and the driver called till they awoke James Murdoch. The poor man came stumbling across the bog, and the priest told him the news." That understatement creates what is the final distinction of the story: its sympathetic but never indulgent depiction of a pathetic decency.

In his preface to the revised *Field,* Moore recounts that before he had finished "The Exile" he had begun writing "Home Sickness," and that the village of Duncannon in the latter led him to imagine the villages around Dublin, from which process sprang the "Parishioners" episodes. "The somewhat harsh rule of Father Maguire set me thinking of a gentler type of priest, and the pathetic figure of Father MacTurnan tempted me." It is apparent, too, that as Moore's imagination was stimulated by the possibilities of the situations he conceived, important stylistic developments also were exciting him. The creation of the *Field* and its revised edition was as much a technical adventure as a thematic one, even if the short story was not the medium most suited to his talent. When Moore arranged the stories in the first English edition, "Julia Cahill's Curse" was placed between the two MacTurnan stories. However, in the revised edition, the story of Julia followed them—in a more appropriate relationship—and both "A Play-House in the Waste" and "Julia Cahill's Curse" were extensively revised. Moore was discovering the shanachie, the teller of tales, and the advantages of a dialogue betwen him and a somewhat more sophisticated interlocutor that he was to exploit in *A Story Teller's Holiday.* In their early versions, "A Play-House" and "Julia Cahill's Curse" were narrated by a persona close to Moore and suggestive of Turgenev's sportsman. But in "A Play-House" as it was revised, the persona is Pat Comer, an agricultural organizer who reports what his jarvey told him; and in the revised "Curse" the dominant narrative persona is again that of the driver, now mediated by the same but less defined narrator, Pat Comer.

In the 1914 preface, Moore pretends to believe that Synge derived the idiom of his plays from the first edition of *The Untilled Field*—a piece of outrageousness of which only Moore was capable. What had of course happened was that Moore had finally seen the advantage of the idiom of Synge and Lady Gregory and had adopted his own version of it. Much of the interest of the revised "Play-House" and "The Curse" rises from the speech of the Irish voices dominant in them. But the matter as well as the manner of the two stories is uniquely Irish, for Moore is drawing upon the myths and fantasies of the folk imagination that Yeats had celebrated decades earlier and which Moore himself had hitherto tended to disdain. So if the *Field* is to be seen as a stage in the transformation of Moore's style, it must also be recognized as a turning back to material that had been well worked over already by other writers.

In "A Play-House in the Waste," another account of human misery, Pat Comer recounts to his listeners how he has seen "pitiful . . . people starving in the field on the mountain side. . . . I call to mind two men in ragged trousers and shirts as ragged, with brown beards on faces yellow with famine; and the words of one of them are not easily forgotten: 'The white sun of Heaven doesn't shine upon two poorer men than upon this man and myself.' I can tell you I didn't envy the priest his job, living all his life in the waste listening to the tales of starvation, looking into famished faces." Father MacTurnan has made a sad little effort, in the face of government policy "that relief works should benefit nobody except the workers," to persuade the government inspector to extend a road and build a theater: his hope has been that he would later persuade the government to dredge the harbor and thus establish the theater as an excursion center for the performance of miracle plays. All these dreams came to nothing, when the roof and a wall of the play-house were leveled by a great wind.

"A Play-House in the Waste" is also a ghost story. Pat Comer's jarvey has described how he and the parish doctor were terrified by "a white thing gliding" which he later identifies as the illegitimate baby of the young woman who was to perform the role of Good Deeds in the play. According to the jarvey, Margaret gave birth to the child in her mother's stable and the child was strangled and buried by its grandmother. Later, he narrates, Father MacTurnan baptized the apparition. All this might have been shaped to punish the folly of the priest and the appalling superstition of the peasants. In fact, it is not. The story of the ghost is linked to the conditions of poverty and squalor; and since we have only the words of the jarvey and no explanation from MacTurnan, as readers, we hold the story in the ironic contemplation of the mind, just as Moore has suspended it in the ironies of his artifice.

"Julia Cahill's Curse" is just such another ironic story. Whereas the original version focused on a most unpleasant parish priest and his stiff-necked defense of his authoritarian rule, the revised version sharply limits his role, shifting the emphasis so that it falls upon the telling of the tale and the symbolic Julia. According to the shanachie-driver, every year as a consequence of Julia's curse, another roof falls in: "most of the people that were there are dead or gone to America. . . . 'tis said that the priest will say Mass in an empty chapel." Julia, who has cursed this land of the dead, resembles Kate Kavanagh of "Some Parishioners," except that she never bows to the priest's demand that she marry as he chooses. From the start of the driver's tale, she is a figure of discord, provoking fights among the young men. She is a rebel, since she is determined to choose her own mate; she is a pagan force not to be checked by priest or parent. According to the driver, she went "into the mountains every night to meet the fairies," and it is they who have given her the power to place a curse on the village; even now she may as well be with the fairies as in America. To his listener, she is "an outcast Venus." If he, in so identifying her, comes close to allegorizing her, it is the voice of the driver that dominates the story. In his marvelously irrational final words, he asserts both that he will look for her in America and that she will not have changed: "Sure hasn't she been with the fairies?" In his words, Julia is part of the lore of the folk; she symbolizes their longings for freedom, instinctual, passional expression, and timeless beauty. She is, if you please, a mythic archetype.

Of the remaining works gathered in *The Untilled Field,* one, "Almsgiving," is an essay and one, "The Wild Goose," is a short novel. It is not enough to say of the latter that it is what critics like to call an artistic failure. It is an artistic catastrophe. If ever there was a work that failed to find its objective correlative, "The Wild Goose" is that work. It is actually an effort to express the themes and concerns later so brilliantly and ironically mastered in *Hail and Farewell;* but it remains a silly, formless, and didactic attempt to fantasize about Moore's Irish experience in terms of realistic fiction. A major episode in the work occurs when the hero insists that his wealthy wife abandon breast feeding "and consider her personal charm for him." As Ned Carmady's views more and more approximate the self-defeating anticlericalism of George Moore, he and his wife drift so far apart that she finally offers him his freedom. As a short novel, "The Wild Goose" is entirely improbable; it is an abortive attempt to express Moore's anticlericalism and his infatuation and disillusionment with the revival, but also to deal with his difficult relations with women.

On the other hand, "The Wedding Gown," "The Clerk's Quest," and "So on He Fares" are very good stories, indeed, and they serve to illustrate the variety of things Moore was able to do in short fiction. "The Wedding Gown," which in its earliest published version (1887) considerably antedates any of the other stories in the volume, remains an old-fashioned tale rather than a modern short story, but it is a particularly good tale. Its leisurely opening, which gives an account of two families (the Big House and its servants), is something few writers after Joyce would permit themselves. Once past that opening, the story concentrates on a brief but powerful and affecting account of Margaret Kirwin, her love affair, the early death of her husband, her years of wandering and derangement, and her final return to her family. Moore's description of this strange survivor of romance and suffering is memorable:

> Margaret Kirwin walked with a short stick, her head lifted hardly higher than the handle, and when the family were talking round the kitchen fire she would come among them for a while and say something to them, and then go away, and they felt they had seen someone from another world. She hobbled now and then as far as the garden gate, and she frightened the peasantry, so strange did she seem among the flowers—so old and forlorn, almost cut off from this world, with only one memory to link her to it. It was the spectral look in her eyes that frightened them, for Margaret was not ugly. In spite of all her wrinkles the form of the face remained, and it was easy, especially when her little grandniece was by, to see that sixty-five years ago she must have had a long pleasant face such as one sees in a fox and red hair like Molly.

The one possession Margaret Kirwin has retained throughout a desperate pilgrimage is her wedding dress, which she has allowed no one to touch. But when Molly, her grandniece, weeps that she cannot attend a ball at the Great House for want of a gown, Margaret startles the family by insisting that Molly wear the wedding gown. For the old woman, Molly in the gown and slippers, her hair "thick and red like a fox's," is herself on her wedding day. Tapping folk legend and fairy tale, Moore brings the story to a climax in which Molly senses that she must leave the ball at the very moment when the old lady fantasizes that she is donning her dress to join her betrothed at the church. Hostile though he was to the church as an institution and skeptic though he might be, Moore was not disinclined in this story—or elsewhere in the collection—to exploit the preternatural. In this climactic passage there is also an ironic use of vegetation myth as Molly plunges home through the woods and fields "clothed in the green of spring":

> The stillness of the night frightened Molly, and when she stopped to pick up her dress she heard the ducks chattering in the reeds. The world seemed divided into darkness and light. The hawthorn-trees threw back shadows that reached into the hollows, and Molly did not dare go by the path that led though the little wood, lest she should meet Death there. For now it seemed to her that she was running a race with Death, and that she must get to the cottage before him.

By the time she reaches the door of the cottage, Molly knows, however, that death has been there before her. Thus at the very moment she had assumed the state of womanhood and in the spring of the year, she not only repeats Margaret Kirwin's experience but recognizes her own features in those of the old woman. She recognizes that she will one day look like Margaret and repeat her death as well, the death she has sought to evade:

> She approached a few steps, and then a strange curiosity came over her, and though she had always feared death she now looked curiously upon death, and she thought that she saw the likeness which her aunt had often noticed.
> "Yes," she said, "she is like me. I shall be like that some day if I live long enough." And then she knocked at the door of the room where her parents were sleeping.

It may be that the opening of "The Wedding Gown" could be handled far more economically than it was; it is difficult to imagine a more understatedly moving conclusion.

"The Wedding Gown" was conceived before the scheme for the collection has developed in Moore's imagination and before his attitude toward the church and the clergy had entered into the shaping of the *Field*. Neither "So on He Fares" nor "The Clerk's Quest" is touched by Moore's struggle to escape the didactic impulse, nor does either of them seem to have been written to deal with specifically Irish problems. Malcolm Brown was surely right in seeing "So on He Fares" as a psychological enactment of Moore's sense of two rejections by Mother Ireland;[24] and it may well be that the story also reveals something of Moore's familial and amatory experiences. However, in whatever psychic experiences it may have originated, the story contrasts with the failed psychic enactment of "The Wild Goose" and is one of Moore's best. Its essential distinction is that it creates both a child's consciousness and a maturing youth's comprehension of rejection. Though the mother is not the protagonist and her consciousness is never rendered in the way that the boy's is, the irrationality of her hatred of her child is boldly imagined and depicted. Frequently in the suddenness with which it reveals the impact and expression of the irrational, the story suggests the mature short fiction of D. H. Lawrence, and always it manifests how little Moore's sense of life was complacent or evasive, how little he deluded himself about the impulses of "a pretty child with bright blue eyes, soft curls, and a shy, winning manner." Here is the child fantasizing a release from a household in which he is not wanted:

He was very unhappy, and though he knew it was wrong he could not help laying plans for escape. Sometimes he thought that the best plan would be to set fire to the house; for while his mother was carrying pails of water from the back yard, he would run away; but he did not dare to think out his plan of setting fire to the house lest one of the spirits which dwelt in the hollow beyond the paling should come and drag him down a hole.

The boy's escape from his mother and her hatred comes when she deliberately puts a bee down his neck. In an anguish of pain and fully returning the hatred he recognizes in his mother, the boy plunges into the canal and escapes on a barge. Moore makes no attempt to explain the mother's hatred; it is merely a given in the story, but it is given so convincingly that we accept it.

Like a number of other stories in the *Field*, "So on He Fares" derives strength from the archetypal situations of folktale and legend it evokes, but to which it makes no overt allusion. Thus the boy, who has identified the barges with his absent but loved father, finds himself almost magically saved from his mother and drowning by bargemen. As if in a fairy tale, he finds a substitute mother who loves him; on her death, as if a questing hero, he becomes a sailor, leading a "rough, wild life," remembering his escape as something "like a tale heard in infancy." The climax of the story, in which he returns to his home to find his father still absent, his mother still filled with hatred for him, and another child, almost his replica, bearing his name but as loved as he was hated, is brilliantly ironic. This questing hero who has returned from the dead is repudiated once again. "In this second experience there was neither terror nor mystery—only bitterness." But while Ulick feels it is "a pity that he had ever been taken out of the canal, . . . life had taken a hold of him." He repeats his original journey. "The evening sky opened calm and benedictive, and the green country flowed on, the boat passed by ruins, castles and churches and everyday was alike until they reached the Shannon." Written ostensibly in the mode of psychological realism Moore had adopted at this point in his career, the story yet taps the archetypal and the mythic. The Shannon, which his father has described to him as the outlet for the canal and which he has always associated with male adventure, is, in effect, the water of life on which he must sail, rejected, unloved, alone, but with the bitter wisdom of understanding.

"The Clerk's Quest" is at the opposite narrative pole from "The Wedding Gown." In it, George Moore is working in the mode of the modern short story. He spoke of it and "Almsgiving" as "two little stories" and of the regrettable "Wild Goose" as a "long story." The drift of his words to his publisher seems to imply the superiority of the longer work.[25] Even Helmut Gerber echoes Moore, speaking of "The Clerk's Quest" and "Alms-Giving" as "both relatively slight stories."[26] "Alms-Giving" may resemble some of Turgenev's sketches, but its discursiveness identifies it, despite its narrative elements, as being an informal essay;

and "The Clerk's Quest," if brief, is not slight by comparison to the best work in the *Field*. It is also a work composed without reference to the original framing stories or to the provincial setting of nearly all the other stories. In "The Clerk's Quest" Moore moved into the heart of Dublin, into the very world James Joyce would depict in *Dubliners*, into the seedy atmosphere of the lower middle class:

For thirty years Edward Dempsey had worked low down in the list of clerks in the firm of Quin and Wee. He did this work so well that he seemed born to do it, and it was felt that any change in which Dempsey was concerned would be unlucky.

The directness with which Moore addresses his subject contrasts sharply with the opening of a "tale" like "The Wedding Gown"; moreover, the milieu that Moore is exploiting has much more in common with Joyce's "Counterparts" or "A Painful Case" than it does with the other stories of the *Field*. Moore's "hero" is a man who has scarcely existed, "An obscure, clandestine, taciturn little man occupying in life only the space necessary to bend over a desk, and whose conical head leaned to one side as if in token of his humility." A single accident transforms what has been Dempsey's existence—but scarcely a life. "One summer day, when the heat of the areas was rising and filling the open window, Dempsey's somnolent senses were moved by a soft and suave perfume." The "insinuating perfume"—it is the fragrance of heliotrope—rises from the check of Henrietta Brown. To Dempsey, fragrance, check, and handwriting are suddenly "pregnant with occult significances." Touched at last by romance and mystery, Dempsey becomes as obsessed a worshipper as Biddy McHale; he writes Henrietta Brown, who is resident in that romantic city Edinburgh; he squanders his meager savings on gifts of jewelry, which she refuses; he neglects his work and grows increasingly careless so that his employers are forced to dismiss him. None of this matters to Dempsey, for his romantic obsession has detached him from reason altogether. He wanders out into the Dublin suburbs. He is headed for Edinburgh! Robbed of the jewelry he carries to Henrietta, Dempsey is "sustained by his dream"; he follows that dream to a moment of ecstasy and release:

He was very tired, he had been wandering all day, and threw himself on the grass by the road-side. He lay there looking up at the stars, thinking of Henrietta, knowing that everything was slipping away, and he passing into a diviner sense. Henrietta seemed to be coming nearer to him and revealing herself more clearly; and when the word of death was in his throat, and his eyes opened for the last time, it seemed to him that one of the stars came down from the sky and laid its bright face upon his shoulder.

The measure of George Moore's success as he worked over the stories of *The Untilled Field* is that he was able not only to liberate himself sufficiently from the demon of didacticism but also from what he regarded as the unifying theme of the collection. "The Clerk's Quest" tells us nothing about the failings of the Irish clergy or the defects of Irish culture or depopulation. Moore's title offers us assurance, if we need any, that he regarded his account of a very silly and ordinary man as archetypal also. With marvelous poise, he shows us the safety and banality of the real world, the danger and ecstasy of romantic illusion. As economical and poignant a piece as he ever produced, "The Clerk's Quest" is an aesthetically balanced ironic reflection on both reality and illusion.

In making the preposterous claim that *The Untilled Field* was the source of Synge's inspiration, Moore, nevertheless, did utter one truth: "*The Untilled Field* was a landmark in Anglo-Irish literature, a new departure." That fine writer of short stories, Frank O'Connor saw Moore's book as one in a series of landmarks. "In 1924 Liam O'Flaherty published *Spring Sowing,* and at once we are back to an interrupted pattern that began in 1903 with Moore's *The Untilled Field* and was briefly resumed in 1914 in Joyce's *Dubliners*—the search for what Samuel Ferguson had called the 'Facts'".[27] Though the publication date of *Dubliners* was no more than an unfortunate feature of publishing history, the pattern O'Connor discerns has its validity; the three collections he mentions were, in truth, part of an artistic effort to get at the realities of Irish life, an effort to which George Moore certainly made the initial contribution. It is not only the case that "The Exile," "Home Sickness," "A Letter to Rome," "The Wedding Gown," "The Clerk's Quest," and "So on He Fares"—to mention the best individual tales or short stories in *The Untilled Field*—are impressive works, not even that *The Untilled Field* marks a stage in the development of the literary revival, but that the book did help to establish a tradition of Irish short story writing in the English language that is there to be assimilated by Irish writers, however much subsequent writers among them may modify the tradition.

Frank O'Connor did not stop at suggesting the place of Joyce's *Dubliners* in a particular tradition, however, for he also argued that Joyce was "not so staggeringly original as he appears in books by students of Joyce. After all, it was only twelve months before [the composition of the first three *Dubliners* stories] that George Moore had published *The Untilled Field,* and it takes a student of Joyce to ignore a simple fact like that. Moore was the only Irish writer of his time who was in touch with continental fiction. He was the first writer in these kingdoms who realized what it was all about and introduced to English fiction the principles of French naturalism. There is no doubt at all in my mind that Joyce was deeply influenced by him."[28] O'Connor is, of course, quite right. Moore was, indeed, a central figure in the development of modern literature in English. But the questions O'Connor forces us to ask are these: what was the actual nature of Moore's influence on Joyce, and was that influence manifest in the *Dubliners* stories?

When Joyce denounced the Irish Literary Theatre and W. B. Yeats in "The Day of the Rabblement," he also had some harsh words for George Moore and a few grudging words of praise. He granted to Moore "wonderful mimetic ability" and then, with all the cruelty of his youth, dismissed him as outdated: "Some years ago his books might have entitled him to the place of honour among English novelists. But though *Vain Fortune* (perhaps one should add some of *Esther Waters*) is fine, original work, Mr. Moore is really struggling in the backwash of that tide which has advanced from Flaubert through Jakobsen to D'Annunzio." Joyce's final stinging comment was that, despite Moore's "quest of a new impulse," that impulse "has no kind of relation to the future of art."[29] Joyce's arrogant words defined both his and Moore's relation as being to the art of Europe rather than to that of England; they also implied that James Joyce himself rode the crest of a literary movement now sweeping beyond D'Annunzio, while poor Moore wallowed in its backwash. However demeaning to Moore Joyce's view might be, it does reveal one influence that Moore had upon Joyce's career. He was, indeed, unavoidably *there* for Joyce—an Irish writer who tapped the central strains of European thought and literary development to which Joyce succeeded as his heir. Moore was the conduit by which the general and pervasive influence of Flaubert, Zola, symbolist poetry, Turgenev and the other Russians flowed through to the young Joyce. On the other hand, Joyce, in his correspondence with his brother Stanislaus, had little to say of *The Untilled Field* that did not suggest his utter scorn for the book. When he announced to Stanislaus (in November of 1904) that he had finally read Moore's stories in the Tauchnitz edition, which did not contain the didactic prologue and epilogue, he also pronounced the book "Damned stupid." He then expressed his disdain for Moore's command of the railway schedule into Dublin and for his punctuation.[30] About a year later, he described the structure he was devising for *Dubliners*— now amounting to ten stories—and he pointed out that no one had yet given Dublin to the world; in the same letter he launched into another attack on *The Untilled Field,* "that silly wretched book of Moore's . . . which the Americans found so remarkable for its 'craftsmanship.' " "Dear me!" he added. "It is very dull and flat indeed: and ill written."[31] During the course of the same letter, Joyce told Stanislaus how much he preferred Lermontoff's *Hero of Our Days* to anything by Turgenev; earlier he had emphatically declared the superiority of Tolstoy to Turgenev.[32] Late in his life, according to Arthur Power's record of conversations he had with him, Joyce continued to prefer Tolstoy and Dostoevski to Turgenev but praised the latter's *Sportsman's Sketches* as his "best work" and "deeper" into life than his novels. But only grudgingly did he permit Power to include George Moore among the great Irish writers: "in prose we have Sterne, Wilde, Swift (if you count him as an Irishman), and then there is George Moore, according to you, and a few others."[33]

Yet Joyce, in the same period, found the opportunity to visit Moore in London. Moore has recorded his impression of the meeting in which he found Joyce "distinguished, courteous, respectful." Moore's added words remind us of how, decades earlier, Joyce had dethroned him from "the place of honour among English novelists," for he writes that Joyce "seemed anxious to accord me the first place. I demurred, and declared him first in Europe."[34] One cannot help but wonder if Joyce had initiated the ritual of compliment in his London conversation with Moore in order to elicit Moore's belated abdication of the throne. Joyce himself had denied his elder in 1901! Certainly there are evidences of rivalry in his attitude toward Moore. Did Joyce dismiss Moore's *Field* and Turgenev (whose book inspired the work), because Joyce wished to regard himself as unindebted to them? When he told Stanislaus (in July of 1905) that he would complete *Dubliners* and then produce another book to be called *Provincials*—an ambition soon abandoned—was Joyce really declaring his wish to rewrite *The Untilled Field* as he thought it should have been written?[35] Even more tantalizingly, why, after he had first indicated to Stanislaus his disdain for *The Untilled Field*, did he plan a translation of Moore's *Celibates* (three short novels that Moore called short stories) and then abandon the work? Was the young Joyce attempting to rival and eclipse George Moore to assert his own independence?

Both in general and in particular the case can be made that Moore was a profound influence on Joyce throughout his career. Joyce's biographer, Richard Ellmann, has even shown that the ending of "The Dead," the final glory in *Dubliners*, is derived from the ending of *Vain Fortune*, which Joyce "adroitly recomposed."[36] There is evidence, we may conclude, that there were tensions in Joyce's attitude toward Moore, even a desire to better him (in all senses of the word). But there is no evidence to support the implication of Frank O'Connor that the influence of Moore was of such a kind as Joyce's admirers have been unwilling to acknowledge as a group. The *Dubliners* stories were not shaped by Moore any more than by Maupassant, Flaubert, Turgenev, or Chekhov, though they reveal the general infuence of both the realist and symbolist traditions. Not only was the form of the *Dubliners* stories arrived at independently by Joyce—who had produced versions of three of the stories before he read *The Untilled Field*—but the structure and unity of *Dubliners*, Joyce's personal disposition perhaps being reinforced by Moore's effort to achieve these in his earlier collection, was definitely Joyce's own.

When Joyce recorded his first impression of *The Untilled Field* for his brother Stanislaus, he complained, referring to "The Wild Goose," that "A woman alludes to her husband in the confession box as 'Ned.'" The same lady, he further complained, "has been living for three years on the line between Bray and Dublin" but "looks up the table to see the hours of the trains. This . . . where the trains go regularly; this after three years. Isn't it rather stupid of Moore."[37]

Joyce's criticism of Moore was anything but picayune; rather it was fundamental, for he was offended that Moore should have so poor a grasp of what seemed to him elementary social facts. It has not generally been recognized that one of the *Dubliners* stories does bear a very definite relation to one of those in *The Untilled Field*.[38] In fact, Joyce's "Counterparts," the sixth in the sequence of composition of the stories, is a total reworking of the only Dublin story in *The Untilled Field*, "The Clerk's Quest." It is a reworking by a writer who was determined that both the inner reality and the surface appearances, manners, and language of Dublin should be scrupulously rendered. Moore's Edward Dempsey works "low down in the list of clerks in the firm of Quin and Wee"; Joyce's Farrington is similarly situated in the firm of Crosbie & Alleyne. Moore's Dempsey is distracted from his life of humble and dutiful service by the scent of perfume on a check, which leads him to the worship of Henrietta Brown, and thence to dismissal and death as he experiences a vision of beauty. Joyce's Farrington, filled with rage against his servile position in a Protestant firm and thirsting for drink, is so tantalized by the perfume of a client that he is tempted to insult Mr. Alleyne, thus endangering his future with the firm. Then he is compelled to offer a humiliating apology in the presence of the perfumed woman who has aroused him.

The elements that the two stories have in common with one another are immediately apparent. The elements that contrast with one another are intriguing. For instance, Moore never quite lets us know what kind of clerical work Dempsey performs, whereas Joyce depicts the frustrating effort Farrington makes to copy a contract. Whereas Dempsey is satisfied with his lot and has even saved up a little nest egg, Farrington seethes with resentment, rage, and lust and even has to pawn his watch to go on a pub crawl with his cronies. Whereas Dempsey is a bachelor, sensitive enough to entertain a romantic love, Farrington is a married man, burdened with children he can scarcely distinguish from one another, lusting after chorus girls he cannot afford. The perfume of Henrietta Brown that assails the senses of Dempsey is the fragrance of heliotrope; the perfume of the voluptuous Miss Delacour—a "moist pungent odour" that leaves its trace on stairs and corridor—is some lusher fragrance. Pathetic Dempsey achieves his release from an indifferent world through romantic derangement; brutal and frustrated Farrington is more trapped at the close of his story than at its beginning: his bout of drinking has resulted only in a succession of humiliations, including defeat in a contest of strength by a younger Englishman. Thwarted, he turns his violence against one of his children. In every respect, Farrington's situation is both more petty, banal, and mean than that of Dempsey and more futile. He is as trapped in the circumstances of his life as is his son who cannot escape Farrington's vicious whipping, though he appeals to the Blessed Virgin for succor. Whereas in "The Clerk's Quest" Moore eschews his effort elsewhere in the revised *Untilled Field* to approximate the cadences of rustic Irish speech, Joyce makes every effort in "Counterparts" to draw upon the colloquialisms and the urban argot of each of the groups he depicts. One comes away from Moore's story with a sense of the pathos of Dempsey's situation and fate. One comes away from Joyce's with a sense of the hopelessness of Farrington's entrapment and with a clear, sharp, detailed knowledge of the social conventions, conflicts, and circumstances of those depicted. Moore, entranced by the irony that Dempsey should worship so ordinary a goddess as a Henrietta Brown of Edinburgh, is indifferent (as he might not have been in an earlier work) to many particulars of appearance and place. We learn no more about Dempsey's appearance than that he has a "conical" head; when he dies, we know only that he is somewhere in the country beyond Dublin. Joyce's picture of Farrington's "hanging face, dark wine-coloured, with fair eyebrows and moustache," of his "heavy dirty eyes," of that face "flushed darker still with anger and humiliation at having been defeated" arm wrestling with an English actor is one that cannot be shaken from memory. The particularity with which Joyce renders the streets of Dublin, the actual pubs that are visited, the series of drinks that are stood, the overtures of an English vaudeville actress, the desperation of a brutalized child, all this is indicative of Joyce's passion not only for verisimilitude but for verity. That Joyce should so have transformed a few key elements he found in Moore's story was neither an accident nor a disguise. In the pursuit of his craft, Joyce was extraordinarily conscious and deliberate. "Counterparts" was his effort to show how much more James Joyce knew about the "facts"—the social and religious conflicts, the language, the emotional texture, the psychology—of Dublin experience than did George Moore.

Joyce left us a kind of *apologia* for what he had done in *Dubliners* in a letter he wrote to the publisher Grant Richards, who was then struggling to get the stories past an English printer. His intention, he wrote in this frequently quoted letter, "was to write a chapter of the moral history" of his country; Dublin was chosen for the scene because that city seemed to him "the center of paralysis." Joyce continued: "I have written . . . for the most part in a style of scrupulous meanness and with the conviction that he is a very bold man who dares to alter in the presentment, still more to deform, whatever he has seen and heard."[39] It is worth noting the slight qualification Joyce introduces into his defense of the style of his stories. That "for the most part" points to his own recognition that the *Dubliners* stories were not all of a piece. Moreover, to these stories he attached the term *epicleti* by reference to an invitation to the Holy Ghost to transform bread and wine into the body and blood of Christ.[40] Earlier, speaking of his poems, he told Stanislaus that "there is a certain resemblance between the mystery of the mass and what I am trying to do ... to give people a kind of intellectual pleasure or spiritual enjoyment by converting the bread of everyday life into something that has a permanent artistic life of its own ... for their mental, moral, and spiritual uplift."[41] Was then Joyce no more than an honest recorder of what he had seen and heard? Or was he a transformer, a transubstantiator of the daily bread of experience? He was not always as assured as he seemed in his letter to Richards that he had simply recorded the truth that was there to be observed. Writing Stanislaus in July of 1905, he complained that the Dublin newspapers would object to his stories as "a caricature of Dublin life." Uncertain at the moment, he asked his brother if he thought there was "any truth in this?" And Joyce made a striking admission: "At times the spirit directing my pen seems to me so plainly mischievous that I am almost prepared to let the Dublin critics have their way."[42] So Joyce himself offers us different accounts of his accomplishment in the *Dubliners* stories. He is a fastidious observer of the facts of experience which he preserves in a mean style appropriate to his subject; he is a mischievous artist offering us distortions and exaggerations designed to ridicule aspects of Dublin life that he disdains. To compound the aesthetic difficulties to which these conflicting views of Joyce's stories lead us, there is, as indicated earlier, the tantalizing phrase "for the most part," suggesting that *Dubliners* may contain more than one kind of story. And then there is that view Joyce had from early on of the artist-priest who transforms gross matter into radiant art.

Almost all who have commented on Joyce's first prose works, his epiphanies, have recognized that there are, among these brief prose passages, distinctly different kinds; and the definition of epiphany that we find in *Stephen Hero* points to two radically different kinds. By an epiphany, Stephen tells us, "he meant a sudden spiritual manifestation, whether in the vulgarity of speech or of gesture or in a memorable phrase of the mind itself."[43] Even a very cursory examination of the surviving epiphanies will reveal a sharp distinction between objective records of conversations and gestures and subjective poetic records of some memorable phase of the mind—for instance, dream experience. In the radically contrasting kinds of epiphanies, there is even something more than the obvious distinction between an objective rendering of the real and an exploration of subjective psychic states. Approached psychologically, Joyce's epiphanies may be said to reveal a hostility to the world outside the self. Indeed, the surviving objective epiphanies almost all reveal some banality, some stupidity, some emptiness, some appalling vulgarity, some fatuous pretension. By contrast, the subjective epiphanies reveal a rich inner world of the imagination. Even when terrors assail that inner world, there are values and emotional significances in it.

Among the fifteen stories in *Dubliners,* there are two distinct kinds, corresponding to the distinctive types of epiphany Joyce recorded. Though there are major exceptions, the least satisfying of these stories are those that emerge from the manner of the objective epiphanies; the most artistically and emotionally satisfying are those that emerge from the manner of the subjective ones. For instance, Joyce is triumphantly successful in the first three stories of the collection—"The Sisters," "Araby," "An Encounter," each of which is a first-person narrative—and in the final story, "The Dead," which is dominated by a central consciousness. All these are among the masterpieces of the short story. But Joyce is most scrupulously mean in style when he is most detached from that which is *other* than the self or when he neither explores nor expresses some significant inner life. What each reader must ask himself about these "objective" stories is whether they are simply a record of what the young James Joyce observed or whether they are the response of a mischievous artist bent upon the exposure of paralysis in the life of Dublin.

Each of the first three stories of *Dubliners* is narrated by the protagonist of the story, but we have to assume—though Joyce's critics usually have not done so—that he narrates at a point in time distant from the events he recounts. In these stories Joyce has already mastered one of his great technical achievements, which was to bring more than one perspective to bear on events. He does not make us conscious that the narrator in each of these stories is no longer an unsophisticated boy or youth, nor does he make us conscious of any contrast between present and past. At the center of each story is the boy and his consciousness of things; we are scarcely aware as we read that a mature narrator is there, mediating between us and the boy, who is progressively more mature in each story.

Frank O'Connor has said that these stories are "what a magazine editor might legitimately describe as 'sketches.'" He finds them "interesting mainly for their style."[44] Indeed, "The Sisters," "An Encounter," and "Araby" left the narrative of plot or action and the old-fashioned tale as practiced by Moore very far behind. Economical, oblique, accruing meaning by implication and innuendo, these are stories in which O'Connor ought instead to have noted the inseparability of matter and manner. They are stories in which apparently very little happens. In "The Sisters" the boy learns of the death of an infirm priest who has taught him about the institutions and sacraments of the church; he attends the priest's wake at the home of his sisters and listens to their clumsy efforts to explain their brother's failure as a priest. In "An Encounter" the boy takes an unauthorized holiday from school with a friend, goes for a desultory walk with him across Dublin, encounters an aging homosexual sadist, whom he does not understand but fears, and hurries away. In "Araby" the boy, now into his teens, falls in love with a neighbor girl, foolishly attends a bazaar she mentions, arrives as it is closing, and is disappointed. Little happens, but everything registers on the sensibility of the boy in each of the stories, as that sensibility is mediated by his older self.

"The Sisters" is the most enigmatic of the stories. Even its title, drawing attention neither to the boy nor to the priest, has tantalized the critics. Whatever is finally revealed about the priest comes to us through the sisters' uncomprehending conversation about him, as that is qualified by the earlier reactions of the boy. As the story opens, the boy knows that there is "no hope" for Father Flynn, who has suffered paralysis following his third stroke. The very word *paralysis* obsesses the boy. "It had always sounded strangely in my ears, like the word *gnomon* in the Euclid and the word *simony* in the Catechism. But now it sounded to me like the name of some maleficent and sinful being." Given his vivid personification of *paralysis,* it is clear that the boy's imagination is excitable and intense. But our attention has been called to his response to two other words as well, words that might well fascinate a boy as responsive and reflective as this one. Along with the word *paralysis* (which describes most of the lives depicted in *Dubliners*), the words gnomon (an incomplete parallelogram) and *simony* (the selling of priestly offices, or the materialization of things spiritual) have been taken as keys not only to this story but to the entire collection. In this triad—paralysis, gnomon, and simony—we find the symbolic crux of the entire work: the lives of most Dubliners are thwarted, incomplete, given over not to the sacredness of life but to futile, material concerns.

At the opening of "The Sisters," as the boy listens to the conversation of his aunt and uncle and their visitor, Mr. Cotter, he is angered and affronted, in particular by the suspicious moralism of old Cotter, a "tiresome old red-nosed imbecile," who raises all kinds of doubts about the priest. Mr. Cotter feels that "there was something queer . . . something uncanny about" Father Flynn. He says that he would not allow his children to spend time, as the boy has done, with the priest; it might be "bad" for a child to be much around a man like Flynn. In fact, the boy's memories of the trembling hands, the green faded garments, the snuff-stained handkerchief of the priest are repugnant, as is his memory of Father Flynn's characteristic smile during which he would "uncover his big discoloured teeth and let his tongue lie upon his lower lip." From a rational point of view, the boy's sessions with the priest can scarcely have contaminated him, even if they manifested certain of Flynn's obsessions: "His questions showed me how complex and mysterious were certain institutions of the Church which I had always regarded as the simplest acts. The duties of the priest towards the Eucharist and towards the secrecy of the confessional seemed so grave to me that I wondered how anybody ever found in himself the courage to undertake them." The priest's scrupulousness is doubtless related to the accident he had during a mass, when he dropped a chalice; but it seems excessive to argue, as some exegetes have done, that the boy may have been corrupted by discussion of these matters.

Interpreters of this story have reached levels of hysteria. Father Flynn has been identified as Ireland's God and as a homosexual; he has been fatuously assailed as "a degenerate old man" transmitting "infectious corruption" to the boy.[45] But if one is able to move beyond interpretation that is itself on the level of Mr. Cotter's perceptions, it can be seen that the boy is made to feel that he is himself unconventional and unusual. When his uncle responds to Mr. Cotter's innuendos, describes him as "that Rosicrucian there," and recommends that he take healthy exercise in the outdoors, he is made to think that his reflectiveness and intellectualism are peculiar. It is not surprising then that in his fantasy he identifies Father Flynn as a "simoniac" and imputes to the pathetic old man romantic qualities he simply does not possess. (Only in the protagonist's fantasy and word play is there a basis for convicting the priest of simony.) In imagination, the boy evokes the visage of the paralytic and understands that the priest seeks to confess to him. "I felt my soul receding into some pleasant and vicious region." Like the boy in "An Encounter" and in "Araby"—and it does not matter whether there are three boys of different ages or one boy at different stages or whether the boy is Joyce himself—the protagonist of "The Sisters" responds to fantasies of the exotic, which may be due to his sense of being different from the drab world that surrounds him. Later, he remembers a dream in which he had seen "long velvet curtains and a swinging lamp of antique fashion." He feels that he has "been very far away, in some land where the customs were strange—in Persia I thought."

The final section of the story is reported by the narrator who offers no explanation or interpretation of its significance. But while the sherry and cream crackers served at the wake by Father Flynn's sisters have been identified as the sacramental bread and wine and fantastic interpretations of the boy's refusal of the crackers have been offered, the real force of the conclusion of the story has often been ignored.[46] Joyce's method was not to provide us with explanations but to expect of us sensitive responses both to what is depicted and what is unuttered. It is up to the reader of "The Sisters" to see that the boy has tried to make of the priest something he was not and to project his own sense of difference and his own longing for the unconventional onto the old man. What we do learn from the conversation of the priest's sisters is that, after the priest broke the chalice (possibly spilling the consecrated wine), he suffered a mental breakdown. He was found "sitting up by himself in the dark in his confession-box,

wide awake and laughing-like softly to himself." Had Father Flynn's accident
caused him to speculate about the relation of spirit to matter, to question the
doctrine of transubstantiation? (Joyce deliberately selected as the date for the
story July 1, which is the Feast of the Precious Blood.[47]) Or had Flynn's clumsiness so affronted his own scruples that he has become deranged? It is impossible
to say for sure. The ambiguity, like the obliquity, is an essential aspect of Joyce's
method. In any case, the boy can no longer indulge in his fantasies about the
priest nor identify his exotic fantasies of escape and singularity with him. No
simoniac—any more than he is the God of Ireland or the homosexual seducer
of the boy or the corrupter of his Catholic faith—Flynn was something more
real than any of these that the boy has to recognize and that all the *Dubliners*
stories depict: a thwarted and defeated human being.

"An Encounter," like "Araby," is less cryptic because the narrator has the
last word in each of these and does make more explicit the consequence of
the experience depicted. Each of these stories is a quest and each of them
contrasts the quotidian world with a fantasy world of romantic release and
adventure; in each of the stories the protagonist moves farther away from
home and into the Dublin world, only to meet defeat in his romantic quest.

The narrator of "An Encounter" describes the play of a group of neighborhood boys, who have been introduced to the Wild West. But to fantasy
play, this timid protagonist prefers fantasy reading about the "fierce un-
kempt and beautiful girls" of American detective stories, and yet he also
hungers for "real adventures" which will satisfy his craving for "wild sensa-
tions." The result of his longing for escape is that he plans with Leo Dillon
and a boy named Mahony "a day's miching," which will include a ferry ride
and a walk out to the Pigeon House on Dublin bay. It seems entirely possible
that the Pigeon House was associated in Joyce's imagination with the Holy
Ghost—for even at this point in his career Joyce had a sense of humor—but
solemn exegetes have insisted upon interpreting this symbolic quest as a
moral allegory in which the youthful protagonist fails to achieve the desire
of the soul for union with the third person of the Trinity.[48] Others may
console themselves with regarding the story as a more subtle symbolic revelation of universal dream and defeat. In any case, the day begins badly when
Leo Dillon fails to show and the protagonist sets out with Mahony. Crossing
the Liffey in the ferryboat, the boys are in the company of two laborers and
"a little Jew," surely an exotic in Dublin but ignored by the protagonist who
seeks some more astonishing manifestation of the remote and the strange.
He seeks, he tells us, not completing his thought, "the foreign sailors to see
had any of them green eyes for I had some confused notion . . ." But the only

sailor whose eyes might be called green is a tall man who clowns for the crowd.

Finally, too tired to reach the Pigeon House, the boys meet "a queer old josser"—Mahony's phrase—in a vacant field where they lie on a bank to rest. This encounter is the climax of their quest. The old josser approaches them "one hand upon his hip and in the other . . . a stick." Described variously as pervert, pederast, and deviant by the critics, he is certainly a sadist and homosexual. Given his love for romantic literature—Thomas Moore, Sir Walter Scott, and Lord Lytton—he is an uncomfortable analogue for the protagonist himself. Soon revealing his yellow and gap-toothed smile, he encourages the boys to talk of the "little sweetheart" he knows every boy to have. The simple fact is that the boy who sought wild adventure is unable to cope with this obscene creature or even to comprehend his obsessive repetition of words and his strange shivering. It is Mahony who calls attention to the old josser's masturbation, when he walks away from the boys for a few minutes. Still, the protagonist does not have the sense to depart. On the man's return, apparently not satisfied by his self-abuse, he indulges in a fantasy that is both homosexual and sadistic, for he describes how he would whip a boy, particularly one who might talk to girls, obsessively repeating allusions to the whip and whipping. It is in the midst of this sick monologue that the boy glances up at the josser's face. "As I did so I met the gaze of a pair of bottle-green eyes peering at me from under a twitching forehead." The protagonist has encountered the exotic he hoped to find—a real one— and he is totally unable to cope with his encounter! Summoning Mahony, who has had the sense to move away in pursuit of a cat, he finds himself dependent upon this more familiar sadist. The conclusion of the story is a brilliant one, a moment in which the young quester achieves the wisdom the hero always does seek. It is a moment of self-discovery:

My voice had an accent of forced bravery in it and I was ashamed of my paltry stratagem. I had to call the name again before Mahony saw me and halooed in answer. How my heart beat as he came running across the field to me! He ran as if to bring me aid. And I was penitent; for in my heart I had always despised him a little.

"Araby" also is distinguished from many of the stories that follow it by the fact that it concludes with a moment of inner realization and spiritual honesty on the part of a growing youth. Nowhere else among the *Dubliners* stories has Joyce used setting more brilliantly, both achieving verisimilitude and establishing the mood of the story that is to follow. The "blindness" of North Richmond Street—a closed street—the vacant detached house at its end, the "brown imperturbable faces" of the other houses on the street, the musty air of the boy's house, the "dark dripping gardens," and the "dark odorous stables" of the lanes in the rear: all these details create the drab, oppressive atmosphere of the neighborhood. In this milieu, little wonder that the adolescent protagonist responds to a neighborhood girl, Mangan's sister. As he introduces the girl, Joyce handles his imagery in such a way that she is both a part of the atmosphere of North Richmond Street and yet something apart from it. The boys watch her from the shadow; she waits for them, her figure partially defined by the light but always hidden by the shadows. The erotic appeal she holds for the boy is expressed in brief, telling images: "Her dress swung as she moved her body and the soft rope of her hair tossed from side to side." And later, "The light from the lamp . . . caught the white curve of her neck, lit up her hair that rested there and, falling, lit up the hand upon the railing. It fell over one side of her dress and caught the white border of a petticoat, just visible as she stood at ease."

Playing off the boy's romanticism—a romanticism as extreme as that of the Irish poet Mangan who is evoked by the girl's name—against the ordinariness of her "brown figure" and playing off the religious intensity of the boy's feelings against the banality of the society that surrounds him, Joyce engages us emotionally in the discrepancy between reality and illusion. It is the narrator's consciousness of the significance of his earlier emotions that permits us to see the confusion of religious and erotic impulses in his feelings about the girl. As he moves through the noisy streets, he imagined, the narrator tells us, that he bore his chalice "safely through a throng of foes": "Her name sprang to my lips at moments in strange prayers and praises which I myself did not understand." When Mangan's sister casually mentions the bazaar Araby and he promises to bring her something from it, the youth identifies all his confused emotions, all his fantasies of the exotic, with it. On Saturday, when he is to attend, he waits the return of his uncle, who is to give him a florin; his suffering is intense, because his uncle is late and even at the moment of the boy's departure frets him with questions about "The Arab's Farewell to His Steed," a very bad sentimental poem that he is about to recite as the boy leaves. The care with which Joyce subordinated all the details of the story to his commanding irony is manifest when we know Caroline Norton's poem, which concludes as the repentant Arab vows that he will fling back the gold for which he has sold his horse. We sense then that the uncle's drunken sentimentalism and the sham romanticism of the poem are vulgar analogues of the boy's emotions. Neither at an Ascendancy charitable bazaar nor elsewhere will this youth be able to purchase the fulfillment he seeks.

Arriving late at the nearly deserted bazaar, Joyce's protagonist finds no Persian opulence, but hears first the sounds of coins being counted and then the phrases of an empty flirtation, which parodies his own conversation with Mangan's sister. That a sign the boy reads is "Café Chantant" and the accents he hears in the flirtation are English reveal that he has, indeed, found a foreign place, and a particularly bogus one. Rebuffed by the young saleswoman, as he seeks something to bring back to Mangan's sister, he is forced to recognize the failure and folly of his quest. But as did "An Encounter," the story ends with a moment of discovery, of self-recognition that is more important than the defeat the boy has experienced. Handling the coins in his pocket, alone in the darkening hall, he gazes up into the darkness and sees himself "as a creature driven and derided by vanity." It is the mediating narrator's voice that gives to this conclusion the imaginative power that pervades the three opening stories: not only a complex and troubling irony, not only an artful and evocative style, but a depth of perception and feeling that is inseparable from the artfulness of the technique.

As the number of his stories grew, Joyce arranged them in a design. He explained to the publisher Grant Richards that the stories were grouped to reveal life in Dublin "under four of its aspects: childhood, adolescence, maturity and public life."[49] (For those who are puzzled that the protagonists of stories like "Two Gallants" and "The Boarding House" are adolescents, though they are over thirty, it helps to know that Joyce derived his categories from those of Greece and Rome, which were very different from those of this century.)[50] Characteristically, Joyce grouped the stories in sets of three, four, four, and three to achieve a formal balance.[51] He then added the last item in the collection, "The Dead," as an afterthought. If it upset the established sequence of triads and quartets and Joyce's intention to begin and end with a story featuring a priest, "The Dead" did not violate the pattern of a life's progression, adding indeed, the kingdom of death.

Just as George Moore insisted upon the unity of *The Untilled Field* so Joyce, when he wrote of *Dubliners* as "a chapter of the moral history of his country," was implying the unity of his work. In providing an arrangement based upon the stages in the development of human life, in emphasizing the theme of individual and social paralysis, in depicting throughout the stories the condition of entrapment, in concentrating, for the most part, on the lower middle class of Dublin, in emphasizing certain harmonies of tone and color and imagery in the stories, Joyce went much further than had Moore to achieve unity.

Far more extensive claims have been made for the underlying unity of *Dubliners,* however, and these claims have tended to suggest that the stories are based upon an extensive network of correspondences, motifs, allusions, parallels, and symbolic significances no less intricate than those in *Ulysses* and *Finnegan's Wake*. Critics and scholars have argued for the manifest presence of an extensive series of correspondences to Homer's *Odyssey*, to the three graces (or theological virtues), to the four cardinal virtues, to the seven deadly sins, to the episodes of Dante's *Inferno*, to Ibsen's *When We Dead Awaken*, to a pattern of eastward and westward movement. If, indeed, at this point in his career, Joyce was able to contain within his imagination all these patterns and associations—as he would in fact have been able to do later in his career—he was an even more extraordinary young artist than has usually been thought. The problem with many of these interpretations is that they depend upon the universal archetypes of Roman Catholic symbology or earlier myth; while they discern ways in which Joyce's imagination was shaped by his religion and make convincing cases for particular allusions or parallels, they so insist upon the consistency of their insights that they turn Joyce's suggestiveness into crude allegory. Furthermore, much of the criticism devoted to the explication of the "unity" of *Dubliners* had been so extremely moralistic that it seems bent upon flailing the pathetic creatures of Dublin's petit-bourgeoisie with a zeal eclipsing Joyce's own desire "to betray the soul of that hemiplegia or paralysis which many consider a city."[52]

The degree to which Joyce's own desire to punish or to caricature his characters effects the quality of his art is an issue that has not been considered sufficiently. But just as Moore's imaginative process while he composed and revised *The Untilled Field* was a struggle between the demands of art and the impulse to instruct, so Joyce's imaginative process as he composed most of the *Dubliners* stories was a struggle between the impulse to reflect faithfully a disdained reality and the impulse to expose to contempt and ridicule. Frank O'Connor, who was often wrongheaded on Joyce, nevertheless recognized a marked difference between the masterful opening stories and "The Dead" and the middle stories, which he described as "harsh naturalistic stories." O'Connor then made a further distinction among these stories, distinguishing between those in which he saw a form of mock-heroic comedy and others, like "Counterparts" or "A Little Cloud," in which he saw the principle of antithesis or ironic contrast at work. All these stories he described as "ugly little stories."[53] One might not want to accept O'Connor's distinctions or discriminations entirely, but he does provide a basis for a rational and critical interpretation of what must often be an emotional response to many of the stories in *Dubliners*, which tend to be depressing when read as a group.

While Joyce, in *Dubliners,* never enters the world of the desperately poor, only rarely the comfortable world of the upper middle class, only once (unconvincingly in "After the Race") the world of the upper class; while the milieu of his stories is never the most prosperous and elegant part of the city; while he scarcely touches happy, smiling, and cheerful aspects of urban life, it has to be granted that he includes in his stories a very wide range of the types of the petit-bourgeoisie. Yet just as Joyce's social range is more restricted than that of Moore in *The Untilled Field,* the emotional range of most of the stories is more limited. In *Dubliners,* no one ever experiences the fulness of love, an escape to freedom, or even a deranged ecstasy. Paralysis and entrapment are everywhere. In the three stories of boyhood and in "The Dead," the degree of moral recognition that comes to the protagonist provides us with an important element of relief from despair. But in the middle group of stories, the control Joyce achieved is largely that of ironic detachment; he himself spoke of "the frigidities of *The Boarding House* and *Counterparts.*" Among these middle stories, where the material is untouched by the consciousness of a sensibility capable of discernment, where no element of mock-heroic lends another perspective, where the naturalistic detail is not given another dimension by the symbolic imagery, the frigidities have a withering quality.

Joyce himself felt that the two weakest stories in the collection were "After the Race" and "A Painful Case," and indicated that he would have liked to rewrite the former, the one totally unconvincing story in the collection. The story depicts, without the sense of fact Joyce ordinarily commanded and with a forced adjectival quality that does not bring a single one of its characters to life, a milieu and a series of events Joyce simply did not know. When the nouveau riche Jimmy Doyle is "taken" at cards by the Englishman and Jimmy senses that he will regret his evening's intoxication and loss, who could care in the least? Not even recent scholarly discoveries that the sudden conclusion is an ironic political comment contrasting the Hungarian independence movement with Irish nationalism and that a political allegory may be discerned in its events have added interest to this failure of a story.[54]

On the other hand, Joyce's own ranking of "A Painful Case" does an injustice to this story. Probably Joyce made a profound artistic error when he attempted to depict a man who is a bank cashier, living the most clerkly of celibate lives, and also a translator of Hauptmann, an admirer of Nietzsche, and an appreciator of Mozart. But the account of the relationship that develops between the repressed intellectual, who has "neither companions nor friends, church nor creed" and "no communion with others," and Mrs. Emily Sinico, the married woman of passionate nature and "great sensibility," who almost brings him to life, is convincingly done. Mrs. Sinico is touched by that quality of oriental voluptuousness that Joyce always associated with the sensual fulfillment Mr. Duffy denies. "Her companionship was like a warm soil about an exotic." But when she makes the error of clasping his hand passionately and pressing it to her cheek, thereby revealing that she has come to love and desire him, Mr. Duffy breaks off the relationship. Four years pass, and then Mr. Duffy reads a newspaper report, "Death of a Lady at Sydney Parade," which reveals that Mrs. Sinico has been killed by a train, while she was returning drunken to her home. The conclusion of the story is perhaps rhetorically overwrought, an effect that stems from Joyce's failure to characterize Duffy consistently; nevertheless, it is moving, because Duffy nearly recognizes and comprehends his failure. He sees the degree of his culpability, sees that he has "withheld life from" Mrs. Sinico. In the story's final lines, Joyce introduces an image of evocative power. Mr. Duffy sees a train "winding out of Kingsbridge Station, like a worm with a fiery head winding through the darkness." Not only does the image evoke sexual failure, decay, and the inexorability of time, but it brings to Duffy's ears the rhythm of the engine, "reiterating the syllables of her name." At the very moment that Joyce has brought Mr. Duffy to the threshold of self-knowledge, he snatches that moment of recognition from him, for Mr. Duffy, we read, "began to doubt the reality of what memory told him." He no longer feels Mrs. Sinico's presence. Then he hears nothing; the night is silent. "He listened again: perfectly silent. He felt that he was alone." But if the concluding lines return us to the bleakness of vision that dominates most of these stories, the power of Mr. Duffy's moment of perception warrants our thinking better of the story than Joyce himself did.

It is interesting to consider "Eveline," which Joyce placed fourth in the arrangement of stories as the first among the stories of adolescence, in relation to "A Painful Case." "Eveline," one of the briefest and slightest of stories, opens with an extended reverie—not stream of consciousness but an early approach to something like it. Eveline's reverie acquaints us with the key facts of her life: the sense of loss she has felt as the city has changed around her, the increasing brutality of her father, her isolation due to the death of her mother and favorite brother, the burdensome nature of her life in business and as a substitute mother for the younger children. Her reverie mounts to a climax, as she remembers the derangement of her mother before her death and determines that she will escape to Buenos Aires with her lover, who is "kind, manly, open-hearted." This reverie constitutes most of the story. Even though we get no sense that Eveline loves Frank or is powerfully drawn to him and conclude that she sees him primarily as an escape, we have been close enough to her to sympathize with her weakness and irresolution, as she tries to persuade herself that she has a responsibility to her father but then is moved by memories of her mother's pathetic end to decide upon exile. The concluding passage of the story, which follows after a break in the text, is hurriedly and dangerously close to a trick ending, for Eveline changes her mind just as she and Frank are to embark. She has not the will to choose a new life and follow Frank abroad. But whereas "A Painful Case" closes with Mr. Duffy's repudiation of his moment of self-recognition and his acceptance of isolation, Eveline's reversal is followed by concluding lines in which an interpretation of her failure is imposed from that element of the narrative that is independent of her consciousness: "She set her white face to him, passive, like a helpless animal. Her eyes gave him no sign of love or farewell or recognition." In the case of "Eveline," it is Joyce himself who has reduced his protagonist to the animal level; it is not Eveline.

In the group of "ugly little stories" to which Frank O'Connor made specific reference, there is no flaw in technique, no failure of Joyce's command of social detail, and no hope for the creatures of his imagination, trapped by circumstances and their own profound limitations. None of the characters in these stories can rise above meanness of condition or vulgar fantasy. The conclusion of "Counterparts"—outstanding among the lot for sheer power of crude naturalism—in which the brutal and brutalized Farrington victimizes his own son, really defines the condition of nearly every significant character in the group of stories. Little Chandler of "A Little Cloud" first idealizes the vulgar journalist Ignatius Gallaher, who has returned to Dublin for a visit, and then resents the contrast between his friend's life and his own, a contrast all the more glaring because he finally admits to himself that he believes he is superior to Gallaher in breeding and education. But aroused by Gallaher's tales of European immorality, Little Chandler indulges in a fantasy of Middle Eastern voluptuousness—of "rich Jewesses," "dark Oriental eyes," and "passion." He sees the primness of his household furnishings, the coldness of his wife. Recognizing that he is "a prisoner for life," he screams at his infant son, whose responding screams elicit from Chandler's wife a glance in which he discerns hatred. But Chandler is a silly little man, who confuses his own sentimentality with poetic sensibility. His story ends with no true recognition on his part of why he is imprisoned.

"Two Gallants" brilliantly characterizes Lenehan, whose "breeches, . . . white rubber shoes and . . . jauntily slung waterproof expressed youth," but whose waistline and scanty hair are better evidence of his jaded spirit, and Corley, with the "large, globular and oily" head, who moves his bulk at an easy pace toward an assignation. While Lenehan waits for the return of Corley, we watch him eat "a plate of hot grocer's peas" at a dingy shop; for a moment we are given a glimpse into the desperation of his spirit. But when he and Corley keep their appointment, following on the latter's meeting with a housemaid, we learn the purpose of the quest the two have shared: a gold coin that Corley has extracted from the girl and will share with Lenehan. Though Corley regards the young woman as "a fine decent tart," Joyce's incisive description of "her stout short muscular body, . . . her fat red cheeks," and her "straggling mouth which lay open in a contented leer" leaves no doubt that she is not quite Corley's victim and that he is more of a "tart" than she.

"The Boarding House" is another story in which Joyce's command of characterization and social detail is quite brilliant. In this story, Mrs. Mooney, a butcher's daughter who has sloughed off a drunken husband and established a boarding house, and her daughter, Polly, "a little perverse madonna," beautifully manage their individual hypocrisies so that Polly may seduce one of the boarders without either mother or daughter admitting she knows what she is doing and the other knows that she knows. The florid and vulgar Mrs. Mooney deals "with moral problems as a cleaver deals with meat." While the Sunday church bells ring, she prepares to confront Mr. Doran with her knowledge of his affair with Polly, reflecting that "she would have lots of time to have the matter out with Mr. Doran and then catch short twelve at Marlborough Street." As mother wields the cleaver, Polly waits in Doran's room, drifting off into so pleasant a fantasy of the future that when her mother calls from below it takes her a minute to remember "what she had been waiting for." Joyce modulates between the consciousness of each of the three characters; and when he gives us access to that of Doran, we discover that while this victim fears he is being had, last night's confession has prepared him to do the conventional and proper thing. "What could he do now but marry her or run away? He could not brazen it out." Given the baseness of motive in the three characters, as in those of "Two Gallants," it is impossible to feel sympathy with any of them. Frigidities, indeed!

But "Clay," Joyce's account of the little old maid, Maria, and a visit she makes to her relatives, the Donnellys, on All Hallow Eve, stands apart from these other stories. Though even poor Maria has been weighed in the moral scales of some of Joyce's interpreters and found wanting, her story is not written with the frigidity of "Counterparts," "Two Gallants," and "The Boarding House." Joyce's narrative technique, if not quite describable by Frank O'Connor's term *mock-heroic,* is of a very special kind, for it places the consciousness of Maria at the center of the story and parodies that consciousness. The narrative voice of "Clay" is a double one, for Joyce manages to suggest the speech patterns of a very limited and naive person of a certain social level and also to convey a delicately satirical mockery of her sensibility.

Throughout the story, the poise of Joyce's irony is remarkable. What happens in the story is, as always in *Dubliners,* very slight. Maria leaves the Dublin by

Lamplight Laundry, a Protestant charitable institution for reformed prostitutes, where she holds a minor post in the kitchen, purchases treats for her relatives, forgets a piece of plum cake on the tram to Drumcondra because she is flustered by speaking to a "colonel-looking gentleman," and spends the evening with the Donnellys "talking over old times." She fails in her effort to persuade Joe Donnelly to make peace with his brother Alphy; in the divining game played for All Hallow Eve, she first touches a saucer of wet clay placed there by a neighbor girl, but, when Mrs. Donnelly intervenes and arranges a second try, she gets the prayer book. (The ritual objects—ring, prayer book, and clay—signify the fortune or fate of the participant: marriage, convent, death.) The evening ends, as Maria sings Balfe's "I Dreamt That I Dwelt," repeating the first verse twice. Her slip is psychologically revealing, for Maria avoids the stanza depicting a maiden besieged by suitors, an experience she has never known and never will, much as she may have longed for it.

Joyce's triumph in the story is that he neither sentimentalizes nor disdains Maria. He permits her to be both funny and pathetic. As Adaline Glasheen has remarked in a sane essay on the story, "When Joyce talked about the spiritual liberation of Ireland, . . . he had forgotten "Clay," an art-for-art's sake piece of work if there ever was one."[55] Yet even Maria, if never quite excoriated by the critics as so many of Joyce's Dubliners have been, has not quite escaped moral obloquy. Unable, in view of Maria's disinterest in food and drink for herself, to convict her of gluttony—which ought to be the deadly sin of the story, given barmbrack, penny cakes, and plum cake with almond frosting—one writer has concluded that Maria's sin is *tristitia* or gloominess.[56] This conclusion has been reached despite the fact that one of Joyce's ways of characterizing Maria is by describing her laugh and depicting her nearly inveterate cheerfulness. That her name and her undoubted virginity evoke the Blessed Virgin Mary, and that her altogether unfortunate nose and chin reminds us both of Punch and of a Halloween witch are undeniable, but most of those writers who have emphasized the symbolic significance of these details have failed to see that they are ironic analogies, meant neither to demean nor condemn Maria but to suggest her predicament. Maria is a simple, homely little creature who would love to marry but never will; who tries to bring peace but is quite inept and cannot really cope with life beyond the laundry; who has a handful of relatives who make some kind of effort—despite Joe Donnelly's overriding interest in the next bottle—to attend to her; but who is quite alone. To imagine that Maria could ever have been a mother, spiritually, physically, and intellectually fulfilled, had not Dublin been so corrupt and she so weak, mischievous, or sinful is as preposterous as to think that Joyce is consigning her to hell. What he has done in "Clay," however, is to create a consciousness that has none of the subtlety of the narrative voice in a story like "Araby" but with whom we can sympathize. He has manifested some of the genius that would later enable him to create a character like Gerty McDowell and to depict Leopold and Molly Bloom in such a way that we both laugh at them and totally accept them.

The three stories—one weak, two superlative—that precede "The Dead" all deal, according to Joyce's scheme, with public life. The problem with "A Mother" is not one of execution but of conception. In this account of Mrs. Kearney's efforts to promote her daughter's musical career through association with the Irish language movement, Joyce's ability to suggest social situation, psychological attitude, and character trait by means of telling details is not diminished. "A Mother," of all the *Dubliners* stories, comes closest to being outright satire. The provincialism of Irish musical culture and the sheer ineptitude of nationalist organizations are ruthlessly exposed to ridicule. Joyce's hand does not falter in his portrait of Mrs. Kearney, and the skill with which he depicts her mounting rage, when she becomes convinced that Kathleen will be denied her contractual fee, is impressive. But the cruelty of the satire and the technical virtuosity of the piece are both in excess of the material at hand. The truth is, the incidents of the story are too trivial to justify the expenditure of satiric spleen and artistic energy that are involved.

By contrast, "Ivy Day in the Committee Room," which was Joyce's own favorite among the stories written before "The Dead," is a flawless work.[57] The setting of the story is a candidate's committee room on 6 October during a municipal election. While the concurrence of the memorial day of Charles Stewart Parnell and such a Dublin municipal election was highly improbable, as Joyce well knew, he was willing to hazard an improbability with the ring of authenticity. Typically, there is no heightened action in the story. The committee room is the headquarters of the Nationalist candidate, Tricky Dicky Tierney; the caretaker and a few canvassers who are sheltering from the wretched weather engage in desultory gossip; a few others drift in and out; a gift of stout eventually arrives from Tierney. And, finally, Joe Hynes (who supports another candidate) recites a poem of his own composition about Parnell. Joyce drew the attention of his brother to the fact that Anatole France had influenced both "Ivy Day" and "The Dead," and it has been surmised that *The Procurator of Judea* suggested to Joyce the effectiveness of allusion to a dead figure who never actually appears but whose presence is felt throughout.[58] It is an added irony that Tierney, nominally a Nationalist but really a publican on the make, despised even by those who canvass for him, is also a present absence. Only gradually do we sense that it is the symbolic presence of the betrayed Parnell that dominates the story.

Joyce never produced a more painterly story than this one, achieving brilliant chiaroscuro effects in which shadow and light contribute to the dramatic and symbolic ironies. The events transpire in the murky shadows of a "denuded" room inadequately illuminated by a fire and a few uncertain candles—and un-illuminated by any present values or belief. Early in the story, Mr. O'Connor tears a strip from one of Tierney's cards, lights his cigarette with it, and thus suggests his real attitude toward his candidate. "As he did so the flame lit up a leaf of dark glossy ivy in the lapel of his coat." This ivy, the emblem of Parnell, is evoked throughout as a symbolic motif that ironically mocks the deathly atmosphere of the shadowy room.

As he develops that atmosphere, Joyce casts into relief the visages of the men assembled or momentarily stopping there: old Jack, his face bony and hairy, his moist mouth falling open at times; O'Connor, a gray-haired young man "whose face was disfigured by many blotches and pimples"; Henchy, "a bustling little man with a snuffling nose"; Father Keon, a defrocked priest whose face "had the appearance of damp yellow cheese"; Crofton, "a very fat man whose clothing drops from sloping shoulders and whose big face "resembled a young ox's in expression."

Just as vivid and far less repulsive is the language these men speak as they gossip, slander, and hypocritically fawn. Mr. Henchy, in particular, has a command of racy abuse and gossip. When Tierney is slow about sending round a promised case of stout, Henchy abuses him with relish:

—O, he's as tricky as they make 'em, said Mr Henchy. He hasn't got those little pigs' eyes for nothing. Blast his soul! Couldn't he pay up like a man instead of: *O, Now, Mr. Henchy, I must speak to Mr. Fanning . . . . I've spent a lot of money?* Mean little shoeboy of hell! I suppose he forgets the time his little old father kept a hand-me-down shop in Mary's Lane.
—But is that a fact? asked Mr O'Connor.
—God, yes, said Mr Henchy. Did you never hear that? And the men used to go in on Sunday morning, before the houses were open to buy a waistcoat or a trousers—moya! But Tricky Dicky's little old father always had a little black bottle up in a corner. Do you mind now? That's where he first saw the light.

It is Henchy, too, who, when Joe Hynes leaves the room, circulates the lie that the latter is in the pay of the opposition candidate to spy on the Tierney committee and then even intimates that Hynes may be in the pay of Dublin Castle and a traitor to the Nationalist cause.

Among the hypocrites, wastrels, and hacks depicted in the story, Hynes, "hard up like the rest of us," according to O'Connor, but denounced by Henchy as a sponger without a "spark of manhood in him," comes off rather well. (The density of Joyce's imagery and his irony may be noted in Henchy's references to "the light" and "some spark," for, despite his loquacity, he lives in darkness.) "A

tall slender young man with a light brown moustache," Hynes is defended by
O'Connor who himself seems to have a faint spark of integrity and describes his
friend as "a straight man . . . clever . . . with the pen." It is Hynes and O'Connor
who most clearly see how absurd it is for Ireland, which repudiated Parnell for
his liaison with Mrs. O'Shea, to greet the English king, a notorious whoremaster.
Of course Hynes is a sentimentalist in his idealization of the working man and
in the language of his poem on Parnell. Yet he is at least capable of passionate
devotion to an ideal, and it is the sentimentalism of his poem that precipitates a
conclusion of great emotional power. When he rises to recite his poem, "The
Death of Parnell," Joe Hynes declaims verses that are laden with the clichés of
popular and formulaic poetry. Before he begins his recitation and at the very
moment he concludes, the sound of corks popping from bottles of stout placed
near the fire is heard. The "Pok!" that resounds when Hynes completes his
recitation is an ironic indication that hot air has been exhaled and that a favorite
political activity of those in attendance has more to do with booze than with
heroism. Still James Joyce, who was something of a sentimentalist himself, was
also something of a genius, and he knew how to turn sentimentalism into a
more intense feeling—the very real passion of Hynes's devotion to his "Lord,"
the Christ-like Parnell: "*Pok!* The cork flew out of Mr. Hynes' bottle, but Mr.
Hynes remained sitting, flushed and bareheaded on the table. He did not seem
to have heard the invitation." Throughout the story, the heroic figure of Parnell
has mocked the futile activities of the shadowy room where there is so little
light; but the evocation of the betrayed leader and the genuineness of Joe
Hynes's feeling, which survives both his own sentimentality and its deflation by
Joyce, give a dimension to the story that its more frigid companions lack.

Like "A Mother" and "Ivy Day," "Grace" is also executed by means of a
detached omniscience, without a single center of consciousness. We are indebted to Stanislaus Joyce (who detested the symbolic interpretations of *Dubliners* that American critics had begun to offer) for the information that Joyce
wrote this story with Dante's *Commedia* in mind. "Mr. Kernan's fall down the
steps of the lavatory is his descent into hell," Stanislaus tells us, "the sickroom is
purgatory, and the church in which he and his friends listen to the sermon is
paradise at last."[59] A tripartite structure is the norm in the *Dubliners* stories, but
Joyce has underlined it by distinct breaks in the text in this instance; it is to be
hoped that Joyce's joke would have been discovered even had not his brother
explained it to us in the pages of *My Brother's Keeper*. But joke the allusion to
Inferno, Purgatorio, and *Paradiso* is; and, though the story has provoked solemn
allegorical interpretations, it is—and surely this is enough—a marvelous piece
of mock-heroic. It is also, among all the stories of the collection, the only truly

comic one, not just because it begins in hell and ends in heaven but because its ironies are subordinate to a controlling vision that is wonderfully funny. It may be that when Mr. Kernan, who has gotten himself "peloothered" altogether, is picked up from the lavatory floor, "his clothes . . . smeared with the filth and ooze of the floor," that he has been rescued from the infernal circle of the gluttonous, or even from the eighth circle of Malebolge, where the flatterers lie in dung and ordure, but it may also be more important to laugh at the resulting comedy than to interpret each of its elements literally, to assign appropriate blame to each of the characters, or to seek particular circles of hell, purgatory, and heaven in the details of the story.[60]

In the final section of the story, Kernan and his friends are described sitting "in the form of a quincunx," as they listen to the dreadful sermon of Father Purdon. Surely the multiple significations of the quincunx (among other things an emblem of fallen man and of the cross and wounds of Christ) are pertinent only to the extent that these foolish men and the ridiculous sermon are made more laughable by the incongruity of the allusion, which is not, after all, arcane but immediately apprehensible by the informed comic sense. In the *Paradiso* section of the story, to be sure, Joyce's comic sense is nudged by a satiric impulse. Father Purdon, whose name would have reminded the Dubliners of Joyce's own time of a particularly notorious street in the red light district, heaves himself into his pulpit to deliver a sermon on "one of the most difficult texts in all the Scriptures": "For the children of this world are wiser in their generation than the children of light. Wherefore make unto yourselves friends out of the mammon of iniquity so that when you die they may receive you into everlasting dwellings." This text he manages to twist into "a text for business men and professional men." If it is not literally true that Father Purdon is a simoniac, as is often claimed, he is an extraordinarily vulgar man who has come so close to the language of his audience that he has joined the children of mammon. "But one thing only, he said, he would ask of his hearers. And that was to be straight and manly with God . . . to be frank and say like a man: . . . with God's grace I will rectify this and this. I will set right my accounts."

Yet it is the second part of the story that is most memorable, for, as Mr. Kernan and his friends set about his reformation by sharing a bottle, they engage in a conversation comically pervaded by the imagery of light. Their ignorance, their misinformation, their self-congratulatory myths about almost every religious and historical subject they discuss are superbly comic. As their conversation draws to a close, Mr. Kernan learns that he must hold a lighted candle during the retreat. A not entirely persuaded convert to Roman Catholicism, he exclaims, "No, damn it all, I bar the candles! . . . I bar the magic lantern business." Probably those who claim that symbolically he, like Father Purdon, rejects the "light" are to some degree correct.[61] But if one is too solemn, one may give the impression that Joyce's theme is one any Jesuit of his time might have expounded in a sermon. A better reading of "Grace" would insist that Joyce's mock-heroic comedy is moving toward the acceptance of human folly that we find in *Ulysses*. "Grace" requires of us only that we be able to join in the laughter of Mr. Kernan's friends, as they react to his comic protest against the candles. To assume that Joyce morally disdains a fellow inebriate like silly Mr. Kernan is excessive. If we are able to respond to comic allusion and to comic tone, we should be able to recognize the inevitability of Mr. Kernan's behavior and the impossibility of the demands myths make on poor mortal creatures.

While Joyce was in Rome in 1906, he expressed for a second time in a letter to Stanislaus some reservations about his collection of stories. "Sometimes," he confided, "thinking of Ireland it seems to me that I have been unnecessarily harsh. I have reproduced . . . none of the attractions of the city for I have never felt at my ease in any city since I left it except Paris. I have not reproduced its ingenuous insularity and its hospitality. . . . I have not been just to its beauty: for it is more beautiful naturally in my opinion than what I have seen of England, Switzerland, France, Austria or Italy."[62] "The Dead" was conceived in Rome but written after his return to Trieste out of a sense that he might "reproduce" certain of Dublin's charms and graces. But Joyce was quick also to assure his brother that were he entirely to rewrite the collection of stories, "I am sure I would find again what you call the Holy Ghost sitting in the ink-bottle and the perverse devil of my literary conscience sitting on my pen."[63] Little wonder that the story he produced was no jolly encomia to Ireland's hospitality but a masterpiece of subtle and complex suggestiveness in which Joyce transmuted both his attitude toward Ireland and his passion for truth. And little wonder, given the richness and density of his material, that he stretched the form of the short story to the point where it became a different thing altogether, a nouvelle, or short novel.

Technically, "The Dead" is a pleasure to explore, for Joyce found the means to move between an objective and detached omniscience and the central consciousness of Gabriel Conroy, the protagonist, without making us aware of any seams in his narrative method. The first two sections of "The Dead" are an account of the Misses Morkan's annual dance, an account that captures all the bustle, confusions, discords, and pleasures of a rather elaborate dance, musical recital, and late supper at the home of three musical ladies, the aunts Kate and Julia and their more active niece, Mary Jane. Mary Jane's pupils belong to "the better class families on the Kingstown and Dalkey line," and this story depicts the most "polished" bourgeois milieu of all the *Dubliners* stories. Gabriel Conroy himself is a university lecturer and a literary reviewer. Throughout the first two sections of the short novel, his consciousness of things gradually grows more dominant and is at the very center of the third section.

One of those double narrative voices Joyce is able to assume opens "The Dead," giving us the expository facts and slightly mocking them by the voice, as it were, of one of the genteel guests: "It was always a great affair, the Misses Morkan's annual dance. Everybody who knew them came to it. . . . Never once had it fallen flat. For years and years it had gone off in splendid style as long as anyone could remember." Joyce does full justice to the festive aspects of so genteel an affair. Many of the most pleasant things in life are there—song, dance, laughter, tribute, food, liquors—and yet there is a monochromatic quality to his rendering of the surface of things. Even the festive board, dominated by a fat brown goose and a ham "peppered over with crust crumbs," though it is touched by various colors, seems predominantly brown. Of Mr. Browne, a tiresome joker, wizened and swarthy, who is in pursuit of Mary Jane, Aunt Kate observes, "Browne is everywhere," adding "He has been laid on here like the gas . . . all during Christmas." At a moment of intense feeling, when Gabriel glimpses his wife, he cannot see her face, which is in shadow, but only "the terracotta and salmon pink panels of her skirt which the shadow made appear black and white."

Below the surface of the festivity, there are constant hints of emotions that do not accord with the season or the occasion. Gabriel is answered sharply by the maid, when he attempts a light compliment; her bitterness shocks and discomposes him. The aunts are concerned that Freddy Malins, who is about to be shipped to a monastery to dry out, will arrive "screwed" and disrupt the party. Mr. Browne attempts a joke in a "very low Dublin accent," which is responded to by the young ladies "in silence." Not a soul at the party really listens to or enjoys Mary Jane's performance of an academy piece, though she is given hearty applause. Gabriel is angered by a triggered memory of his mother's disapproval of his marriage. Molly Ivors quarrels with Gabriel over nationalist issues and the language question; she leaves the party early, refusing to share the supper. In a temper following his exchange with Miss Ivors, Gabriel snaps at his wife. Aunt Kate has a little outburst of temper at the papal decision to ban females in choirs. Mr. Browne and Freddy Malins foolishly make far too much of the youthfulness of the voice of the aged and failing Aunt Julia, when she sings "Arrayed for the Bridal." The tenor Bartell D'Arcy is offended by the disparagement of contemporary singers. Gabriel devises a speech to get back at Miss Ivors, but his effort is futile since she is not present to take his barb. Bartell

D'Arcy, who suffers from a bad cold, has another fit of temper over the state of his voice, as the party is breaking up. The cumulative effect of all these details is to suggest how little real communication or communion there is in society.

An ironic progression of images also complements these details. When Molly Ivors opens her conversation with Gabriel, during which she accuses him of being a West Briton—that is, an Irishman whose culture is English—she tells him that she has "a crow to pluck" with him. Later, after her little spat with Gabriel, she refuses Mary Jane's appeal that she stay for the supper, "To take a pick itself . . . after all your dancing." At the table, as the conversation about singers angers D'Arcy, Aunt Kate, "who had been picking a bone" of the brown goose, praises the voice of a long dead and unknown tenor; and when D'Arcy offends her at the close of the evening, he snaps out, "Can't you see that I'm as hoarse as a crow." To allegorize these secondary images would be absurd, for they are suggestive, modifying one another and the context in which they appear, bringing into focus the underlying elements of conflict, and implying the proximity of life and death. Death, the dead, the past, memory, these pervade the story in allusion, detail, and incident: a long dead writer such as Shakespeare, a more recent dead poet, Browning; the dead singers who are remembered at dinner; Gabriel's mother, who returns to him in memory; the "absent faces" of the past to whom he alludes in his speech; grandfather Patrick Morkan, Johnny, his horse, and King Billy's statue, about whom he tells a funny story; the Wellington Monument and O'Connell Bridge, reminders of Irish history and of the dead hand of the past on the present; and finally the boy, Michael Furey, Gretta's first love, who died, after standing out in the rain, for love of her, and whose memory fills her with grief, when she hears D'Arcy sing "The Lass of Aughrim."

Upon Gabriel's arrival at the party, a fringe of snow lies across the shoulders of his overcoat, and he is seen to be scraping the snow from his galoshes. Indeed, he has insisted that Gretta wear galoshes to protect her against a cold, even though he says she would "walk home in the snow if she were let." That Aunt Julia does not know what galoshes are and that Gabriel says "everyone wears them on the continent," merely gives us information, on the level of circumstantial realism, about the differing levels of sophistication in Dublin and about Gabriel's orientation toward Europe. But the differing attitudes of Gabriel and Gretta toward contact with the snow also reveal some fundamental emotional differences between a woman who is spontaneous and impulsive and a man who is far more staid and cautious. As Joyce further develops snow imagery in "The Dead," these contrasts begin to take on highly suggestive symbolic implications, though no more than elsewhere in *Dubliners* is Joyce's imagery translatable into a single corresponding meaning. Following his unpleasant encounter with Molly

Ivors, Gabriel, warmed by the dancing, unsettled by the Ivors spat, and distracted by his self-conscious preparation of the tribute he is to pay his aunts, finds that he is attracted to the snow. "Gabriel's warm trembling fingers tapped the cold pane of the window. How cool it must be outside! How pleasant it would be to walk out alone, first along by the river and then through the park." At this point the appeal of the snow is escapist and isolationist, as it is when Gabriel recalls the snow a moment before he speaks. However, in this third passage of snow imagery, Joyce adds a detail that is to be important later. Imagining the purity of the snow in Phoenix Park (and thus moving further from the habitations of men), Gabriel thinks of the "snow that flashed westward over the white field of Fifteen Acres." But when the Conroys leave the party, it is Bartell D'Arcy rather than Gabriel who is concerned about contact with the snow. Gabriel has been seized, while watching Gretta in the shadow, with a feverish desire to possess her, and he longs for the moment of embrace when they reach their hotel in central Dublin.

As it turns out, at the moment he expects Gretta to come to his embrace, she stuns him by breaking away from him and weeping. Gabriel, self-conscious and egoistic as ever, catches a glimpse of his gilt-rimmed eyeglasses in the cheval glass, before Gretta pours out her tale of Michael Furey, alluding in particular to the passionate appeal of the boy's "big dark eyes." The last pages of the story depict Gabriel's moments of self-discovery and recognition, moments more intense than those at the conclusion of either "An Encounter" or "Araby." With the miraculous power of his maturing craft, James Joyce transmutes the conflict between the self and the other that has dominated his early career. Now neither reporter nor caricaturist, he gives us a passage in which the everyday bread of experience is surely transubstantiated into imperishable art. From having regretted that he had not revealed Dublin's "ingenuous insularity," Joyce progressed to a revelation of the insularity of the soul. The party of the maiden Morkans took place on Usher's Island. Gretta had been secluded from Michael Furey at her grandmother's house on Nun's Island. Michael Furey died for her a week after she had arrived at her convent school. Gabriel's consciousness of his own isolation proceeds in stages. He sees himself now as "a ludicrous figure, acting as a pennyboy for his aunts, a nervous well-meaning sentimentalist, orating to vulgarians and idealising his own clownish lusts, the pitiable, fatuous fellow he had caught a glimpse of in the mirror." But at this point in the discovery of the self, he remains ego-bound. As Gretta sleeps, he progresses further in his journey of discovery. He recognizes how little he has known about his wife, recognizes that she may not have "told him all the story," senses that poor Aunt Julia may soon be a shade, understands that Michael Furey has loved more deeply than he himself ever has the woman who lies beside him. Beyond the discovery of the self, there is the discovery of the other. Gabriel sees Michael Furey "standing under a dripping tree. Other forms were near. His soul had approached that region where dwell the vast hosts of the dead." Having discovered his insularity, Gabriel transcends it, experiencing selfless emotions of pity and generosity, in an imaginative union with death-in-life.

Joyce is now prepared to bring the expanding metaphor of snow to its completion. Gabriel has heard that snow is general all over Ireland: "It was falling . . . upon every part of the lonely churchyard . . . where Michael Furey lay buried. It lay thickly drifted on the crooked crosses and headstones, on the spears of the little gate, on the barren thorns. His soul swooned softly as he heard the snow falling faintly through the universe and faintly falling like the descent of their last end, upon all the living and the dead." The ambiguity that was at the heart of James Joyce's mature genius is inseparable from the linguistic power of this conclusion, which is an opening out for his readers into troubling and insoluble questions at the very moment that Joyce's artistry reconciles life and death. Gabriel Conroy has learned to sympathize with others, but he has learned the essential solitude of the soul. He has come to a sense of the oneness of life, but he has attained this vision through identification with death. In setting "out on his journey westward" he may be moving toward old age and death himself, but his acceptance of the cosmic and universal mantle of snow, which brings water and life, may imply a rebirth. One should exclude none of these possibilities. An art that approaches the complexity of life and death themselves will not permit us to do so.

In 1916 the volatile George Moore told a correspondent that he found some of the stories of *Dubliners* "trivial and disagreeable." But he also felt that all of the stories had been "written by a clever man." And of one of the pieces in *Dubliners,* he said, "the longest story in the book and the last seemed to me perfection whilst I read it. I regretted that I was not the author of it."[64] Richard Ellmann has pointed out the appropriateness of Moore's admiration, given the influence of *Vain Fortune* on "The Dead." And though one cannot avoid the ironic reflection that "The Dead" was the first work of Joyce that justified his arrogant assumption in 1901 that he rather than Moore was riding the crest of a movement fusing realism and symbolism, it seems altogether appropriate that Moore should have appreciated the nouvelle in which Joyce so superbly resolved the conflict within him between his resentment of Ireland and his love of art, between his sense of self and his sense of everything that was *other,* for the same conflicts had raged in Moore as he worked at *The Untilled Field.* Yeats believed that the poet could make out of a quarrel with others mere rhetoric, but out of a quarrel with the self, poetry. In the opening years of our century, as Moore and Joyce worked on *The Untilled Field* and *Dubliners*, books that grew out of their quarrel with Ireland, each managed to produce a number of stories in which a struggle within the self resulted in Irish works of art that now belong to the entire world.

SETTING THE STANDARDS:
WRITERS OF THE 1920s AND 1930s

James F. Kilroy

By the 1920s, the short story had been established, particularly in England and America, as a literary form especially suited to modernist expression. Perhaps its very constraints, limited action, potent details, and highly charged expression were best adapted to certain notions of the economy of art. Or, as has been suggested, its fragmented action and characterization reflected the disillusionment of the postwar generation. Even more likely, the development through influential magazines of a new readership for the art provided a new market and an eager audience. Finally, the recognition of the new form by critics and teachers may have raised it to respectability. For the same and probably many other reasons, the new form was nurtured in Ireland in the 1920s and 1930s.

Three masterful short story writers, Liam O'Flaherty, Frank O'Connor, and Sean O'Faolain, set the standards, the high water markings of artistic achievement, although they are so dissimilar in their techniques and favored themes that the common linkage of them as "the three O's" is not fair to any. Their dominant tones, the thematic equivalents of ruling passions, are widely varied: O'Flaherty's social commitment and natural vehemence contrasts sharply with O'Faolain's cool intelligence and with O'Connor's ironic but warm humaneness. But in at least one important respect they are properly linked as the conscious molders of the genre, three who transformed the traditional forms of short fiction and even reshaped the short story as developed by Moore and Joyce. Two of the three wrote critical studies of the form; all three have consciously experimented with structure and narrative technique throughout their careers.

But perhaps there was something indigenous to Ireland in the troubled period of the 1920s and 1930s that nurtured the growth of this form, or some experience or attitude shared by the three as Irishmen that accounts for their eminence. They came from the provinces and wrote frequently of their native areas: O'Flaherty's Connaught, particularly the Aran Islands, and O'Connor and O'Faolain's Cork. All three quarreled with their native religion and occasionally expressed anticlerical sentiments. Although they all took part in military actions, they grew to mistrust the fervid nationalism they had felt as young men. But the greater common quality of the three, and of the best of their contemporaries as well, was an acute self-consciousness, a tendency to examine their own national identities, religious affiliations, and vocational choices that is parallel to Ireland's own self-scrutiny in this period. Even more than the long struggle toward independence culminating in the Easter Rising and treaty, the Civil War transformed mass attitudes, for it brought disillusionment and a recognition that under a different flag there was still in Ireland dissension and corruption. Because of the continued warfare, as well as its agrarian economy, Ireland seemed not to have entered the modern world. Like the writers of the American South of the same period, the impression of being part of a troubled and alienated society made the writers invest their art with particular energy, making it a means to assert their identity before a quite foreign and possibly hostile world, or to write for an Irish audience that they had already grown to disdain. With such motives for self-expression, literary art acquires great importance, and its development is in turn enhanced.

Just as Joyce and Beckett, Shaw and O'Casey, and Yeats were reshaping other literary forms in the 1920s and 1930s, O'Flaherty, O'Connor, and O'Faolain, and several less eminent of their contemporaries were reshaping and perfecting the form of the short story.

• • •

Of "the three O's," Liam O'Flaherty is the most forceful and bold. His stories treat violent and painful subjects, and their ethical implications are more profound than those of O'Connor or O'Faolain. Like Zola and Dreiser, he is a naturalist who views man's attempts to counteract natural forces as futile, and who regards social institutions as essentially corrupting. Expressing such forceful convictions, his stories are less subtle than those of his two well-known Irish contemporaries, for they aim at an immediate impact.

Growing up on the Aran Islands, O'Flaherty knew nature at its most violent; in his stories it is most often an oppressive force. He observes and describes the sea, winds, and seasonal changes fastidiously but warily, acknowledging their destructive power. A farmer's efforts to work the recalcitrant soil or a fisherman's attempts to escape from a stormy sea appear as no more than animal responses, in which distinguishing human characteristics are ignored. Because man's innate powers are regarded as far inferior to antagonistic natural forces, plots tend to be lopsided when man is pitted against nature. Likewise, if reason is feeble in such conflict, human communication is largely futile, or merely self-deceptive, making the stories rely less on dialogue than on gestures and action. Sophisticated narrative techniques are absent, inappropriate as they are to the elemental subjects of the stories, and the structures tend to be simple, focusing attention directly on a single or a few incidents.

Although most of his publications are novels, the short story is the form in which O'Flaherty's harsh vision is most forcefully conveyed. He has published fifteen novels, several of which achieved international popularity. But they tend to seem longer than their themes justify; furthermore, the didactic aspect often dominates the novels. The constraints of the short story are consonant with O'Flaherty's single-minded, bleak vision.

He has published four major collections of short stories, plus several smaller gatherings and some selected editions. They fall into two periods: the first three collections, published in the first five years of his literary career (*Spring Sowing,* 1924; *The Tent,* 1926: *The Mountain Tavern and Other Stories,* 1929), and then, nearly twenty years later, *Two Lovely Beasts and Other Stories* (1948). Because he regarded the short story as less challenging than the longer fictional form, he neglected it for much of his writing career. Yet since he returned to it, the stories have expanded in scope, and even employ more ambitious narrative techniques.

Because the early stories were written within a few years of each other and reveal no technical development within that period, they may be discussed together.

"Spring Sowing," the title story of his first collection, reveals the dominant thematic concern of the early stories: the subjection of man to nature. Young newlyweds set forth on their first day of working the land. The husband is determined to prove himself a man "worthy of being the head of a family," while his wife is terrified at the prospect of being subjected to the pitiless earth; yet they set to their exacting, tedious work. The physical effort is not glossed over as being ennobling: they complete the day's tasks, ending only with the anticipation of "sleep and forgetfulness." In such a barren context the characters are little more than animals, slaves to the cycles of nature, hoping merely to stay alive. Only there seems to be no alternative to submission to a cruel natural order. In "Poor People," a later stage in such a married life is presented, as a couple desperately seek food to keep themselves and their four-year-old son alive; at the story's end they are left, the son having died, sitting together and weeping. The naturalistic theme dominates such stories. Action is minimal, setting so stripped of appeal as to seem preternatural, and the conflict for survival is sharply, relentlessly focused. Individualizing characteristics are omitted, so that the people sometimes even lack names; background information is irrelevant to the immediate concern; distracting literary techniques are eschewed. Yet such stories have great force, for with so few details included, the stark natural images acquire great suggestiveness. In "Spring Sowing" the young couple's work suggests fruition and reproduction ("they were to open up the earth together and plant seeds in it"), and the husband's contention with the wife reveals his desire to achieve a dominant role as master, just as her ultimate submission reveals her willing acceptance of an inferior position. In this short, unrelieved story, the last sentence achieves special power: "Cows were lowing at a distance," reflecting the couple's animal state, their inevitable suffering, and yet their participation in natural processes.

Such animal behavior and primitive instincts tend to dominate rational concerns or civilized behavior. In "Blood Lust," a man in a fishing boat with the handsome brother he envies struggles with a growing, nearly irrepressible desire to murder him. Eventually he crushes a fish to a shapeless mass, and when he has done so, he sighs; "his blood lust was satisfied." The most basic of instincts, the will to survive, is vividly conveyed in "Trapped," in which a man escapes after being stranded on a mountain. The intense psychological frenzy of such characters is well conveyed, but their actions, extreme as they may be, are made to seem spontaneous and inevitable.

Man is depicted as so small and insignificant a creature in a cruel and indifferent universe that it is not really surprising that in several of O'Flaherty's best stories animals replace humans as characters. A cow jumps to death after losing her calf; a conger eel is captured and wrestles with a pair of cruel sailors, but heroically escapes back to the sea; a sea bird struggles, not only against wind and sea, but against the other birds, which reject a wounded animal. In the last of these stories, "The Wounded Cormorant," the rejection and even attack by the healthy birds is horrifying, but it does not seem morally reprehensible, for human moral codes are irrelevant to a conflict with nature. The bird resists as long as it can and then falls off a ledge to the sea below, where "it disappeared, sucked down among the seaweed strands." That closing statement reveals how dispassionate the narration is, for the other cormorants are portrayed as no more cruel than the waves and weeds. O'Flaherty even wrote one story in which a wave, attacking the land and eventually destroying a cliff, is the sole protagonist.

Consistent with his naturalist intentions are O'Flaherty's unambiguous endings, the generally direct narrative techniques, and his rejection of stylistic elaboration.[1] Stories tend to begin abruptly, with no historical background or topical commentary, and to end sharply, often with accounts of death or separation, or with some other full closure. Between those poles only essential action is described—perceptions, episodes, events, but little commentary. Yet even in such unadorned, skeletal accounts, a strong impression of the writer's authority is conveyed; the abrupt turns of plot, the selectivity of detail and incident, and the strength of the endings all give the impression of a sure-handed, controlling sensibility. Paradoxically, the more restricted the narrative, the greater the sense of such authority; for defying conventions of storytelling, an author, such as O'Flaherty, who presents only the least ambiguous actions, makes a statement that is so strong as to be distinctive.

O'Flaherty's implied criticism of Catholicism is consonant with his naturalist convictions; to him the institution of religion is unnatural in that it enforces conformity, weakness, and slavery. Cruel, uncharitable, and even perverse priests appear, but O'Flaherty's exposure of them is not much more vigorous than what is found in many pieces of Irish fiction or drama. What O'Flaherty most consistently denounces is the tyranny exercised by the clergy rather than the priests themselves. In "The Inquisition," for instance, a young postulant is denounced by an old priest for buying cigarettes for his friends. When the postulant rebels, within his mind at least, he becomes free, but he has also become as deceitful as his oppressor, showing the poisonous effects of institutional victimization. Human tyranny in this and other forms is the target of some of O'Flaherty's most forceful stories. In "The Tent," a tinker extorts complete control of his two wives and then of the man who wanders into the scene; in "The Tyrant" a woman decides to leave her ambitious, controlling husband; and the lecherous lawyer in "The Sensualist" is brought to realize his own baseness by discovering that the woman he planned to seduce has already deceived him.

At times the force of O'Flaherty's denunciation of such tyrants is so strong that the stories become melodramatic. (The last-named story ends with his vision of the "whole world . . . watching him . . . and crying out insanely, 'Shame, shame, shame.' ") But in those stories that are most pared down, in which the satiric target is clearly established and the responses sufficient, O'Flaherty's strong voice and conviction elevate the stories to true artistry. In "The Outcast" a young woman confesses to a priest that she has given birth to an illegitimate child. When he drives her away, she walks to a lake, says some prayers, and goes to jump off the brink. But when she hears her baby cry, she returns to him "joyfully," picks him up, and then . . . jumps headlong into the lake. As the story's inscription, "I am the Good Shepherd," is applied to the insensitive priest, it is ironic; but in refraining from abandoning her child, the mother herself becomes such a model. Kitty's realizations that she will not be forgiven and that her child will be similarly abandoned are not articulated, nor does a narrator comment upon them. But clearly the tyranny of the priest is set in contrast to her human concern for her child.

Other forms of social control beyond those imposed by the church are likewise vigorously exposed. The stratification of society into classes is one such satiric target. In "The Terrorist," a story that reveals O'Flaherty's early Marxist sympathies, a theater audience into which a bomb is thrown is neatly divided into three classes, corresponding to the orchestra and two balconies. In "The Fireman's Death," the men tending the engines utter "curses on the sea, the fires, God, and the rich men who make slaves toil in the bowels of ships." In such stories, the exposure of injustice often determines the shape of the narrative, with plot and character development sacrificed to theme.

However, such social reactions and political convictions, striking as they may be, are not the elements that distinguish O'Flaherty's art. Naturalist tendencies are common in the literature of the period, and O'Flaherty's criticism of institutions and human tyranny are no more vehement than those of many other writers of the early twentieth century. Rather, what dignify the best stories are strange and powerful contrasts: between moral outrage and an irrepressible lyric impulse in some stories, between a conviction of men's subservience to nature and a celebration of life in others.

"The Mountain Tavern" includes some strong statements spoken by characters denouncing the Civil War which had occurred only a few years earlier. In particular, the family members whose home and place of business have been burned to the ground are victims of both the Republicans and Free State soldiers. The tavern owner's wife, Mrs. Galligan, is explicit in her denunciation: after the years of the Troubles, the two forces have turned on one another "like dogs after a bitch," she cries. Even the two exhausted soldiers who survive give up their will to fight. But such comments and conclusions do not determine the story's shape, for the narrative is more concerned with natural description than the people who traverse this desolate setting. It opens with a long, detailed description of falling snow which smooths, silences and obliterates all vestiges of humanity: "Up above was the sky and God perhaps, though it was hard to believe it; hard to believe that there was anything in the whole universe but a flat white stretch of virgin land between squat mountain peaks and a ceaseless shower of falling snow-flakes." Human beings impinge on the scene: three soldiers looking for shelter and food at a public house they know to be safe. But they find it burned to the ground, and when one of the three Republican soldiers dies, the people show their hatred, looking steadily and pitilessly, "with the serene cruelty of children watching an insect being tortured." The story moves to its conclusion when a lorry of Free State soldiers arrives, and the two Republicans surrender. Both groups are denounced by the old woman as robbers who have taken the possessions and even the lives of the common people. At the story's conclusion, the human characters disappear from the scene and nature reclaims the land, erasing the traces of man, a ruined tavern, and a bloodstained piece of ground where the soldier had died: "Night fell and snow fell, fell like soft soothing white flower petals on the black ruin and on the black spot where the corpse had lain."

O'Flaherty's expression, even when rough and imprecise, suits the combination of pessimism and lyric enthusiasm which appears in such stories. He favors similes over metaphors, thus suggesting that any proposed comparison is not quite adequate. He repeats words, not so much to expand meaning incrementally but to reveal the urgency and recognition that his intended statements are just beyond his power of expression. The impression of struggling to express one's self is particularly appropriate to the stories in which the characters themselves find verbal expression difficult. The parents in "Going into Exile" speak only in platitudes when they try to articulate their feelings of grief at the approaching emigration of their two children. In fact, the moments of strained silence are the most evocative: "They stood in silence fully five minutes. Each hungered to embrace the other, to cry, to beat the air, to scream with excess of sorrow. But they stood silent and sombre, like nature about them, hugging their woe." When the child departs, the mother can do no more than cry. But given the skeptical view of language the characters have expressed and the sparse use of dialogue in the story, the last comments of the neighbors—"There is nothing that time will not cure . . . Time and patience"—is painfully ironic, for such consolation does not relieve the suffering; in fact, this is a grief that neither time nor patience may alleviate.

O'Flaherty's insistence that men have only very limited power to control their lives or to combat natural forces severely limits possible modes of action in his early stories. Very few stories center on conflict between humans; more often, men struggle with the insurmountable forces outside, or with ungovernable impulses within themselves, the outcomes being predictable from the story's start. Thus the narrative form is determined by the explication of a conflict or the presentation of a theme, rather than by action. In "The Tramp," for example, the title character tries to persuade inmates of a workhouse to join him in the freedom of wandering through the natural world; the inmates refuse to do so, so bound are they to social notions of propriety and respectability. Animals, in other stories, free from social re-straints, can reconcile their own desire for freedom with nature's laws. The conger eel, in the story of that title, clearly escapes human bonds for the sea's depths, where it can enjoy unlimited freedom. In such animal fables, the narrative line is slight, serving aims of social criticism and moral instruction.

In stories about human beings, similar elements of fable are abundant; moral instruction is so predominant that detailed depiction of characters or complicated narrative lines are often sacrificed. "The Fairy Goose," built upon a patently contrived plot, presents a forceful comment on folk super-stition and religious belief. Such moral tales can have great force, as does "Red Barbara," a celebration of natural vitality and even violence. But that story of a vivacious woman's marriage to a saintly, disciplined man is nar-rated with such strong moral implications that it becomes a kind of pagan sermon. In this regard, O'Flaherty's resemblance to D. H. Lawrence is strik-ing: both authors occasionally abandon their considerable descriptive powers and their challenging theories of the integrity of human instincts in order to preach in a simplistic manner. In one of O'Flaherty's weakest early stories, "Beauty," a man, having rejected the woman with whom he had fled into the wilds, turns from her and kisses a tree, which is supposed to symbolize an absolute, independent, life-affirming spirit.

Although a selected edition of earlier stories appeared in 1939, and three stories were published in a limited edition, *The Wild Swan and Other Stories* (1932), O'Flaherty's literary activities in the thirties and forties were entirely devoted to novels and political prose. Finally, in 1948, a collection of new stories, *Two Lovely Beasts and Other Stories,* was published, most of which had appeared in periodicals in the ten years preceding. O'Flaherty's interests had evidently broadened, and his analytical powers sharpened, so that in these stories he recognizes more complex motives for human actions and subdues his anger at social institutions. The narrative forms are looser, accommodat-ing varied incidents.

The title story, "Two Lovely Beasts," is his longest, most complex and yet most balanced short story. The main character, Colin Derrane, succumbs to material ambition as he acquires a second calf, one more than he can easily support, and more than the community regards as permissible, since he will have to use his cow's milk to nurture the two calves and will have none left for his poor neighbors. O'Flaherty's criticism of him is never directly stated, but the implications are clear and forceful. Derrane claims God's providence on his side, but he is clearly brutalized by his success; at the story's end, as he drives away from the fair after selling the two beasts for top prices, "his pale blue eyes stared fixedly straight ahead, cold and resolute and ruthless." By allowing the villagers to present the direct condemnation of him as a "bloodsucker" who has taken the food from the country to sell to foreigners, O'Flaherty can deflate their condemnation as well, for guilty as Derrane is of greed, his neighbors are driven by envy more than justice in accusing him of such crimes. This detailed presentation of Derrane's ambitions, their slow growth and destructive consequences, is made possible by the more ample form of the story. The efficacy of human actions is neither denied nor is it contrasted to the superior power of nature as insistently as in earlier stories, thus allowing wider narrative interests and thematic variety.

The author's more extensive treatment of the varieties of human responses in the later stories is seen in "The Wedding," in which a celebration in a house only two hundred yards away is observed and commented upon by a mad, crippled woman and her alcoholic cousin. Their distorted, bitter view is contrasted to the vitality of three young girls who are excited about the event. By the story's end, the older women have revealed their frustration at being unwed; they are left hugging each other, the one weeping but the other pealing in "idiotic laughter." The story avoids both sentimentality and cynicism by such careful balance, yet presents a forceful contrast of youth with age, and sanity with madness.

Several of the stories in other volumes were written in Irish as well as English, and ten of these were published in 1953 as *Duil (Desire)*. A comparison of versions in both languages reveals how conscious O'Flaherty was of achieving such balance and avoiding facile moral implications. In the earlier, Irish version of "The Touch," for example, the young man who is in love with the vivacious daughter of a spiteful man for whom he works as a day laborer is much weaker than in the later English version of this story. The effect of the final version is to balance the young man's cowardice against the father's cruelty, so as to give prominence to the girl, who is symbolically identified with the spirited horse she rides. She is being sold like livestock, doomed to marriage with a man she does not love and separation from the man she does love, but who is too weak to carry her away.[2]

The balance O'Flaherty achieves in his late stories is not gained by compromising his convictions or decreasing the intensity of the emotions expressed. In fact, the late stories return to many of the subjects of the early works: animal tales, accounts of man's contention with nature, and stories of death and violence. They are less vehement and provocative, so that some critics regard them as inferior to his earlier stories, but they treat subjects and attitudes that are more complex and subtle than such favored early themes as brute struggle and resentment. "The Tide," a late story, deserves comparison with his earlier "The Wave," in that both describe a natural phenomenon of water's motion. The early story is undoubtedly forceful in its vivid description of a wave acquiring enormous force and then breaking against the shore; but the later story, although quieter indeed, is more comprehensive in surveying the curative effects of the regressing and progressing tide. The humans who invade the beach are gross and voluptuous, attacking it selfishly; but the tide that drives them away at the story's end restores all to its original beauty. Critical as the story is of human rapacity, nature is seen as a positive force, not a destroyer, and the tone is austere, yet reassuring rather than angry.

"The Parting" represents the considerable achievement of his last collection of stories. Its main character, a thirteen-year-old boy leaving for the seminary in compliance with his family's plan, sees himself as one of the livestock being hoisted aboard the steamer to be sold for profit. His desire to remain home on the island, his need for his family's affection, and his inability to understand what is happening in this strange setting all turn at the end to an awful recognition of finality and the irreversibility of his fate. Criticism of the practice of taking such a young boy away from home is not disguised, yet it does not displace or prevent the reader's sympathy for the victim. For all their lack of perception, the characters are complex, affected by contrary motives and desires. When the boy, for instance, speaks "gruffly" to his mother, the narrator explains, "Indeed it was the intensity of his love that forced him to be gruff and almost brutal when he spoke to her. If he allowed any tenderness to creep into his voice, it would mean the collapse of his resistance." The boy's awareness of conflict within the family and his embarrassment are no stronger than his fear of leaving them. Yet the story's conclusion is as forceful as any of O'Flaherty's, as the boy realizes the "dark vows" he is about to take will make this parting "final, forever and forever."

O'Flaherty's expression in the late stories is no more polished or graceful than his early ones. But the rough style, the spare dialogue and the brutal commentary are well adapted to his mature outlook, one that is balanced and complex, but vivid and vehement. Like the rough landscapes of Jack Yeats, O'Flaherty's stories rely on violent contrasts and bold strokes to convey their energetic visions. They are striking, sometimes disturbing, but never pallid.

• • •

In the conclusion to *An Only Child,* the first volume of his autobiography, Frank O'Connor refers to storytelling as a "celebration" of such exceptional people as his mother who "represented all I should ever know of God"; such joy and wonder at the variety of human beings characterize O'Connor's stories through-out his career. Despite the sufferings of his early years caused by the family's poverty and mistreatment by his father, and his sense of alienation from his native country during most of his adult life because of his unpopular political and religious views, O'Connor's optimism never seemed to falter. He was well aware of his separation from his countrymen as well as his personal alienation as an artist; in fact, he argued that the short story has for its essential or most characteristic subject an "intense awareness of human loneliness." Yet his stories are neither morose nor morbid; they are infused with respect for man's abilities to adapt, to survive adversity, and to learn from experience. Few of his charac-ters ever rise to heroic action; they are more often hurt into recognizing life's cruelties. But victimized or victorious they are admirable.

In teaching college students to write short stories, O'Connor insisted that each writer carefully articulate the themes of his or her story in no more than four lines before proceeding to compose further. His own stories give evidence of being carefully planned along such lines. Narrative development is usually not extensive and only the barest hints at setting are provided, so that theme, as revealed by action and dialogue, determines structure. Yet every subject is qualified by a strong personal element. Whether O'Connor employs a personified narrator or presents the story directly, a distinctive voice is heard, commenting and interpreting if only by innuendo. The per-sonal voice that he consciously sought to restore to fiction not only estab-lishes intimacy with the reader and evokes compassion, but in itself it reflects the author's regard for personality. The range of his characters is not wide; they are almost all Irish men, women, and children of the middle classes. Yet they are sufficiently varied as to reveal a comprehensive catalog of human aspirations and weaknesses. He focuses on individuals, rather than on fami-lies, communities, or nations. In fact, in *The Lonely Voice,* he argues that no concept of a normal society is necessary in the short story, although it is essential to a novel, because the shorter form typically is concerned with individuals and their inner conflicts, not broad social concerns.

From his earliest collections to his last, O'Connor favored the most efficient narrative form in which exposition is kept to a minimum or is expressed through action, with all elements leading to a climactic moment, an incident that changes a person's life. There are notable exceptions, stories with no dra-matic climaxes and ones with much broader plots, but more consistently than O'Flaherty's or O'Faolain's, the stories of Frank O'Connor follow an efficient and effective formula. Few physical details are given; natural imagery and de-scriptions of place are sparse. Even human beings are sketched only minimally, with a few comments on size, weight, or extraordinary facial features. But speech patterns are widely varied. In a *Paris Review* interview, O'Connor agreed that he lacked concern for sense details, explaining that he himself noticed primarily cadences, distinctive phrases, and figures of speech rather than visual details.[3] In his early stories, speakers are typically distinguished by speech patterns so suggestive as to uncover subtle aspects of character. Extensive use of dialect and colorful speech could easily become distracting, he came to recognize, and so in revising the most serious early stories, which he did very extensively, he often flattened speech and narrative tone in order to maintain a mood of sobriety. Like his friend Yeats, O'Connor boldly revised his works years after first publication, a practice that O'Faolain considered improper and even offensive, but one that usually resulted in sharper focus and greater economy. He exercised severe restraint in selecting stories to be reprinted in cumulative volumes, so that only after his death were many stories gathered into his collected works.

O'Connor's first collection, *Guests of the Nation* (1931), reveals his impressive command of literary technique even at the start of his career. The characters in the title story are established primarily by gestures and speech patterns; the confusion and anxiety of the central character, the narrator, are made evident by the urgency of his account. Simply and even naively his first sentence outlines the intimate and sympathetic relationship that had developed among the Irish soldiers and their English captives; they had become "chums," appreciative of each other. But their spontaneous friendship comes into fatal conflict with duty, action prescribed by fidelity to nation or abstract cause. The narrator, ironically named Bonaparte, participates in the execution of two Englishmen and realizes his own guilt and corruption because he has violated personal claims under pressure of abstract patriotism. Although the only killing he does is to finish the job when one of the victims is not fully out of pain, Bonaparte is clearly guilty by complicity and is finally overwhelmed with a feeling of isolation and insignificance. That climax is expressed in powerful, poetic language in which a series of visual images are presented in a hurried manner, leading to a recognition of self as "somehow very small and very lonely." And this incident has an indelible effect on him: "And anything that ever happened me after I never felt the same about again."

Powerful as that conclusion is, the theme of desolation caused by the failure of both human bonds and national concerns has been sounded from the first paragraph on. The initial setting is dusk, the end of the day, when Belcher and 'Awkins would play cards with Noble and Bonaparte, supervised on occasion by Jeremiah Donavan. The last named, the only one of the Irish with a common Celtic proper name, does indeed supervise the games of contention, being the one who later insists on the execution. The names of his compatriots suggest inflated patriotism, in contrast to the earthy names of the English prisoners, Belcher and 'Awkins. Although they argue over a question of "capitalists and priests and love for your own country," they are all "chums," making the final act of destruction most painful. The narrator's disillusionment colors the entire account; long before the final incident he comments on how shameful he would have regarded disloyalty to his nationalist "brothers" but adds, "I knew better after." Yet there is a strong forward movement, advancing through four stages from premonitions of death at dusk to an evening argument to a third stage of confusion in which the inevitable order of execution is given. In this episode the conflict is most clearly articulated; against 'Awkins's insistence that they were all "chums" among whom there was no deadly enmity is posited the "usual riga-marole about doing our duty." The theme having been stated, dramatized, and amplified, the action of the final episode is as inevitable as that of a classic trag-edy, and the action transcends temporal bounds, shifting from the past tense to the present tense at the most intense moments. Thus narrative rules are sus-pended, the storyteller merging past with present as he relates incidents that not only changed his life but continue to torture him, a conflict between com-peting claims that cannot be resolved. Yet however compelling either individual friendship or national loyalties are, neither justifies taking a human life, for in succumbing to fear of his superior and becoming an accomplice to the execu-tion, Bonaparte, the narrator, is alienated from all comfort. The old woman who falls to her knees on learning of the execution may pray not only for the dead but for the living guilty.

O'Connor's personal experience in the Troubles and the Civil War, described in *An Only Child* (1961), shattered his idealism about warfare and made him exceptionally sensitive to the horror of violence. While a prisoner of the Free State government in 1923, he was one of only a few who voted against the staging of a hunger strike, a controversial stand motivated by his conviction that the proposal was inhumane. A moral conviction that human destruction is never justified by political ends appears often in the early stories and raises them above political partisanship, even at a time when allegiances were so strictly drawn that neutrality itself was regarded as suspect. In "Jumbo's Wife," sympathy is even afforded the wife of an informer who had been responsible for the death of an Irish neighbor. Although this story ends with the execution of the spy, its focus is the persecution of a wife mentally unequipped to comprehend her hus-band's actions yet protective of him on an animal level, despite his violent mis-treatment of her. The story's underlying theme is violence itself, horrifying no matter for what cause, noble or ignoble, it is committed. However, as in the early works of many fiction writers, the style of this story and most others in *Guests of the Nation* is so studied, so reliant on imagery and delicate impressions, that it becomes distracting in its beauty.

As though aware of the stylistic excesses of the first volume, O'Connor experiments with more direct and sparse styles in his next collection, *Bones of Contention* (1936). In it appear stories that gently mock his earlier romantic idealism, such as "Lofty" and "A Romantic"; these stories also prefigure O'Connor's continuing fascination with impractical, doomed figures who are motivated and defeated by dreams. Two stories, among O'Connor's very best, reveal his early command of form and technique: "In the Train" and "The Majesty of the Law." The first of these employs narrative techniques that he later admired in Turgenev's *A Sportsman's Sketches*: the suppression of plot, "episodic interest," and its replacement with "the static quality of an essay or poem." The story of the trial from which the villagers of Farranchreest are returning on a train is disclosed gradually through comments of policemen and peasants, leading up to the crucial disclosure that one passenger, Helena, has been acquitted of murder because others lied to protect her. The conversations in each compartment of the train are linked by the appearance of a passing drunk and by cross-references to each other which reveal the loneliness of these characters returning to their desolate village surrounded by bogland. Although the villagers have protected Helena to spite the police, they now plan to turn against her and drive her away; and clearly she realizes the suffering that lies ahead for her. She sees herself at the story's end as having been caught up, mastered, and thrown aside by life and love. Thus the train compartment in which she sits alone, talking only to herself, becomes an evocative image of her isolated state, and her comment that a purported future mate is no more to her "than the salt sea" likewise becomes metaphoric. Cady Driscoll, the man she loved, embodies the force that has used and ruined her; like the bitter sea, he has been ruthless and oblivious to her suffering. The subject of personal isolation has been explored from the first episode in the complaints of the sergeant's wife, and his responses on the need for security; it is echoed in subsequent episodes in the comments of both the disgruntled policemen and the contented country people. As the focus advances from one train compartment to the next, the theme is developed by repetition and parallels rather than by relying upon narrative outcomes.

In a similar manner, "The Majesty of the Law" explores by incrementation a single subject, announced in the title but unidentified in the plot until the last page. After genial conversation about country traditions, a policeman ever-so-gently gets around to inquiring whether his host, Dan Bride, will pay the fine imposed on him or whether he will go to jail; the story ends with Dan, a few days later, heading for the jail. The policeman treats him with extreme politeness, as do the neighbors who bid him farewell; he himself does not feel guilt, for in his own words he had only "had the grave misfortune to open the head of another old man in such a way as to require his removal to hospital." The responsible party, he is convinced, is his victim, who had an "unmannerly method of argument," so, like the ancient Irish poets who punished their enemies by starving on the doorstep in order to mortify them, he will go to jail to shame and thus punish his enemy. While the polite manners of both parties seem humorous at the start, by the story's conclusion the law has come to seem majestic indeed, the code of a closed community, reinforced by formalized behavior and strengthened by rituals, a primitive law that recognizes the integrity of the individual.

In both stories, the sparse details and indirect presentation cause the focus to narrow gradually to a single person, one who is indeed lonely, but is determined to survive and even take dominance. Set against such self-realization are laziness and cowardice, not forces of social conformity; in fact, despite his objections to such institutions as the Roman Catholic church and political or nationalist parties, O'Connor rarely attacks them even indirectly in his stories. Instead, conflict tends to be internalized and undramatized, and the stories rely less on dramatic conflict than on gradual lyrical disclosure of theme. Several of the best stories in *Crab Apple Jelly* (1944) reveal this simpler, more lyric form. The two religious brothers in "Song without Words" acknowledge the attraction of the secular world, but they feel they have triumphed over the demon adversary when they conform to the rules of their order and forsake their little worldly pleasures. Thus their story does not reflect struggle with rules as much as with their natural selves; and their victory leads to their song of celebration. Abby Driscoll, in "The Long Road to Ummera," achieves a similar internal triumph by reaching the place in which she has long wished to be buried, so that she may lie beside her husband and among her neighbors. The reader's involvement in plot, what O'Connor termed "episodic interest," is minimal, for once Abby determines to return to her village the outcome of the action is quite predictable. Instead, a sense of triumph dominates the story, deriving from the knowledge that Abby will get her own way, and asserting the importance of tradition and order and the most primitive, simple, and intimate relationships. Although its form, similar to that of Eudora Welty's "The Worn Path," resembles a heroic quest, ending victoriously with a symbolic return, the triumphant, celebratory note has pervaded the story from its first words.

"Uprooted" is built upon a different kind of quest pattern, as two brothers return to their homes in search of stability, order, and happiness. Although they find desirable elements in the simple country life, neither feels he can return to it, one because he is a priest and the other because he has been changed by living in the city. Yet their perceptions are more limited than the reader's. The second brother, the story's main character, is "tired to death" of the city to which he has moved. He recognizes that his failure to realize his ambitions has been due to his own cautiousness and lack of boldness. His father had once had "the gumption" to win for himself a good wife, but both sons admit to lacking power to direct their own lives. Ned entertains the notion of marrying an island woman and moving back from Dublin, but in the sobering light of morning he rejects the idea, saying his decisions of the past have foreclosed a return home. Having done so, he sees his home as brightly colored, like one in a children's picture book; home is now inaccessible to him and therefore is unbelievably attractive just as at an earlier time the city must have appeared. Excluded from his dream-invested past and temperamentally incapable of achieving a more satisfying life in the future, Ned comes at the story's end to recognize that he is permanently uprooted.

Such a narrative structure is found in many of O'Connor's stories: carefully controlled action leading to a momentary realization of one's impotence, an impression of the irretrievability of past joys or the finality of earlier actions. The self-recognition experienced by the focal character is set in contrast to a stable, contented social group, in this case the island people who follow a simpler form of existence in which one's place is determined, a life that accords with nature's cycles. The typical story ends abruptly with realization of alienation, presented tersely but with great power, experienced and reported directly as Bonaparte does in "Guests of the Nation" or indirectly as in the case of Helena in "In the Train" or Ned in "Uprooted." With some variations, this pattern is seen in many of the best stories throughout O'Connor's career: in "The Frying Pan," "The Ugly Duckling," and "The Martyr," for example.

The intensity of such a realization, a recognition in the Aristotelian sense, varies with the situation, but in this collection one may note a development from greater toward less finality in such scenes, allowing the characters greater opportunities for change in their lives. In "Guests of the Nation," the discovery absolutely mars and indelibly changes the speaker's life, while in the later stories there is a mature, if disillusioned, acknowledgement that humans adapt and thrive despite early shattering experiences. But the recognition scene is nevertheless climactic. In "The Mad Lomasneys" it occurs when Ned Lowry learns that Rita Lomasney spurned him out of sheer carelessness, and silently but "savagely" throws his cigarette in the fire. Even at this intense moment of recognition he cannot deliberately hurt her, just as he could not earlier articulate his love or claim possession of her; but he does, it is reported in a single line, marry someone else. By attributing her devastating action to impetuosity rather than a rational or even irrational motive which the reader could understand, the story suppresses narrative interest, focuses intensively on a single recognition scene, and then reiterates the irrelevancies of plot by merely reporting a subsequent action, the marriage, which would otherwise have been explained. An impression of illogicality or discontinuity results, instead of the more usual artistic impression of order and balance.

The title of the next collection, *The Common Chord* (1947), points to the dominant expressive element of its stories: irony. The humorous tone of most of the stories, the use of carefully contrived contrasts between the reactions of characters and those of both narrator and reader, the reliance on reversed expectations, and the tendency toward multiple levels of meaning make them more complex and subtle. Characteristic of this more ironic art is the employment of a focal character whose response to the climactic realization is inadequate or inappropriate. The smug priest who hears the confession of a spirited young woman in "News for the Church" is, indeed, brought to learn something about both sexual passion and the limits of his authority, but he responds vindictively. As the representative of a repressive institution he effectively assaults and destroys her self-confidence. Although she takes an early lead in their verbal sparring match, describing her transgression as a matter of no great importance, he triumphs in the end by making her feel ashamed of the physical act. She embraces dreams and tries "to pull the few shreds of illusion she had left tighter about her," as though protecting her own chastity from the priest's assault. What makes Father Cassidy assume the aggressive role is her nonchalance, and his sudden realization of her insecurity, her romantic need to tell someone about a long dreamed-about event. She comes to confession not ashamed, but nearly proud; she leaves the church "a tiny, limp, dejected figure." While criticism of the church for imposing a rigid sexual code which threatens self-esteem and individuality is undeniably conveyed, the story is amusing and the tone light and far from ponderous. The priest does learn something from the vivacious ingenue; he too is changed by the encounter, aware at the end of his own "heavy policeman's feet," and troubled by what has happened. But in the story's final sentence, as he passes a statue of St. Anne, "patron of marriageable girls," the priest, established as both a tyrant and a naive, threatened old man, is nevertheless lighthearted: "he almost found himself giving her a wink."

O'Connor's quarrels with church and state are well-known; his two volumes of autobiography reveal the extent of his resentments, but the stories are never strident. And although his book-length studies of fiction have led some critics to view his stories as somber studies of alienated man, his humanity never wavers. The admission of multiple levels of significance and the irrepressible tendency to find amusement even in conflict relieve the stories from any narrowly focused, intense social criticism. Concern with ethical questions, moral issues, and political principles are presented in the stories, but the ironic juxtaposition with lighter elements changes their effects, making them no less moving but more comprehensive.

In the stories' treatment of marriage, a rich balance is struck between serious analysis of interpersonal dynamics and a gentle, ironic tone revealing amusing incongruities in personal behavior. In "The Frying-Pan," for instance, a dinner table conversation among a priest and his closest friends, a young married couple, leads to the revelation of the frustration of each individual: the married man has wanted to be a priest, the priest is in love with the man's wife, and she suffers from the strict religious code that makes her seem adulterous whatever she does. The story ends with a shared recognition that the three characters would "die as they had lived, their desires unsatisfied." Thus the twisted perspectives of the characters that make natural, impulsive actions seem sinful, perpetrated in this case by the layman rather than the priest, put all three characters in the same situation: the "frying pan" referred to in the title from which the only escape is the fire of damnation or death. The final realization of their dilemma serves as the story's climax. No personalized narrator is employed, and characters are just adequately enough developed to convey their common, inescapable solitude. The theme of loneliness, cited by O'Connor as the essential subject of the short story, dictates precisely that narrative structure, rapid exposition, limited plot and character development, leading to a realization of isolation.

Even those stories that proceed beyond that subject to consider the effects of loneliness or its relation to social and emotional ties, follow a similar pattern. "Don Juan's Temptation" is a middle-aged roué's simple account of his attempts to seduce a young woman; but because his experiences are reported by a narrator who reflects the narrow views of a provincial society, rich dual interpretations are allowed. To win young Helen, the town's Don Juan, Gussie, argues against not only her moral attitudes but her romantic hopes of absolute love, while admitting to himself the continuing idealistic love he feels for his first sweetheart. His extended suffering is truly pathetic, but the framing objective narration expands the subject beyond personal experience to provide a humorous view. The auditor who asks whether Gussie sent the girl home when she turned up at his apartment is described as "probably some middle aged man with a daughter of his own"; yet he is clearly fascinated by the sensual man because of his greater experiences with women. The narrative ends after the realization of inevitable loneliness, although relevant ironic commentary follows.

The narrative scheme of "Judas" is unusually complex, for both a personalized narrator and a named auditor are employed. A pathetic bachelor, Jerry Moynihan, relates what is for him the unforgettable incident in his life: his single encounter with love for a woman his own age, which he interprets as a betrayal of his mother. He rejects his sole chance of leading a normal adult life and ends by reverting to childish behavior, enjoying the coddling but stifling attentions of his jealous mother who makes him into her own "little man." A crippled product of maternal possessiveness, Jerry repeatedly refers to self-destruction and violence in what seem to be flippant figures of speech, but that reveal his near desperation and even suggest a degree of masochism, for he seems to take some pleasure in self-denunciation. The fact that Jerry is now relating this tale to an identified auditor, Michael John, raises another question: why does he tell such a painful story? Perhaps to claim some experience of love in his past life; to account for his present single state; to attempt to make sense of an experience for which he still feels guilt, identifying the party sinned against as his mother, when it was obviously himself? All these are satisfactory explanations, but another impulse is as strong: the story is, indeed, incriminating, and he is continuing to destroy his self-esteem by dwelling on such errors and guilt. The story's climax is Jerry's recognition of the complex ·intertwining of mother and son. When they are reunited neither can accuse nor apologize: "all she could do was to try and comfort me for the way I'd hurt her, to make up to me for the nature she'd given me."

O'Connor refused to distinguish the short story from the novel on the basis of mere length; the difference, he said, was more fundamental, determined by the wider thematic scope and more complex assumptions of the novel. "The Holy Door," at about 24,000 words, and with its extensive plot covering years of experience, tests the validity of O'Connor's critical claim. The personal focus, the story's center of consciousness, shifts from one to the other among three characters, each of whom is sufficiently presented in one part of the story as to be sympathetic. The action is so extensive that ten numbered episodes are required to record it, and as the story progresses, the perception of minor characters such as Father Ring changes. Yet by O'Connor's standards it is a unified short story, one that even employs the familiar structure, culminating in self-recognition. Although a single subject, the nature of marriage, is explored through various episodes, the basic structure is that of typical O'Connor short stories, culminating in a revelatory episode. The theme of sexual repression and its effect on personal integrity is the story's most powerful subject, and the fuller plot and multiple characters serve to elaborate that familiar theme further than in any other single story. Even the story's ambiguous title includes among its several references the sanctity of a door that opened (the Holy Door in Rome) and the undeniable and disturbing fact of doors that separate individuals from each other. Each isolated character harms himself or herself as severely as the friends and partners. Polly's inhibitions and her refusal to surrender herself to her husband kill her own spirit as well as his. He is no more accommodating, with equally dire effects. When, after his wife's death, he claims Nora for his next wife, he overcomes his guilt and his fear of a curse, and asserts his mastery by joining with Nora: "The pair of us are a match for anyone and anything." She agrees to marry this man she first refused years ago and goes to it "like a Christian martyr offering herself to the lions," yet paradoxically satisfying her own desires. Thus the question raised at the start of the story, whether surrender of autonomy is required in marriage is answered with a recognition of the paradox that in relinquishing dominance, self-realization is achieved and happiness gained by both parties.

Traveller's Samples (1951) does not have the thematic unity of the previous collection: as the title indicates, the collection is more varied. Two of the stories, "First Confession" and "Legal Aid," had appeared even before the previous volume was completed, but most are stories from the late forties and early fifties. In the first several, the childish perceptions conveyed by a mature narrator juxtapose complementary and contrasting perspectives, just as Joyce does in the early stories in Dubliners; however, the effects of O'Connor's technique are typically humorous. In "First Confession," the narrative voice closely approximates the childish perception of a little boy: the image of a damned soul, who made a bad confession and after returning to earth left the mark of a pair of hands burned into a bed, recurs several times in comic phrases such as the boy's fear of "burning people's furniture." But except for a more precise vocabulary, the narrative is confined to a child's naive and amusing perceptions. Viewed from a child's eyes, the threats of hell and strict moral codes seem less disturbing, so the effect is a softening of somber subjects.

The same childish perspective, when applied to more troubling subjects produces more complex effects. In "The Drunkard," a boy's account of his own first experience with drink, while amusing in itself, casts the subject of his father's alcoholism and the family's suffering against the boy's pretended sophistication. Overcome with drink the boy unwittingly mimics his father at his most belligerent and outrageous and, in the end, symbolically replaces replaces the father, earning his mother's pity and affection. Even the father's weakness of character is revealed through the boy's pathetic self-pity. What would other wise be a maudlin account of drunkenness and familial discord is broadened when viewed from the fresh perspective of youth, yet the father's "weakness" can still be viewed as symptomatic of deeper character traits. O'Connor uses the same technique in "The Thief," with harsher and less artistic results. A boy discovers his parents' poverty, his father's cruelty and drunkenness, and his mother's desperate hopes that her son will not turn out like her husband through what had seemed merely an amusing account of discovering the truth about Santa Claus. But in this story the contrasts between ideals and faith are so strong as to restrict the thematic application only to the boy's experiences. A connection between such harmless faith in benevolence and the dark world of adult irresponsibility is not clearly established. Unlike Joyce's "Araby," in which the explosion of a boy's childish idealism leads to profound implications about other kinds of belief, most importantly at the conclusion of religious faith, "The Thief" does not extend significance beyond the surface subject of the story: relations within one family. That narrative technique of employing an ingenuous narrator to recount complex subjects, characteristic of this volume, appears in many stories in later collections.

"Legal Aid" is narrated from the perspective of a limited provincial society. In the views of a small town which cares about classes and respectability and which measures success in material terms, Delia Carty was "ruined" because the "whole family was slightly touched," and Tom Flynn is irresponsible. Thus in the town's view the paternity case she brings against him becomes primarily a match between lawyers. Even when the foolish lovers are finally brought together, Delia's sorrowful realization of "the poor broken china of an idol was being offered her now" is muted by the amusing social commentary and satire. Yet the story's conclusion, which returns to discussion of the social standing of the two pompous lawyers, has the ironic effect of mocking itself. The reputations of the two men of law have been threatened by the marriage of their clients. But reputations gained by unethical and merely theatrical tactics are not worth having, so that the perspective turns ironically on the provincial society itself in an amusing and clever manner.

A central tenet of *The Lonely Voice* is the claim that, unlike the novel, a short story requires no measure of a normal society against which characters are judged. But just as it is more difficult to create a believable good character than a functional villain, one can quite easily expose the distorted values of a provincial society, and O'Connor does so frequently and with ease in "Legal Aid" and many other stories. In "The Masculine Principle" the smug attitudes of a narrow society are even more effectively exploded. "Old Miles Reilly in our town was a building contractor, . . ." the story begins, leading us to surmise at the start that the intimate tone of "our town" will be shared by reader and narrator throughout. But the town, its spokesman goes on to say, admires Reilly for his money and even tolerates the tyrannical Father Ring, a pure, unalloyed materialist who equates pretty girls with pound notes. When Jim Piper refuses to be intimidated by the priest, he asserts an independent spirit so rare in the town that he is regarded as a worthy mate for Reilly's fiery daughter, Evelyn. At each stage of the action, she too opposes the town's standards—by running off to London with her fiance's money, by returning shamelessly, having spent it all, and by conceiving a child out of wedlock. But Jim is an even greater iconoclast, for he acts on his own will throughout, most triumphantly at the end when he claims Evelyn for his wife. Having determined he would not marry until he had two hundred pounds in the bank, he quietly persists and succeeds in asserting his individuality, earning the respect of Evelyn's father, the paragon of the town. The narrative voice, while approximating that of the community, is ironically exposed as inadequate. As close as O'Connor comes in the stories of the forties and fifties to depicting a desirable kind of society is the last story in *Traveller's Samples,* "Darcy in the Land of Youth," in which wartime England, for all the bombing and rationing, is pictured as Tir-na-nOg. A young man working in an English defense factory falls in love with an uninhibited girl who represents a very desirable alternative to the cramped, stifling life of Cork.

For all its warmth and congeniality, the narrative voice in O'Connor's stories only rarely serves as spokesman for a stable community, and in this respect O'Connor does not build upon the Irish oral tradition, and his narrators do not resemble the traditional shanachies. Although he consistently sought to restore the oral quality to storytelling and includes what seems to be local lore, O'Connor typically views society as corrupt, narrow, and repressive in his stories; it is most often a destructive force against which O'Connor's individualists, iconoclasts, or victims testify.

After *Traveller's Samples,* O'Connor's popularity in England and America as well as in Ireland prompted the publication of *Stories* in 1952; because new and republished works are combined in this and later collections, the development of O'Connor's craft is harder to trace. However, the original stories in this collection continue to reveal the author's growing command of narrative technique and show important shifts in subject matter. A few changes in subject matter appear; because he left Ireland in 1951 to assume a teaching position in America, the later stories reflect the greater objectivity that comes from viewing home from far away. Even the subject of relations—among mothers, fathers, and children, about which O'Connor had written so sensitively but with barely concealed bitterness against fathers—is treated with greater balance and more healthy humor in "My Oedipus Complex," which first appeared in *Stories*. The possessive love of a mother is made to seem slightly ridiculous and the diction of the narrative mocks itself as the boy wages warfare with his father, conducting "skirmishes" with him. The story ends with a reconciliation of father and son, the end to his oedipal stage: but the boy even asserts mastery over the father, drawing from him gestures of love and even gifts. Compared with "First Confession," the story is harsher but more mature, qualifying the naive perceptions of a child with the disturbing recognition that there is an element of possessiveness in all love; this is surely a more complex and troubling aspect of experience than spats between siblings or a child's embarrassment at his grandmother's manners, subjects of the earlier story. "The Genius" in *Domestic Relations* (1957) presents an even more critical view of youth. While the boy's belief in his own superior powers and his confusion about matters of reproduction are amusing, what he learns in the story shatters his childish optimism: "I saw that love was a game that two people couldn't play at without pushing, just like football."

Many of the stories in *Domestic Relations* employ a familiar narrative technique of relating experiences of childhood or adolescence through a purportedly naive perspective. But the perspective becomes much less restricted, shifting to mature judgments so as to qualify and contrast naive interpretations. Commentary by a mature interpreter becomes more frequent, often appearing as opening and closing statements to stories that otherwise recapture youthful, idealistic visions. But the sober, disillusioned commentary forms the real subject of such stories. "The Duke's Children," for example, closes with a mature interpretation of the idealism of two young people who consider themselves so much more sophisticated than their parents that they regard themselves as nobility. The narrative seems amusing, but the commentary extends the significance of their dreams to a universal observation: the narrator sees himself and the young girl he once loved as "outcasts of a lost fatherland who go through life living above and beyond themselves like some image of man's original aspiration." Aspirations, anticipations, plans for the future are recurrent concerns of stories in this volume, and the exploration of such subjects requires a more extensive time frame to contrast early aspirations with life's outcomes. "Expectation of Life," for example, traces the marriage of Shiela Hennessey to a man twenty years older than herself. Unhappy with her placid, stolid husband, she begins after only a few years to look forward to marrying an earlier suitor after her husband's death; but when she is close to death herself, she realizes what she missed in not enjoying present experiences, and her discovery provides the story's thematic conclusion. By the late 1950s the dominant narrative voice in O'Connor's stories had become more confident and authoritative. In the last mentioned story, comments such as "Women are like that" appear; ironic or not, such authorial interjections, assigned to no identified narrator, extend the subjects beyond the simple narrative. Likewise after the climactic self-realization, multiple responses, often alternatives to the main character's responses, are offered. In the same story two men who had loved the same woman respond to her death in ways so different from each other that neither one can understand the other.

As their themes expand to include the consequences of self-realization and to recognize multiple perspectives, the stories are often much longer and the plots more complicated. In "The Ugly Duckling," the usual recognition scene is effectively muted by being unspoken by the main character; it is a lyrical evocation of interior experience, of love sustained by imagination, so rich that it becomes invulnerable. Here the authoritative, lyrical, authorial commentary serves as the story's conclusion. In other stories of this period, plot is so extended as to include a complete cycle of changes in characters. Joan, the title character in "The Little Mother" in *Collection Two* (1946), moves from childish simplicity to domineering hardness when she takes charge of her family, but returns finally to childlike dependence on others. In "A Sense of Responsibility" in the same volume, Jack Cantillon, who feels inordinate compunction to help others while not surrendering one degree of self-will, nevertheless is so fully developed as a character that he, as the title indicates, comes to personify that rare quality of responsibility. Inscrutable aspects of human nature are given greater play in stories of the last ten years of O'Connor's life, and the variety of human attitudes is celebrated. Such humane appreciation even replaces social criticism in such stories as "The Sorcerer's Apprentice"; while orthodox attitudes toward marriage are exposed as restrictive, this story focuses attention on character, a young woman discovering "the business of love" as a natural activity, reconcilable with religious belief even when considered immoral by strict religious codes. The discoveries characters make in stories of this period are likely to spur them toward more positive efforts at living. Even the strong ending of "The Weeping Children," in which a husband who has traveled to Cork to bring home his wife's illegitimate child sees four other abandoned children weeping silently, pleadingly evokes in him sympathy and love rather than resentment at their mistreatment. He is exceptional in respecting a responsibility to care for his wife's child, but the unfeeling world who could ignore such needs does not become a subject of outrage. The several stories about the bishop of Moyle expose that clergyman's vanity and love of material comfort, but the criticism is gentle, and the point of the stories is to explore a quite human desire for power or control of others.

After his death in 1966, O'Connor's widow collected twenty-six of his previously published stories to form *Collection Three* (1969), published in America in slightly different form as *A Set of Variations*. These are all stories of the last fifteen years of his life, the period of his most mature art. "A Story by Maupassant," written in 1945, is included because it had been thoroughly revised shortly before his death. As we might expect, a mood of retrospection dominates this story. Human aspirations are viewed as futile, but those who sustain them are treated with compassion so that the story's tone is not bitter. In fact, the heroic potential of even quiet lives emerges as the story's main concern. The woman who regards the two illegitimate boys she raises as her real children, more dear than her own progeny, is made to seem heroic by her stamina and independence. Similarly, the husband in "The American Wife," who is left alone because his wife cannot adapt to the cynicism and sterility of Ireland, is not merely a victim. Ireland's history, his own family, the provincial society, a multitude of forces have shaped his character years ago, yet from personal defeat he has earned "fortitude and humour and sweetness." Such stories move inevitably toward clear thematic conclusions without sudden realizations or dramatized recognitions.

The several stories about Father Fogarty even reveal a more accommodating view of Irish Catholicism, a change confirmed by a story unusual in its directness on the subject of religion: "A Minority." What starts off as a typical O'Connor study of friendship between two boarding school boys who are both isolated because neither is a Catholic turns into a sober consideration of the need to maintain the faith of one's fathers. Denis Halligan turns from atheism to Catholicism in order to gain social acceptance in the school, while his friend Willy Stein remains faithful to his Jewish heritage, even though his parents have been killed. But when Denis resorts to anti-Semitic denunciations, he realizes his own guilt and even confesses to envy, for Stein has been "transfigured by a glory that he himself would never know." In its admission of heroism and in the unrelieved intensity of the conclusion, the story recalls pieces in O'Connor's first volume, but by the end of his career mature acceptance has replaced disillusionment as the usual response.

One of the last stories O'Connor completed culminates in another direct and forceful statement about religion. Dick Gordon, the main character in "The Cheat," steadfastly holds to his disbelief, although his wife is converted to Catholicism and various priests attempt to win him over or frighten him into submission. But his friend Father Hogan delivers the story's forceful conclusion. Gordon is an optimist, he says, one who sees no evil in others because he is so consistently faithful to his own standards, and thus he is certain of salvation. The final development of O'Connor's narrative technique is well revealed in the last paragraph of this story, in which complementary themes—love, regret at past mistakes, responsibility to others and to self—are integrated and resolved. The perspective of the priest is syntactically linked to the expression of love by the wife to form a coherent thematic conclusion, expressed in a stately, confident manner: "He still had a duty to the living as well as to the friend who was about to die."

The 1981 publication of *The Cornet Player Who Betrayed Ireland* provides a series of stories which span O'Connor's career. Although none of the stories is among his very best, the collection, arranged in order of their composition, describes the course of O'Connor's development. "War," the first story, dated 1926, consists of a single incident of warfare, presented objectively and focusing upon a young soldier who cannot comprehend the violence around him. His realization of the futility of war and of his own inability to change the world is presented with greatest force as the story's climax. Following that statement, he is wounded and ends crying to be left alone. The structural formula of the early stories is made evident here. The introduction of first-person narrators in later stories intensifies the emotional impact, while limiting the implications to those a single person could accommodate.

"There Is a Lone House," dated 1933, extends from personal discovery to a consideration of interpersonal concerns, requiring a less compact narrative structure, so that a pair of viewpoints may be adequately represented. Imagery is presented in greater visual detail and hints are provided to foreshadow the discovery that the woman in a lonely glen who takes in a traveling man and eventually claims him as her husband has earlier murdered her uncle. These two main characters vie for mastery of each other, so that the story records multiple stages of their relationship, ending in their marriage.

One remarkable story, "May Night," dated 1935, deserves comment as being unique in O'Connor's canon in its surrealistic treatment of the fear of death. The story consists primarily of dialogue between two tramps who quarrel and fight, yet rely upon each other for their lives. When they encounter a young man who plans to kill himself, they try to posit reasons for staying alive, even in their miserable state. The literary analogues to this situation are obvious even in summary: the characters are like Yeats's quarreling tramp and blind man in *On Baile's Strand* and like Dunsany's tramps in *The Glittering Gates*, both published earlier; the resemblance to Samuel Beckett's Gogo and Didi in *Waiting for Godot* is even stronger.

The middle period of O'Connor's career is reflected in several stories that employ personified narrators, often looking back at their own childhood experiences. Such stories tend to center on a single incident that shatters pleasant illusions, and so they end with strong scenes in which some permanent loss or painful realization is presented in strongly emotional terms. By the time of the first publication of "The Cornet Player Who Betrayed Ireland" and "The Adventuress," that is, 1942 and 1948, the narrative voice, while reporting childhood disillusioning experiences, is itself made more complex and is subjected to ironic interpretation for misunderstanding or magnifying the importance of the events related. In 1953's "Adventure," the narrator's voice has grown much more authoritative, as he delivers interpretations before and after the narrative account. The basic plot reflects the author's interest in failed marriages and the possibility of starting over, but this tale ends with suicide and the emotional destruction of all parties involved. Although the story's dramatic focus seems to be a triangle, consisting of an attractive woman, her steadfast but unassertive suitor, and her blustering successful suitor who, in the end, turns out to be a bigamist, it shifts in the last paragraph to the narrator who has for the first time experienced a true adventure. Thus the story's actual subject emerges as a result of a complex narrative scheme and is presented directly as a more intellectual and complicated observation.

In the continuing analysis of political, religious, and ethical questions, the development of O'Connor's thought is remarkable. In his command of technique, particularly the manipulation of naive narrators so as to achieve multiple levels of irony, an equally notable growth may be traced. His analysis of the short story, *The Lonely Voice* (1965), is one of a half dozen critical works on this genre that are genuinely instructive, a book that confirms the impression that O'Connor studied the form and perfected techniques over his years of writing. Yet one constant element continues to attract attention: his celebration of the individual, and that characteristic so determines the form as to distinguish O'Connor's art as a short story writer. Impressions of the variety of human types and the unpredictability of personal responses dominate his best works. Men, women, and even children, who tenaciously hold to their ideals and aspirations, who respond boldly in triumph or defeat, and even those who fail, having acted with full exercise of will, appear in many stories throughout his career. In those works, action reveals character, setting reflects it, imagery and style amplify it, and theme springs from character. Yet O'Connor's are much more than sketches, for in celebrating unique character he reaches a universal comment: the world of action, and places, and ideas, rich as it is, does not correspond to the inner world which each individual maintains. Exploration of "interior worlds" and juxtaposition of them with the contrasting outer worlds provides a potent form for O'Connor's short stories, and an elegant model for subsequent writers.

• • •

If intelligence may be defined as the capacity to recognize equal validity in contradictory statements and the ability to recognize complexities and dilemmas, Sean O'Faolain is the most intelligent of Irish writers. Puzzles, human contradictions, and unresolved problems dominate his collections of stories over a career of more than fifty years, and the development of his literary craft may even be traced by considering the various ways in which he deals with the complexities of human experiences.

The son of a pious mother and a father who thought of himself as British, John Whelan very early learned to recognize and deal with what he regarded as irreconcilable differences in political convictions. Yet he also learned to develop and defend his own beliefs. At age eighteen, having become committed to the nationalist cause, he changed his name to its Irish equivalent, Sean O'Faolain. He enlisted in the Irish Republican Army, and after the treaty continued to serve on the republican side in the civil war. Thus, before he wrote his first published story, he had acted on his convictions, but had come to see how untenable for him were intense and simple political allegiances. Yet his disillusionment did not lead to cynicism or despair. When he found he could not wholeheartedly support nationalist causes, and later, when he had to face the objections of the Censorship Board and religious authorities to his works, he responded strongly, with conviction of the moral integrity of art and the importance of intellectual analysis. Most notably, as editor of the *Bell* from 1940 to 1946, he encouraged the open and thorough discussion of the most controversial topics of the day: nationalism, censorship, the language movement, and other political issues. Similarly, in his stories, he never shies away from controversy nor does he submit to sectarian or parochial views.

His first collection, *Midsummer Night Madness* (1932) conveys most vividly varied responses to the political and military events that had recently transformed Ireland. The confused atmosphere of the Troubles and of the Civil War are reflected in many of the stories. His own wartime experiences enabled him to describe the fear, dedication, and intimacy among conspirators in "The Bombshop"; and the vivid emotions of fright expressed in "The Fugue" surely comes from personal experience. Such stories even aspire to ambitious structural forms. "The Fugue," for example, balances precise descriptions of nature with accelerated action in which a young rebel flees from British soldiers and with a lyrical interlude in which he meets and falls in love with a country girl. The story ends almost as it started, so that the musical form indicated by the title is accurate. Instead of presenting a consecutive plot, a single encounter between soldier and girl is placed between contrasting settings: the placid natural scene and the relentless threat of violence and death. These three planes are so juxtaposed as to reflect obliquely one another, with recurring motifs of loneliness pervading all. By the story's end, the three are harmonized, with nature depicted as both loving and destroying, resuming its "ancient, ceaseless gyre."

A similar but less comprehensive structure is seen in the title story, "Midsummer Night Madness." The opening paragraph efficiently positions the narrator between two settings: the confining city and the open countryside. As he makes his way to Henn Hall, the symbol of the Anglo-Irish Big House, the narrator provides information on the house and its owner. Such formalized exposition marks the story as apprentice work, as do the attempts at foreshadowing. The narrator is inadequately defined, but Henn, awkwardly described as a hen, although dissipated and foolish, is presented in greater detail as a cowering fallen aristocrat. Set in contrast to him are the new men of the emerging middle class, Stevey Long and the rebels who have taken occupancy of Henn Hall. Finally, in the person of the tinker woman, Gypsy, the lowest class is represented. The contrast among these three, all occupying the same house, is sharp enough that the story could dispense with the long, contrived conversations between Henn and the narrator, which reiterate without amplifying the theme of class differences. The narrator seems disturbed, nearly frantic much of the time, so that his responses to Long and Henn are confused, rather than ambivalent. His self-conscious, literary expression reflects the absence of a clear focus to the story. Yet the story achieves real power through the superimposition of three classes: the faded aristocracy pretending to continue their genteel ways; the cruel young soldiers driven by patriotic ideals, but ignorant of history and confused in their goals; and the purely sensual tinkers, more worldly but hopeless. Gypsy's concluding evaluations of both Stevey and Henn contrast her desire for love with their political and social concerns.

A juxtaposition of love with nationalist feeling underlies most of the stories in O'Faolain's first collection, making them similar to much European fiction of the twenties and thirties; but while French and English authors tend to contrast personal relations with the inhumanity revealed in the First World War, O'Faolain and his compatriots naturally refer to the Irish revolution and even more vividly to the Civil War which followed. In "The Patriot," the most technically ambitious story of this volume, the love of two young people, Bernie and Norah, is contrasted with the nationalist fervor of his former teacher, Edward Bradley. In a series of encounters among the three characters, the recent decline from revolution to civil war provides an oppressive contrast to the growing love of the couple. By the final episode, the newlyweds merely observe their enthusiastic nationalist friend and mentor as he passes on the street, but they do not join in the cheering. Yet the forces of love and patriotism are, even to the end, treated as equally compelling. The final picture of Bradley driving out of town shows him as no less passionate, dedicated, and attractive than he had been at his first appearance. In turning away from Bradley to his new wife smiling to him in the dark, Bernie chooses love; but neither he nor the narration denies the force of the call of patriotism. Because no moral conclusion is presented, the story's episodic form is justified: each incident brings love and patriotism into sharp contrast but not into conflict. The two impulses inspire different people and dignify them equally. Thus there is no scene in which the two impulses are set in direct opposition to each other; Bernie, who has become Bernard in the last episode, simply grows out of patriotism because of his experiences as a guerrilla and his discovery of love, whereas Bradley does not.

Apparently some of O'Faolain's Irish readers in the thirties bristled at his frank and unflattering treatment of the nationalist cause, or considered his descriptions of sexual relations dangerous to morals, for the book was banned by the Censorship Board. Edward Garnett's introduction to the collection, praising the stories but taking swipes at Ireland as "the most backward nation in Europe," no doubt fed the suspicion of the book's first readers that O'Faolain was expressing antinationalist sentiments.[4]

By the time he finished his second collection of stories, O'Faolain had published biographies of De Valera and Constance Markiewicz and had begun work on his book on Daniel O'Connell, so his interest in Irish history had been even further developed. His first two novels had appeared, both treating the intense and destructive power of Irish society. At this stage of his life, O'Faolain seems to have expended considerable energy in asserting his minority stand in opposition to dominant or at least prevailing Irish social attitudes, and some of his alienation from society is reflected in the stories in *A Purse of Coppers* (1937). Here the language is more controlled and the tone less lyrical than in the first collection, and most stories center on tightly limited action, usually on a single episode. Attention has shifted from questions of the relations between social demands and human needs to a greater interest in isolated individuals. The first story in the collection, "A Broken World," consists of a train-trip conversation among a priest, a farmer, and the narrator on the barren state of modern Ireland. The priest's pessimistic view that the structured society which has been overthrown has not been replaced by a world of shared values, what he calls "moral unity," haunts the narrator and dominates the story. The imagery is that of Joyce's "The Dead," with the snow a "white shroud, covering the whole of Ireland," under which "life was lying broken and hardly breathing." The narrator ends his account hoping for an image that could rekindle the world, a resurrection call for which we all wait, perhaps vainly. The story ends with a series of powerful questions and aspirations, expressed in striking images, making it resemble one of Yeats's poems looking toward a second coming or a resurrection from the dead. There is no substantive communication or interaction among the characters nor any resolution—only vivid impressions and a lyrical outburst at the end.

A similar view of human loneliness is presented in "Egotists," in which an Irish sailor, stopping at a motor camp in Texas, meets a professor and his niece, and a French priest. Each tells about his or her life, revealing profound loneliness and longing for the unattainable. As in the previously mentioned story, the brief conversations bring no persons or views into conflict, and the story ends with a striking natural description of a silent, mysterious night. To some extent the self-absorption and personal dreams of the various aliens isolate each from the other, as the title indicates. Likewise, in "Discord" a newlywed couple visiting a Dublin priest observe his loneliness and pettiness, and realize their own isolation from each other. The young wife feigns innocence and cheerfulness, thus regaining some share of contentment for them both, but her recognition of discord constitutes the story's climactic event. The isolation and alienation treated in many stories in *A Purse of Coppers* are presented in vivid detail, particularly through a few evocative images: snowy landscapes, barren deserts, buried crypts, and similar settings. But the stories do not progress beyond depiction, making them resemble in this regard romantic lyric fragments.

In O'Faolain's next collection, *Teresa and Other Stories* (1947), fuller narratives are provided, and more complex subjects than alienation and loneliness are raised and examined. In "The Man Who Invented Sin," a curate objects to the quite innocent fun of a group of monks and nuns studying Irish in the Gaeltacht. But years later the effect of his moral judgment is still felt, as one of the participants concludes, "It's not good to take people out of their rut, I didn't enjoy that summer." O'Faolain's already established skill in character portrayal and the economy of incidents are enriched by going beyond such personal emotions as loneliness to considering the consequences of human actions. In the title story, Teresa, a wide-eyed, enthusiastic nun on a pilgrimage to Lisieux believes she must renounce the world by becoming a Carmelite in order to become a saint; discouraged from that, she eventually leaves the convent and marries. When she returns to visit the convent with her husband, her sense of alienation and loneliness is strongly expresed, as she tells him, "You will never know what I gave up to marry you!" As though loneliness is inevitable, she realizes how irrevocable her decision has been, and her husband sees how separated they are from each other. Teresa's reasons for wanting to join the Carmelites are made clear enough: she had wanted to become a saint. But her decision to abandon that and to leave the convent is motivated by much more complex impulses. Attempts to interpret such decisions and their consequences are central concerns of O'Faolain's stories at this stage, expanding the narrative structure of the stories and making the tone more subdued and reflective. In "Lady Lucifer," three men rowing on a river casually discuss the problem of distinguishing pride from humility in human actions; this leads one of them, a doctor, to tell about a nurse who had married a wealthy man who soon proved psychotic. His account of the nurse, called Lady Lucifer, seems to have little to do with the peaceful boat trip which frames it, nor with the purported issues of pride and humility. But there are subtle connections among the narratives, such as a pair of female characters, the nurse and the woman at the lock house where the three travelers rest. In the contrast between those two women, one idealistic but dissatisfied, the other contented and humble, the question of how to distinguish pride from humility is explored.

The natural descriptions in this and many of the stories in O'Faolain's first three volumes resemble the lyrical passages in Turgenev's stories. As in *A Sportsman's Sketches,* a narrator provides commentary and even judgments. Instead of presenting a complex plot, the stories tend to focus on one or a few episodes, which reveal incongruities in human experience, discrepancies between human aspirations and actions, or contrasts between nature's order and man's ambitions. Alienation is a recurrent theme, conveyed by employing a narrator who reports on behavior that he does not adequately understand; yet there is very strong sympathy for characters, particularly for the lower classes. Furthermore, in this third volume may be discerned a shift toward another literary model, Chekhov, whose stories deal with more intellectual questions in which the complexities of human actions are more extensively explored, and personalities investigated in greater depth. Both Turgenev and Chekhov reduced plot to a minimum, and both tended to contrast idealizations with actual life. But the narrative angle of Turgenev, that of a concerned but relatively uninformed reporter, differs from Chekhov's more immediate, scientific portrayal, one suggesting superior knowledge, if somewhat less emotion.

"The Silence of the Valley" is the first of O'Faolain's stories to bear a strong resemblance to Chekhov's works. Five guests in a hotel in the Gaeltacht pass the time in casual conversation, while in a cottage nearby the wake of an old cobbler is held. Speakers in both places express concern for the passing of old ways, but the pleasure-seeking hotel guests and the county folk seem worlds apart. All around them nature, the silent valley, overshadows and reduces them, so that their words sound feeble and trivial. The vacationers go to the wake and even watch the funeral, but they never come to understand the primitive life which reminds them of their isolation. Although one of the hotel guests, a young man who has apparently come to learn Irish, praises the simple folk life, he cannot reconcile that nostalgia with his hope for seaplanes on the lake and increased tourism. In fact, the group of hotel residents represents the modern world, concerned with efficiency and novelty, which is displacing the simple country world of religious faith and tradition; yet the modernized world itself is already under threat of annihilation. The atmosphere at the end is dark; although it is May, it feels like autumn, says one, but the American provides the more fitting term: the fall, the end of a world. Contrasting this depressing atmosphere is the story's final ambiguous statement. When the American soldier predicts tomorrow will be another fine day, the red-haired Scots girl who has been the most alert, vocal, and responsive of the guests replies, "Yes . . . it will be another great day—Tomorrow." But the narrator adds: "And her eyebrows sank, very slowly, like a falling curtain." The ending, in its expression of hope despite overwhelming defeat, resembles that of *Uncle Vanya* and *The Three Sisters.* The silence of the valley, marred only by noises from the farmhouses on one side and the hotel on the other, is eternal and irresistible, reducing all human concerns to trivial sounds.

By mid-century, O'Faolain had earned recognition not only as an accomplished literary craftsman, but as a social commentator on Ireland. His books on Irish history and contemporary society, his frequent contributions to English and American periodicals, and his forceful arguments in the *Bell* made him a well-known but controversial figure. He even took on the Irish puritan attitudes toward sex and marriage, which had resulted in later marriages and a declining birthrate, in a particularly explosive article in *Life.*

His study, *The Short Story,* which appeared in 1948, reflects his mature views of his own craft. Essential to a short story, he argues, are "punch and poetry," an immediate impact and the impression of verbal felicity. The book's four chapters on literary conventions and techniques are lucid and specific, making it one of the few comprehensive and useful studies of this genre. He considers the relative merits of various kinds of short story forms, of openings and closings, and of authorial interventions, while acknowledging the need to present vivid impressions of the actual world of recognizable characters. Yet he argues that realistic detail "is a bore if it merely gives us an idle verisimilitude"; it should provoke the imagination, suggesting greater meanings and leading to broader associations. But the element he regards as even more integral to artistry in the short story, the author's conviction, what he calls "personal voltage," is more difficult to define or describe. The short story is "an emphatically personal exposition," the product of a "unique sensibility"; it is the author's "counterpart, his perfect opportunity to project himself." In such claims it is clear that O'Faolain considers this an essentially romantic genre, for which the genius of the inspired artist is the single most important determinant. The author's voice must be distinctive, revealing a personality that strikes the reader as unique and interesting. However, pressures of living in the present complex society make such distinctiveness difficult to maintain. Furthermore, the writer is affected by the reactions of his readers, his friends, and his critics, and even, ultimately, by his own growing critical sense of art. Few writers, he claims, can maintain what he calls the "simple, natural self" for long; inevitably a more complex and compelling personality must be developed. Although he does not specify characteristics of the artist's created personality beyond being distinctive and memorable, O'Faolain seems to assume that it conveys conviction and intense emotions. In the choice of incident to be reported, in his or her implied relations with the reader, the writer assumes authority. Authority, the power to affect a reader's thought or feelings derives from the very act of making the story, yet such authority is amplified, made stronger by the felt presence of a distinctive personality. Thus the writer's authority is measured by the interests of his or her convictions and feelings. In Ireland, O'Faolain argues, two "divinely appointed spiritual plumbers, the Church and Cathleen ni Houlihan," mitigate against developing such an independent personality with both distinctive and intense feelings and ideas: those oppressive forces must, of course, be overcome. What is most remarkable here is the implied importance O'Faolain gives to intensity, as well as uniqueness, an emphasis that he himself has grown into, a quality reflected in his mature fiction, but absent in his earliest work.

In the preface to *The Stories of Sean O'Faolain* (1958), he comments on his own development of such an authorial identity. Looking back at the work of his twenties, his first stories, he sees himself as extremely romantic. The diction of those early stories reveals his idealism and lack of perception of the essential aspects of life; words like *dawn,* he argues, evoke stock responses, while weak connectives such as *and* and *but* attempt merely to carry on and expand emotional effects after meaning has been conveyed. He does not disclaim the early stories; they just emanated from a personality quite different from that which he created for himself in later years. "Fugue," for instance, he calls "a lovely story," adding, "I wish I felt like that now." Given the conviction that the writer's self is consciously created and that it changes as it is developed, he cannot allow himself to rewrite his stories years later, when he is a different author.

Of the new stories in the 1958 collection, "Lovers of the Lake" best reveals his progress in realizing his goals; it is, in fact, the finest story of his entire career. This account of two middle-aged lovers who go on a pilgrimage to Lough Derg is not only most comprehensive and objective in its exposure of middle-class modern attitudes but most intense as well, in recognizing the compulsion of religious faith. The plot is efficiently constructed, with the request to go to Lough Derg presented in the first paragraph, followed by brief incidents from the voyage there, the pilgrimage itself, and the return from it, concluding with a powerful, but ambiguous end to the pilgrimage, as the lovers walk back to their separate rooms in a Salthill hotel. Each of the two main characters, Jenny and Bobby, is vividly presented; although middle-aged, they are both immature, even childish, as is suggested by their diminutive names. While they both praise spontaneity as a virtue, they are tradition-bound and provincial: Jenny's first words criticize some tennis players for neglecting to wear the expected whites. Neither she, the childless wife of a man she does not love, nor he, a successful surgeon, have interests or passions beyond each other. As Jenny says, "All I have is you, and God." Her religious conviction, almost submerged for years, is nevertheless what keeps them apart and makes her aware of her sinfulness. Bobby, on the other hand, says he, like all doctors, believes in the Devil; but he cannot see what is wrong with the world and the flesh. As he progresses, his religious faith intensifies and becomes more troubling. To the extent that the story has a dramatic conflict, it reaches its climax in his reformation, and their shared realization that they *cannot* give up everything for each other: they will never be able to marry and each will retain a secret self hidden from the other. By the story's end, when they hesitate before going to bed, filling hours with activity so as not to face themselves and each other, they have both changed and are on an equal level. Whether or not they resume their relationship after this one night's abstinence, and it seems likely they will, Bobby has decided to return again for another pilgrimage, indicating that they will both live in the consciousness of sin.

The inconsistencies of both characters are made obvious. Their petty prejudices and materialistic tastes are easily exposed; yet they are religious idealists, absolute in their beliefs, if inconsistent in their practice. Eventually the intensity of their religious passion, like the strength of their love, is conveyed in full force. In simpler, more transparent minor characters, the conflict within the two is echoed. The young woman with goat's eyes with whom Jenny talks confesses to lust, causing Jenny to admit the same. The Englishman who has been coming here for twenty-two years admits to guilt for not loving his wife; as he put it, love is "godly," not human but foolish, thus presenting the story's dominant concept of love, both human and divine. As though the story contains two planes of action, the main ideas are more directly, more simply stated in the background level of action, yet made bold, more vivid and complex in the main section, the affair between Jenny and Bobby.

Disillusionment, frustration, boredom, doubt, and uncertainty are conveyed throughout the story, while only a few expressions of hope or positive emotion or thought are given. Yet the story affirms the strength of the most noble inclinations, such as love and faith, while recognizing the insurmountable separation of characters from each other. While not denying the ironic implications conveyed by the courtly title, it accurately describes a pair of lovers who experience the conflict of religious faith with sexual impulses, as did the lovers of Arthurian legends.

Predictably, O'Faolain's subsequent collections of stories reflect more mature and complicated concerns, becoming even more reflective and retrospective.

The dominant subject of his next volume, *I Remember! I Remember!* (1961) is, as the title indicates, the complex functions of memory. In the title story, that subject is presented directly in the first paragraph, in the form of a claim made by the narrator of the effect of memory or subsequent action. To illustrate his point, the narrator remembers a crippled woman with an infallible memory, and he then recounts the story of how her relations with her sister had broken down. The early description of the invalid is slightly exaggerated, as though she will become a comic figure; and much of the plot consists of accounts of trivial irritations because of her recollection of embarrassing or incriminating details of her sister's past. But as it is exposed in this story, memory's function is cruel. Although the crippled sister living in Ardagh enjoys preserving memories of other people's lives, her sister, who has had an unhappy love affair and whose marriage seems to have failed, cannot stand to be reminded of the past. The infirm sister knows that Mary has houses in New York and Zurich, friends named Gold, Barter, and Cash; what she does not realize is how lonely and desolate the woman is. Thus, although the invalid sister is not aware of the suffering she causes by her reminders of the past, her digging for information about painful relationships make her oppressive. The physically dependent sister becomes the tyrant from whom the independent sister struggles to escape. The intellectual subjects proposed at the start are dramatically explored: memory is revealed as complex and sometimes cruel, and it can provoke, even subliminally, important action.

Several other stories in the volume reiterate the view of memory as a destructive or at least a disturbing force, both shaped by personality and affecting it profoundly. "A Touch of Autumn in the Air" opens with a claim by its narrator that personality determines what may be recalled; he then illustrates his claim by describing an encounter with a successful merchant and presenting that man's seemingly random recollections. The story's conclusion is also given by the narrator: the claim that even our memory is subject to "the uncharted currents of the heart." The narrator intervenes to ask why did the old man recall precisely the trivial events of one childhood autumn? One answer he gives is that an impression of littleness, insignificance was the man's most evocative memory; it was an impression that might well have been painful and might still seem inescapable and troubling to a man regarded by the world as wealthy, powerful, and important. The narrator, whose assessments and commentary are undisputed, implies that not only memory but subsequent desires and actions are determined by such unarticulated but evocative experiences as the striking impression of one's insignificance within the natural world. Plausible as that observation is, it undermines one of the foundations of fiction: the claim that a simple event directly causes another, so that an entire string of causes and their effects may be traced in what is usually called a plot. But if the causes of certain

intense experiences cannot be so neatly linked, if we sense instead only correspondences between present and earlier events or impressions, then plot, as we
have known it, disappears. A set of individual perceptions, recording incidents
and feelings in what seem to be plausible ways, themselves evocative in their
associations, comes to constitute the narrative line of fiction.

A related denial of causality is presented in "A Shadow, Silent as a Cloud," in
which a middle-aged architect, in a conversation with a waitress whom he knew
as a child, comes to realize his own insignificance. Deprived of love because he
has committed his whole life to his career, he realizes that he has not directed
his own life; but now when he sees his errors, it is too late to reverse them. The
encounter severely upsets him, but it cannot change him this late in his life, and
around him are others who are also unwittingly destroying their own lives. But
if humans have no control over their destinies, then narratives about their actions are severely restricted. Events that in retrospect reflect each other or res-
onate in striking ways are all that can be recorded. However, even restricted by
such a loose narrative structure, these stories are remarkably effective. The dominant tone is appropriately subdued, echoing the futility of human aspirations,
and the stories make effective use of natural images that remind us of nature's
repetitive motions: waves lapping, stars moving, the sun's setting.

A versatile writer, O'Faolain has continued to write compelling stories with
more traditional forms and strong plots. In the *I Remember! I Remember!* volume,
"One Night in Turin" is a good example of a traditional tale, so familiar in its
form that it seems an Irish provincial version of a short work by Henry James.
A successful Irish lawyer, Walter Hunter, resumes a relationship with Countess
Maria Rinaldi, the Irish widow of an Italian count, a woman he has loved from
a distance for sixteen years since he first knew her as Molly O'Sullivan. The
story's point of view shifts back and forth, making us aware of Molly's perception of him as vain, Hunter's hesitation to reveal his love to her, and the contrasting views of her younger suitor, a crass, insensitive creature who plans to
marry an unknown American girl solely for her money. The story, the longest
in this collection, traces three days of Walter's wanderings as he tries to decide
whether to tell her of his love. But even at the end of this more heavily plotted
story, the theme of the cruelty of memory and the futility of human aspirations
returns. The Countess explodes his pleasant memory and tells him that we do
not find happiness, we make it. Indulging in fantasies of the past, he has merely
sought love, not actively risked himself by loving. Thus the retrospective art of
remembering is contrasted to the activity of loving, showing the hazards and
destructive power of memory.

Instead of implications and vivid imagery, the stories in the next volume, *The
Heat of the Sun* (1966), rely more clearly on plot, often involving complex, surprising twists of action. In his introduction, O'Faolain presents a useful distinc-

tion between the short story and the tale. The former, he says, is consciously limited in place, time, and character in order to convey a "brief, bright moment" within a narrow space; the tale is freer, more spacious, allowing more changes of mood, a greater variety of characters and more plot. The proposed distinction is to some degree self-justifying since more episodic, broader ranging narratives outnumber sharply focused, economical stories in this and the following two volumes; but O'Faolain did not need the justification, for the best of his recent stories are what he might call tales, yet they still deserve the title of short story.

The title piece, he labels a short story, and true to definition, its plot is compact and tone consistent throughout. A narrator, speaking in a conversational tone and even using direct address at the start, describes his return to a local pub whose barman, Alfie, had been the friend and confidant of all the young men who gather there. Discovering that Alfie is no longer working because he is dying, the young narrator, himself confused and troubled about whether to marry a materialistic girl who does not love him, goes to visit Alfie's estranged wife. There, in a long confessional conversation, he comes to realize the futility of his love and his similarities to the older woman, now awaiting notice of her husband's death. Yet his subsequent realization does not stop him from loving the woman with whom he knows he is ill-matched; instead he just feels exhausted, and he longs for the relief that Alfie's widow now must feel or the eternal rest Alfie has attained. The lines from *Cymbeline* that he recalls—"Quiet consummation have; and renowned by thy grave"—express his tribute to Alfie, but another phrase from the play, the title of this story, proposes a freedom from fear which the narrator may have acquired now that he has achieved self-realization. Such Shakespearean echoes reinforce the dominant subject of the story, a consciousness of futility and death which leads to acceptance. The subject is developed through imagery and random comments, rather than through action, and even the main character's recognition does not lead to an effectual reaction or character change.

"The Bosom of the Country," on the other hand, fits O'Faolain's definition of a tale. Its plot is more extended, and the characters change within the course of the reported action. The story begins when Frank, a retired major, and his mistress of ten years learn, in their bed, of the death of her husband. The opening description of the characters is lively and their situation ironic, for by now this love has faded badly. Nevertheless, he agrees to marry the widow and even agrees to convert to Roman Catholicism to do so. But after their marriage he becomes scrupulous in his devotions, which his new wife never was, and so their union nearly dissolves. That turn is a familiar comic development. But another reversal occurs on Easter Sunday, when Frank experiences a miraculous revival of sensual love for his wife, and even realizes "the heart is the centre."

He justifies his lapse from religion, becoming as lax as his wife for whom super-stition was all, and in their lapsed faith and lazy pleasure they resume their life together, a life as sensual but dissatisfying as it as at the story's beginning.

Such a tale is no less powerful in its impact nor less incisive than the more compact short story discussed before. The main character changes twice, so that the ironic plot reveals a man's ascent and subsequent fall from faith, while at the same time recognizing the hazards of scrupulous devotion and the strong attrac-tions of the flesh. For such a complex subject, a full plot and changing perspec-tives are fitting, because in allowing various faults to be seen, they provoke an analytical response. On the other hand, a short story such as "The Heat of the Sun" explores a single subject through parallel or harmonious characters and incidents, so that a single limited action and heavier imagery are appropriate. Its strict selection of detail and incident calls greater attention to the writer's au-thority, leading to the use of a personified narrator. The short story presents its single subject as a complete tableau in which all elements ideally echo and am-plify a single complex theme. The tale, on the other hand, proceeds beyond a chord to a melody, in which man's capacities for change and adaptation, or at least acceptance, are emphasized. The tale celebrates life's variety, just as classical comedy does. Thus action is more extended, and the narrator's presence less essential. Without authorial intervention, the plots lead the reader to logical conclusions about the effectuality of the actions presented.

The best stories in O'Faolain's most recent two collections are tales, in his sense of the term, and so they offer more explicit conclusions. "The Time of Their Lives" in *The Talking Trees* (1970) is an amusing account of the courtship of a middle-aged, frumpy Irish woman by an Italian count, who seems at first to be after her money, but who turns out to be sensitive and loving. She refuses his proposal of marriage when she decides that he only pities her, leading to an explicit conclusion on what they had both learned from their encounter, a lesson hinted at in the story's title. Such a tale differs from the short stories in its range, although not in its subject, for in her own analysis of what her Italian lover had signified by his proposal, the Irish spinster recognizes how much it was a plea for help, yet how futile the proposal had been. Their relationship was "some-thing precious, brief and almost true," she concludes, with an emphasis inevita-bly falling on the word *almost*. By this quiet deflation of sentiment the story's thematic conclusion is not really different from that of "The Heat of the Sun" and other short stories.

Likewise, "Our Fearful Innocence," while clearly a tale in its range and struc-ture, treats familiar O'Faolain concerns of memory and perception. A provincial country engineer recalls his attraction to a married woman who had left her husband and lived alone, a development the engineer was unable to comprehend. But when a mutual friend accounts for her behavior by informing him that the husband was impotent, he regards his earlier feelings as romantic and imprecise; as a result, he becomes aware of the limits of human understanding and memory. Throughout this story, fairy tale elements appear that in retrospect seem to be subtle comments on how little the narrator knows and how much is imagined. The woman, for instance, is associated with the sea; she looks out toward it in crucial scenes, like a mermaid who emerges from the sea, but discontented on earth, returns to death in the water. By including a greater number of incidents and expanding meaning by multiple levels of imagery, this tale presents a full and powerful analysis, for it allows a set of contrasts which expose the dangers of innocence, the subject specified in the title.

In his most recent collections, *Foreign Affairs* (1976) O'Faolain experiments more freely with fictional conventions and fundamental assumptions about story telling. In "How to Write a Short Story," a naive apprentice writer whose first aspiration was to become a poet, hears an older friend's account of childhood love, a homosexual encounter with a schoolmate. Having recently read Maupassant and wanting to outdo him in ironic interpretations, the young writer exhibits many of the most ridiculous tendencies of apprentices: he revises his own phrases as he presents them to the reader, making them more "poetic" but also more distracting. He interrupts the doctor's account with anticipations of what will follow, predictions that fail to be accurate. Searching for dramatic order in imitation of Maupassant, the novice cannot see the inherent thematic order of the doctor's account: a view of life as a series of related, but not causally linked episodes, in which early experiences are repeatedly reexamined, but never fully understood. Aiming at a pleasant or startling dramatic form, the inexperienced writer cannot accurately describe actual life, so that in the story presented his attempts illustrate how *not* to write. However, by contrasting his foolish attempts with the doctor's understated version, the story constitutes a unified, more subtle, and satisfying narrative. Proclaiming the superiority of art over life, the foolish young poseur of a writer misses sight of the order found within actual life and fails to recognize its relevance to true art, in which even such desperate elements are harmoniously interrelated.

"Falling Rocks, Narrowing Road, Cul-de-sac, Stop" further subverts familiar notions of narrative structure by presenting a complicated account of six characters, two of whom were the main characters in "How to Write a Short Story," and then ending with a numbered list of subsequent events, none of which logically or dramatically results from the story's events. Despite clear hints that one character, the daughter of a German couple with whom three cronies in a provincial town get involved, is attracted to the young writer, we are told she married another of the three men, a priest. And the third man, the doctor, marries her mother, which is no less a startling outcome. Thus the expectations presented in the story are nearly reversed by the enumerated set of concluding events. The narrator's statement of the story's intention, to show that "table-thumping decisions" rarely conclude anything, explodes another assumption of the genre: powerful experiences of self-discovery, moments of revelation, or decisions to change one's life are often only momentary. Men live by their images of self, but at the mercy of immense forces that often defy their aspirations. But equally strong and destructive are the impediments men themselves set up, the roadblocks referred to in the title.

Such a conclusion about perception is implied in "An Inside Outside Complex," in which a middle-aged man falls in love with a woman when first seeing her through her picture window. Although their subsequent marriage fails, he is drawn back again, and at the story's end they have propped a large mirror outside the large front window, so that they can, by looking outside, see themselves inside, a clear representation of his and all men's need for an objective image, a view of self from an outside vantage point.

By contrasting O'Faolain's treatment of the human need for self-realization, and the arbitrary definition of self on which it is based, with his earlier treatments of the same theme in the stories in *Midsummer Night Madness* and *A Purse of Coppers,* the course of his development as an artist may be discerned. In his early stories, such themes as human loneliness and the conflict of abstract beliefs with human relationships predominate; more theoretical issues such as the function of memory and the nature of spiritual aspirations take precedence in work of his middle period; now, in the latest stage of his career, as he is aware of the impossibility of exact expression, analogous to the unattainability of one's ideals of self or notions of perfect love, the stories reflect a mature acceptance of life in its apparent variety, while asserting subtle relationships among events as perceived by individual characters. At each stage, the fictional structure reflects theme, so that the precise musical forms of the earliest stories give way to forms appropriate to intellectual dialectic, emphasizing contrasts and balances, and most recently to much looser narrative structures, in which episodes are thematically linked but not causally related.

• • •

Once the direction of the short story was first determined by Moore and Joyce and then broadened, refined, and reasserted primarily by the works of O'Flaherty, O'Connor, and O'Faolain, it rivaled drama as the dominant genre in Ireland for at least a generation. It was a sophisticated, highly developed form, almost unrelated to such native forms as the folktale and sketch; symbolic expression, highly controlled narrative techniques, and attention to vivid details were its hallmarks, just as peasant speech and simple realistic settings tended to dominate Irish drama of the period. Naturally, there were many of merit who continued to write short fiction of the older, simpler sorts, and scores of very popular writers of humorous, fabulous, and sensational prose. James Stephens, a writer of undeniable charm, achieved a level of artistry in old fashioned fictional forms. In both the light, fantastic air of his fables and the pared-down, flat style of his sketches, he skillfully created imagined worlds through manipulation of literary styles. His first collection of short prose works, *Here Are Ladies* (1913), is a series of character sketches that graphically expose the meanness of urban life; his second, *Etched in Moonlight* (1928), includes some memorable fables, particularly the title story, a vivid nightmare, reminiscent of Maturin or Le Fanu. However, Stephens's moral convictions and humane sympathies make him sacrifice realistic intentions, so that character and setting are unduly simplified. Such pieces as "Desire" and "Hunger" are moving and even lyrical, but they do not resemble the artistic short stories of this period because they are too direct in eliciting emotional responses. The prose works of Lord Dunsany tend in a different direction—to emphasize plot and fantastic effects purely for their own sakes; they are often spectacular, skillful, and entertaining, but limited in scope to plot rather than expanding to broader themes. The absence of such aspirations toward greater meaning disqualifies the work of many other writers of short fiction. The action of the Censorship Board in banning Eric Cross's collection *The Tailor of Ansty* (1942) earned it notoriety at the time, but granting the liveliness of the narrative voice and the amusing effects of the tales, these are no more than anecdotes—similar to the amusing sketches of Seumas MacManus in their exaggeration of dialogue and characterization for humorous effects.

• • •

Daniel Corkery's place in literary history would be assured solely by the fact of his personal and literary influence on both Sean O'Faolain and Frank O'Connor, for they testified to the importance, early in their careers, of his encouragement and even his instruction in writing. A generation older than them, he warned both his fellow Cork writers of the dangers of becoming provincial, which he defined, oddly enough, as writing for alien audiences; and to learn their craft he encouraged them to read the Russian masters, particularly Gogol, Babel, Turgenev, and Chekhov. By the time O'Faolain and O'Connor met him, Corkery had published one collection of short stories which are so efficient in structure and so simply expressed that they could serve as models of the genre. An ardent nationalist, Corkery promoted a pure Irish culture which must have impressed the younger artists, at least in exposing them to forgotten works of their native literature. But as he came to insist on the exclusive claims of Ireland, admonishing others to write only for their own people and then only in the Irish language, both younger writers expressed their disagreement. His intense prejudices against English and Ascendancy cultures distorted his critical judgments, making such works as *The Hidden Ireland* and *Synge and Anglo-Irish Literature* extremist and unconvincing.

His four volumes of short stories are strikingly uneven in quality, despite a continuing display of craftsmanship, as though Corkery knew the rules well, but chose to violate them at some stages of his career. The stories focus clearly on single incidents, or several such, arranged as discrete but related episodes; they employ an absolute minimum of action or background so as to keep the focus clear. Although a few employ indirect narration, the stories seem written rather than spoken; there are few verbal embellishments or evidence of dialect savored and enjoyed. At times they are somewhat too literary, with effects too obviously calculated and symbolism unnecessarily explicit. When thematic concerns predominate, moral conclusions are insisted upon, making the stories merely mechanical. But particularly in his first and third collections, Corkery produced stories generated by intense feeling yet skillfully controlled and understated.

Most of the stories in the first volume, *A Munster Twilight* (1916), treat the familiar modern theme of alienation from society, but in a curiously reserved manner. While feeling for the victims of alienating experiences is surely conveyed, the stories afford equal or greater sympathy to society: the community, family, or group. In "The Bonny Labouring Boy," only four pages long, an exhausted construction worker, resting in a pub, hears of the death of his wife. Although his own confused reactions are presented, more details are given of the annoyance of his fellow workers at his weakness and lack of spirit, and of the consternation of his female relatives and neighbors that he stopped in a pub instead of directly returning home. As a result, he seems pathetic, a victim of his own weakness, and the community's vigorous impatience with him seems appropriate. Such a social perspective on character and incident is found in most of the stories in this volume. In "Storm-Struck," John Donovan returns home from America, blinded from an explosion in a copper mine. Yet the narrative undercuts the personal impact and stresses the reaction of the village; news of his arrival and his crippled state spreads by gossip: "from hedge to hedge—an empty story." The first of the story's two parts establishes Donovan as embittered by his blindness. Then one afternoon he gets lost in a storm but is rescued and brought home by Kitty Regan, his former love, now unhappily married into a parish, as the villagers say. Although the story's fullest action appears in the first section, its second part contains the climax in which Donovan, angry that Kitty does not come back to him, mocks her, comparing her to sea-birds that take shelter at a lighthouse window but will not enter when the window is opened to them. At the story's end, the perceptions of the village dominate: they "could not understand; they stared in wonder at his bitter lips, his stony eyes." A sympathetic emotional response to Donovan is not allowed because the controlling view is that of the Irish village, which can "stare in wonder" at his blindness, but offers no real sympathy to the victim; to the village he seems to whine, "like a boy who failed halfway in an adventure."

A similar witholding of sympathy concludes "The Spancelled," a story of a widow, miserable because she will lose her inheritance if she remarries, who meets an equally unhappy man, who is already an outcast from society because his uncle was a "grabber." They meet and finally kiss, but the closing sentence specifies the motive for their choice and reveals the controlling, unsympathetic response of the community: "And so they leaped from their pit of sorrow, as the spancelled will until time be over; in no other way is it possible for them—this is their sorry philosophy—to revenge themselves on fortune, to give scorn for scorn." A moral conclusion, appropriate to the community rather than the couple, is imposed upon the story.

The best story in the volume, the finest Corkery ever wrote, "The Ploughing of Leaca-na-Naomh," pits community values against the greed of a farmer who ends utterly defeated. Traditional belief makes a certain *leaca,* a mountainside meadow, sacred, for the graves of saints are said to be there. Thus, the main character's desire to plough it shocks his workers and neighbors because such a deed seems sacrilegious. The fact that the actual crime is committed by a fool, acting out his master's greed and even his madness, makes the deed even more offensive to the community; when the fool falls to his death, their premonitions seem justified. But the story transcends folk morality through the narrative device of an uninformed, confused narrator, one incapable of formulating a moral message, but fascinated with the action itself.

Their focus on society rather than individuals makes the stories of Corkery's first volume deemphasize the importance of human aspirations and suffering, so that they lack emotional intensity. Yet they are carefully constructed, employing a bare minimum of exposition, only a few incidents in each story, and efficient use of setting.

Corkery's second collection, *The Hounds of Banba* (1920), suffers from being too obviously calculated and shaped to inspire nationalist feelings. Because the stories describe contemporary events, when guerrilla warfare with the English was widespread, anti-Sassenach sentiments inspire the most unbelievably heroic statements and actions. In "The Price," for example, a woman revives a wounded patriot with Lourdes water and then saves the entire town from being burned by devil-like English soldiers. At the end, we are told she has become a nun, and a narrator, reviewing the action, concludes, ". . . all miracles are the fruit of love." But that platitude is inadequate and inappropriate to the story, as are the exaggerations of character and the heavy symbolism—or attempts at symbolism. Yet Corkery's architectonic skill is still demonstrated in the parallelism of episodes in this and several other stories; he even uses a musical structure in one story, "An Unfinished Symphony." The stories are not loose or anecdotal; they are clearly focused. Usually a narrator, himself a nationalist, is used, which might justify some of the extreme bias within stories; but that insistent authorial voice seems shrill and unconvincing.

In presenting subjects as volatile as nationalism, the strong authority of an author who seems to know more, or at least have thought more, is desired. But Corkery is an enthusiast, and the stories reveal his resentments, hopes, and fears—his emotional rather than actual experiences. Instead of presenting the perceptions or even convictions of a community, he advocates an abstract belief, an -ism. Of course, in every narrative some degree of conviction is manifested. A principle of selection of detail and incidents, as well as interpretation and emphasis of those elements, is determined by an author imposing significance on certain actions and objects; the author expresses some degree of conviction of the importance, benefit, or meaning in every word included in a literary work. A conviction of the importance of allegiance to a nation is one that informs some of the greatest works of literature. Thus it is not the relevance of Corkery's themes but his mode of presentation that undermines these stories. In *The Hounds of Banba,* political interpretations are imposed upon the actions; a predisposition to side with one faction makes some characters nearly superhuman and others diabolical. The author provides too many interpretations beyond what the reader could formulate. The narrator is so adamant in his political convictions that his characters tend to lose their individuality, the actions their credibility—all gives way to exhortation to heroism for Ireland.

The tone of his next collection, *The Stormy Hills* (1929), is darker and more depressed, but nevertheless more genuine, human, and moving. As in his first collection, the perceptions of a community are in several stories given prominence over interest in the varieties of individual behavior. In "The Wager," the gentry vies with the laboring class, "them" versus "us," culminating in a triumphant symbolic victory for the farm workers who have been so mistreated that a jockey is urged to risk his life merely as part of a wager. But in this and other stories, individual suffering is not overshadowed by social concern, resulting in more balanced and powerful stories. In the best story in this volume, "The Eyes of the Dead," the depiction of a shipwreck victim is presented directly and vividly. The two-part construction nicely separates the narrative background, given in the first few pages, from the true subject: John Spillane's withdrawal from active life after a shipwreck in which he was the lone survivor. When he reveals to his family that he is haunted by the sight of the stormy eyes of those who drowned, the family and the wider community, by inference, are left impotent to help: "Transfixed, they glared at him, at his round-shouldered sailor's back disappearing again into his den of refuge. They could not hear his voice any more, they were afraid to follow him." But by slowly building to Spillane's revelation of anxiety, a degree of sympathy for him is evoked. The story does not rely on any overt conflict between the main character and the rural society; instead, those contrasting concerns are set against each other, so that the loneliness of such men as Spillane seems inevitable. In "Nightfall," an old man who has returned from New Zealand flirts with a young girl and is tricked by her and her village suitor, so that he is left at the end of the story lost in the dark hills; although the old man is foolish, he earns some compassion by the story's end. In such stories the division into numbered episodes, characteristic of this volume, reflects the balanced juxtaposition of elements. The narrative style is appropriately muted; the passive voice and past tense are favored, as though the narrator is an alien anthropologist reporting on folk ways he has to strain in order to understand. In some cases this leads him to exaggerate the roughness of landscape and character and to glorify brute strength, a tendency in this volume with which Sean O'Faolain found fault, calling it "gigantism," which is a "confession of weakness."[5]

Corkery's last collection, *Earth Out of Earth* (1939) is a miscellany of strained, trivial stories, lacking both the intensity of even his worst early tales and the architectonic polish of his best stories. Quite uncongenial subjects are tackled: a young boy's perspective in going to a fair with his father in "Vision"; a village gossip's story of circus people in "The Sisters Dufreno"; and a father feeling guilt because he has discouraged his son from entering the seminary in "Richard Clery's Sunday." Such ill-fitting points of view and the subjects themselves call forth an artificial, folksy style, and even his control of structure is lost.

Historical importance, then, is due Daniel Corkery as a short story writer. The carefully devised structures of his best stories, their understated tones, sparse imagery, and clear focuses resemble the Continental models of Chekhov and Turgenev more than the native folk tradition. At his best, Corkery presents communal attitudes with a sympathy and understanding that lead to a recognition of complexity and the interdependence of man and his communities. If at times nationalist passion distorts his presentation and makes him suspend his artistic control, he nevertheless has extended the short story's subject matter beyond its concentration on incident and individual character to an awareness of the legitimate claims of family, village, and nation.

. . .

If only for a single masterpiece, "The Weaver's Grave," Seumas O'Kelly deserves critical recognition. In his short life, he published five collections of short stories, only few of which are true examples of the form, most being folktales, anecdotes, and even tales of leprechauns. But his range and skill, evidenced in even such a few stories, are impressive.

Although only a sketch, "The Rector" reveals the breadth of O'Kelly's concerns and sympathies. The title character, a Church of Ireland clergyman, is aware of his alienation from the majority of people in his district; he even recognizes that his speech gives him away as an outsider. Unable to converse, even casually, with a stone-breaker on the road, but noting that his Protestant gardener has gained acceptance and merged into Connaught life, the rector experiences a painful, frightening realization: that the peasant class of both religions may feel a common bond that sets them against the controlling upper class. The impression is only fleeting, but his perception of even familiar scenes is transformed, making the trees appear as torpedoes and the rectory become a fortress. The story ends with his resolution, " 'I must write a letter to the papers,' he said, 'Ireland is lost.' " His gesture is ineffectual, and it confirms the impression throughout the story that he represents the colonial spirit. But the story, presented without rancor, presents a theory of working-class solidarity that found some favor in the years before and after the Easter Rising, depicting the alienation between classes. The main character is indicated by just a few gestures and details; the slight action is sufficient to reveal his inner anxiety.

"The Sick Call," another story in *Waysiders* (1917), contrasts a Spanish Friar, called from his monastery to visit Kevin Hoober, a flute player, who lies sick. Most of the story is taken up with description of the journey to the house, making the story resemble one of Turgenev's sportsman's sketches. An altar boy serves as narrator, which makes the descriptions fresh and vivid, since he does not fully comprehend what is happening, and is unfamiliar with the remote district to which they travel. When the house is reached and the flutist is ministered to, his impressions are not entirely reconciled. The boy is told that Hooben had been moody and solitary, playing his flute, or *fideog,* and had sunk into paralysis and unconsciousness. "Some of the people also having knowledge say he is lying under a certain influence," the musician's sister intimates. The priest, after seeing Hooben, says only "He should have more courage." As a result, when the flutist says he will be playing the fideog the coming April, his mother exclaims, "The cross of Christ between him and that fideog!" The boy, as in Joyce's "The Sisters," cannot understand whether the flutist is cursed or doomed. For the reader, the picture of Hooben becomes an emblem of the artist, inspired and determined to live, but doomed, and perhaps damned as well.

A six-part series, "The Golden Barque" (1919), shows O'Kelly's interest in more violent subjects. The crew of a canal barge seem driven by hatred of one another as they pass through lovely inland countryside. But the stories are mere anecdotes, which do not progress beyond concern for plot and character.

"The Weaver's Grave" (1919) is undoubtedly one of the best stories of this period. Through its slow description of the graveyard, Cloon na Morav, the Meadow of the Dead, an atmosphere of timeless mortality is built. The place is so fully described and assigned such importance that it becomes as potent a force as any of the characters who come to it seeking the proper place to bury the weaver; in fact its description constitutes the first of the story's five parts. The two old men who come to identify the site seem at first caricatures; Meehaul Lynskey, the nailer, and Cahir Bowes, the stone breaker, mimic the actions of their occupations, and come to represent the builder and the destroyer. They fail to find the right plot, despite many attempts; in their vicious quarreling and feebleness they come to seem proper inhabitants of Coon na Morav. The third part of the story establishes the present state of the weaver's widow, his fourth wife; she is a woman who never experienced much passion or love, but who now wants to give her dead husband the proper burial he deserves. Attempting to learn the location of her husband's grave site, she visits the cooper, Malachai Roohan, the only living person entitled to be buried in the revered graveyard, now that the weaver has died. The old, bedridden man speaks of hope and of life's illusions, yet in his anger he reveals his own terror at approaching death. The first sentence of the final section of the story reveals the widow's change, when she says, "The day is going on me." Now the graveyard, as she approaches it, seems monstrous, while the single star in the evening sky seems to be very young. The twin grave diggers emerge in her consciousness as individuals, and the renewed search for the grave site is successful. Her awakened senses make her respond to the advances of the handsome young grave digger; she speaks like a girl at the end, when she utters the comprehensive concluding statement, "I'm satisfied."

Like "The Dead," the story's theme is death and resurrection, and psychological death is as final as physical dying. The widow clearly chooses life, as offered to her by the young grave digger, in the very graveyard where she will now bury her husband. The story's strongest comments are implied by gesture, not provided by the author. The stylized repeated actions of the two old men, the old cooper raising himself in bed by pulling himself up by a rope, and, most suggestive of all, the young grave digger leaping over the black grave to embrace the young widow—such gestures acquire meanings that may not be fully articulated, but they all indicate grasping for life. The amplitude of the story's theme, the vitality it celebrates, made more precious by setting it in the place of death, and the masterful use of symbolism to extend meaning, make the story comparable to the masterpieces of this genre.

• • •

In the 1920s and 1930s, encouraged by the activities of the Gaelic League and other groups promoting the revitalization of the language, writers published great numbers of short stories in the Irish language. Of the several writers in this genre who achieved literary recognition in this period, Padraic O'Conaire was both the most accomplished and the most popular. The romantic story of his adult life wandering through the country, like one of Synge's tramps, and his facility in writing fanciful children's stories, no doubt added to his fame as a writer of realistic short fiction. Throughout his works a knowledge of and sympathy for country folk are evident, but in writing exclusively for an unsophisticated audience, he limited his powers and confined his art to tales and anecdotes, rather than the more sharply focused stories of the Russian masters whom he himself admired.

The most popular of his stories, "M'Asal Beag Dubh" ("My Little Black Ass") is amusing and uncomplicated, expressing the narrator's simple pleasure and love of nature. His characteristic literary techniques are seen here: direct address to the reader, hyperbole, and an amused tone. Its humor derives from accounts of tricks, both those perpetrated by the tinkers and those devised by the narrator. But it claims to be no more than an anecdote, and a sentimental one at that. In its conclusion the ass is compared with the narrator: "He has lost some of his bad habits in the course of time—something I failed to do myself. And I think my little black ass knows that as well as anyone." Such direct emotional appeal and folk humor characterize many of O'Conaire's stories.

His more realistic stories tend to be grim in their subject matter, treating familiar Irish themes of conflict with nature, loneliness, and physical impairment. In "Paidin Mhaire," for instance, a young man who loves the sea, indeed feels himself as a sea creature, goes blind and is confined to a poorhouse until his death. In their relentless progress toward catastrophe and their subdued depressed narrative tone, such stories have undeniable force. However, the plots are too obviously contrived so as to reach a climax in death or a similarly shocking incident. Episodes are loosely strung together, even in very short stories, with no subordination of one event to another, yet in the end some climactic event always occurs, a surprise ending or a too-strong conclusion. In "Two Brave Women," for instance, we learn that each of the title characters had known of the death of the young man they both loved, although for years each had carried on a pretense of his being alive to console the other.

In their simple descriptions and recognition of human suffering, the stories in ways resemble O'Flaherty's, but they lack the intensity of his works. Writing, as he seemed to do, for a peasant audience, O'Conaire's stories are ideal for textbooks, indeed for school-age readers, but their historical importance in the development of the Irish short story is negligible.

• • •

The writers who rose to prominence in the 1920s and 1930s were not experimental as was either Joyce who preceded them or Beckett who followed, but their achievements are not the less, for they perfected narrative techniques they had adapted from earlier Irish and Continental authors, provided models of structure, and set the dominant subjects that drew international attention to the Irish short story.

MARY LAVIN, ELIZABETH BOWEN, AND A NEW GENERATION: THE IRISH SHORT STORY AT MIDCENTURY

Janet Egleson Dunleavy

By the end of World War II, the Irish short story had become an established subgenre of twentieth-century literature. Its form and content, pioneered before World War I by George Moore and James Joyce, had been redefined by Frank O'Connor and Sean O'Faolain ("the Romulus and Remus of Irish short fiction," in the words of Mary Lavin, whose later achievement drew praise from them both). In Irish and in English, Liam O'Flaherty had extended the range of models against which writers who began publishing in the thirties and forties might measure their own work. Continued experimentation as well as imitation characterized the early work of these younger writers who, following the example of O'Connor, O'Faolain, and O'Flaherty, imposed their own individual style on the subgenre, further contributing to expansion of its potential. They introduced new concepts of literary craft; they attracted new readers in Ireland, England, and the United States; they projected new images in literature. By the mid-1940s, periodicals dedicated to introducing sophisticated readers to changing concepts in literature and art—for example, *Atlantic Monthly,* published in the United States, but widely read in England, and both the English and the American editions of *Harper's Bazaar*—had begun to include an Irish short story in almost every issue. Editors of fashionable magazines bid against one another to attract not only the "three O's," as O'Connor, O'Faolain, and O'Flaherty came to be known in the trade, but also new Irish names that represented the best new work in the field. Little magazines of the period, sometimes called "shoestring" publications, also bid for their stories, offering smaller audiences and less money than their well-heeled rivals, but also a more enduring prestige, plus an opportunity to treat topics that did not, in the opinion of editors of more widely circulated magazines, appeal to the general reading public.

As the first half of the twentieth century drew to a close, O'Connor, O'Faolain, and O'Flaherty remained, among living writers, the acknowledged masters of the Irish short story (George Moore died in 1933, James Joyce in 1941). Recognized as writers of outstanding ability not only by critics but by the "three O's" themselves, however, were five newer voices in Irish short fiction: Mary Lavin, Elizabeth Bowen, Benedict Kiely, Bryan MacMahon, and Michael Mc-Laverty. As these writers added to the body of their published fiction year by year, the validity of early opinions of their work was confirmed. Today they continue to be regarded as eminent literary artists. Indeed, as indicated in the following brief accounts of their careers, together these five have been awarded almost all the honors and literary prizes for which writers of short fiction in English are eligible.

• • •

Hailed by Joyce Carol Oates as "one of the finest of short story writers" of the twentieth century and by V. S. Pritchett as an artist "with the power to present the surface of life rapidly, but as a covering for something else," American-born Mary Lavin (1912–) is, of the five, the one uniquely committed to short fiction.[1] Although she has published also two novels, several poems, two children's books, and three or four critical essays, it is as a writer of short fiction— both the short story and the longer novella, or tale—that she prefers to be known. In this genre she is represented by twelve separate volumes, each containing new stories as well as stories previously published in periodicals, plus four retrospective collections. A number of stories published in periodicals has not yet appeared in book form.

Born in East Walpole, Massachusetts, Mary Lavin has been a resident of Ireland since the age of ten, except for short visits to the United States (most of them to teach or lecture on creative writing in American universities). Although her American origins are reflected in some of her stories, for the most part she sets her fiction in Ireland and identifies her characters as Irish men, women, and children. Her dual national experience no doubt has contributed to the "double vision" observed by some critics, the ability to sustain a narrative tone that is simultaneously universal and particular, objective and subjective. It may also explain why, with few exceptions (e.g., "The Patriot Son," "The Face of Hate," and the charming and whimsical tale entitled "A Likely Story"), nationality is not a significant identifying factor in her characterizations, and why she is able to focus so skillfully on the true landscape of her stories, the human heart. The extent to which her stories are published, read, and studied in other countries and cultures testifies to their universality.

Mary Lavin's earliest efforts in fiction were encouraged by Lord Dunsany, who first knew her as the daughter of Tom Lavin of Bective House, an estate belonging to an Irish-American, Charles Bird, not far from Dunsany's own estate in County Meath. At her father's request, Dunsany read her first unpublished stories in 1938, finding in them "astonishing insight . . . reminiscent of the Russians." It was Dunsany who introduced her work to Ellery Sedgwick, just as the well-known editor of the *Atlantic Monthly* was about to retire; through Sedgwick it reached the desk of Edward Weeks, Sedgwick's successor. It was Dunsany also who advised Mary Lavin to submit her first stories for publication, disregarding letters of rejection but heeding the editorial advice that accompanied them, and Dunsany who helped her find her first literary agent. It was he who supported her admission to the Dublin literary circle, dominated by Frank O'Connor and Sean O'Faolain, in which her concepts of writing as art, fiction as craft, and the short story as a product of the disciplined imagination were reinforced.

No adviser could have been better suited to the needs of the young writer than Lord Dunsany, who refused to recommend changes in her fiction, lest he alter for the worse either her style or her content. Instead, he suggested authors she might read, as examples of writers in full command of language and the skillful ways it can be used in the service of the short story (Tolstoy, Chekhov, and Maupassant were among them). Only in her use of punctuation would he agree to be her mentor, as his letters reveal, but even in this he moved cautiously, noting by example rather than by instruction what differences in meaning might be achieved by the addition or deletion of a comma, or how altering a mark of punctuation might resolve problems of ambiguity.

Prior to her first attempt at writing short fiction, Mary Lavin had not thought of herself as a creative writer. A teacher of French at the Loreto School in Dublin, where she herself had received her secondary education, she had earned first-class honors at University College Dublin in 1936 for her M.A. thesis on Jane Austen. In 1938 she was at work on her Ph.D. dissertation on Virginia Woolf. One day, trying to understand Virginia Woolf, to think as the older writer might think, Mary Lavin speculated on what, at that moment, Virginia Woolf might be doing—whether and what, for example, she might be writing. Picking up her own pen and turning over the pages of her dissertation in progress, she drafted her own first short story, "Miss Holland." The experience fascinated her: creative writing, she found, drew on facets of her personality and intellect very different from those required for literary scholarship. Immediately she set to work on several more stories, among them those read by Lord Dunsany and those she sent, at the request of Ellery Sedgwick and Edward Weeks, to the *Atlantic Monthly*. The *Atlantic* became the first publication to accept a Mary Lavin story ("The Green Grave and the Black Grave," which appeared in May 1940). The *Dublin Magazine,* edited by Seumas O'Sullivan (James Starkey), became the first to print an example of her work ("Miss Holland," April–June 1939). Meanwhile, the dissertation on Virginia Woolf was set aside, never to be submitted in fulfillment of the Ph.D.

By 1942, when the Atlantic Monthly Press brought out *Tales from Bective Bridge,* Mary Lavin's first volume of short stories, six of the stories that she had written rapidly between 1938 and 1941 had appeared in magazines, and more were scheduled for future periodical publication. In 1943, *Tales from Bective Bridge* was republished in England; this edition won the James Tait Black Memorial Prize for the year's best work of fiction and was selected for distribution as a Readers Union book. Since then Mary Lavin has had two Guggenheim Foundation Fellowships (1959 and 1960) and has been awarded the Katherine Mansfield Prize (1961), the Ella Lynam Cabot Award (1971), the Eire Society of Boston Gold Medal (1974), the Gregory Medal (1975), and the American Irish Foundation Literature Prize (1979). In 1964 and 1965 she was elected president of Irish PEN. In 1968 the degree of Doctor of Letters (*honoris causa*) was conferred on her by the National University of Ireland. In 1971 and 1972, she was elected president of the Irish Academy of Letters, and in 1981 she was named to the Aos Dana, Ireland's newly constituted equivalent of the French Academy. In 1982 she received a five-year grant, as a member of Aos Dana, that freed her to pursue the art of short fiction without concern for its commercial potential.

As a native-born American long resident in Ireland, Mary Lavin belongs to both Ireland and the United States, a fact that has been recognized by the American universities that seek her participation in creative writing programs and by successive Irish governments that have appointed her to such quasi-public bodies as the Arts Council and the Cultural Relations Committee of the Department of External Affairs. She has long been a member also of the Board of Trustees of the National Library of Ireland. These appointments indicate the esteem in which she is held in her country of residence, where she is regarded as a major influence on younger writers, a link not only between them and the generation of O'Connor, O'Faolain, and O'Flaherty, but also between contemporary writers and those European masters of short fiction recommended to her by Lord Dunsany when she herself was young. Indeed, it is because she continues to experiment with the forms of short fiction, in language, length, content, and narrative mode, that she remains very much a contemporary writer of international reputation, despite a career that extends over nearly half a century. She also represents, among women writers, a continuation of a line of descent from Jane Austen to Virginia Woolf, a distinction she shares with her older contemporary, Elizabeth Bowen, whom she also admires.[2]

Because Mary Lavin's fiction reflects the sights, smells, and sounds of places where she herself has lived and presents characters that follow patterns of life familiar to the people of such places, she is sometimes regarded as a naturalist or as an autobiographical writer. Similarly, because her stories are built around events that have a beginning, middle, and end, she also has been described as an old-fashioned storyteller, a traditionalist with a talent for recreating milieu, conveying verisimilitude, and eliciting, through what appear to be documented representations of reality, the reader's willing suspension of disbelief. Analysis of themes, characters, forms, and narrative modes, however, reveals subtleties beneath the surface of Mary Lavin's fiction, the "extraordinary sense" described by V. S. Pritchett "that what we call real life is a veil." Reviewers have noted also the skill with which she suggests rather than discloses the story beneath her surface story and hints at stasis beyond kinesis, permanence beneath change.

In discussions of her work, Mary Lavin has confirmed observations by scholars and critics of a still point beyond the physical, emotional, and sometimes intellectual eddy and flow of her fiction. Indeed, it is in this still point that a story has its genesis, she declares. As she herself describes the creative process, as she knows it, a story begins when she is struck by what appears to her to be a universal truth: "That happens." A question forms in her mind: "To whom does that happen?" It sharpens her observations, it makes her keenly aware of the people around her. Gradually an answer suggests itself: "That happens to that kind of person." It is followed by other questions: "Why?" "Under what circumstances?" When they are answered to her satisfaction, she has the nucleus of the story, the insight that will attract readers of different cultures in different countries. It remains only for her to form a situation around that insight, to make real and believable the people to whom "that happens," to fix them in time and place. From the storehouse of her memory, she draws the physical features of people and place; the discriminating details of gesture, voice, and action; the play of light and shadow on a landscape; the quirky moods of household pets; the squeaks of doors and groans of floorboards; the rhythmic patterns developed through habit and imposed by custom that make her fiction, art imitating life, seem to be life itself. If the same views of city or country appear in story after story, if her characters seem to inhabit similar if not identical houses or flats, the reasons are easily given: Why should the author try to imagine a house she has never seen, try to estimate the number of steps in a staircase that she never has climbed, try to position doors, or furniture, or a fireplace, when her home in Bective in County Meath or her Dublin townhouse or her mother's family's shop in Athenry has appropriate rooms in which her characters can live their fictional lives, with only minor changes needed to suit their taste, income, or background? Why wonder how far a character might have to go from home to store, school, neighbor, church, hospital, or post office, when the distance can be measured in the author's own real world of the present or can be remembered from the past?

Mary Lavin's early stories—those written in the late 1930s and 1940s—focus on the universal truth of restricted vision. In stories such as "The Green Grave and the Black Grave," "At Sallygap," "Sarah," "Brother Boniface," "Brigid," "The Small Bequest," "The Cemetery in the Desmesne," and "The Nun's Mother," she treats relationships assumed to be intimate and reveals the gulfs that exist between husbands and wives, parents and children, sisters and brothers, long-term neighbors, childhood friends, and others who think of themselves as really knowing each other. Sometimes their unperceived misunderstandings simply leave each feeling lonely and isolated; sometimes there is friction and a sense of betrayal that leads to chronic irritation or bursts of anger; sometimes separation seems to be the only solution, but lies must be told to justify the leaving; sometimes the truth is revealed, but always without hope that anything can be changed. And in one story at least—"The Small Bequest"—truth alone is not sufficient: the claim of close ties is not merely rebuffed but rejected with vengeance.

Many of the stories written during the 1950s and early 1960s test the universal truths Mary Lavin explores in her early writings: if this kind of thing happens to this kind of person under these circumstances, what happens in similar circumstances to a different kind of person? What happens to the same kind of person in different circumstances? Mary Lavin's fascination with these questions is revealed in such stories as "The Widow's Son," in which the author actually provides the reader with alternate endings, then discusses the implications of each. For the most part, however, she tests her truths in different stories: "A Tragedy" may be read as an alternative to "Frail Vessel"; "The Long Holidays" may be seen as a comic version of what might have happened to another Miss Holland (albeit one with somewhat more self-confidence, more inclination to manipulate others).

During the 1950s and early 1960s, Mary Lavin also began to develop story cycles, individual tales that are connected through use of the same characters: for example, the Grimes family (for which the Mahons of Athenry, Mary Lavin's mother's family, served as models) appears, in this period, in "A Visit to the Cemetery," "An Old Boot," "The Little Prince," "Frail Vessel," and "Loving Memory"; Vera, a recurring character who sometimes shares traits and experiences of the author herself, is portrayed in "What's Wrong With Aubretia?" and

"One Summer." Critics who view Mary Lavin's work as autobiographical also describe her widow stories as a group belonging to this period, for in the decade following the death of Mary Lavin's first husband, William Walsh, in 1954 (she was remarried in 1969 to Michael MacDonald Scott), she wrote "Bridal Sheets," "In A Café," "In the Middle of the Fields," and "The Cuckoo Spit." But "Love Is for Lovers," "Lilacs," "The Dead Soldier," "Brigid," and "The Widow's Son" all concern widows, too, and all were written long before the author herself experienced widowhood. Nor can these stories be read as related in the way the Grimes family stories are related, for although superficial similarities of detail invite comparisons between some of her widows, others are unlike in all respects but their widowhood. What probably is true is that Mary Lavin brought to her widow stories of 1954 and after insights gained from her personal experience, always the raw material of her art (but always, as she emphasizes whenever she discusses her conception of writing as art, *only* raw material until it is synthesized and universalized). Finally, in the 1950s and early 1960s, Mary Lavin returned to some of the themes she had explored in her early work and to some collateral themes that had been suggested by them. For example, in "The Great Wave" and "Bridal Sheets" she evokes again the world of "The Green Grave and the Black Grave." "Brigid" also might be read as a related story, for although its central character is a farmer's wife, she is as unprepared for the shock of her husband's sudden death as the wives of the islanders of "Bridal Sheets" and "The Green Grave and the Black Grave."

Since the late 1960s Mary Lavin has preferred to write in the form of the short novel or tale rather than the short story: that is, the form that generally ranges from approximately seventy to nearly two hundred printed pages. As a result she has published less frequently in periodicals such as the *New Yorker,* in which stories usually run between five and fifteen pages in length and rarely exceed forty pages. Instead, following the practice familiar to readers of Henry James, D. H. Lawrence, and Joseph Conrad, she has turned increasingly to book publication, reducing the number of titles included in a single volume to between three and five (cf. *A Memory and Other Stories,* 1972, and *The Shrine and Other Stories,* 1977) instead of twelve or thirteen, as in her earlier volumes. (While this change possibly has made her work less accessible to readers of periodicals, it has assured her more recognition among readers of books.[3]) Her first experiments with the tale were published in *The Becker Wives and Other Stories* (1946), in which the title story is seventy-one pages long and "A Happy Death" is but a slightly shorter sixty-eight pages. These short novels were preceded by her first full-length novel, *The House in Clewe Street* (1945), which had been serialized in the *Atlantic Monthly* in 1944–45 before it was published in book form. They were followed by *Mary O'Grady,* a second full-length novel, published in

1950. At this point the author returned to writing short stories of conventional length, partly because she was dissatisfied with her novels (critics did not share her dissatisfaction), partly because she found writing short fiction more satisfying. For a time the length of her stories was influenced, no doubt, by the fact that in 1958 the *New Yorker* had taken a first-reading option on her new work; the number of its issues in which a tale or novella could be published was limited. But again and again Mary Lavin was tempted by the form of the longer tale or novella, which allowed her to develop themes she felt she could not handle adequately within the conventional length of the short story. The success of such stories as "Happiness" and "A Memory" testifies to the accuracy of her artistic judgment.

Mary Lavin's art is economic, disciplined, compressed. Her working method is to allow her imagination to range freely, often over hundreds of pages of rough draft, until her characters and their backgrounds have been established, details of her story have been worked out, and the causes of the action have been analyzed. At this point she attacks her manuscript ruthlessly, discarding everything that is not essential to the central story she wishes to tell. Stripped of all but essential text, her stories emerge as brilliant, hard, gemlike. The quality of her art is her major contribution to the Irish short story. Important also is the nature of its content. She neither romanticizes nor trivializes the Irish experience, as did so many writers of the nineteenth century. Nor does she share the odi-atque-amo attitude toward Ireland familiar to readers of Moore and Joyce. Her work is closest perhaps, as they themselves observed, to that of O'Connor, O'Faolain, and O'Flaherty, but it transcends the national and historic context of their stories to present a world that is externally Irish but beyond time, place, and event in its understanding of that which is universally human in the Irish experience. In making this contribution to Irish literature, Mary Lavin has enhanced both the significance and the dignity of the Irish short story.

• • •

More than thirteen years her senior and a seasoned writer well before Mary Lavin began publishing fiction, Elizabeth Bowen (1899–1973) is known less for her short stories than for her novels, especially *The House in Paris* (1935), *The Death of the Heart* (1938), and *The Heat of the Day* (1949).[4] Although born in Dublin, Ireland, and distinctly Anglo-Irish by heritage, she is often discussed by literary critics as an English writer because so little of her fiction explicitly concerns Irish life. Of her eleven novels, only *The Last September* (1929) is set in Ireland; of the seventy-nine titles in *The Collected Stories of Elizabeth Bowen* (1981), only ten focus clearly on Ireland or its people. Yet, as Victoria Glendinning points out in a biography published in 1977, Elizabeth Bowen's entire life was

divided between Ireland, her native country, and England, where she was educated, a fact that is reflected in her fiction. Moreover, her achievement in the
short story is at least as important as her achievement in the novel. For her, as
for Mary Lavin, short fiction was a literary form different from the novel in its
demands on the author and its impact on the reader.

Elizabeth Bowen was the daughter of Florence Colley of Mount Temple,
Clontarf (a fashionable north Dublin suburb famed as the site of the battle
in which Brian Boru defeated the Vikings in 1014) and Henry Charles Cole
Bowen of Bowen's Court (a magnificent eight-hundred-acre estate in
County Cork). On her mother's side she was related to Arthur Wellesley,
Duke of Wellington, who defeated Napoleon at Waterloo and served as
prime minister of England from 1828 to 1830. Another Colley ancestor had
been solicitor general and surveyor general of Ireland in the sixteenth century. On her father's side, she was descended from a Bowen who was an
officer in Cromwell's army. The County Cork estate had been Cromwell's
reward to this seventeenth-century ancestor for his part in Cromwell's Irish
campaign.

By birth, therefore, Elizabeth Bowen was a member of the privileged class
in Ireland; family circumstances confirmed her social standing, shielded her
from that other distressful Ireland that existed beyond the world of Dublin
Georgian houses and country estates, and determined her early associations.
During the winter, the family lived on fashionable Herbert Place in Dublin,
while Henry Bowen pursued a career in law, first privately and then as an
official with the Land Commission. In the summer, father, mother, and
daughter moved to Bowen's Court, where they entertained and were entertained by other Big House families. Winter and summer, young Elizabeth
visited with an army of aunts, uncles, and cousins with whom she felt at
home. An Anglo-Irish life, familiar in general outline as well as specific detail
to such Big House predecessors of Elizabeth Bowen as Maria Edgeworth,
George Moore, and Edith Somerville, it was interrupted abruptly when Elizabeth was seven. Her father, suffering from a deteriorating psychological
condition, was hospitalized; with her mother she moved to Kent, on the
west coast of England, near Colley relatives. Six years later, Henry Bowen
had regained his health sufficiently for the family to be reunited in Ireland,
but Florence Colley Bowen had contracted cancer. She died in Kent in 1912,
when Elizabeth was thirteen years old. The extended family that had provided emotional support for herself and her mother during her father's illness rallied once more: it was decided that during the school term Elizabeth
would continue living in England with her mother's unmarried sister and
brother in Hertfordshire, where she could attend Harpenden Hall, a good

day school; summers she would spend with her father and one of his sisters at Bowen's Court in Ireland.

From Harpenden Hall Elizabeth Bowen was enrolled at Downe House, a boarding school in Kent in which the headmistress, Olive Willis, believed that young ladies should be stimulated intellectually, encouraged to articulate their ideas, provided opportunities for artistic expression, and trained to handle all aspects of life with graciousness and aplomb. Elizabeth read voraciously (Jane Austen, the subject of Mary Lavin's M.A. thesis, was one of her favorite authors) and became an active member of the literary society. Like Mary Lavin, however, she did not at first perceive that her taste in literature, her talent for imaginative re-creation, and her way with words might suggest a writing career. Rather, upon completing the prescribed course at Downe, she thought first of studying art, for which she also had a flair. But her two terms at the London County Council School of Art were as disappointing for her as George Moore's similar experience in the ateliers of Paris had been for him; sensibly, like Moore, she looked elsewhere for the career that would save her from her worst fears, a "useless life." As Victoria Glendinning has suggested, Elizabeth Bowen's conversations with the author Stephen Gwynn (brother of Mary Gwynn, who married Henry Charles Cole Bowen in 1918) might have helped awaken her interest in writing: she next took a course in journalism. Meanwhile, between finishing her last year of school in Kent and enrolling in her journalism class in London, Elizabeth Bowen had been much in Ireland, working as a volunteer among the war wounded in Dublin hospitals and dancing with British garrison officers (among them, one to whom she was briefly engaged) in Cork. These experiences, as well as those belonging to a winter spent in Italy with an aunt and several cousins, provided setting, situation, and character for the fiction she began to write in her early twenties. Her stories and novels were informed also by perceptions of the world and human relationships derived from the unique combination of personal, social, and historic events that was the matrix of her early life.

Despite the superficial serenity of her adolescence and early adulthood after the illness of her father and the death of her mother, Elizabeth Bowen's early life was not untroubled. A violent strike, its repercussions felt in England, disrupted Dublin in 1913. In 1914 World War I began: England declared war on Germany while Elizabeth was still on her summer holiday in Ireland. Less than two years later much of the Dublin she knew was riddled by bullets and set aflame in the Easter Rising of 1916. In its aftermath a relative, Captain John Bowen-Colthurst, was court-martialed for having ordered the execution of Francis Sheehy Skeffington, a pacifist writer sympathetic with the Republican cause; Sir Roger Casement was hanged. Joy following the armistice in 1918 was short-lived in England: on its heels came an influenza epidemic that took almost as many English lives as had the war. In Ireland it was followed by the bloodshed and violence of the Anglo-Irish war of 1919–21. The Treaty of 1921 ended the conflict; however, by establishing the Irish Free State in the twenty-six counties, it also ended the power of the Ascendancy. On the date on which the treaty was signed, Anglo-Ireland, as it was known to Elizabeth, her family, and her friends—the Ireland of her ancestors—vanished as a political and social reality. During the Anglo-Irish war many of the Big Houses in which she had attended dances had been burned; many of the Big House families with whom she had lunched and played tennis had fled to England. Still there was no peace: for two years more Ireland was ravaged by the Civil War, in which brother fought brother, both sides threatened the safety of the citizenry, and Bowen's Court was again at risk. Bowen's Court, however, survived the Troubles, and passed from father to daughter in 1930 to become, as Elizabeth Bowen's reputation as a writer increased, a literary landmark. (It was later razed, to her dismay, by the man to whom she sold the estate in 1959.) Elizabeth Bowen survived, too, but like other events of 1913–23, the wars that changed the face and character of Ireland were forever woven into the fabric of her existence.

Most critics discount the significance of historical events in Elizabeth Bowen's life, pointing as evidence to her own few remarks concerning their disruptive effects in her autobiographical writings. They cite instead the death of her mother (also little discussed by her) as the major traumatic event of her childhood. There is little doubt that her mother's death was indeed deeply disturbing, especially given the intimacy Florence Colley Bowen and Elizabeth Bowen shared (depicted in an early story, "Coming Home") in the years of Henry Bowen's illness; other biographical sources have established that fact. But there is evidence also that the destruction of her Anglo-Irish world was deeply felt, too. For one thing, instability charac- terizes the lives of the men and women of her short fiction (most of them people of her own social class). Seldom are they depicted in a settled home. Some live in respectable rooming houses or flats (cf., "Breakfast," "Daffo- dils"), or are just returning from or going somewhere (cf., "The Return," "Joining Charles"), or are in the process of moving (cf., "The New House," "Attractive Modern Homes," "The Last Night in the Old House," "The Dis- inherited"). Their emotional lives are also in flux. Some are trying to adjust to the death or departure of one with whom they had shared an intimate relationship (cf., "Requiescat," "Making Arrangements"). Intimacy, when it is achieved, may be but a brief moment during a chance encounter, unlikely to be repeated (cf., "Lunch"). Isolation may be a pathological condition (cf., "Dead Mabelle," "Telling"). Although their affluence enables them to travel, many Elizabeth Bowen characters are unable to cope successfully with a foreign environment (cf., "Contessina," "Shoes: An International Episode"). Wherever they are, marriage is precarious (as in "A Love Story"); love is uncertain (as in "Look at All Those Roses"); and charity is suspect (as in "The Easter Egg Party").

Elizabeth Bowen's first stories were returned by editors with the usual letters of rejection until she was taken up by her old headmistress from Downe House. Prompted by Olive Willis whom she had known at Oxford, Rose Macaulay, the critic and novelist, read Elizabeth Bowen's stories, encouraged her talent, and introduced her to Naomi Royde-Smith, editor of the *Saturday Westminster,* who first accepted one of her stories for publication. This in itself was a milestone, but the relationship produced another of equal significance. Rose Macaulay recommended Elizabeth Bowen's work to Frank Sidgwick of Sidgwick & Jackson, who published *Encounters,* her first volume of short stories, in 1923.

After *Encounters,* in addition to her novels, autobiographical and critical writings, and histories, Elizabeth Bowen published five more volumes of short fiction: *Ann Lee's and Other Stories* (1926); *Joining Charles and Other Stories* (1929); *The Cat Jumps and Other Stories* (1934); *Look at All Those Roses* (1941); and *The Demon Lover and Other Stories* (1945). In addition to depicting unsettled lives, these volumes are remarkable for their perceptive and sensitive portraits of children. In "Coming Home," twelve-year-old Rosalind returns from school to relive with "Darlingest," the mother that is "exclusively" her own, the excitement of having her essay read aloud by her teacher. Her joy crumbles like the macaroons she has brought for them to share when she finds that her mother is not at home. In "Charity" and "The Jungle," Rachel seeks companionship as she struggles to cross the uncharted country between early and late adolescence. In "The Tommy Crans," Herbert and Nancy, children who were never young, accommodate Mr. and Mrs. Crans, who have never grown up. In "Maria," a fifteen-year-old girl expertly manipulates to her own advantage the adults who try to manipulate her. Howling, weeping, seven-year-old Frederick of "Tears, Idle Tears" embarrasses his elegant mother in Regent's Park—and grows up a little, unexpectedly, after a conversation with a stranger. Geraldine of "The Little Girl's Room" returns her grandmother's hypocrisy with her own. Critics, who prefer to comment on novels rather than on short fiction, have drawn attention to the remarkable characterizations of Leopold and Henrietta of *The House in Paris* and Portia of *The Death of the Heart.* The children of Elizabeth Bowen's short stories are drawn with the same fine understanding, the same awareness of the resilience of the young in the face of situations that most adults would find untenable.

Although all Elizabeth Bowen's fiction has a sense of place, an appropriateness of background detail, her short stories differ from her novels in that geographical setting is not always specific. Her characters speak and behave for the most part as one might expect upper-class English or Anglo-Irish characters to speak and behave (exceptions are the young woman on the park bench in "Tears, Idle Tears" and the distraught source of the monologue of "Oh, Madame"), but the reader is not always told whether their dining rooms, sitting rooms, and bedrooms are in England or in Ireland. Even when the setting is specifically English, so alike are the speech and behavior patterns of the Anglo-Irish educated in England and the native upper-class English, and so often do the Anglo-Irish move back and forth between Ireland and England, that the exact background of specific characters may not be determined. Nor does it really matter. In fact, the very sense that on the surface these well-behaved people maintain their composure and relate to one another in the predictable ways prescribed by social class, the very sameness of their manners and chit-chat, heightens the contrast between what they appear to be and what they are. It is in this contrast that the power of Elizabeth Bowen's short fiction may be found.

In eight stories, however, published in *Elizabeth Bowen's Irish Stories* (1978), setting is clearly and identifiably Irish. A ninth, "The Happy Autumn Fields," is also included in this volume, despite the fact that its Irish setting is not identified, because (as Victoria Glendinning explains in her brief introduction) the author herself had written in her preface to *The Demon Lover and Other Stories* that it was, for her, "unshakeably County Cork." Given this flimsy basis for selection, a tenth title could have been included: the story-within-a-story of "The Back Drawing-Room" also has an Irish setting. In these ten tales, Elizabeth Bowen's descriptive passages are more vividly rendered, more painterly in style, more nostalgic in mood, than those usually found in her short fiction. None of the so-called Irish stories, however, is useful in analyzing Elizabeth Bowen's impressions of or attitudes toward Ireland. For these the reader must turn to other sources: her only Irish novel, *The Last September*; her two histories, *Bowen's Court* (1942) and *The Shelbourne: A Centre of Dublin Life for More Than a Century* (1951); her essays, reviews, and autobiographical writings.

Through Rose Macaulay and Naomi Royde-Smith, Elizabeth Bowen had been introduced, while still an unknown young writer, into a literary circle that included, among others, Edith Sitwell, Walter de la Mare, and Aldous Huxley. In 1923 (the year in which *Encounters* was published) she married Alan Cameron, an educational administrator. Two years later he was appointed secretary for education for the city of Oxford, they took a house in the village of Old Headington, and her circle was enlarged to include Lord David Cecil, Maurice Bowra, Evelyn Waugh, Anthony Powell, and a host of others. Elizabeth Bowen was first introduced to Virginia Woolf, whose work she admired, by an Oxford friend, Susan Buchan. Eventually she came to know others of the Bloomsbury group, too; theirs was an intellectual and artistic circle in which, when her own success enabled her to overcome her awe of them, she was comfortable. These were the men and women she often entertained at Bowen's Court between 1930 and 1970, together with well-known Irish and American writers of the period.

Elizabeth Bowen's work was widely read and well received by critics on both sides of the Atlantic. In England, where she took as one of her subjects daily life in the face of wartime death and destruction, she was made a Commander of the British Empire in 1948; Oxford University, whose academic circles also provided material for her short stories, conferred upon her the degree of Doctor of Letters (*honoris causa*) in 1957. In Ireland, where she chronicled with Chekhovian objectivity the last days of the Anglo-Irish and analyzed the ways in which individuals respond to uncertainty and change, she was elected in 1937 to the Irish Academy of Letters and received an honorary Doctor of Letters from Trinity College in 1949. Across the Atlantic, in the United States and Canada, readers were attracted by her narrative skill, her psychological insights, and what Angus Wilson has described as her "instinctive formal vision."

• • •

Benedict Kiely (1919–   ) brought to Irish short fiction a perspective different from both Mary Lavin's and Elizabeth Bowen's.[5] Born in County Tyrone during the Anglo-Irish war, he grew up in Northern Ireland, the British province that came into being as a political and social entity just before Elizabeth Bowen's Anglo-Ireland was eliminated by the Treaty of 1921. Her County Cork and Mary Lavin's Counties Galway and Meath were included in the twenty-six counties of the Irish Free State (later, the Irish Republic); his County Tyrone, together with five other northeast counties of Ireland, remains to this day under British rule. Although often called Ulster, this newly constituted British territory comprises in fact only part of the Irish cultural and geographical entity of that name: the ancient province included also the counties of Donegal, Cavan, and Monaghan. Because "home" traditionally has been, among Irishmen, the province of birth, Benedict Kiely grew up at "home" in Omagh, a market town in County Tyrone, Northern Ireland, but also at "home" in Donegal in the Irish Free State. This second home, the county of William Allingham and Seamus O'Grianna, was where he spent his summers; where he practiced speaking the native Ulster dialect in the Irish-speaking district (called the Gaeltacht); and where he often sat near the fire in an Irish cottage and listened to the centuries-old tales of the traditional Irish storyteller, the seanachie.

But if Omagh was in Northern Ireland by an Act of Parliament of 1920 and in Ulster by historical imperative, it had also another dimension: it was an Irish town of a kind well known to Mary Lavin and Elizabeth Bowen. Not unlike Athenry, to which Mary Lavin had been brought when she was ten and where her mother's people, the Mahons, had kept a shop, it had been headquarters for a British garrison since well before the turn of the century. Nor was it unlike the garrison towns of County Cork from which officers used to come to attend dances at Bowen's Court. Omagh's recent past therefore provided the young Benedict Kiely with another overlay of Irish history through which he might look forward and back to learn who he was and to what people he belonged. He learned of his County Tyrone heritage also from the works of William Carleton, the nineteenth-century author from a neighboring valley, whose storytelling abilities he admired, and whose background and traditions he shared.

Perceiving analogies between the personal art of the seanachie and the art of Carleton's *Traits and Stories of the Irish Peasantry,* Benedict Kiely began to shape, while still in Omagh, his own portrait of the writer he was to become. This portrait later served as archetype for the ficelle character of much of his short fiction: for example, "The Little Wrens and Robins" and "A Room in Linden," both originally published in the *New Yorker* and included in *A Ball of Malt and Madame Butterfly* (1973). However, like Mary Lavin and Elizabeth Bowen, he did not begin adult life as a writer; his first vocational choice was the priesthood. When he discovered that he did not have a calling for the religious life, he turned next to the study of literature and history at University College, Dublin. There, where he continued in the graduate program in history following receipt of his arts degree in 1943, his talent brought encouragement and opportunities for literary achievement. *Counties of Contention: A Study of the Origin and Implications of Partition* (1945) was one of the fruits of his academic work. Recognition of his ability resulted, in 1945, in his being offered a position as leader writer and literary critic for the *Irish Independent,* a Dublin daily newspaper.

In another city, in another country, to be labeled a journalist is often a liability for an aspiring young writer. (Twenty-three years earlier, Gertrude Stein had advised Ernest Hemingway to give up writing for newspapers if he intended to be serious about fiction.) But in Ireland, where arts graduates of exceptional ability traditionally have begun their careers as staff members on Dublin newspapers, and even letters to the editor are written with style and imagination, such an offer was an opportunity. For Benedict Kiely, it meant becoming a colleague of such men as Brian O'Nolan (a.k.a. Flann O'Brien/Myles na gCopaleen), whose irreverent humor, subtle wit, and curious ability to combine the lyric and satiric were not unlike his own. It meant being turned loose to investigate the city that had produced such disparate talents as Sean O'Casey (whose ability to laugh at the edge of the grave Kiely shares) and James Joyce (from whom Kiely may have learned the technique of objectifying, through his older writer's eyes, the personal feelings and emotions of his younger, remembered self). A year later, in 1946, Kiely's own reputation as a creative writer was publicly launched by the appearance of a novel, *Land without Stars,* and the publication of a short story, "Blackbird in a Bramble Bough."

Today Kiely's principal works include nine novels, a novella, three collections of short fiction, the historical study mentioned above, a biographical-critical study of William Carleton, an appraisal of modern Irish fiction, and a personal memoir of his journeys throughout Ireland. He continues to write; he is often heard on Irish radio and television, where he is an articulate and perceptive commentator on contemporary Irish culture; he occasionally teaches at American colleges and universities; he also has served on the faculty of the School for Irish Studies in Dublin; and he is often invited to speak at academic meetings and before university audiences. In 1980 Kiely was the recipient of both the Allied Irish Banks literary prize and the literature award of the American Irish Foundation.

For Benedict Kiely, as for George Moore (a predecessor about whom he frequently writes with a certain ambivalence), it is the story that always holds him in thrall; in his fiction, as in Moore's, there is always the sound of a man's voice speaking. Yet his short stories have been called uneven by some critics. Daniel Casey, who prefers Kiely's novels, describes the narrative mode of the early stories as straightforward and conventional and at times finds his situations contrived, his characters stereotyped, his descriptions "unnecessarily elaborate." These are, of course, characteristics of oral narrative, the type of storytelling Kiely would have learned from listening carefully to the seanachie in Donegal; they are characteristics also of Carleton's *Traits and Stories of the Irish Peasantry,* to which Kiely has acknowledged a debt. Perceived as purposeful, they become not flaws but evidence of a stage in Kiely's development. A comparison of his two volumes of short fiction, *A Journey to the Seven Streams: Seventeen Stories* (1963) and *A Ball of Malt and Madame Butterfly: A Dozen Stories* (1973), confirms this judgment.

"Blackbird in the Bramble Bough, " from the first volume (published originally in September 1946 in the *Irish Bookman*), is a tale of a young man's disillusion with a visiting poet. It begins with the young man looking at a clipping from an American newspaper, which contains a picture of a poet who had visited Ireland not many months before and a critic's description of his poetry as "like the song of a blackbird on a bramble bough." The rest is recollection: of the evening when the poet had come to lecture at the local convent school, of the young man's excitement when he, a young teacher, had been assigned to look after the distinguished visitor. The poet's stature had diminished in direct proportion to the time they had spent together; by the end of the evening, as the young man recalls—with amusement, chronicling the highlights for himself and the reader, but also with a certain sense of superiority—the poet had been completely demystified. Kiely's vivid descriptions and earthy humor leave the reader amused, too, but the story, a slight effort, provides neither insight nor heightened understanding.

"The Little Wrens and Roses" (first published in the *New Yorker,* collected in Kiely's second volume of short fiction) is also about a young man and a poet. The narrative I, Ben, is the young man; Cousin Ellen, the poet, is a "nonstop talker" who used to try his father's patience during her visits to the family. Ben mocks her to himself, to the amusement of the reader, by quoting lines from her sentimental verse and by reciting a parody of a typical Cousin Ellen monologue. But he also recalls that, to himself as well as to others, she was once something of a local celebrity, because her poems were published in the local newspaper. By the time he was eighteen he had realized that these poems were crude and banal. Still he had enjoyed Cousin Ellen's visits, for the show they provided: Cousin Ellen talking, talking, talking, apparently without need of breath; his father muttering that he was drowning, "drifting slowly, sinking slowly, brain and body numb, . . . but teetotally helpless." Ben remembers Cousin Ellen in the hospital, shortly before she died. In her usual fashion she had rattled on, a comic figure, threatening to make a poem out of every second observation. Later, he had walked to the station, talking of Cousin Ellen with the new servant girl from Mayo, a young woman with a sweet singing voice but an unfortunate birthmark on one cheek. To the young woman, as unsophisticated as once he had been, the published poet was an awesome figure. Tongue in cheek, he had declaimed one of Cousin Ellen's sentimental verses, but his mocking condescension had been lost on her: she had sung the words to a slow sweet tune that the narrator had "never heard before or since."

Far more sophisticated than "Blackbird in the Bramble Bough," "The Little Wrens and Roses" is an example of Kiely's ability to play with narrative focus, first inviting the reader to regard Cousin Ellen as silly, self-centered, and vain; then asking the reader to admire her as a great character in the Irish meaning of that term; then making her an object of pity; and finally giving voice to her "poetic soul" in a tune that expresses the emotions Cousin Ellen could not convey. Another story from the same collection, also first published in the *New Yorker,* reveals a different but equally skillful handling of narrative technique. "A

Great God's Angel Standing" begins as a straightforward narrative, a fairly conventional tale of the friendship of a priest and a rake, with the narrative focused on the rake (he, of course, has the greater capacity to amuse the reader; he, like Milton's snake, gets all the good lines). Little by little a narrative presence enters the story, until "I" becomes a character deserving of the reader's attention. The jokes cease; the story develops an unexpected poignancy as the focus shifts to the priest; "I" has the last word. Whose story has been told? The reader—the humor still echoing in his mind, but with an unexpected pang in the heart—is left with the question.

For the most part critics have concentrated on Kiely's novels, noting his short fiction only in passing, pointing to the fact that, to date, he has produced only three volumes of short fiction—a total of twenty-nine stories—plus another uncollected handful. Exceptions are John Wilson Foster, who regards Kiely as "the equal of O'Faolain and within hailing distance of O'Connor"; Thomas Flanagan, who perceives in Kiely's Omagh resemblances to Faulkner's Yoknapatawpha; and Mervyn Wall, who calls attention to the evidence in Kiely's short stories of his commitment to the traditions of Irish storytelling. Certainly, one significance of Kiely's short fiction is its debt to the techniques of the Irish storyteller. His contributions to the genre are notable also for the sheer poetry of their descriptive passages, especially those detailing the splendors of Ulster river valleys and countryside; for the skillful juxtapositon of humor and pathos, used by the author not just for effect, but to maintain subtle control of the narrative; and for a lustiness and earthiness that, according to Vivian Mercier,[6] belong within a well-documented Irish comic tradition even older than that of the Irish folktale.

Like Mary Lavin, Benedict Kiely recently has begun to write fiction that is shorter than the conventional novel, longer than the conventional short story. *Proxopera* (1977), his first effort to employ the format of the novella or tale, also represents a departure in style and content. In its attack on terrorism it is more topical than Kiely's other work. Instead of subtle irony or witty satire, Kiely's usual verbal weapons, it depends on the evocative power of language more commonly found in Kiely's descriptive passages to achieve its effect. Whether it will remain a single work in the author's corpus or indicates a new direction for his shorter fiction remains to be seen.

• • •

Like Benedict Kiely, Michael McLaverty (1907–   ) is an Ulsterman, but the perspective he brings to Irish short fiction is different from either Kiely's or Mary Lavin's or Elizabeth Bowen's.[7] Born in Carrickmacross, County Monaghan, another Irish market town not unlike Mary Lavin's Athenry and Benedict

Kiely's Omagh, he lived during an impressionable period of his childhood on remote Rathlin Island, off the coast of County Antrim. The fiction derived from these Rathlin Island years, especially that which depicts the relationship between island child and the wild creatures of his environment (cf., "The Wild Duck's Nest"), invites comparison with the stories of Liam O'Flaherty. Educated in Belfast, where he became a teacher of mathematics and then headmaster of a secondary school, he draws also on his observations of life in Northern Ireland's principal city, often contrasting rural and urban experiences (usually to the detriment of the latter). Not surprising, given his career as an educator, McLaverty also has used the schoolroom as a setting for his fiction. Both schoolmasters and schoolchildren are among his memorable creations.

Despite his responsibilities as teacher and headmaster, McLaverty has published seven novels and two volumes of short fiction. His work has been well received among critics and reviewers on both sides of the Atlantic. For more than twenty years, however, except for anthologized stories, his short fiction was out of print. Now, fortunately, it is available in two collections, *The Road to the Shore and Other Stories* (1976) and *Collected Short Stories* (1978).

In an introduction to the *Collected Short Stories,* Seamus Heaney notes evidence of McLaverty's fondness for Gerard Manley Hopkins, without "that merely verbal effulgence that Hopkins can . . . inspire." Heaney's estimate of the durability of McLaverty's short fiction echoes that of John Wilson Foster, whose essays on Northern Irish writing are among the most perceptive that have appeared in recent years. Analysis of the strengths and shortcomings of McLaverty's published fiction confirms these judgments; like Mary Lavin, he has the disciplined imagination and talent for artistic compression better suited to the short story than to the novel. In 1982, in recognition of his contributions to modern Irish literature, Michael McLaverty received the American Irish Foundation annual literary award.

The *Collected Short Stories* contains twenty-three examples of McLaverty's short fiction. Although all were published previously, some more than forty years ago, none seems dated or old-fashioned in either subject or style. His technique is that of the miniaturist: on a restricted canvas he paints in careful and minute detail portraits of his fictional characters. Everything contributes to heightened understanding of and sympathy with his subject, even though, in the world of justice and law, neither might be deserved. So compelling is his treatment, for example, of the hopeless alcoholic in "Aunt Suzanne," the compulsive miser of "A Schoolmaster," and the faithless orphan of "Look at the Boats" that it is difficult not to regard these violators of trust and love with charity. Yet in McLaverty's probing of human problems and of the uncomfortably personal area that lies between judgment and emotion, there is nothing to soften reality, not even blame or feelings of revenge. Old Tom O'Brien of "Uprooted" loses the farm that he created from barren fields when the army chooses to build an airstrip on the headland that has been home to him and his family. He will never be happy in Downpatrick, where his son has bought a shop with the compensation money. Like his sheep dog, he languishes in the town, scarcely venturing out-of-doors, until the day when, without a word to son or daughter-in-law, he returns to the headland. He finds his house razed, his land leveled; only church and graveyard remain. There he stands, confronting both literal and figurative reality.

In another story of old age and change, Paddy of "The White Mare" is loath to give up working the farm in which he has taken such pride all his life. His sisters scold, his muscles rebel, his old bones ache, but he stubbornly continues to do his chores. Then one last heroic effort to plough his fields puts him in bed, too weak and sore to get up for several days; while he is unable to interfere, his sister Kate sells his white mare. Still unable to face the fact that his sister is right and that no longer can he or the mare do the work of a young farmer and his horse, he jumps from his bed and races to the strand to try to stop the dealer who is taking the mare to the mainland. It is a harsh moment for old Paddy when he discovers that he is too late. But it is his moment of reality. Mary Lavin's men and women may make a hell of heaven and a heaven of hell; Benedict Kiely's may use satire to deflect the slings and arrows of misfortune. Inevitability plays a more active part in Michael McLaverty's stories. In the face of it, his poignantly human characters do the best they can.

Although many of McLaverty's most successful short stories are, as these observations suggest, sensitive fictional portraits, as a craftsman he is by no means confined to this technique. "Pigeons," for example, a story very different from "Aunt Suzanne," "A Schoolmaster," and other portraits, owes its form to the art of the ballad singer. Its various episodes, like the stanzas of a ballad, form an incremental narrative made up of Frankie's recollections of his brother, Johnny: Johnny kept pigeons; he brought home sweets and other surprises for Frankie on Saturday night; he shared a bedroom with Frankie; he shared his Saturday sausages, too, bought with the money he brought home on payday; he let Frankie help him with the pigeons; he died; he was buried. Each recollection contributes to the story; each ends with a refrain that varies only slightly from one episode to another: "but Johnny is dead; he died for Ireland," "because he died for Ireland," "it was on Saturday that Johnny died for Ireland," "our Johnny died for Ireland." Structure enhances meaning: the lives of Irish heroes often are recounted in Irish ballads; structure therefore establishes, more than anything said in the story, that Johnny was a hero.

In another story, "Stone," McLaverty employs metaphor as a narrative device: James Heaney, a miserly bachelor, is obsessed with the idea of recording his name for all future generations to see on the largest stone monument in the churchyard—larger even than the one that marks the grave of another stony-hearted bachelor, McBride. It will be, he avows, his answer to his neighbors, who are always telling him that after his death he will be forgotten, because he has never married and has no child. The sight of McBride's monument is his daily comfort; it strengthens his stony resolve; it is his symbol of eternity. Then one night a violent storm fells the tree outside his miser's cottage and shatters McBride's monument in the graveyard above on the hill. "Stiffened with awe," himself like a stone monument, he regards the ruin in stony silence before he returns to his cottage.

"The Game Cock" uses metaphor similarly, but with a different technique. For most of its length the story seems to be about a feisty rooster who is being trained for the spring cock fights. Elaborately, McLaverty prepares the scene; Dick, as the rooster is called, is victorious. But when the bird dies of his injuries after his one day of battle, the focus shifts suddenly to Mick, father of the boy who tells the story. Is he the *real* game cock? The question is left to the reader; the author does not say.

• • •

Of the five authors considered in this brief study, Bryan MacMahon (1909–   )[8] is the most indebted to Gaelic tradition. His books include *Peig*, his 1973 translation of Peig Sayers's autobiographical account of life on the Great Blasket and nearby mainland. (A renowned storyteller, it was she from whom Robin Flower and Seamus Delargey obtained folktales and recollections of the people of the Gaeltacht of the Dingle Peninsula.) Phrases from the Munster dialect often appear in MacMahon's novels and stories, usually in translation (cf. the triads recited by Xandy, the traveling man of "King of the Bees"), but at times in the original Irish, as simple expressions skillfully woven into the text (cf. the snatches of dialogue, repeated in English in the narrative, in "The Kings Asleep in the Ground"). Well-known Irish stories, some of them from the manuscript tradition,[9] are adapted in whole or in part (cf. the motif of a life replaced by a life in "The Gap of Life"). Gaeilgeoir-thumping, that indoor sport indulged in by one-half of the bilingual writers and scholars of Ireland against the other half, supplies the essential leaven of humor in a blood-chilling tale within a tale (cf., "The Story that Spins"); its dimensions include its debt to Myles na gCopaleen's *An Béal Bocht* and the Irish writings of Maurice O'Sullivan, Thomas O'Croghan, and Séamus O'Grianna which *An Béal Bocht* parodies. MacMahon also has a knowledge of Shelta, the language of Irish tinkers. Among Irish writers he is noteworthy for his well-documented, sympathetic portrayals in fiction of the traveling people of Ireland.

In addition to novels and stories, MacMahon has written poems, plays, ballads, and children's books; he also has designed historical pageants, and he is one of the principal organizers of the Listowel Writers' Week, a conference featuring discussions and workshops that, under his direction, has become an annual international literary event. Long a member of the Irish Academy of Letters, in 1972 he received an honorary doctorate from the National University of Ireland.

Like Michael McLaverty, Bryan MacMahon has spent most of his life teaching as well as writing. Born in Listowel, County Kerry, where he has lived most of his life, he trained as a national schoolteacher at St. Patrick's College, Drumcondra, but never heeded the siren song of Dublin, possibly because Listowel has its own strong centuries-old literary traditions in both Irish and English. (In addition to MacMahon, it has nurtured, to cite just a few twentieth-century authors, George Fitzmaurice, John B. Keane, Brendan Kennelly, Maurice Walsh, and Seamus Wilmot.) Nor did he ever consider seriously life outside Ireland, although for a brief period during World War II, he worked in a factory in the English midlands, and he has made successful tours of the United States as a writer and lecturer.

MacMahon's writings first attracted attention when they appeared in Dublin literary magazines in the 1940s. Among those who singled him out for special attention were Sean O'Faolain and Frank O'Connor. His first collection of short fiction, *The Lion-Tamer and Other Stories*, was published in Toronto and New York in 1948 and 1949 and was republished in New York and London in 1958. By then he also had established a reputation among American readers and critics: a novel and a children's book had been published in the United States, and his stories had appeared in American periodicals. A second volume, *The Red Petticoat and Other Stories* (1955), followed the first; it enhanced his reputation as a writer of short fiction. Selections from both these early collections, plus new uncollected stories, were included in his most recent volume, *The End of the World and Other Stories* (1976).

Most of MacMahon's short fiction follows the pattern of the particular type of Irish folktale that focuses on rural or village life. Its outstanding characteristic is its vivid evocation of the landscape of western Ireland; hill and valley, coast and riverbank, come alive, vibrant not only in visual description but evocative also of sound and smell. In "The Gap of Life," a bicycle is heard long before it is seen, by the "lock-lock" of wheels and gears straining up the hill. In "King of the Bees," morning sunlight after a soft rain has thrown a "vinegary smell of soot and mortar and rotten thatch and nettle-bed" in the air near a ruined cabin. In "By the Sea," a troop of boy scouts from the midlands is taken to the coast on a camping trip: at their first sight of the sea they stop to admire "the squirming and crawling of it, the slithering and sidling of it, the terror and delight of it"; situation rather than character is the focus of the narrative. In "The End of the World, " a prediction published in an English newspaper is brought to the attention of the local lads by one of their number: it gives them a subject for their evening's banter and mutual abuse: it provides a reason for the owner of the clipping and the local publican to stay up drinking until the hour appointed for the apocalypse has passed; it offers the excuse with which the lad greets his mother when she asks why he has stayed out so late. In "Ballintierna in the Morning," the story is off and running as soon as a hare is let loose in Dublin on O'Connell Street. In "The Bull Buyers," the new widow of a man killed by his bull is not the easy mark the professional dealer thinks she will be.

If a criticism of these stories is that their plots are contrived, it also is one of their strengths. Contrived they are, indeed, for that is one of the requirements of such folktales, and the best among them provide both the pleasure of anticipation and the pleasure of surprise that Henry James considered the mark of the satisfying story. In such tales, because the narrative focuses on situation, character often is stereotyped. The priest in "Evening in Ireland" is driven by one thought alone: to get the passionate young safely into matrimony as soon as possible. The priest in "The Sound of the Bell" uses his parishioners' complaints that they cannot hear the new church bell as an excuse to go out for a day's shooting. The widows of "The Crab Tree" and "The Bull Buyers" are intent upon snaring a husband. The men of "A Woman's Hair" know better than to try to understand the mysteries or romance of a woman's nature or the bonds of womanhood.

MacMahon is also capable of transcending the conventional form and content of the folktale to write stories of greater depth and insight. "By the Sea" is one such story: the boy scout camping trip ends after just one night when one of the boys wakes up violently ill and suddenly dies; the others fold their tents, on the one hand in childlike disappointment at having to leave the beautiful coast without having had the chance to swim in the sea, on the other hand with no heart to remain, for the death of one of their number has destroyed the spirit with which they set out and has introduced something mysterious and terrifying. "The Ring" is another: an old woman, widowed when young, has learned to be strong and hard in order to bring up the six children with whom she was left to cope alone. Neither child nor grandchild ever has dared to disobey her or to question her rules. But when she loses her wedding ring during haying, she herself breaks all her own rules to find it, holding up the work, refusing all help, methodically searching through a haystack day after day, one wisp at a time. The ring is found at last. Exhausted, she sits by the fire, her face "cold as death." And then, to the astonishment of her grandchildren, she sobs out her husband's name and cries "like the rain." Finally, there is "The Gap of Life," an imaginative reweaving of the classical myth of Orpheus and Euridyce and Irish folk and manuscript tradition. These stories leave no doubt about MacMahon's ability to create memorable characters and to refashion traditional themes with the skill of the file, the poet or maker, as well as with the narrative power of the seanachie.

• • •

As developed in the work of these five writers, the Irish short story at midcentury has proved a versatile and elusive form. Its length extends from the brief sketches of Elizabeth Bowen and Michael McLaverty to the novellas of Mary Lavin and Benedict Kiely. Its models and influences may be found in the work of nineteenth- and early-twentieth-century Irish writers of short fiction; in European and American literature; and in Irish myth, legend, and folktale. It may take as its subject anyone, anywhere in Ireland: farmers and fishermen, shopkeepers and servants, priests and nuns, landlords and tenants, army officers, policemen, immigrants, emigrants, returned Yanks, tinkers, old people, young people, the married and unmarried, children, the dead, the dying. Narrative perspective may be that of the rich, the poor, or the middle class, from country, town, or city, from Irish Republic or Northern Ireland, from Ulster, Leinster, Munster, or Connaught. The authors themselves are similarly varied in background, education, and artistic vision.

From 1950 to 1970, the United States and England provided Irish writers of short fiction with the largest readership for their work. The situation has now changed with the demise of many of the magazines and journals that used to publish short stories, with alterations in editorial policies among those remaining, and with diminishing interest among book publishers in collections of short fiction. Radio plays adapted from short stories, once popular in America, are now few, although both readings and dramatizations continue to be presented in England and in Ireland. Television has not been a substitute, for it tends to use scripts written especially for the medium rather than adaptations of published short fiction. Mary Lavin, Benedict Kiely, Michael McLaverty, Bryan MacMahon, and other established Irish writers committed to the art of the short story are unlikely to be affected by these changes. Whether and how they will affect the future state of the art remains to be seen.

OLD BOYS, YOUNG BUCKS, AND NEW WOMEN: THE CONTEMPORARY IRISH SHORT STORY

Robert Hogan

An intelligent common reader might plausibly turn to dozens, even hundreds, of modern Irish short stories whose authors have been greatly lauded by critics in Ireland and even abroad. But if that common reader persisted and read through those dozens, or even hundreds of stories, he would stagger away with an overall feeling of intolerable depression and dreariness. The reason is that perhaps 95 percent of those stories would deal with personal relations and the individual psyche, rather than with any broad social or public concern; perhaps 96 percent of them would be grimly serious, rather than comic or satiric or whimsical; and perhaps 97 percent of them would finally end in failure, futility, fatality, meanness, madness, misery or a wide variety of appalling and fertile beastliness.

In the nineteenth century, Charles Lever had popularized the fable of the dashing and rollicking Irish blade and buck; Samuel Lover had popularized the cliché of the amiable and gormless *bosthoon* and *omadhaun*; and Dion Boucicault had set the pattern for the witty and sentimental rogue and *shaughraun*. But, although the Irish themselves took Harry Lorrequer and Handy Andy and Myles na Gopaleen to their hearts, they also realized that such portraits had but a tenuous relation to reality and were mainly for export to England and America.

In the first years of this century, George Moore and James Joyce set a different, a much more critical and condemnatory, pattern. There might still flourish an isolated, sometimes sunny soul like James Stephens, but the estimable lightheartedness of George A. Birmingham or Somerville and Ross could now only appear the negligible stuff of middle-brow entertainments.

In fiction, the second generation of modern Irish writers is usually preeminently represented by O'Flaherty, O'Faolain and O'Connor. These writers wrote of an Ireland still under the darkling shades of an old patriotism. Whenever their then obscure contemporary, Samuel Beckett, was forced to return to the island, he was apparently instantly stricken down by an utterly debilitating psychosomatic illness. Indeed, Ireland from the 1920s through the 1950s might well be summed up by a remark of Beckett—not directly aimed at Ireland, but it well could have been:

What constitutes the charm of our country, apart of course from its scant population, and this without help of the meanest contraceptive, is that all is derelict, with the sole exception of history's ancient faeces. These are ardently sought after, stuffed and carried in procession. Wherever nauseated time has dropped a nice fat turd you will find our patriots sniffing it up on all fours, their faces on fire.

And there also, irresistibly if reluctantly drawn, will be found the best writers of De Valera's Ireland.

The best writers of this time—among whom one must include O'Casey and Johnston the dramatists, Clarke and Kavanagh the poets, and O'Duffy and Wall the satirists—could never escape the worst symptoms of the time. De Valera's Irishman had been inoculated by an idealism that was insular and a republicanism that was rabid; he had been hobbled by his prelates' puritanism and by his hierarchy's Jansenistic jeremiads; he had been bullied and contemputously deluded by paternalistic politicians whose main virtue was that they were, by a short head, more inept than they were venal. Many of the best writers of the time escaped, sometimes permanently, from the country; but none of them could escape from the debilitating aesthetic effects of their country on their art.

The best writers of De Valera's Ireland continued the Moore-Joycean tradition of criticism with a decidedly pessimistic tinge. The best post-1950 writers—say, the third-generation moderns—have retained and even deepened the pessimism, but it has been more inner-directed. There were still writers who wrote of the past and its traditional values. Walter Macken wrote of rural Galway; Seamus de Faoite and John B. Keane wrote of rural Kerry; the Americans, Robert Bernen and Anthony Glavin, went to live in the Blue Stacks in Donegal and described the old ways that lingered on there. But the more characteristic writers, at first James Plunkett and William Trevor, more recently Desmond Hogan and Neil Jordan, simply piled up examples of the modern Irishman's psychic malaise. The liberated new women writers, of whom there have been many, wrote mainly the female equivalent of what the men were doing.

A prime reason is doubtless that the new writer lives in a really new Ireland. Since the Lemass government began to attract money into the country, both the face and the mind of the country have been quickly transformed. Uncensorable British television, Japanese motor cars, French bikinis, American Burger Kings, and movies about grease and hair and James Bond and Kung Fu and intergalactic battles all gave rise to the homogenous modernity of the postwar Western world. But, around the beginning of the 1980s, when the new desires had hardened, the money began to dry up. Inflation outpaced the pocketbook; unemployment rose; the national debt zoomed overnight to twelve billion pounds as the government borrowed from foreign banks to finance its day-to-day expenses. Ireland, economically and spiritually, was in hock. Bank robberies increased, and so did murders, and so did that once incredibly rare phenomenon, rape. The Irishman had become the modern man, but the modern man's desires were now almost unattainable. And the characteristic writers reacted, not by asking why, but by delineating their moaning.

Apart from the voluminous work of Yeatsians and Joyceans, who are mainly foreigners and mainly unread by the common reader, there has been little effectual criticism of modern Irish literature. There is considerable interest in writing, but the debut of a wretched writer may be greeted with the same orgiastic laudations as the debut of a good one.

For forty years or more, the great arbiter, and the great standard, of literary taste in Ireland was Yeats. And he was formidable enough to be the cause of some admirable minor dissentients—A. E., Susan Mitchell, Ernest Boyd, W. J. Lawrence, Con Curran, even the impossible Daniel Corkery. Since Yeats's death, however, the standard of criticism has almost totally collapsed and may be symptomatically gauged by the recent (28 January 1982) presentation of a bust of a journalistic ballet critic to the Irish Ballet Company.

What determination of literary taste exists is really in a few hands. Theatrical taste is determined by the coterie of aging civil servants, actors, set designers and professors of economics who run the Abbey Theatre, and by one or two imitative professional entrepreneurs. Poetical taste is determined by whom Liam Miller publishes in his Dolmen Press, and by the poets who review and publish each other in one or two small presses or journals. Prose fictional taste is, at least in the proliferating short story, determined by David Marcus, of whom more presently. Perhaps the brightest spots are that English Old Boy reviewing has not made much of an impact, and that American academic criticism is only just beginning to be felt.

David Marcus deserves an honorary degree from one of the nation's universities. He has become as distinguished a literary editor as Arthur Griffith, A. E., Seamus O'Sullivan, or Sean O'Faolain; and he, more than anyone else, is responsible for reinvigorating the Irish short story in our day. He was born

in Cork city in 1924; he has been a novelist, and he has published a translation of Merriman's *The Midnight Court.* His great impact, however, has been
as an editor—first of the fine literary magazine *Irish Writing,* then of *Poetry
Ireland,* and now of the publishing house the Poolbeg Press. Also, in 1968,
Marcus became literary editor of the *Irish Press* and inaugurated the New Irish
Writing page which each week publishes some new poems and a new story
or two. This page in a national newspaper gave enormous impetus to the
short story, for before it there were very few places in which a short story
writer, unless quite established, could publish. Since then Marcus has published many anthologies of short stories, and since 1976 his Poolbeg Press
has brought out many collections of established writers and of new people
who have been developed by his New Irish Writing page. What Marcus has
done, more than anyone else, is to develop writers and to create an audience.
What he has not quite done, except by the example of what he himself
generally publishes, is to establish standards.

·   ·   ·

Any discussion of the postwar short story must start with Samuel Beckett. Then
it must start over again.

Beckett's thematic stance seems to have changed little from his earliest work
to his latest. In *Murphy* of 1938, he wrote:

All this was duly revolting to Murphy, whose experience as a physical and rational
being obliged him to call sanctuary what the psychiatrists called exile and to think
of the patients not as banished from a system of benefits but as escaped from a
colossal fiasco.

In *Company* of 1979, he wrote:

Then on from nought anew. Huddled thus you find yourself imagining you are not
alone while knowing full well that nothing has occurred to make this possible. The
process continues none the less lapped as it were in its meaninglessness.

What has changed somewhat in Beckett is his aesthetic stance. An early
novel like *Murphy* or *Watt* or the collection of early stories, *More Pricks Than
Kicks,* is already recognizably Beckettian; but the plots still have dramatized
incidents, the characters are not entirely divorced from the Dickensian, and
the twists of phrase are capable of making you laugh. There is a fertility of
comic invention which is bleak but not entirely muted. The early Beckett is
eccentric, but not so outré as to function entirely unconventionally. Thus,
the stories in *More Pricks Than Kicks,* which are chronologically outside the
period of this discussion, are the ones that more closely approach function-

ing traditionally, that are the most easily apprehensible, and that the common reader is going to value most.

Beckett's middle period, after the war, produced his best-known writing—*Waiting for Godot, Endgame, Molloy,* and *Malone Dies.* It also produced short fictions like "First Love," "The Expelled," "The Calmative" and "The End," which really seem preliminary attempts at the famous, longer works. In this period, Beckett seems more purposefully to make the aesthetic punishment fit the crime of reality. The situations are bizarre, but the drama is more minimized, and the always lucid prose begins dully to undercut the fancy. In such plays as *Godot* or such novels as *Molloy,* not much happens twice. Thus, the reader's response is purposely dimmed; he is asked not so much for empathy as dimpathy. Still, there are brilliant comic moments, such as the sucking stones episode in *Molloy* where boredom is raised to a high comic pitch. There are still enough flashes in the long works and even in the short fictions for the common reader to receive, at lengthening intervals, dramatic comic jolts. In "First Love," for instance: "She began stroking my ankles. I considered kicking her in the cunt." Or in "The End":

> What he called his cabin in the mountains was a sort of wooden shed. The door had been removed, for firewood, or for some other purpose. The glass had disappeared from the window. The roof had fallen in at several places. The interior was divided, by the remains of a partition, into two unequal parts. If there had been any furniture it was gone. The vilest acts had been committed on the ground and against the walls. The floor was strewn with excrements, both human and animal, with condoms and vomit. In a cowpad a heart had been traced, pierced by an arrow. And yet there was nothing to attract tourists. I noticed the remains of abandoned nosegays.

In his most recent phase, Beckett has gone yet further in making the punishment fit the crime, and the aesthetic form fit the subject. In his late, increasingly briefer works, such as the "dramaticule" called *Come and Go* or the forty-five-second play called *Breath,* he accomplishes a kind of dramatic stasis. The action becomes a circular rumination, the characters scarcely exist, the prose deflates itself to a repetititve ritual, and the reader is pushed in shorter and shorter time to an exacerbated boredom which verges, at its most successful, on hysteria. Short fictions, such as "All Strange Away" or *Company,* both of 1979, consummately embody this technique.

By traditional literary standards, what Beckett is so successfully doing is a perverse dead end; and one is only astonished that he can so continually find ever more aesthetically deadening variations. For writers of short fiction, his technique is as unutilizable as Synge's or O'Casey's dialogue; and there has been little close emulation of Beckett in modern Irish fiction—principally Alf Mac Lochlainn's 1977 novella *Out of Focus,* and a few short squibs by Tom MacIntyre.

There are, however, Irish echoes throughout Beckett's work. As one critic has remarked elsewhere, "There are so many Irish overtones, faint Irish allusions, and Irish words and turns of speech, that the bleak Beckett landscape seems to be the Irish landscape after someone had dropped an H-bomb on it." In one significant way, therefore, Beckett remains the quintessential postwar Irish writer, and that is in his apathetic disgust toward the world. That attitude has been to the modern Irish storywriter, whether consciously or unconsciously, a pervasive influence; and much modern Irish fiction is but a conventional embodiment of a Beckettian theme.

• • •

The somewhat flip title of this essay is an attempt to impose some faint organization on the voluminous amount of short fiction written during the last thirty years. If even that attempt seems too arbitrary, it might be added that the writers grouped together as "old boys" share two qualities in common. They generally established themselves in the 1950s, and they look back to the themes and techniques that O'Connor, O'Faolain, and O'Flaherty had consolidated in the 1920s and 1930s and 1940s.

An exception is Anthony C. West who is not to be confused with the British novelist Anthony West with whom he has little in common. Anthony C. West was born in 1910 in County Down where he spent the first twenty years of his life and which gave him the material for most of his work. After some years in America, he served in the R.A.F. during World War II, and has since lived with his large family in North Wales.

West is a writer of such extraordinary talent that his work, while never receiving broad public approbation, has certainly overwhelmed some of his critics. Sean O'Faolain has written of him, "We must hold our breath in the presence of one of the most tremblingly sensitive imaginations that has yet ventured into the jungle of Irish life." The critic John Wilson Foster has called him "the most fertile and imaginative writer the North has produced since Carleton." *Esquire,* which in its distinguished past counted Hemingway and Fitzgerald among its contributors, thought his "River's End" to be one of "the greatest stories in its history." His poetic prose has reminded other commentators of Dylan Thomas's *A Child's Christmas in Wales*; and it seems to suggest, at its most Westian, the prose of Faulkner and the poetry of Hopkins. Among modern Irish prose writers, only Juanita Casey approaches and Christy Brown rivals West in the pursuit of eloquence.

Despite all of this, West seems a deeply flawed and a profoundly amateurish writer; and, curiously, his deepest flaw and his profoundest amateurism derive from his seemingly greatest strength—his prose. To a powerful, lushly evocative, and thickly poetic prose style, West sacrifices every other major component of storytelling—plot, theme, and character. Like Faulkner occasionally or Thomas Wolfe usually, he writes prose that diminishes, even just flattens, everything else.

This quite individual prose contains a high proportion of outré words, such as: scraffled, ginned, ferine, fulgor, lacery, gurge, glar, bouting, meniscus, freckened, coenobium, morkin, queachy, brumbles, bearden, caol. Some of West's words, like "progging," are defensibly local-colorish; and some others, like "sub-lacustrine," are just giddily pedantic; but none of the list above is to be found in the *Penguin English Dictionary* of eight hundred closely printed pages.

West is also fond of yoking words unusually together. For instance: boy-free, scorn-pity, breast-valley, lust-longing, life-lust, life-warmth, death-crunch, Eve-greed, rut-drowsed, death-indifferent, sap-sour, trundle-song, shadow-savoured, flow-moved. Sometimes this makes him sound like Hopkins, and sometimes like the author of *Beowulf,* but always it makes him sound mannered. Consider this particularly Hopkinsish passage:

And the bird, broken but unbroken, ruined but quite perfect still, sits there and inwardly disdains the torture, knowing the pain of the upper air's rafale, the limp wingtip trailing, the unblinking eyes, the hauty hawk-lord hateless facebeauty without plea for better death: wings, scimitars of skill, once close as love to winds' unseen tumble-fall and steep rake, bragging stoop, swoop, twist and tight spiral in sun-turned air.

West's most individual mannerisms, though, are strangely akin to the phrasings of the most tiredly romantic female fiction. For instance: her proud young breasts; the rich cupboard of her maidenhood; the aisles of evening when every bird held up its torch of song; Passion's solitary marker on the dull plate of memory; the panorama of summer's mature beauty; night was a maiden queen upon a throne of ebony; crystalled by star-shine; the twin flames of our lives flickering round the dusty doorsteps of night and day; the hallowed crucible of my years; the moonlit fields of life-love and heart-intimacy; the thick mysterious nights of moon-brewed perfumes; when passion blows his trumpet on the hills; the breast of the scented meadow; spring's proud, restless satiety—and innumerably more.

Add to these characteristics the personifications, the Homeric echoes, the occasional self-conscious alliterations. Add also the casualness of punctuation and the casual use of pronouns ("Each evening I shut up my ducks and on fine ones I would sit on the wall . . .") And finally the prose-clotting imagery:

> Her heels caught up on the stool's worn rung, thighs foreshortened by her pose as if she knelt upon her heels, barelegged and cool on moist grass in tree shadow [she is actually in a classroom] or a prow's profile gliding forward on sun's great incandescent waves, poised above a sea emotionlessly; a galleon's prow laden with fantastic treasure bound surely for a shore that waited for the gentle give and take of tide.

Against these faults one would wish to set an example of real eloquence, for one can read hardly a page of West without becoming aware that such acute arousal of emotion is the author's nearly constant intention. Yet, really not one passage is undebilitated by some of the above faults. Everything is tinnier than Donn Byrne, hollower than Vivian Connell; everything is undercut by spurious taste, poor models and unbridled romanticism.

In his many attempts to evoke the Ulster countryside of his youth, West would seem to be more outward-looking than his contemporaries. But he so sensuously wallows in that landscape that it becomes less a photograph of land than a portrayal of his own reactions. He is always individual, always romantic, and always quirky. In perhaps the most emotionally drenched of his stories, "The Turning Page," the protagonist mourns more for the loss of his duck than for the loss of his girl. And then one remembers Jane, the hero's duck, in the novel *As Towns with Fire,* and the hero's ferret in the novel *The Ferret Fancier*—and one becomes ever more conscious of the strange and finally private world of this greatly aspiring, yet greatly flawed writer.

Terence de Vere White was born in Dublin in 1912. He matriculated from Trinity with a B.A. and an Ll.B., and then entered a legal firm in Dublin. After publishing several books, however, he resigned in 1962 to become literary editor of the *Irish Times,* a post he held until 1977. White is a prolific writer who has published a pleasant autobiography, several chatty biographies, some travel books, a volume on the Anglo-Irish, about a dozen novels, a couple of collections of short stories, and hundreds of urbane book reviews.

He is well-read, cultured, entertaining, and a dedicated worker who has done something for the improvement of literary taste in Ireland. Nevertheless, one critic, Martin Ryan, has written of him: "White holds a minor place in Irish letters. In future years, his works will likely appeal more to the social or literary historian than to the general reader." And unfortunately with this judgment one must agree. In White's subjects and ideas, there is a promise of wit which is seldom fulfilled. His novels, perhaps even more than his stories, have contemporary subjects that seem to demand an infusion of high comedy or at least satire; however, White's treatment tends to be bland, dull, and undramatized. His stories, such as the often anthologized "Desert Island," are sometimes told at a Conradian distance from the drama. A curious number of stories takes place at lunch or dinner—among them, "After School," "Lunch with Tom," "Bang," "Fair Exchange," and "Caesar's Platter"—and basically in such stories we get a conversation rather than an action. In such stories, and in a piece about neighborhood gossip, "Miss Collins," the quality of the dialogue is of paramount importance. But here, for instance, is an exchange from "Miss Collins":

> "You met her out in Canada?"
> "What say?"
> "I said, *you met her out in Canada?*"
> "I wonder what gave you that idea. We met on a Swan cruise to Greece. You know them? They bring professors along to lecture. Trouble is, I can't hear half they say."
> "Was that long ago?"
> "Long ago?"
> "Long ago—since you met Miss Collins?"
> "Don't ask me. Time rushes by so fast."

This is not champagne but flat beer; savorless, phlegmatic stuff.

Nevertheless, in descriptive and narrative passages, White sometimes rises to a witty and engaging sentence. For instance:

Tom has the fragmented beauty of a recently excavated and unidentifiable god.

Even after she lost the appearance of a recently startled hen, there was about her a humble awareness of insufficiency.

Overheard, the conversation would have recalled early intercourse between Robinson Crusoe and Man Friday.

These examples are all from the volume of stories, *Big Fleas and Little Fleas*; and they are the best and indeed probably the only examples to be found in the 158 pages. Any random page of Julia O'Faolain will exhibit one or two wittier comparisons.

Wit, if we are to take Congreve and Sheridan and Wilde and Shaw as our touchstones, does not entirely depend upon striking diction and startling comparisons; it also depends upon the tightly controlled form of a sentence, that more often than not leans strongly on balance, parallelism, and antithesis. Not only are these qualities quite missing in White, but actually a high proportion of his sentences contains matter interpolated between double dashes or parentheses.

What one can say affirmatively about White is that he conscientiously applies the manner of William Trevor to a Shavian subject. The ebullient Shaw would have dazzled us with sparkling fireworks; the pessimistic White sheds a gray light from a guttering candle.

Walter Macken was born in Galway in 1915 and died there in 1967. He was a play director for the Galway Gaelic Theatre, the Taibhdearc, and toward the end of his life the artistic director of the Abbey. He was an actor for the Abbey as well, and also appeared in films and on Broadway. He was an effective playwright in Irish and in English; but, above all, he was a forceful novelist and short story writer.

Much of his widely read fiction remains in print. His finest achievement he considered to be an historical trilogy comprising *Seek the Fair Land* set in Cromwellian Ireland, *The Silent People* about the Great Famine, and *The Searching Wind* about the Easter Rising. To my mind, however, his best work is in the novels, *Rain on the Wind* and *The Bog Man*.

His several volumes of stories are more diverse in tone and manner than his longer and mainly serious fictions, but the short work equally reflects his varying merit.

His subject matter, however, is constant, and it is the depiction of country life in the West. He wrote of farmers and fishermen, poachers and priests and small shopkeepers. These people live by mountains and bogs, by cliffs and strands, in tiny villages or on islands. Like his Galway neighbor, Michael Molloy (in whose masterly *The King of Friday's Men* he took the leading role), he wrote of a fast-fading Ireland, in which entrenched customs and even superstitions die slowly. His people cling to ancient attitudes about birth and love and marriage and death and land and honor. Unlike the modern city dweller, they have a respect born of knowledge and love and legitimate fear about nature, which they cannot change, ignore, or control. Indeed, they are a part of it, and so they have a gentle kindness for and empathy with dogs and cows and sheep. They take a droll delight in pranks; they believe in poetic justice according to their own lights; they have a startling propensity for brutality. They are, in short, a nostalgic anachronism.

Macken recreates this world in the most traditional manner of the storyteller, at best like Maupassant and at worst like O. Henry. His stories are not post-Joycean or Lawrencian or Woolfian. They are strongly plotted, social, and extraverted; and they are written in a muscular, unfussy prose. Too often, though, realism gets engulfed by romance; and then Macken writes of brawny giants who could lift you above their heads and throw you six feet.

Such entertainments will keep Macken as popular in Ireland as Canon Shee-han or Charles Kickham or Donn Byrne or George A. Birmingham; but his merits could be both distinctly better and considerably worse. At his most usual, he was a middlebrow popular entertainer like the delightful Birming-ham and Walsh. At his occasional worst, he could be as false as Donn Byrne and as jocularly folksy as John B. Keane at his more journalistic. But at his occasional best, he has written stories that will stand up to the work of George Moore or Frank O'Connor. Because of his popularity, and his occa-sional real dreadfulness, and his avoidance of modern Ireland as a subject, Macken is not really considered much of an artist. Yet from his best stories, one might compile a short volume of solid accomplishment that would show his traditional virtues of clear writing and strong plotting to be a deal more satisfying than much of the more sophisticated stuff by his cleverer successors.

James Plunkett was born James Plunkett Kelly in Dublin in 1920. His stories appeared in Sean O'Faolain's magazine, the *Bell,* in the early 1950s and were collected in a volume called *The Trusting and the Maimed* in 1955. This was such an impressive collection that Plunkett was generally seen as the most important successor to O'Flaherty, O'Faolain, and O'Connor. However, other than a handful of fugitive stories, some radio plays and a play about the labor leader, Jim Larkin, there was no new work of substance until 1969. Then a long novel, *Strumpet City,* appeared and became something of a best-seller in Ireland, England, and America; it was followed in 1977 by a sequel called *Farewell Companions.* Also in 1977 a *Collected Stories,* containing the pieces in his first volume and a few later ones, was published in paper-back in Dublin.

It is unusual for an Irish novelist to have anything like an international success, but Plunkett's novels are, despite their popularity, only a disappoint-ing fulfillment of the promise of his early stories. The novels are good reads, but, after the controlled artistry of many of the stories, the novels seem little more than seriocomic entertainments on no more than a Book-of-the-Month Club or even a Literary Guild level.

Plunkett's stories are not, of course, all of a piece, but they maintain a generally high level of excellence, and several must be ranked among the finest Irish achievements in the genre. Oustanding among these is "A Walk Through the Summer," which on a narrative level tells how a young folk-song collector becomes hobbled with probably the most repulsive and ob-noxious blind man in modern fiction, and takes him to a musical evening at the home of a well-to-do friend with whose wife he is planning to spend the weekend. The blind man becomes drunk, vomits, and to the young Polish girl who cleans up his mess, makes boorish remarks about the staunchness of his Catholicism and the fecklessness of hers. A young friend of the folk-song collector, who has tagged along, succeeds in touching the well-to-do husband for ten pounds. When everyone prepares to leave, a distinguished professor, sodden with drink, cannot be found; and so the other two guests, a shallow businessman and his wife who were to give him a lift, leave without him. The folk-song collector borrows a car, takes the blind man home, and gives him his bed. He himself decides not to pursue the affair with the rich wife and goes to spend the rest of the night in the car. In the back seat he finds the drunken professor, and they settle down to sleep as the sun comes up.

Told baldly, this seems a pointless narrative, but onto it Plunkett grafts a subtle, almost allegorical summation of Irish society in the 1950s; it seems—in its rightness of detail, in its inventiveness of situation, and even in the Joycean reminiscences of the dialogue between Casey and Ellis—a story fit to rank with "The Dead."

The best of Plunkett's other stories present a telling recreation of the narrow and depressing Irish society of the 1950s—a time of public puritanism and personal hopelessness, a time in which jobs offered only a precarious existence and little future, a time in which marriage was virtually impossible for the young, and in which drink was one of the few anodynes for frustration. Occasionally, as in "The Trusting and the Maimed" and "The Wearin' of the Green," Plunkett underscores his point by an ending that is overly ironic and needlessly melodramatic, when his points about personal desperation and Jansenistic morality had been made so well that they needed no such underscoring. Occasionally in pieces like "The Trusting and the Maimed" and "The Trout," he is a little too academic in his manipulation of the symbolic. But he is also capable, as in "The Half Crown," of a depiction of tongue-tied, surly, suffering adolescence that is impeccably done and unforgettable. And he is capable, as in "The Scoop" or "The Plain People," of embodying his condemnation of the 1950s in comedy that only at the very end becomes mordant.

One might easily hazard a guess about what happened to James Plunkett, for it has happened to others of his generation, men who began brilliantly and then became less than they should have. But perhaps the best thing to say is the most general: the 1950s saw the culmination of everything that was most awful in De Valera's Ireland; but the 1960s and 1970s, with their outward-looking and transitory affluence, had an effect upon artists that was finally more devastating, subtle, and insidious to combat. Perhaps, finally, it was impossible to combat. In any event, the career of James Plunkett, who began aloof, paring his fingernails, and who ended in the marketplace, may well embody something of Ireland's own change.

Aidan Higgins was born in County Kildare in 1927 and came to international attention with his first book, a volume of stories published in 1960 as *Felo de Se* and subsequently reissued as *Killachter Meadow* and *Asylum.* This book was followed by four novels and a travel diary about Africa. His work has been much translated and has won many prizes, including the James Tait Black Award.

From his first book, Higgins has spoken in a distinctive voice, and most critics have noted his individual style and his somewhat experimental technique. What has possibly not been noticed is his thematic affinity with Beckett. The reason may be that Higgins keeps one foot fairly firmly embedded in reality, and thus he stands about halfway between Beckett and such conventional realists as William Trevor, John McGahern, or the novelist John Broderick. What all these writers share in common, however, is a glumly, darkly pessimistic view. Higgins's characters, whether they live in Ireland, England, or the Continent, inhabit a grayly depressing Beckettian milieu. The notable difference is that, instead of living by a Beckettian withered tree or in a compost heap, Higgins's characters inhabit a realistic landscape. Nevertheless, they regard it Beckettianly. When day breaks, it breaks "wretchedly." Places give off "a succession of offensive cold-surface smells: an unforgettable blend of rotting newspaper, iodine, mackintosh, cat." City dwellers live in hovels among "slush and fog," and their mornings are

fouled with countless impurities, the air thick and lichenous, full of ice and soot. A rank-smelling pillar of cloud extended into the atmosphere for a mile above Greater London. A dead night wind was blowing from Acton Town . . . intermingled with the reek coming from . . .

Even when people go to the beach, they descend upon it "with the measured tramp of the damned." Such people can only, "at the bottom of the earth, among the used tickets and grease . . . stir a little, broken up, beyond hope, mutilated." They inhabit a "world loathsome beyond words, from root to flower."

Of such a lugubrious prospect, Higgins can sometimes write with a bleak wit: a pianist will "hit the keys as though he detested them all"; an antique dealer will run his "small not remunerative business hard by the hospital in a fashion that carried vagueness to the point of amnesia." However, Higgins's style is mainly made distinctive by a penchant for quoting German and by a penchant for rare words—sebaceous, pyknic, crenels, pleurae, skéne, aphesis, rufous, frass, quassia, lammergeyer, faience, silicified, and so on.

His reputation for experimentation is probably due less to fancy about his matter or gimmicks in his manner than to one or two minor affectations and one major predilection. For instance, in a minor way, he uses the Joycean initial dash, rather than quote marks, to indicate dialogue. In a major way, however, he minimizes plot. Stories such as "Lebensraum" or "Tower and Angels" or "Killachter Meadow" are combinations of character sketches and illustrative essays about attitudes or situations. When he does have a narrative, as in the long "Asylum," it is not really a plot, but a temporal succession of incidents whose proportions are difficult to defend. When Higgins verges toward plot at the end, he seems to omit the essential portions of it.

There is a good deal of the precious in Aidan Higgins, probably too much for him to overcome. However, in his best short pieces, "Killachter Meadow" and "Asylum," his talent is certainly evident. And a foppishness about form and style, when allied to a grimness about content, is interestingly distinctive, no matter how unsatisfactory.

Of the small handful of modern fiction writers who have established a considerable reputation outside of Ireland, William Trevor must be among the most highly regarded. He received the Hawthornden Prize in 1964 for his novel *The Old Boys,* the Royal Society of Literature award in 1975 for his story collection called *Angels at the Ritz,* the Allied Irish Banks Award for Services to Irish Literature in 1976, and the Whitbread Literary Award also in 1976 for his novel called *The Children of Dynmouth.* He was awarded a C.B.E. by Britain in 1977 for his services to literature, and he is a member of the Irish Academy of Letters.

Born William Trevor Cox in County Cork in 1928, he studied at Trinity College, Dublin, became a sculptor before turning to writing, and now lives in Devon. Although he has written stage plays and plays for television and radio, his best work is in the novel and the short story. Much of this work is set in England, but perhaps a third of it occurs in Ireland or concerns Irish people.

Although Trevor seems at his best in depicting the small-town lives of clerks, teachers, and shopkeepers, he writes well of children, of university students, of farmers and of the elderly Anglo-Irish, as well as of the Irish in Britain and the Irish on vacation. But, no matter what the social milieu, he writes with precise, authentic detail; and he does not mind halting his narrative to describe. For instance, from "The Raising of Elvira Tremlett":

We lived in a house next door to the garage, two storeys of cement that had a damp look, with green window-sashes and a green hall-door. Inside, a wealth of polished brown linoleum, its pattern faded to nothing, was cheered here and there by the rugs my mother bought in Roche's Stores in Cork. The votive light of a crimson Sacred Heart gleamed day and night in the hall. Christ blessed us halfway up the stairs; on the landing the Virgin Mary was coy in garish robes. On either side of a narrow trodden carpet the staircase had been grained to make it seem like oak. In the dining-room, never used, there was a square table with six rexine-seated chairs around it, and over the mantlepiece a mirror with chromium decoration. The sitting-room smelt of must and had a picture of the Pope.

There is nothing striking about this typical passage other than its solidness— that is, its conventionality, its clarity, its rightness. And a solid conventionality, even in his occasional ghost stories, is what may be expected from William Trevor. If he does not always tell a story, he at least presents a dramatized situation in which his main characters are caught at some climactic and painful moment. If the characters do not always realize their plight or its point, the reader certainly does, and the reader's response is frequently powerful and rarely less than disturbing. Trevor's stories may lack excitement in style or narrative technique; they may even lack much sense of auctorial individuality, for Trevor usually remains detached. What they never lack, however, is a worthy craftsmanship. There is an impressive and growing bulk of stories from Trevor; and it is both inevitable and right that they have been collected in a fat Penguin that fills an honorable place on one's shelves beside the volumes of O'Connor, O'Faolain, Bowen, and Lavin.

What limits Trevor is also what binds all his work together, and this is that occupational hazard of Irish writers of his generation, a pervasively dreary attitude toward contemporary life. And, as he adds a new volume of stories each three years, few major facets of life now escape his increasingly comprehensive moroseness. Indeed, he has become so morose about so much, that his comment has expanded into a condemnation. In "Mr. McNamara," a character remarks of Ireland, "The whole country had ivy growing over it . . . like ivy on a gravestone." One typical Trevor story, "The Time of Year," ends with this:

> In the garden of the hall of residence the fallen leaves were sodden beneath her feet as she crossed a lawn to shorten her journey. The bewilderment she felt lifted a little. She had been wrong to imagine she envied other people their normality and good fortune. She was as she wished to be. She paused in faint moonlight, repeating that to herself and then repeating it again. She did not quite add that the tragedy had made her what she was, that without it she would not possess her reflective introspection, or be sensitive to more than just the time of year. But the thought hovered with her as she moved towards the lights of the house, offering what appeared to be a hint of comfort.

Note that it is not "comfort," but a "hint of comfort." Note too that it only "appeared to be a hint of comfort."

In a Trevor story, that possibility of a hint of comfort, that qualification upon qualification, is the very most that his characters can expect—any of his characters, no matter what their age or state.

For instance, in "Miss Smith," a baby is maliciously and probably hideously killed by a fiendish schoolboy. In "The Death of Peggy Morrissey," a boy kills a girl in his daydreams and then she actually dies. The fifteen-year-old boy in "An Evening with John Joe Dempsey" is urged to give up his one close friendship, which is with the town's crazed, sex-obsessed dwarf; so the boy replaces friendship by going to bed: "In his bed he entered a paradise; it was grand being alone." In "The Raising of Elvira Tremlett," the schoolboy winds up in an insane asylum. "School," we are told in "Mr. McNamara," was "ordinarily dreary."

Marriage offers little hope either. In "Teresa's Wedding," the bride "felt that she and Artie might make some kind of marriage together because there was nothing that could be destroyed, no magic or anything else. . . . there was nothing special about the occasion." The thirty-six-year-old Bridie in "The Ballroom of Romance" decides to settle for the "lazy and useless" Bowser Egan, whenever his mother and her father die; but she decides to marry him only "because it would be lonesome being by herself in the farmhouse." In "Attracta," the young wife's husband is killed by the I.R.A., and his head is sent to her in the mail, "secured within a plastic bag and packed in a biscuit tin." Later, after the wife has joined the Women's Peace Movement as a kind of testimonial to her dead husband, she is raped by seven men. She then commits suicide, and when she is discovered four days later, "mice had left droppings on her body."

Family life is little better. Husbands kiss servant girls, and wives are ashamed of their husbands and themselves. Parents are uninterested in their children in "The Death of Peggy Morrissey." Children hate their fathers in "A Choice of Butchers" and "Mr. McNamara." They hate their guardians in "Memories of Youghal." There is incest in "The Raising of Elvira Tremlett."

The upperclasses get their unjust deserts, and servants get what is coming to them, except money. In "The Distant Past," a small town turns against an aged, now impoverished Anglo-Irish couple, and Trevor reflects that "because of the distant past they would die friendless. It was worse than being murdered in their beds." In "Last Wishes," some contented servants lose their places because their mistress has died before signing a codicil to her will, and Trevor reflects, "And yet it seemed cruelly fitting that the loss of so much should wreak such damage in pleasant, harmless people"—certainly one of the more sadistic views that an author might take toward his characters.

Trevor's characters, no matter of what age, are physically unattractive. The little boy in "Miss Smith" looks like "a weasel wearing glasses." A university student looks like "an etiolated newt." The still youngish woman in "The Ballroom of Romance" has a browned, wind-toughened face; "her neck and nose were lean, her lips touched with early wrinkles." An aunt "had a grey look about her and was religious." Successful priests are fat, red-faced, and drunken; unsuccessful priests are "so thin you could hardly bear to look," and their flesh is "the colour of whitewash." Even dogs, if they are not old and blind and deaf, slouch "in a manner that was characteristic of the dogs of the town."

Houses are gray, riddled with woodworm, suffused with damp; their roofs leak, and their drains are clogged. Food is awful, for butchers sell tainted meat and even give short measure of it. In restaurants the soup has "quite large pieces of bone and gristle in it," and mashed turnips are inevitably the main vegetable. If a town has a ballroom, it is seedy; if it has a cinema, it is closed and "a ruin now."

Lovers are false. All professionals are venal. Teachers, for instance, are boring and arrogant, and their wives pusillanimous and pathetic, as in "The Time of Year" and "The Grass Widows." Postmen probably open letters. The weather is bad. Trees are "bleakly bare." . . . this catalogue could be considerably expanded.

But perhaps the point has been sufficiently made that, in every aspect of life that Trevor has discussed—whether great or small, momentous or trivial—there is no respite from the seedy, the sordid, the disillusioning, the depressing, the ghastly, and the horrible. In story after story, he relentlessly accumulates new examples of awfulness. He is like a phlegmatic Poe, and perhaps even more pernicious because no one ever takes Poe's romances seriously. To a Poe or a Hawthorne, or to a Monk Lewis or an Ann Radcliffe, horror was romantic or glamorous, or at least interestingly odd. To Trevor, however, horror is the dull, realistic stuff of everyday life; and in his low-keyed, businesslike fashion he quietly proceeds, story by story, to transform the entirety of modern life into a gray, dank, commonplace asylum.

Amazingly, some critics have compared Trevor to Dickens, but no Dickens could have written of Christmas as dismally as has Trevor in "The Time of Year" and "Another Christmas." Astonishingly, some critics have commented upon Trevor's humor; but what sounded to them as laughter strikes this commentator as a death rattle.

Yet Trevor is steadily prolific and always careful of his technique; because of his application and his solid virtues, he will continue to be read and admired by perceptive and depressed people. Such readers, if they are Irish, could hardly fail to be depressed by their world; yet they may mistake pessimism for tragedy and glumness for the entirety of truth. Still, no one could deny that William Trevor is a consummate, understated symptom of the malaise of Ireland and of our time. If he were to write a "Christmas Carol," his Tiny Tim would say—softly but definitely—"God damn us, everyone."

John B. Keane has not nearly the command of technique of Trevor, but it is a distinct relief to turn to him. Keane was born in 1928 in North Kerry, in an area that gave Ireland a very popular writer in Maurice Walsh and a once popular one in George Fitzmaurice. Keane made his initial impact, like Fitzmaurice, as a folk dramatist, but he has gone on, in many plays, to dramatize various contemporary problems. A prolific writer, he has also published much humorous journalism, an autobiography, collections of poems, stories, and essays, as well as several epistolary novellas like *Letters of an Irish T. D.,* which contains the drollest satiric caricature of an Irish politician since the Eloquent Dempsy.

Because much of Keane's output has appeared in newspapers, because there is so much of it and it is so uneven, and because he has always determinedly retained his base in Kerry, he is probably considered more of a popular entertainer than an artist. Nevertheless, uneven as Keane's work has been, the best of it, in whatever genre, is of considerable merit.

A typical example of his short fiction is the small 1976 collection of eight stories, *Death Be Not Proud.* These stories, like all of Keane's, can be divided into those told by a distanced general observer and those told by an involved personal voice. In the first and less successful group, the language is simple and lean but flat and inexpressive. To note two telling symptoms, rarely will the author burden a noun with more than one adjective, and he is capable of writing a page with no more than two commas, as well as with occasional misspellings and mistakes in grammar. (This is not to single Keane out as a literary Tony Lumpkin; the current secretary, for instance, of the Irish Academy of Letters writes much more ungrammatically and is turgid to boot.) The richer stories are those, however, in which a personal narrative voice rings distinctly out. There, the combination of disengaged simplicity and faint awkwardness is entirely lost. For instance:

It was a fair year for primroses, a better one for hay and a woeful year for funerals.

The writing does not get more complicated, but it does get more vivid:

Through the yellow whins that stood out against the green hedges I could see his small fields, some still glinting sogginess in the height of summer.

That "glinting sogginess" is superb, as is also much of the dialogue.

Keane's stories are unpretentious in technique and small in scope. They always tell a tale and are mainly based on memories of a dying rural culture. But, if his culture is dying, Keane is at least, unlike Trevor, not having a wake over it. He has a humorous, observing eye and a riper voice than many of his contemporaries; and it would be an arrogant condescension to ignore these simple, straightforward pieces.

Brian Friel, the playwright, began his career as a quite successful short story writer. Born in January 1929 in County Tyrone, he became for ten years a teacher in Derry and wrote stories and plays in his spare time. Many of the stories appeared in the *New Yorker,* and Friel published two collections, *The Saucer of Larks* in 1962 and *The Gold in the Sea* in 1965. However, after the international stage success of his *Philadelphia, Here I Come!* Friel turned entirely away from fiction, and he has grown into probably the most important contemporary Irish dramatist.

Nevertheless, his early fiction has much merit. In subject and technique, he seems something of a rural, Northern O'Connor; and some of the stories of childhood seems very O'Connor-like indeed. Compare, for instance, "The First of My Sins" to O'Connor's "First Confession." Also like O'Connor, Friel wrote nearly as many comic stories as serious ones; however, many of the comic stories are tinged with ruefulness, and many of the serious ones contain even broadly comic moments. This blend of light and dark seems characteristic of Friel's best stories and contributes greatly to the success of "The Illusionists," "The Flower of Kiltymore," and "Ginger Hero." Friel is also knowledgeably evocative in set pieces like the salmon fishing of "The Gold in the Sea," the cock fight of "Ginger Hero," the pigeon racing of "The Widowhood System," or the water diviner searching for a drowned body in "The Diviner." Even more than O'Connor does he establish the details of a world. His second collection, *The Gold in the Sea,* must rank with Plunkett's *The Trusting and the Maimed* and Montague's *Death of a Chieftain* as the best work of the time; and "The Death of a Scientific Humanist" and "Ginger Hero" are among the finest of postwar stories.

Despite his accomplishment, Friel shows no sign of adding to his smallish number of stories. However, the extraordinary accomplishment of his recent plays, particularly in their technical inventiveness, so far outstrips his work in fiction, that one cannot feel Irish literature is in any way the loser.

John Montague, the poet, is nearly the same age as Friel and has a similar early background. Although born in Brooklyn in February 1929, he was raised in County Tyrone. Like Friel also, he has published a small number of impressive stories, but he has mainly devoted himself to another literary genre. With his seven or eight volumes of poems, he is generally considered to rank with Seamus Heaney and Thomas Kinsella as one of Ireland's most important contemporary poets.

I am no great admirer of Montague's poetry, but his 1964 volume of stories, *Death of a Chieftain,* contains some of the most important short fiction of its time. Like Friel, Montague writes of the rural North—in a childhood story like "The Oklahoma Kid" or a drinking story like "The New Enamel Bucket." These stories, like Friel's, seem caught in a traditional, unchanging past; Montague, however, also writes more broadly of society's problems and of contemporary events that disrupt the placid waters of the past. See, for instance, "The Cry," which predates the current northern violence, but accurately diagnoses its intractable background; or "A Change of Management," an eerily prophetic piece about the modernizing of Ireland.

One of Montague's best-known poems, "The Rough Field," discusses the North by juxtaposing certain significant recreations of the historical past. This same preoccupation is apparent in his rather Conradian title story which is set, surprisingly but effectively, in Central America.

When Friel abandoned the short story, he more than compensated by the remarkable achievement of his plays. My opinion of Montague's poetry is undoubtedly a current heresy, but it is no heresy to wish that he had given us two or three more volumes of impressive short fiction.

John Jordan was born in Dublin in 1930 and seems to have been, more perniciously than some of his generation, affected by his times. Certainly his three collections of poems and stories are disappointingly slim, and yet the quality of the stories is very fine. The stories appeared over a period of thirty years in various Irish periodicals, and were uncollected until 1977, in a volume of 109 pages entitled *Yarns.* This little book contains thirteen quite short pieces, all eminently readable, and two or three brilliantly capturing facets of Dublin in the 1950s. Among the best are "First Draft" and "Not Quite the Same" which memorably portray the pub crawls of the overripe Mrs. McMenamin and her male satellites. These and "Tango," a brittle and sad depiction of a gay party, are so fine that one really deplores the minimal output of this talented writer.

Patrick Boyle might appropriately be considered the last of the Old Guard, for his stories only began to appear as late as 1965 when the author was sixty years old. Nevertheless, the stories really look back to O'Faolain and particularly to O'Connor in their range of tone, in their variety of subject, and in their thoroughly dramatized and distanced control.

Born in 1905 in County Antrim, Boyle was more a contemporary of O'Flaherty, O'Connor, and O'Faolain than of White, Trevor, or Plunkett. However, most of his adult life he was not a writer. He worked for forty-five years in the Ulster Bank, and it was only after his retirement that he seriously and vigorously turned to writing. In 1965 he submitted pseudonymously fourteen stories to a contest sponsored by the *Irish Times,* and de Vere White later wrote, "When I came to look at the entries I found an extraordinary thing. The first, second, fourth, fifth had all been written by the one man, Patrick Boyle." As the judges of the contest were White, Mary Lavin, and Frank O'Connor, Boyle may certainly be said to have been launched with the approbation of the Old Guard.

In 1966 Boyle published a novel and followed it by three collections of stories: *At Night All Cats Are Grey,* also in 1966; *All Looks Yellow to the Jaundiced Eye* in 1969; and *A View from Calvary* in 1976. These three collections are remarkable for their mature accomplishment and their generally consistent excellence. Indeed, it is difficult to single out Boyle's best work, but such an attempt does bring a rather startled awareness of Boyle's diversity. One finds satiric farce in "Pastorale" or "In Adversity Be Ye Steadfast." Or something that borders on eccentric fantasy in "Dialogue." Or blackish comedy in "Interlude" and "Shaybo." Or rueful stories of childhood in "Age, I Do Abhor Thee"; of adolescence in "Sally"; of middle age in "The Rule of Three." The writing is ever fluent and sometimes admirable—see the comic description of singing in "Interlude" or the long, serious description of piano playing in "A View from Calvary." There is a gallery of quickly caught, memorable character types and stereotypes.

Boyle, of course, had his failures and his faults. The novella, "A View from Calvary," is too leisurely and too long; and "All Looks Yellow to the Jaundiced Eye" is too silly. But he has so many successes and so many excellences that he needed only to have started earlier to loom as large in importance as his most distinguished contemporaries. He died in February 1982.

• • •

The "young bucks" of this section are not all of them young in years, but most of them came to notice as short story writers in the middle 1970s, and some of them had lived through or reacted to the student unrest of the late 1960s. If one were to pick a year when one first became strongly conscious of a rather newer breed of writer than Plunkett, Trevor, and Boyle, 1976 would be a plausible choice. In that year a number of young writers formed a new publishing house, the Irish Writers' Co-operative, to publish the works of their members. Their first books were a novel and a collection of stories by two young men who were born in 1951, Desmond Hogan and Neil Jordan. And in the same year the newly formed Poolbeg Press brought out the first collection of a somewhat older but more accomplished writer, Gillman Noonan. It was an interesting year for fiction.

If there be notable differences between the old boys and the young men, it might partly reside not so much in a deepening gloom—for one could hardly be gloomier than Trevor—but in a more romantic view of gloom. It might also partly reside in a greater focus on the psyche of the speaker who is sometimes hardly distinguishable from the author. And it might partly reside in a greater slovenliness of, and perhaps even a contempt for, form; fortunately, there are some notable exceptions.

A semi-exception is Eugene McCabe who was born in Glasgow in 1930. He was educated at University College, Cork, and became for ten years a dairy farmer in County Monaghan. After the success of his play, *The King of the Castle,* which won the Irish Life Drama Award in 1964, he turned to writing and produced several other plays for the stage, considerable work for television, and a number of stories and novellas which he has sometimes dramatized. He writes with authenticity and strength of the modern North and its troubles; and his story "Cancer" and his novella "Heritage" have a persuasive and despairing sense of the intractable actuality that exists along the border of Ulster and the Republic.

McCabe's most impressive qualities are a firm sense of structure, an ability to draw truly and firmly etched character types, and a reliance on strong themes. His major fault lies in the ultrasimplicity of his prose. The diction is lean to gauntness; the syntax is inevitably simple; the sentences are almost invariably short. "She put a plate of beans on the table" is typical; and, whenever McCabe ventures beyond a three-line sentence, his sense of punctuation quite deserts him. Such prose is quickly, easily readable, especially when interspersed with much short, terse dialogue; but it is no medium for any but the simplest of presentations and the most blatant of statements. Perhaps it is McCabe's stage and television work that has fostered such compressed, bare statement; but the effect upon his fiction is to keep as melodrama what often should rise to tragedy. If such a writer took the tools of his trade as seriously as he took truthful observation, he might produce a work of art instead of a painful tract for the times.

Brian Power was born in 1930, has taken a master's degree in sociology from Boston University, and is a Roman Catholic priest who has been based in and about Dublin. He has published two collections of stories, *A Land Not Sown* in 1977 and *The Wild and Daring Sixties* in 1980. His stories usually reflect aspects of urban living of the 1960s and 1970s, and they cut across class lines, embracing both the poor and the well-off. They are written in various techniques and from different attitudes. That is, Power is capable of straightforward and depressing realism as in "Two Hundred Greeners," told from the view of an adolescent delinquent from the slums. "The Pursuer," in the form of a letter from a spinster schoolteacher, describes that modern and frightening phenomenon, the adolescent monster from the middle class. "The Godmother" is a realistic comedy, told in the semipretentious, semigauche voice of a middle-class youth studying for his Leaving. Power is also capable of dramatized didacticism as in "All God's

Children," a story about school busing in Boston; and he is just as effective with satirical burlesque in "Games Children Play," told from the view of a sociological researcher. Some pieces, like "Pyromaniacs," are quite simple—in this case an O'Connor-like comedy about young children and the church. But other pieces, like "The Wild and Daring Sixties," are a subtle playing off of the narrator's density against the opinions of other characters. "Amanda," which is set in New Mexico, gets considerable comedy from point of view, as a priest indulges in imagining how he will defend himself from a parishioner, all the while it becomes clear to the reader that the priest cannot in the least handle the situation.

In subject, in attitude, and in technique, Power is obviously a versatile writer. He is sometimes a bit long-winded, and sometimes a bit broad; but he can put himself into the minds of his disparate narrators with great effect. One looks forward with real interest to his new work.

John Morrow was born in 1930 in Belfast. After leaving school at fourteen, he had a variety of jobs, from working in the shipyards to selling insurance, and so did not make his mark as a writer until the 1970s. Since 1977, however, he has published two novels and a collection of stories; and, other than the journalistic humorist Sam McCaughtry, he is the only comic writer to emerge from the modern North. Despite the cliché of the dour Northerner, Ulster in years past has produced an impressive group of comic writers, among them Rutherford Mayne, Gerald MacNamara, Lynn Doyle, George Shiels, and whether she knew it or not, Amanda McKittrick Ros. Morrow differs from these earlier writers in possessing sardonic, fanciful, and fluent prose which is in some respects reminiscent of both Wodehouse and Perelman. His collection of short pieces, *Northern Myths*, 1979, contains sketches, vignettes, and comic essays as well as stories, and is one of the most drolly written collections of recent years. In his first novel, *The Confessions of Proinsias O'Toole*, Morrow seemed to strain, like Perelman, for a gag in every line; but in *Northern Myths* his prose has become less frenetic and more effective and relaxed:

One of the enduring legends in our family concerns a distant cousin whose mother ran a house catering mostly for singers of the popular operatic sort. Being hard of hearing herself, it was natural that she should corner the market in this very unpopular type of guest. With an eighteen stone tenor practising in your drawing room it was very hard to keep putty in the window frames.

However, Morris is at his best in his heightening of Belfast speech. For instance:

"I've heard tell there wasn't a barman in Belfast that didn't know all about Bella's grief. Between the pair of them they gave that claims money the quare guttin', though big flyshit there was cute enough to keep out of the light for fear the other widdas would start talkin'. Bella gargled her way roun' the snugs in her weeds an' then hawked home a bottle up her shawl. But they were foolin' nobody; sure I believe on a quiet night the whole street could hear the bedboard knockin' bricks outa the chimney."

Sometimes Morrow takes a sardonic view of the current Troubles, a valuable stance; for, if this talented writer faces any dangers, the chief is that he might congeal into a popular entertainer who only serves up the flavors of the Belfast slums of years past. He does that so well that he could easily become trapped by it. So far he has not.

At his best, Tom Mac Intyre, who was born in the early 1930s in County Cavan, is also a humorist. He has published a novel, an account of the Dublin Arms trial, two collections of stories, and some free verse translations of Irish poetry, and he has written some plays. Despite such varied and seemingly prolific activity, there was a gap of ten years between his two most recent books; and his two collections of stories were published so far apart and are so little akin that they seem written by different people. His 1969 novel, *The Charollais,* was, for Ireland, an avant-garde fantasy written in a far-out comic style which was as initially dazzling as it was cumulatively dull. However, his first collection of stories, *Dance the Dance,* 1970, was quite conventional. If most of the stories seemed too short for much substance or too trivial for much effect, his one developed story, "Epithalamion," suggested that the author had a talent for social comedy that did not turn brittle or uncompassionate. His second collection was not issued until 1982, a sixty-four-page booklet called *The Harper's Turn* which contained a rather baffled introduction by Seamus Heaney and fifteen very short pieces—some of less than two pages. The more striking pieces were rambling, pointless fairy sketches, with a lot of dialogue surrounding descriptive passages like this:

Dawn-light or thereabouts (this child takes minding) and a garden sliding away from the garden a woman and her daughter, the garden pool, a dog surfacing, friend, pointer, swims clear, white and brown, and is the child who strolls where wild orchids, winnowed blue, lacemaker texture, grow: among them, turn of the hand, breath, he gathers pollen, pollen, pollen, ambles on.

Of such writing, Seamus Heaney remarks, "Language left to play so autonomously is reaching for the condition of poetry." Indeed, if Mac Intyre would chop this stuff up into arbitrary lengths, it could pass for much modern Irish poetry. But no matter whether it be bad poetry or worse prose, such writing is a depressing indication that one of the few modern Irish writers capable of being clever with words has opted for a foppish fooling around with them.

John McGahern's first book was a dour, moving novel about adolescence. Called *The Barracks,* it was published in 1965 and won several awards. It was also banned by the Irish Censorship Board, an event that caused McGahern to lose his teaching post and that subsequently probably played some part in the considerable easing of the censor's standards.

McGahern was born in 1934 in Dublin and brought up in County Roscommon. He has published three novels since *The Barracks* and two collections of stories, and is generally considered one of the leading fiction writers. However, his second novel and the best parts of his third were really variations on the theme of his first. The poor parts of his third novel and his generally ineffective fourth novel were attempts to widen his subject matter, but to date McGahern's best work seems rather autobiographically tied to a condemnatory depiction of provincial Irish life. To this extent, he seems something of a modern Brinsley MacNamara.

His first collection, *Nightlines,* was published in 1970, and his second collection, *Getting Through,* in 1978. The stories, whether set in Ireland or on the Continent, are more successful than the novels in escaping from the confines of the author's own life. Their only mild success, however, is probably partly due to their being as gloomy as Trevor's work but not as consistently achieved. A character in "Doorways," for instance, remarks of Ireland, "This country depresses me so much it makes me mad." And depression is the overriding feeling that one takes away from these accounts of death, futility, and disillusionment.

In the stories, though, McGahern has attempted some distancing, some aesthetic paring of the fingernails, some experimenting with the tools of his trade. He attempts to dramatize by using quite a lot of dialogue. Occasionally, as in "The Beginning of an Idea" or "Doorways," he attempts a rather heavyhanded and academic use of symbolism. Often he writes effectively, but equally often he can descend to such muddiness as, "They would have to know that they could know nothing to go through the low door of love, the door that was the same doorway between the self and the other everywhere."

In sum, McGahern has written one painful, moving book out of his own experience. His later books seem attempts to broaden his subject matter and to acquire technique to deal with it. But so far the issue is in doubt.

Bernard Mac Laverty was born in Belfast in 1942. He has published two collections of stories, a short novel, and two books for children. His adult fiction is justifiably highly regarded; and his novel, *Lamb,* except for a too-arbitrary ending, was one of the most successful and gripping volumes of recent years.

The stories in his first collection, *Secrets,* have several strong merits. Like William Trevor, Mac Laverty writes detached observations of several kinds of people—children, university students, housewives, men on the dole, a man who artificially inseminates cattle, old ladies who are dying. Unlike Trevor, however, Mac Laverty has several kinds of stories which are written to produce different kinds of effects, ranging from the Trevorian study of accumulating failure of "Hugo" to the jokey fantasy of "The Miraculous Candidate." Some people lose in Mac Laverty, but some people win: the husband and wife in "The Pornographer Woos" do go happily to bed. But rather more interestingly, in Mac Laverty, sometimes even the losers win a battle. In "A Present for Christmas," the down-and-out McGettigan accidentally comes into a sackful of drink to lighten a few days of his wretched life. In "The Bull with the Hard Hat," the depressed and even ineffectual artificial inseminator does still have his Walter Mitty fantasies. Mac Laverty's view of the world can be sometime as gray as Trevor's or Higgins's or McGahern's; but for Mac Laverty gray is not the only color in the spectrum. His overall view, then, is more balanced, less misanthropic, and finally more convincing.

In fictional technique, Mac Laverty tries for nothing ambitious or exceptional. He writes observed, dramatized scenes, and he does them as well as Trevor or Plunkett or Montague. He uses a lot of dialogue, and his descriptions and narrations do their tasks quietly and briskly.

In his second collection, A Time to Dance, 1982, most of the pieces are static sketches of character rather than stories. As sketches, they are generally successful and provocatively contrasting both in subject and in tone. The best are probably "A Time to Dance" in which the boy's eyepatch becomes a telling symbol of what his mother does not want him to see about life; "Life Drawing" in which the dead relations between an artist and his father are neatly summarized by the artist's failure to realize his father has died while being sketched; "Phonefun Limited" in which two middle-aged ex-prostitutes carry on their business of glamorous titillation from their most unglamorous flat; and "Language, Truth and Lockjaw" in which a husband more interested in abstract analysis than emotion gets his jaw locked. Some pieces, such as the too-short "Father and Son" or "The Beginning of Sin," which is about a drunken priest, have predictably Trevorian endings. However, others, such as "Phonefun Limited," "Language, Truth and Lockjaw" or even "The Daily Woman" are either amusing or upbeat. The one piece that is a developed story is "My Dear Palestrina," about a talented boy and his music teacher and how a narrow Northern society pulls them apart. In this story, Mac Laverty is an accomplished and mature writer, but even in his many less ambitious sketches there is a more varied view of life and a more evident craftsmanship than is to be found in most of his contemporaries.

Desmond Hogan was born in 1951 in County Galway and first came to widespread attention in 1976 with his short novel, The Ikon Maker. Since then he has had some plays produced and published a second novel and two collections of stories which have been well received in England. Indeed, his first collection, *The Diamonds at the Bottom of the Sea,* won the John Llewellyn Rhys Memorial Prize in 1980; and his British publishers have easily been able to amass such admiring testimonials for their book blurbs as, "No one will ever push Joyce or MacNeice off my raft; but Mr. Hogan joins them" (*Times*). Despite such journalistic extravagance, the fairly general opinion now is that Hogan is one of the most exciting new Irish talents of the last ten years. Although the subject matter of his successive books has slightly broadened and the quality of his prose has somewhat improved, he remains to this commentator among the most florid, puerile, boring, ungrammatical, and overpraised of the recent Irish writers.

His subject matter has broadened as his heroes have aged. At one time he wrote obliquely of the suppressed homosexuality of twelve-year-old boys, and how the death of one blighted the others' lives into young manhood. Then the heroes became Grafton Street Byrons, sitting in Stephen's Green in the aftermath of the late 1960s, sipping coffee in Bewley's, smoking pot in seedy bed-sits, having unsatisfying and glancing relations with wraithlike characters who were doing the same thing, and ever and always brooding, brooding, brooding. (One Grafton Street novel by a contemporary of even less ability refers to Hogan as "the sad poet.") More recently, the heroes have achieved success of some sort and have transferred their broodings to Shepherd's Bush or San Francisco. However, the details of their milieu are a bit more effectively evoked. There are, for instance, lots of allusions to such popular preoccupations of recent years as Thomas Merton, Herman Hesse, Jack Kerouac, Allen Ginsberg, Malcolm Lowry, Charlie Parker, Bob Dylan, and so on.

Hogan's constant and obtrusive faults are basic ones. He does usually narrate a story rather than slap down a sketch, but the story meanders shapelessly, without architecture, without proportion. His characterization, save for that of the protagonist, is thin; and the protagonist is usually a journalist, an artist, or someone called Desmond. The other characters are so sieved through the psyche of the protagonist that they remain tersely described, undeveloped, and lifeless. For instance, in "Southern Birds," Hogan uses his favorite triangle of two young men and a woman. Here, the woman embodies some of the most recognizable characteristics of Juanita Casey, who is probably about the most personally individual Irish writer since Brendan Behan. But even here, he flattens the character out, reduces it even to a wispy ectoplasm; and, considering his model, this is quite a dreary accomplishment. In another triangle story, "A Poet and an Englishman," the female

character is as unbelievable and as manipulated as D. H. Lawrence's absurd
wish fulfillment of a heroine in "The Woman Who Rode Away." Hogan's
story ends:

> She'd never known how Peader had picked up a young boy from Cahirciveen
> who's been drunkenly urinating and made love to him in the tent, kissed his white
> naked pimples as Michael Gillespie had kissed his years before.
>
> She'd never know but when she woke in the morning between Peader and a
> young boy she knew more about life's passion than she'd ever known before. She
> rose and put on a long skirt and looked at the morning, fresh, blue-laden, as she'd
> never seen it before.

Like a Lawrence with no talent for words, or a Tennessee Williams with no
ear for dialogue, Hogan twists the world into a private fantasy.

Yet to say Hogan has no talent for words is not quite accurate. There is
an erratic flair that makes his prose his most individual and even intermit-
tently appealing quality. Originally he wrote mainly in fragments and one-
sentence paragraphs containing lyric, unusual, and arresting comparisons.
His more recent work is less telegraphic in sentence structure; and his diction remains engaging and, at its rare best, sardonic. At the typical worst,
however, he utilizes the incongruous word that does not quite coalesce into
sense. For instance:

> There'd been one particular tree there, open like a complaint.

> . . . there was a sense of inflation about her movements.

> In the painting her neck swung towards her nape like a swan's neck. Her eyes rang
> with laughter. Her face was thin and pinched and her lips smote the vision like a
> paper rose.

However, if we forgive the bad grammar (smaller than him . . ., neither
tinker or gipsy . . ., Hopefully, there would be . . .), and pass over the
wrongly used words ("They'd always deigned to live in the West, but they
never made it"), we can hardly ignore the purple passages and the exuberant
romanticism that would deter even a Barbara Cartland. For example:

> . . . the wet urgency of sex in the grass always inspired or threaded by dew.

Or:

> Gradually it became more real to me that I loved him, that we were active within a
> certain sacrifice. Both of us had been bare and destitute when we met. The two of
> us had warded off total calamity, total loss. "Jamesy!" His picture swooned; he was
> like a ravaged corpse in my head and the area between us opened.

This vague, flatulent, and tasteless drivel is bought, read, and admired—a fact beyond satire. Today, Thomas Wolfe begins to look like Goethe.

Neil Jordan was born in Sligo in 1951. His slim volume of stories and sketches, *A Night in Tunisia,* was published in 1976 and received, like Hogan's work, much favorable comment. Since then, he has published a short novel, but most of his recent work has been in writing and directing for films and television.

One of his better sketches concerns a young builder's laborer in London who is so depressed by his life and surroundings that he kills himself in a public shower. Another is about a middle-aged man who remembers how his wife deserted him and gets maudlinly drunk. But most are about adolescents and young people who are battered and blighted by love. There is a good deal of frantic, inchoate emotion, such as:

. . . he couldn't see my tears or see my smile.

She was crying, great breathful sobs.

He was crying, and his face looked more beautiful than ever through the tears.

The sight of his tan overcoat and his dark oiled hair brought a desolate panic to her.

. . . I stopped my hate and felt baffled, sad, older than I could bear.

Generally, Jordan's style is an understated lyricism, à la Hemingway, much less florid than Hogan's, and with fewer sentence fragments. However, there is little sense of the architecture or sometimes even of the basic syntax of a sentence. In fact, the basic conventions of writing are either ignored or simply not understood: the grammar is careless, the spelling is a little faulty, and the punctuation is confusing and inconsistent. One Irish reviewer mildly deplored the spelling, but all the others—even Sean O'Faolain—rapturously gushed about the brilliant debut of a consummate talent.

How do people read books? Even if they read only for content and statement, what about the sentences that demand you back up and disentangle the most plausible meaning? On any page of Jordan's book, there are several examples of writing like this, complete with errors:

He knew as he approached the baths to wash off the dust of a weeks labour, that this hour would be the week's highpoint.
"Have you got the time" Jamie burst in. "Have you eyes in your head," she countered.
The tinker was on the burrows now, pulling the donkey by the hair of it's neck.

He felt that somewhere he knew as much as she. . . . And the boy saw the naked figure, smaller than him.
. . . a ladies drink.

. . . his father would stop and let him play on, listening. And he [who?] would occasionally look and catch that look on his [whose?] listening eyes, wry, sad and loving his [whose?] pleasure at how his son played only marred by the knowledge of how little it meant to him. And he [who?] . . .

Then the front door opening, the sound of the saxaphone [a saxophone is quite significant in the story] case laid down.

She thought of all the times they had talked it out, every conceivable mutation in their relationship, able and disable, every possible emotional variant, despision [?] to fear, since it's only by talking of such things that they are rendered harmless.

All minor flaws, but there are six or a dozen on every page, and hundreds and hundreds within the book.

The rather undramatized stories and short sketches otherwise show hints of sensitive observation; and there are doubtless needles in the haystacks. The Irish reviewers have admired the quality of the few needles and ignored the vast quantities of hay.

In any event, Jordan may have found his proper metier in films and television, where characters do not have to speak too many words, and anguish may be expressed with a sound like "Argghh!" But if his first book has any point in a literary discussion, it is a sobering symptom of the standards of the day.

1976 also saw the first collection of Gillman Noonan. Most collections of recent Irish stories are either thoroughly bad or thoroughly mediocre; but a few books, particularly those by women, contain one or two memorable stories. Noonan's *A Sexual Relationship* is especially notable, for he has five or even six quite striking pieces—the title story, "Goodbye Gran," "Dear Parents, I'm Working for the EEC!" "Money for the Town," "The Wedding Suit," and the fantastic sequences of "Writer Story."

Noonan was born in 1937 in County Cork. He graduated from University College, Cork, and worked for several years on the Continent. No new book of his appeared until *Friends and Occasional Lovers*, 1982, and he has not had as subsequently successful a career as Hogan or Jordan, but his first work is to theirs as night is to day.

Nevertheless, he does not entirely escape the occupational blight of being a modern Irish writer. As he describes the work of the writer in "Writer Story," "it was still the language of wanting to escape, of resentment, of frustration that smothered all joy." And certainly the first story in his book, "Between the Cells," is the quintessence of Irish dreariness. The pejorative connotations of the writing equal anything in John McGahern or John Broderick or St. John of the Cross. For instance, from only ten lines on page 8:

> . . . a thousand paunchy insects all carrying bags of stout . . . dry flaking skin . . . closing in . . . tormented . . . slow decay beneath the mucus of a smelly cubicle . . . slime eddying around my feet while men prowled and grunted outside at the urinals.

In a writer who can so successfully reproduce such conventional and solemn hysteria, it is surprising to find two stories about youth that are as sunny and droll as Frank O'Connor's "First Confession" and "My Oedipus Complex." These pieces, "Goodbye Gran" and "The Wedding Suit," are sane, sad and funny, mature and beautifully observed.

O'Connor, admirable as his work was, had a somewhat limited range of observation, mainly the youth and young manhood of the lower middle class. Noonan, in his first collection, is more varied in subject and in attitude. His "Money for the Town," in the hands of a Broderick or McGahern or Trevor, could be another tritely depressing story of the cumulative tediums of marriage among the dull horrors of a small Irish town. Noonan, without sacrificing such valid points, has his trapped and middle-aged hero decide not to act bastardly.

The best piece in Noonan's first collection is a strongly characterized two-hander in which a young Irishman learns to be less conventionally chauvinistic about casual sex relationships. Though understated, the piece is authentic and quietly funny, and the German girl is an immensely better creation than any of the unreal girls in Hogan or Jordan. "Dear Parents, I'm Working for the EEC!" is ineffective as story, for the narrator is too detached from the action. As a sketch, though, of a young man who cannot decide whether to be in with the establishment or out with the kooks, the narrative strategy is defensible enough. A charming daydream involving Yeats, Joyce, Beckett, and other luminaries similarly saves "Writer Story" from being an indulgent and plotless rumination. For instance:

> Beckett had strolled over to where what looked like the torso of a human being protruded from the sand. The head was in the shape of an egg and utterly featureless.
> —Remarkable, he said to Stephens, the things one sees on Irish beaches.
> —A sad case that, said Ahearn. He was a good mate of mine before he turned into an egghead.
> —Amorphous, don't you think? said Stephens.
> —Very Irish, said Beckett. Indehiscent..
> —Jasus, indecent! Ahearn exclaimed. He's for the fuckin' National Geographic.

In the literary bogland that comprises much of modern Irish fiction, simple fun and silliness are as welcome as they are rare.

Noonan's second collection, *Friends and Occasional Lovers,* disappointingly does not extend or develop the good qualities of his first book. The second book is mainly about varieties of sexual nonexperience, in which things never happen, or stop happening, or happen without being important. The author's attitude seems mainly depressed, and his gift for comedy is much more muted than in the first volume. The name of Henry James pops up in the quite Jamesian story called "Plato and Passion," and the ghost of James seems to brood over the entire collection. This genteel presence seems particularly evident in the undramatized quality of most of the stories. Little usually happens, and it happens obliquely. In one of the best stories, "Haiku and High Octane," the interesting leading character is not even quite sure what did happen; and most of the stories are rather embalmed in the main characters' ruminations.

Sometimes the writing gets noticeably turgid, as in the following sentence from "Salvage Operation," which contains double dashes, three sets of parentheses and an italicized word:

Nor was it a question of Fran bringing missionary zeal to bear (though she tried her damndest to save the marriage) on the hedonist—Alice continued to have her lovers, once even "babysitting" in their home with one of them, a young man she had met at an extramural course (Allan: "Ha, ha, very good, " shaking his hand)—it was that he, randy Al, was no longer one of them while *they* (and now the word was Fran's, linking Alice along a beach in Kerry) had become "sisters."

This is an extreme but symptomatic example; and elsewhere Noonan will fall occasionally into a pretentious lyricism, as in "Excerpts from the Journal of a Confirmed Bachelor," where the concluding sentence in part reads:

. . . and I thought how knowing I was, perched like a cocky bird on the gargoyle of some doomed church, untouched for all my concern by the anguish in the stone, by hope, its wild guttering and death.

The strengths of *A Sexual Relationship* were the dramatized quality of the best stories, and a style made lucid by a comic view. These strengths are rarely evident in this second collection which flounders in sensibility and technique. If this means that Noonan is learning from his contemporaries, he should immediately return to his old school—himself.

John Macardle, born in 1939, is a County Monaghan filmmaker who has published one volume of stories, *It's Handy When People Don't Die,* 1981. He chiefly writes of country life and of moral, social, and cultural attitudes that are rooted in the Irish past. Sometimes, as in his intriguing title story about Vinegar

Hill and the '98 Rising, he actually returns to the past. Sometimes, as in "The Warmth and the Wine," a story set in modern Amsterdam, he may venture into the European present; but even then his main character carries the Irish past anachronistically into a modern world which disturbs but only mildly changes him. The best of Macardle resides in his nice eye for detail and in his occasional, highly evocative word—qualities particularly evident in his "A Growth of Some Kind." The worst of Macardle is in the often inordinate leisureliness in developing his stories—a quality irritatingly present in "Light Signs."

Of the short story writers who have published a first collection in the 1980s, the most lauded young man is probably Dermot Healy. Healy's *Banished Misfortune*, 1982, was greeted in both Ireland and England with such encomia as "impressive," "admirable," "unique talent," and "the mastery of the form breathes through every line."

Healy was born in County Westmeath in 1947, received two Hennessy Awards for his short stories, and has worked in the theater and in films. A novel has been announced for 1983, and he seems likely to repeat the success of Jordan and Hogan.

The twelve stories in his collection are of various lengths and two manners. "Reprieve" and "Betrayal" are less than two pages long; the remainder range from about five to fifteen pages. "Reprieve" and particularly "The Tenant" are told in a conventional manner; the remainder, which really set the tone for the book, are written with a denser obliquity than that of Hogan or Jordan and may owe something to writers like Higgins and MacIntyre. Healy does not, however, depend upon unusual or foreign words or upon startling images, but rather upon an eccentric punctuation linking or, more usually, curiously separating sentences, clauses, and fragments of sentences. A typical passage is one like this from "First Snow of the Year":

It stopped snowing, the brittle stars came out. Would the dead forgive him if his hand wandered over Helen's face in the darkness of the mourning house, touching and parting flesh here, and folding his body around her against death. The canoe to the sea. He walked across a new planet, journeying inwards, without thought of his fellows. There were so many clear stars that he found the gravel track on the far side of the bog as in a dream, all beaten up and restored, like the others of his tribe.

Not a totally baffling paragraph but, if regarded closely, in part a puzzling one. The attractions of such a style are its freedom, its individuality, and its suggestion of a sensitive, mysterious, and wildly inexplicable persona. However, the dangers are obvious: certain phrases lose their syntactical anchor so that their position gets puzzling and their meaning murky; the public presentation of a narrative gets camouflaged, and indeed the narrative becomes less prominent than the narrating. Many modern Irish poets, either through a desire to be more widely heard or through simple incapacity, have cast off conventional form in favor of the occasional jeweled phrase strewn through writing whose essential prosiness no chopping up into arbitrary line lengths can disguise. Conversely, some fiction writers, like Healy, seem striving for the personal voice of poetry rather than the public voice of prose. But, as prose must still have a justified right-hand margin, it is the syntax of the sentence rather than the length that must be chopped. Both attempts often seem like shortcuts to individuality; but to a talent as tender as Healy's, the critic is tempted to hold up a sign that reads "cul de sac."

From the time of Maria Edgeworth, there has always been a handful of notable women writers in Ireland. Preeminently, there were in this century Somerville and Ross, Lady Gregory, Elizabeth Bowen, and Mary Lavin. Lady Longford, Kate O'Brien, Mary Manning, Molly Keane, Teresa Deevy, and Anne Crone have all contributed occasional works of striking merit. And, of course, there has always been a legion of popular writers like Rosa Mulholland or Annie M. P. Smithson. There have been two candidates for the crown of legendary badness in Amanda McKittrick Ros and Lizzie Twigg.

In the last two decades, however, there is a notably larger number of women whose work commands high respect. Perhaps the reason may be laid in part to the influence of the women's liberation movement in the United States. Certainly, in Ireland, where the social, economic and legal position of women was rather medieval, that influence could only be beneficial. One dramatic symptom of a greater militancy among Irish women was the women's peace movement in Ulster which was for a time a real force, and which won for its founders the Nobel Peace Prize.

In fiction, there seem about as many fine new women writers as men, and the general quality of the women's work seems consistently higher. Overwhelmingly, of course, the content of their fiction is an investigation of Irish life as it affects women. To the male mind, there appears an occasional horrific story such as the Julia O'Faolain one in which the wife chains her husband in the cellar, but generally the content of these stories and novels is adding a sane new dimension to Irish literary experience. Molly Bloom is long overdue to have some sisters.

Pride of place as the first of the "new women" must surely be given to Edna O'Brien. She was born in County Clare in 1930 and made an immediate reputation with her first novel, *The Country Girls,* 1960. When her country girls came up to Dublin, they were dazzled and delighted by the modern world. They sloughed off their provincial puritanism; they exuberantly discovered sex; they were utterly fresh and charming. Since that first book, Edna O'Brien has published about ten more novels, four collections of stories and some travel literature, as well as doing much work for the stage, television, and films. In practically all her work—in book after book, play after play, and story after story—Edna O'Brien has remained obsessively faithful to the themes of love and sex. If there has been growth in her work, it is mainly that, as the author has grown older, so too have her heroines. Although the frankly treated themes of love and sex have been Edna O'Brien's great strength, her preoccupation with them only has become her major limitation as a writer.

This preoccupation may even be responsible for the considerable unevenness in O'Brien's work. What was initially treated lightheartedly has come to be handled with increasing seriousness, and the seriousness has tended to deteriorate into the mushy seriousness of romanticism. Still, she remains capable of writing with considerable drollness and of fashioning startling images:

. . . as if the black crows had turned into great black razors and were inside his head, cutting, cutting away.

Or:

. . . yet out in the street the concrete slabs were marshy and the spiked railings threatening to brain her.

As Edna O'Brien has more and more come to treat sex sentimentally or melodramatically, such startling images are more frequent than her earlier droll turns of phrase. But in recent books her style has not grown so much blacker as purpler, and is increasingly reminiscent of the bathetic and banal style of cheap romantic fiction. For instance:

Her arrival was blessed with magic. Trees, the sound of running water, flowers, wild flowers . . .

In the morning the world was clean and bright. There had been rain and everything got washed, the water mills, the ducks, the roses, the trees, the lupins and the little winding paths. She bent down and smelt some pansies. A pure sweet silken smell, like the texture of childhood.

Or in her worst melodramatic vein:

One night as she lay in the bed, a little breathless, he came in very softly, closed the door, removed his dressing-gown, and took possession of her with such a force that afterwards she suspected she had a broken rib. They used words that they had not used for years. She was young and wild. A lovely fever took hold of her. She was saucy.

Or:

The zip of his trousers hurt her but he was mindless of that. The thing is he had desired her from the very first, and now he was pumping all his arrogance and all his cockatooing into her and she was taking it gladly, also gluttonously. She was recovering her pride as a woman.

This essay has perhaps given inordinate space to problems of style. People do not read fiction for style, but for story. The blockbuster best-sellers of our time, by people like Arthur Hailey and Leon Uris, may be childishly written, may have cardboard characters, may have a banal and truistic theme, but their galloping story carries them through—at least for thought-less readers. Nevertheless, style is a symptom of quality of mind and quality of general craftsmanship.

The recent style of Edna O'Brien is particularly worth attention, for it suggests her increasing deterioration as an artist. Like D. H. Lawrence, who also had intense powers of observation and great capacities for drollery, Edna O'Brien became more compulsively somber about her major topic. She also became a sillier and lesser writer than she could have been.

Nevertheless, the success of her delightful best work opened the door for a lot of later women who were now able to write frankly and sensitively of areas of experience that even Somerville and Ross, in *The Real Charlotte,* were only able to treat obliquely.

Val Mulkerns was born in Dublin in 1925, and her novels published in the early 1950s are distinctly pre-O'Brien in their romantic treatment of love. However, after a long publishing hiatus, Mulkerns brought out two volumes of stories, *Antiquities* in 1978 and *An Idle Woman* in 1980, which are quite post-O'Brien in attitude and in quality. The difference is not a matter of one writer's influence upon another, but of the influence of a changed world.

Antiquities contains several loosely connected stories about several genera-tions of a single family, and its best pieces are more controlled and distanced than anything in Mulkerns's early novels. *An Idle Woman* breaks into two halves. In the first and poorer part, there are stories of vital, brittle women and gentle, ineffectual men. The women love to plunge ecstatically into the chilling waters of the Atlantic; the men wade out a few feet, return, and shiver on the shore. The women bound over bogs from tussock to tussock, or leap like goats from rock to rock; the men either sink in up to their ankles or scuttle breathlessly around. These stories are conventionally well done and conventionally depressing.

The second half of the book is more distanced and more impressive. "The Birthday Party" is a horrendous little fable about some tinker children being invited to a birthday party for a middle-class child and being run down by the mother's automobile. Although specifically realistic, it has some allegorical resonance. "Phone You Some Time" is uncharacteristically lighthearted and a small comic triumph. "Home for Christmas" is a brief, brutal vignette, seen through a child's eyes, of unnecessarily penurious living. "Memory and Desire" is a study of middle-aged loneliness contrasted with the making of a television film by bright, virile young people—and the protagonist is a man. Unlike Edna O'Brien, Val Mulkerns shows healthy signs of escaping the confines of liberated woman's fiction.

Eithne Strong was born in 1923 in County Limerick, raised a large family, and so began to publish after O'Brien and Mulkerns. In recent years she has published a novel, some volumes of verse in English and Irish, and one collection of stories called *Patterns*. Her evocations of family life, particularly in "Patterns" and in the uncollected "Red Jelly," are telling reminders of the squalid and wearing aspects of domesticity, but they are also her liveliest writing. The cumulative effects of domesticity upon her heroines is to drive them, however, to irascibility, to much needed if unsatisfying vacations abroad, and to much needed if abortive love affairs. Her usual themes and attitudes might be suggested by these conclusions to five of her stories:

I cannot sleep.

Minnie and Sheamus were asleep. She was in miserable isolation.

Tomorrow she would be gone from the country. They merged into sleep.

He looked sad in the empty street. She drove the other way.

. . . in the darkened chapel I know my smile is gone and I feel a wetness on my cheeks.

One has a mild wonder that a liberated woman should write such conventionally trapped and depressed stories. If such a woman writes such stories, we might expect that much modern woman's fiction in Ireland is going to be examples of exorcism.

Maeve Kelly was born in Dundalk in 1930; her stories, collected in *A Life of Her Own*, 1976, are generally about strong-minded, even self-sufficient women who are inured to harsh country lives. The wife in the moving story "The Last Campaign" admonishes herself, "Tears are for townie women with no guts." Even when it seems that the sister in "Journey Home" has lost the farm, she does not give up: "Josie, she thought. Josie's my trump card. Josie will crack first." In "Lovers," the wife is struggling along through a brutal wind and thinks, "It was a strange and fearful thing to be able to walk almost upright against this challenge." And that sentence might well be taken as a general summation of Maeve Kelly's women.

Her characterization is often striking, and several of her strong women linger in the memory: the island woman with the deaf mute brother in "Amnesty"; the dying woman who leaves her backward son a dose of poison in "Love"; the aged and indomitable cousins of "The Sentimentalist." The titles of some of the stories—"Amnesty," "The Last Campaign," "The Fortress"— indicate that these are embattled lives. Sometimes, as in "Lovers," the battles are won; sometimes, as in "The Last Campaign," they are lost. But whatever the outcome, it is never greeted with the Byronic melancholy and the narcissistic whining that pervades the writing of many of Maeve Kelly's male contemporaries. Nor does she opt, like some of her female English and American contemporaries, for a simplistic solution. When one character is asked if she is a woman's libber, she replies:

"You make it sound like a disease. . . . I don't know what you mean. I told you before I don't know what I am. I only know I am. That's all. It's enough for me. It is enough for you."

Rather than imposing a facile theory on trivial lives, Maeve Kelly writes of beleaguered characters whose stories embody their tough and traditional virtues. She is reminiscent less of Edna O'Brien or Maeve Binchy than of Liam O'Flaherty or Peadar O'Donnell.

She writes in generally much longer paragraphs than one is used to in modern, media-afflicted fiction, and she uses much less dialogue. Yet she is capable of irony, as in her presentation of the thoughts of the young girl in the title story:

He aroused in me a passion of resentment I had never before experienced. He was ten and I almost fourteen but an aeon of civilisation separated us. The bus journey was no improvement. He was a bad traveller and was sick most of the time, spewing out of the window with an abandonment totally in character. I ministered to him from a safe distance but could not avoid some pollution. "Poor little lad," a passenger said. "But aren't you the lucky fellow to have such a good woman to look after you." Instinctively I resisted the role being thrust upon me. At his age, I reflected, I travelled by myself. I would not allow myself to be his mother figure or wife figure or whatever a "good woman" should be. But the pain of mustering a polite smile to cover my spleen was almost unbearable. To have to carry the wretched boy into my territory was one thing, to watch him infect the beautiful landscape with the out-pourings of his greedy, chocolate-filled stomach was another, but to have to grin at the banalities of his sympathisers was the ultimate in suffering.

Too long to be sparkling, but quite effective; and she is capable of the short statement that evokes a lyric shock, as in the concluding sentence of "Lov-ers": "Annie saw them as they came over the rise of the land, man, calf and cow riding the wind."

Maeve Kelly's book does not really attempt to ride the wind, but it does solidly walk the earth, and in modern Irish fiction that is a real achievement.

Julia O'Faolain's mother is an excellent writer of children's stories, and her father is one of the masters of the modern Irish short story. She herself was born in 1932 and received a B.A. at University College, Dublin. Since then her life has been largely lived on the Continent or in America; and her writing often more reflects her adult life and preoccupations than her youth in Dublin. Indeed, her most recent Irish novel seems rather out of touch with the country. Of the seven stories in her second collection, *Man in the Cellar,* 1974, only two—and those not the strongest—reflect Ireland. The most gripping pieces are the disturbing women's lib title story which is set in Italy, the suavely desperate "I Want Us to Be in Love" which is set in Paris, and the telling contrast of a rich American marriage and a middle-class Italian one, "A Travelled Man," which is set mainly in Los Angeles. The Irish stories are "It's a Long Way to Tipperary," which is really a leisurely char-acter sketch, and "The Knight," which is a more dramatized piece about a middle-aged man who joins a lay religious society only to find that its vows of celibacy conflict with his up-to-then inadequate marriage.

Her earlier collection, *We Might See Sights,* 1968, contains more Irish sto-ries and rather better ones. "A Pot of Soothing Herbs" and "Chronic" are delightful studies, one from a woman's and one from a man's view, of the sexual nets in which Irish society entangled its young in the 1950s. Both stories so beautifully catch the times, the tone of voice, and the typical frus-trations of their protagonists that their characters transcend types to become two of the finest comic creations of the modern Irish short story.

A chief delight of reading Julia O'Faolain is that she is one of the few modern Irish writers who can write. She has a witty eye for just but unex-pected resemblances. Copulation is described as "a repetitious undulation, disagreeably similar to the agony of a grounded fish." Students have "necks like plucked quails" and faces "like babies' bottoms." And when one such boy picked up the books from the heroine's desk, "the brush of his sleeve

against my cheek had the toad pressure of jellied frogspawn." Slates on roofs
"might have been shards of solidified winter sea." A girl "puts lipstick on as
though it were jam. Men converge on her like bees." There are roads in
France "where mistletoe hung hairy smudges on the limbs of poplars, and
sounds were spasms in the air."

Now and then she exuberantly overwrites. One could, for instance, make
a small anthology of zany descriptions of her characters' eyes. And one too
often comes across lines like:

Pitiful and repellent, the wrinkles in her face moved in the sun like the long-jointed
legs of agonizing insects.

Chewing, her lips, bunched in an interrupted kiss, moved across her face like a fish
form on sand.

. . . hair . . . came out in handfuls of knots like rutting spiders which she saved to
make a bun.

Her 1982 collection, *Daughters of Passion,* has also a few lush lines like "Evergreens
bulged like steamed artichokes"; but generally the style has been pared back to
a tight casualness, and the favorite narration is now the colloquial evocation of
someone's thoughts.

However, in *Daughters of Passion,* it is not the style that is most arresting,
but the material and the author's attitude toward it. The author seems less
to have grown than to have congealed. Indeed, with this latest collection, it
has become possible to describe a Julia O'Faolain story, just as one might list
the characteristics of an Edna O'Brien story or even a Tennessee Williams
play.

An O'Faolain story is about a woman in her thirties who is in some uncomfortable, unattractive, or unpalatable situation. If the situation changes,
it will change, sometimes melodramatically, for the worse. An O'Faolain
story depicts a world with a high incidence of ugliness, eccentricity, violence,
impotence, madness, and rage. Even art becomes ugly; a painter is told, "you
muck dirt around like, I don't know, a kid playing with faeces." Even kindness becomes cruelty; the gauche, pitiful Mr. Rao of "Will You Please Go
Now" arouses only dislike and is banished from the family whose Christmas
dinner he has been invited to. The spoiled brat in "Diego" screams that her
parents should kill a dog which she thinks does not like her, and the parents
are not unwilling. The heroine of "Mad Marga" will end up in jail, and the
heroine of "Daughters of Passion" is already in jail and on a hunger strike.
The hero of "Why Should Not Old Men Be Mad?" is not mad but is forceably

hurled into a lunatic asylum; the heroine and most of the other characters in "Oh My Monsters!" conspire to keep a violent schizophrenic out of an asylum.

This catalogue of horrors suggests that O'Faolain has become a feminine, perhaps even a darker Trevor. So far, however, Trevor is capable of developed narratives with a glum plausibility; and O'Faolain's most dramatic bits of action seem melodramatic and arbitrary, as if the action must be bizarrely wrenched to fit a fable. Thus, "Why Should Not Old Men Be Mad?" seems more fabulous than realistic; and the most realistic piece, "Legend for a Painting," is a grisly fable about a knight, a lady, and a dragon.

In this latest collection, there are only three Irish stories, and only one of them is actually set in Ireland. But Ireland itself seems less set in Ireland, and one might well conclude that what has happened to the country has also happened to Julia O'Faolain—a cosmopolitanizing process that has brought subtlety and awareness, as well as a loss of innocence and a growth of malaise.

Emma Cooke was born in County Laois in 1934 and has published one collection of stories, *Female Forms*, 1980. In "Halcyon Days," she writes that her heroine's life "was encrusted with men, cornices, blue dungarees, measuring tapes, anoraks, jeans and jumpers, clogs and dressing gowns." An Emma Cooke heroine leads a commonplace life; she marries and tends to get caught in a trap of domestic duties. There is Beattie, the constantly pregnant wife of "A Family Occasion"; there is Geraldine, the tired, middle-aged wife who is visited by an affluent American relative in "Cousins"; there is Greta, the mother overwhelmed by the minutiae of domesticity in "Halcyon Days." Nevertheless, marriage is better than spinsterhood; in "The Foundress" the spinster sister winds up in an asylum, and the married sister concludes that a servant girl who was raped and murdered led a better life than her sister did. A further testimonial to marriage appears in the title story where the life of a bachelor who has gone through a succession of mistresses is shown to be bleak and pointless. And, finally, marriage does not always reduce women to brainless automatons; when they go on vacations to Tenerife or to Greece with their successful husbands, as in "Winter Break" or "The Greek Trip," they can have affairs. The affairs may solve nothing, but what does?

Emma Cooke's view has few heights and no depths; it seems an unhysterical coping with the fairly unsatisfactory. Her stories, too, have few heights or depths, but they reveal a consistently fine observation that gives them considerable merit. The accumulation of small details in "Trinity Sunday" and "Halcyon Days" shows her at her most effective, and keeps her commonplace world from seeming commonplace.

Helen Lucy Burke is the author of a novel, *Close Connections*, and a volume of stories called *A Season for Mothers,* 1980. She writes a fluently unobtrusive prose that eschews the gaudy effects of a John Morrow or the glittering comparisons of a Julia O'Faolain. Nevertheless, the effect of her best stories is as witty as Morrow and, in one case, as mordant as O'Faolain. Probably it is not the devices of her prose but the stance of her mind that makes six of the eight stories in *A Season for Mothers* ripe candidates for anthologizing. Her title story, set in Rome, exhibits and flays the stereotype of the provincial Irish widow. "The Greek Experience" flays the vulnerability of the New Irish Woman, as much as her "Grey Cats in the Dark" lacerates the sexual mores of the typical Irish bachelor. "Sensible Middle-Aged Men" contrasts the old provincial politician with the young, media-oriented breed and gives a savagely accurate account of an election. "The Last Infirmity" is an equally deft account of aging sexuality and literary politics that succeeds in being both satiric and plausible. What could be more on target than:

"And what was Yeats anyway, when all is said and done? A randy parson of a fellow, with seedy ideas of grandeur. Our greatest poet indeed, moryah! Any more than that fellow Kavanagh that they are all raving about now, that tramped down from Monaghan with cowdung on his boots and kept it all his years in Dublin."

In such a passage, and in the best of her stories, Helen Lucy Burke achieves what Terence de Vere White attempted. And for once one must agree with the blurb writer: she is "a shining talent."

Maeve Binchy, who was born in 1940, made a reputation as a journalist for the *IrishTimes,* and her warmly humorous column is so popular that she has culled a couple of paperback collections from it. A prolific writer, she has also turned her hand to novels, plays, and stories. Her *Maeve Binchy's Dublin 4* refers to a Dublin postal district on the south side of the city; it contains four stories, and reflects her usual preoccupation with modern urban life. Her characteristic quality of accurate detail embodied in a clean and lean prose is best evident in "Murmurs in Montrose," about the inevitable backsliding of an alcoholic who was once a successful photographer, and the equally inevitable collapse of his marriage. The other stories contain well-chosen situations rather less well presented. "Dinner in Donnybrook," about an affluent matron's subtle plot to break up her husband's affair, suffers from being much too long in its build-up, and its eighty pages offer much accurate but little memorable detail or dialogue or characterization. "Decision in Belfield" seems, on the narrative level, to be about how the girls of a liberal middle-class family cope with their unmarried pregnancies, but more basically is probably about noncommunication among people who love each other. Part of its problem is that the author does not completely communicate with the reader who never really knows how one of the girls has coped with her problem. "Flat in Ringsend" is a sweet story about a naive country girl who, after being alarmed by city ways, is soothed by city sympathy. There may still be girls like the heroine, but they seem distinctly anachronistic in the 1980s.

Maeve Binchy's stories are more professional than much modern Irish fiction, but their faults rise out of their professionalism. They are too slick, too thin, too easy, and give the impression of having been written with too much haste and too little correction. The characters are seldom memorable, for the details of their lives are only typical. In her plays and journalism, Maeve Binchy has often caught the individual note, the exact detail, the witty phrase, the just satiric touch. Such qualities are her own highest standards, and her stories do not quite attain them. Nor indeed does her blockbuster 1982 novel, *Light a Penny Candle*, which aspires to be little more than conventional romantic fiction.

There is a yet unfilled niche in modern Irish writing for social comedy. In the drama, Hugh Leonard has sometimes veered toward it, but has usually opted for broader, farcical effects. The modern poets are mainly too self-absorbed to be interested in it. In fiction, Terence de Vere White in a long series of novels and stories has had fine ideas but too phlegmatic a touch to make them come alive. If Maeve Binchy would work more seriously at the texture of her work, rather than settling for an easy fluency, it is a niche that she might fill.

Ita Daly was born in Country Leitrim in 1944 and is married to David Marcus. Her single collection, *The Lady with the Red Shoes,* 1980, contains ten stories of about a dozen pages each. Two of them have won Hennessy Literary Awards and one an *Irish Times* short story competition. All are about women, and all but one are narrated by women. Daly's strong points are her characterization and her effective manipulation of the reader; and both points appear in "Hey Nonny No" and "Compassion" when the reader is pushed to judge the narrator's value differently from the way that the narrator does. Many but mercifully not all of the stories are about dreary lives, failure, and disaffection. However, all are written in a terse, trim, professional prose; and all contain terse, precise, and well-considered detail.

With Maura Treacy, I have great difficulty. I have read her collection of stories, *Sixpence in Her Shoe,* twice. I have then laid it aside and returned to it in a few days, only to discover each time that I cannot recall what the stories are about until I have skimmed them through once more. With other authors, a glance at the first paragraph or even at the title is usually enough to bring their best stories back into focus; and I suspect that my vagueness about Maura Treacy is more her fault than mine.

She was born in County Kilkenny in 1946 and published *Sixpence in Her Shoe* in 1977. Her stories are mainly about farm life, and there are fifteen of them in a little book of about 125 pages. Some, such as "A Time for Growing" or "Sadness is Over the Fields," are descriptions or character sketches rather than stories; but even the legitimate stories have something of the blandness of sketches. Partly the problem is that her writing is often only sparely, flatly functional. Here, for instance, is a randomly picked paragraph:

> Fionnuala and her mother were home from Mass and had the dinner ready but her father still had not come up from the new building. He had let them out of the car there and they had walked the rest of the way home. Another car drew up at the site as they left and before they reached home yet another had arrived. Later her mother sent her down to tell him the dinner was ready.

Now and then she is stronger—as, for instance, in the conclusion of one of her better pieces, "Separate Ways":

> There would always be an echo of wonder at the way he re-emerged to carry on the routine of his days, since effort hardly seemed possible without optimism.

But generally the best that can so far be said of Maura Treacy is that she is a serious, careful writer—and that so far she is a little dull.

Kate Cruise O'Brien is the daughter of the multitalented Cassandra of modern Irish life, Conor Cruise O'Brien. She was born in Dublin in 1948, and has published one collection, *A Gift Horse,* 1978. Most of her rather short stories are about the female experience: her Sarahs, Elizabeths, Jennifers, and Joannas rarely have last names, but they include the very young girl being shocked by her first introduction to the grislier aspects of Christianity; the young girl combating the restrictions of school and the queerness of parents; the university student coping with the responsibility for the suicide of a boyfriend; the young woman coping with old lovers, new lovers, and new husbands; the matron coping with old husbands, deserting husbands, babies, mothers-in-law, money, the lack of it, depression, alcoholism, and something quite as normal as the difficulty of getting along with the person you are living with. So baldly stated, this sounds like another typical and depressing catalog of female tribulations. However, most of Kate Cruise O'Brien's women are fuller than mere types. The tipsily flirtatious wife of "The Wedding Party" and the depressed, frigid, and deserted wife of "A Just Desert" are as accurate, more individual, and much more economically described than Maeve Binchy's women. Her young Sarah in "Sackcloth" and her younger Elizabeth in "Hurt" are authentic glimpses into childhood, and her two girl university students make "Henry Died" one of the memorable accomplishments of recent Irish writing.

Generally, the women writers are not quirky in form or style. Generally, the authors' personalities do not intrude as a substitute for substance. They have, in only about fifteen years, created an impressive body of solid new work; and they are adding a rich new dimension to modern Irish writing.

It is now necessary to append a coda about some notable writers who eluded this chapter's rather loose net of organization.

Juanita Casey did not appear in the last section, partly because her 1966 volume of stories, *Hath the Rain a Father?* predates the other women's stories by about ten years, and also because individually she is quite unclassifiable. She was born in England in 1925 of an Irish tinker mother and an English Romany father. The other details of her life, which include being an animal trainer in a circus, make it clear that she never became a liberated woman because she was never caught. After her first book of stories, she published two short novels, a slim collection of verse, and another slim collection of verse and stories. Her novels, *The Horse of Selene* of 1971 and *The Circus* of 1947, are weak in plot, but eloquently lyrical about animals and nature. The stories in her collection, as well as several uncollected pieces, seem, however, her best work. Not only does the short form give a healthy emphasis to her narrative, but also in it she becomes much more playful, and her zany imagination produces a comic style unlike anything else in Irish fiction. She unfortunately does not write enough, she probably writes too quickly and carelessly, and in many ways, therefore, she remains an amateur. But an amateur of something akin to genius.

Nearly as individual as Juanita Casey is Caroline Blackwood who was born in 1931 in Ulster and who is a direct descendant of Richard Brinsley Sheridan. Perhaps she should properly not be included in this essay, for she has only a very few stories which are printed with some sketches and some journalism in her slim volume of 1974, *For All That I Found There.* Her reputation has been made by three short, faulty, dark novels, such as *Great Granny Webster* of 1977. As with Juanita Casey, there is much that is wrong with her work and much that is brilliant.

Certainly also should be mentioned a few writers whose work appeared originally in Irish. Perhaps preeminent is Máirtín Ó Cadhain (1907–70) whose *Road to Bright City* was posthumously translated by Eoghan Ó Tuairisc. Ó Cadhain was much admired for his complicated, eloquent Irish style, but in translation it appears florid and more of a distraction than an aid. The same point might be made of Seamus de Faoite's stories of Kerry, *The More We Are Together.* These stories are told with a command of the devices of eloquence, including parallelism, balance, and so frequently heavy a rhythm that every other quality is submerged in romance and rhetoric. Críostóir Ó Floinn, or O'Flynn when he writes in English, has published poems and plays and fiction. His English collection of stories, *Sanctuary Island*, 1971, has as its first story an account of a writer resembling Edna O'Brien who returns to her native village and gets viciously raped. I found this such a repugnant tale that I have never been able to finish the book.

And finally there is the cultural curiosity of two Americans who went to live in Donegal and wrote books of stories about the still primitive life that they found on mountainy farms. Of these two volumes, Robert Bernen's *Tales from the Blue Stacks*, 1978, is by far the best. It is, in fact, a little gem of sensitive observation and civilized writing. It is written with the scrupulousness of a sociologist and the taste of an artist. Bernen makes us share that "odd sensation to walk along through that remote, primitive region of Europe, in those hills where everything seemed scarcely starting to struggle out of the boundaries of the eighteenth century." We are not only introduced to new facts, but also to realized characters in developed narratives with pertinent themes: the book should become a small classic.

The second American, Anthony Glavin, was born in Boston in 1946 and published his collection called *One for Sorrow* in 1980. Several of his stories reflect old customs and ways, but the author seems a bit like Lady Gregory searching out the quaint. One problem of Glavin's stories is that they are not about very much; one, perhaps symptomatically, is called "Killing Time." A second problem is that the author is less interested in Donegal than in himself; one story, "Of Saints and Scholars," is about an American writer in Donegal who is trying to write a story about Donegal. The texture of Glavin's work is professional enough, but the substance is often arbitrary or thin. But of Bernen's book, one can only say that here is a contribution to Irish literature.

A few writers who have not been touched on perhaps should have been. F. D. Sheridan's slim volume, *Captives,* 1980, starts out with some very slight pieces, but concludes with a couple of substantial ones. Lucile Redmond's *Who Breaks Up the Old Moon to Make New Stars,* 1978, gets overwhelmed with sensitivity, but has one impressive piece. Peter Luke, the English playwright, has recently lived in Ireland; and his *Telling Tales,* 1981, has one memorable comic Irish story. John Feeney's *Mao Dies,* 1977, is pretty slovenly, but one story, which contains a horrendous account of the disposal of a foetus, sticks indelibly and unfortunately in the mind.

● ● ●

After about forty insular years, from the twenties through the fifties, Irish writing has not only been reinvigorated but even to an extent reinvented. When the green curtains began to be opened to the world, both new subject matter and new techniques found an entrance.

What has not, however, happened is the growth of taste and judgment to accommodate the new writing. Pretense and pretentiousness are often valued as highly as solid accomplishment; and several poetic, dramatic, and fictional repuuations have been built on flimsy foundations indeed.

In Ireland, literary judgment about new writing is basically confined to the news media—primarily to a book program on Telefis Eireann, a radio program or two, and the reviews and interviews that appear in the press. The *Irish Times* has for years given considerable space to literature, and the now defunct *Hibernia* for a few years printed some longish reviews of substance. Nevertheless, the media is a poor medium to erect literary standards; of journalistic reviewers only Terence de Vere White has written enough and consistently enough to build up, through his wide knowledge, a sense of credibility. More often, the standards of reviewing are vastly lower, and of the nature either of puffery or of ill-natured and ill-considered dismissal.

The effect of such reviewing on a rapidly changing reading public is alarming. The Republic today has the highest proportion of young people in the E.E.C. Indeed, the *Irish Times* of 5 July 1983 estimated that in Ireland one person out of three is a full-time student. In other words, the reading public is an increasingly young and untutored one; and recent Irish best-seller lists already suggest that this youthful and untutored public is ever more coming to value or at least to accept the meretricious.

This cultural debasement is often abetted by publishers and writers as well as by critics. Some books are published that ought never to have been accepted; some books, particularly from the smaller presses, appear to have been edited by chimpanzees. Simultaneously, some poets, playwrights, and fiction writers thankfully abandon the arcane mysteries of syntax; and the general result is that the literary public grows ever less literate.

There is real merit in the new Irish writing, particularly so in the genre of fiction, but much of the strange new growth flourishing in literary Ireland's four green fields is weeds.

Notes and References

INTRODUCTION

1. V. S. Pritchett, Preface to *New Irish Writing*, ed. David Marcus (London: Quartet Books, 1976), p. 13.

2. J. H. Delargy, "The Gaelic Story-Teller," *Proceedings of the British Academy* 31 (1945); reprinted in 1969 by the University of Chicago for the American Committee on Irish Studies.

3. Vivian Mercier, "The Irish Short Story and Oral Tradition" in *The Celtic Cross*, ed. Browne, Roscelli, and Loftus (West Lafayette, Ind.: Purdue University, 1964), p. 107.

4. Sean O'Faolain, *The Short Story* (Old Greenwich, Conn.: Devin-Adair, 1951), p. 172.

5. Elizabeth Bowen, "Rx for a Story Worth the Telling," *New York Times Book Review,* 31 August 1958, p. 1.

6. Royal A. Gettmann, *Turgenev in England* (Urbana: Illinois Studies in Language and Literature, 1941), p. 148.

7. Leonard Shapiro, *Turgenev: His Life and Times* (New York: Random House, 1978), p. 89.

TALES FROM BIG HOUSE AND CABIN: THE NINETEENTH CENTURY

1. Thomas Flanagan, *The Irish Novelists 1800–1850* (New York: Columbia University Press, 1959), p. 38.

2. Frank O'Connor, *The Lonely Voice: A Study of the Short Story* (New York: World Publishing Co., 1962), p. 37.

3. Edgar Allan Poe, "The Short Story," rev. of *Twice-Told Tales* by Nathaniel Hawthorne; rpt. in *The Portable Edgar Allan Poe,* ed. Philip Van Doren Stern (New York: Viking Press, 1945), p. 566.

4. William Butler Yeats, Introduction to *Representative Irish Tales* (1891; rpt. Atlantic Highlands, N.J.: Humanities Press, 1979), p. 25.

5. *The Autobiography of William Carleton*; quoted in Patrick Rafroidi, "The Irish Short Story in English: The Birth of a New Tradition," in *The Irish Short Story* (Gerrards Cross: Colin Smythe, 1979), p. 34.

6. Ibid., p. 34.

7. Walter Scott, General Preface, *The Waverley Novels* (1829); quoted in Flanagan, *Irish Novelists,* p. 100.

8. Flanagan, *Irish Novelists,* p. 68.

9. Walter Scott, *The Lives of the Novelists*; quoted in O. Elizabeth McWhorter Harden, *Maria Edgeworth's Art of Prose Fiction* (The Hague: Mouton, 1971), p. 63.

10. *The Life and Letters of Maria Edgeworth,* vol. 2 (1895); quoted in Flanagan, *Irish Novelists,* p. 103.

11. Frank O'Connor, *A Short History of Irish Literature: A Backward Look* (New York: Capricorn Books, 1967), p. 146.

12. Thomas Davis, *Essays Literary and Historical,* ed. D. J. O'Donoghue (1914); quoted in Colin Meir, "Voice and Audience in the Early Carleton," *Etudes Irlandaises* 4 (1979):271.

13. Introduction to *Representative Irish Tales,* p. 29.

14. Quoted in Ernest A. Baker, *The History of the English Novel: The Age of Dickens and Thackeray* (London: H. F. & G. Witherby, 1936), p. 32.

15. Flanagan, *Irish Novelists,* p. 256.

16. Ibid., p. 255.

17. Ibid., p. 33.

18. Quoted in Robert E. Lougy, *Charles Robert Maturin* (Lewisburg, Pa.: Bucknell University Press, 1975), p. 66.

19. V. S. Pritchett, Introduction to *In a Glass Darkly* by Joseph Sheridan Le Fanu (London: John Lehman, 1947), p. 8.

20. Ibid., p. 10.

21. Edith Somerville, *Irish Memories* (1917); quoted in John Cronin, *Somerville and Ross* (Lewisburg, Pa; Bucknell University Press, 1972), p. 14.

22. O'Connor, *The Lonely Voice,* p. 34.

IN QUEST OF A NEW IMPULSE:
GEORGE MOORE'S *THE UNTILLED FIELD* AND JAMES JOYCE'S *DUBLINERS*

1. John Eglinton, ed., Introduction to *Letters of George Moore* (Bournemouth: Sydenham, n.d.), p. 14.

2. Richard Ellmann, *James Joyce* (New York: Oxford University Press, 1982), pp. 144–47, 163, 210–11.

3. Helmut E. Gerber, ed., *George Moore in Transition: Letters to T. Fisher Unwin and Lena Milman, 1894–1910,* with a commentary by Helmut E. Gerber (Detroit: Wayne State University Press, 1968), pp. 226–27, 253–54.

4. Introduction, *Letters of George Moore,* p. 14.

5. Joseph Hone. *The Life of George Moore* (New York: Macmillan, 1936), p. 251.

6. George Moore, *Letters to Ed. Dujardin* (New York: Crosby Gaige, 1929), pp. 46–47.

7. Gerber, *Transition,* pp. 231–32.

8. Ibid., p. 221.

9. Ibid., p. 238.

10. Ibid., p. 251.

11. George Moore, *A Communication to My Friends* (London: Nonesuch Press, 1933), p. 83.

12. Gerber, *Transition,* p. 234.

13. Anthony Farrow, *George Moore* (Boston: Twayne, 1978), pp. 114–15.

14. Gerber, *Transition,* pp. 251–52.

15. Ibid., p. 246.

16. Ibid., p. 247.

17. Ibid., p. 249.

18. Moore, *Communication to My Friends,* p. 83.

19. Gerber, *Transition,* p. 247.

20. Avrahm Yarmolinsky, *Turgenev: The Man, His Art and His Age* (New York: Collier Books, 1961), pp. 109–10.

21. Charles Burkhart, "The Short Stories of George Moore," *The Man of Wax: Critical Essays on George Moore,* ed. Douglas Hughes (New York: New York University Press, 1971), pp. 218–25.

22. Moore, *Letters,* p. 62.

23. Gerber, *Transition,* p. 253.

24. Malcolm Brown, *George Moore: A Reconsideration* (Seattle: University of Washington Press, 1955), pp. 168–69.

25. Gerber, *Transition,* p. 263.

26. Ibid., p. 273.

27. Frank O'Connor, *A Short History of Irish Literature: A Backward Look* (New York: G. P. Putman's Sons, 1967), p. 222.

28. Ibid., p. 196.

29. James Joyce, "The Day of the Rabblement," in *The Critical Writings,* ed. Ellsworth Mason and Richard Ellman (New York: Viking Press, 1964), pp. 70–71.

30. James Joyce, *Letters,* vol. 2, ed. Richard Ellmann (New York: Viking Press, 1966), p. 71.

31. Ibid., p. 111.

32. Ibid., p. 106.

33. Arthur Power, *Conversations with James Joyce* (New York: Barnes & Noble, 1974), pp. 56, 94.

34. Ellmann, *Joyce,* p. 617.

35. Joyce, *Letters,* p. 92.

36. Ellmann, *Joyce,* p. 250.

37. Joyce, *Letters,* p. 71.

38. See Karl Beckson, "Moore's *The Untilled Field* and Joyce's *Dubliners*: The Short Story's Intricate Maze," *English Literature in Transition* 15 (1972):291–304; John Raymond Hart, "Moore on Joyce: The Influence of *The Untilled Field* on *Dubliners,*" *Dublin Magazine* 10 (Summer 1973):61–76; Sister Eileen Kennedy, "Moore's *Untilled Field* and Joyce's *Dubliners,*" *Éire-Ireland* 5 (Autumn 1970):81–89. Although both Beckson and Hart compare Dempsey to Joyce's Little Chandler, only Sister Eileen Kennedy develops parallels between "The Clerk's Quest" and "Counterparts," but she refrains from describing Moore's story as the source of Joyce's, as I would do.

39. Joyce, *Letters,* p. 134.

40. Ellmann, *Joyce,* p. 163.

41. Stanislaus Joyce, *My Brother's Keeper: James Joyce's Early Years* (New York: McGraw-Hill, 1964), p. 103–4.

42. Joyce, *Letters,* p. 99.

43. James Joyce, *Stephen Hero* (New York: New Directions, 1963), p. 221.

44. Frank O'Connor, "Work in Progress," in *Dubliners: Text, Criticism, and Notes,* ed. Robert Scholes and A. Walton Litz (New York: Penguin, 1969), p. 305.

45. Edward Brandabur, "The Sisters," in *Dubliners,* pp. 336–37. For a useful summary of these critical excesses, see Thomas E. Connolly, "Joyce's 'The Sisters,'" *James Joyce's Dubliners: A Critical Handbook,* ed. James R. Baker and Thomas F. Staley (Belmont, Calif.: Wadsworth, 1969), pp. 79–86.

46. See Connolly on these interpretations, ibid., pp. 80–81.

47. Florence L. Walzl, "A Date in Joyce's 'The Sisters,'" *Texas Studies in Literature and Language* 4 (Summer 1962):183–87.

48. Brewster Ghiselin, "The Unity of Dubliners," *Twentieth Century Interpretations of Dubliners,* ed. Peter K. Garrett (Englewood Cliffs, N.J.: Prentice-Hall, 1968), pp. 70–71.

49. Joyce, *Letters,* p. 134.

50. I am indebted for this information to Florence L. Walzl's chapter on *Dubliners* in the forthcoming *A Companion to Joyce Studies,* ed. Zack Bowen and James F. Carens.

51. Walzl.

52. James Joyce, *Letters,* vol. 1, ed. Stuart Gilbert (New York: Viking Press, 1957), p. 55.

53. O'Connor, *Dubliners,* p. 307.

54. Zack Bowen, "Hungarian Politics in 'After the Race,'" *James Joyce Quarterly* 7 (Winter 1969)):138–39.

55. Adaline Glasheen, "Clay," in *James Joyce's Dubliners,* ed. Clive Hart (New York: Viking Press, 1969), p. 323.

56. Ghiselin, *Twentieth Century Views,* p. 323.

57. Joyce, *Letters* 1, p. 62.

58. Joyce, *Letters* 2, p. 212.

59. Joyce, *My Brother's Keeper,* p. 228.

60. I am indebted to Florence Walzl's forthcoming chapter in *A Companion to Joyce Studies* for a summary of the various Dantean interpretations.

61. Ghiselin, *Twentieth Century Views,* p. 56.

62. Joyce, *Letters* 2, 166.

63. Ibid.

64. Ellmann, *Joyce,* p. 405–6.

SETTING THE STANDARDS: WRITERS OF THE 1920s AND 1930s

1. O'Flaherty once wrote to his editor Edward Garnett, "I have no style. I don't want any style. I refuse to have a style. I have no time for a style. I think a style is artificial and vulgar." Quoted in Patrick Sheeran, *The Novels of Liam O'Flaherty* (Atlantic Highlands, N.J.: Humanities Press, 1976), p. 104.

2. For a discussion of O'Flaherty's Irish works, see Tomas De Bhaldraithe, "Liam O'Flaherty—Translator?" *Éire-Ireland* 3 (1968):149–53; and Maureen Murphy, "The Double Vision of Liam O'Flaherty," *Éire-Ireland* 8 (1973):20–25.

3. Anthony Whittier, "The Art of Fiction, XIX" *Paris Review* 5, no. 17 (1957):42–64.

4. Edward Garnett, Introduction to *Midsummer Night Madness and Other Stories* (New York: Viking, 1932), p. vii.

5. Sean O'Faolain, "Daniel Corkery," *Dublin Magazine,* n.s. 11 (April 1936):56–57.

MARY LAVIN, ELIZABETH BOWEN, AND A NEW GENERATION: THE IRISH SHORT STORY AT MIDCENTURY

1. Biographical and critical information concerning the life and work of Mary Lavin has been drawn for the most part from the results of research undertaken with the assistance of grants from the American Philosophical Society and the University of Wisconsin-Milwaukee in connection with my full-length study of the genesis and development of Mary Lavin's novels and short fiction (in progress). Specifically, I should like to acknowledge permission to consult Mary Lavin correspondence and manuscripts in the possession of the author; in the Mugar Memorial Library, Boston University; in the Morris Library, University of Southern Illinois; and in the Library of the State University of New York at Binghamton; and I wish to thank the author and the directors of these libraries for their assistance and cooperation. Portions of this essay repeat conclusions expressed in my published essays on Mary Lavin's working methods and achievement as a writer of short fiction (see Bibliography) and my evaluation of her career as a novelist in the *Dictionary of Literary Biography.* I have consulted also studies of Mary Lavin's work by Zack Bowen, Richard F. Peterson, and A. A. Kelly and the Mary Lavin bibliographies discussed below.

2. Mary Lavin's short stories have appeared in a wide variety of English-language magazines, journals, and newspapers, chiefly in Ireland, England, and the United States but also in other parts of the world. Many have been reprinted in textbooks and anthologies; usually revised, most have been collected with new stories not previously published in periodicals in books under the author's name. Entire collections as well as selected stories have been translated for publication in Dutch, German, Hebrew, Walloon, French, Italian, Polish, Russian, and Japanese. Two stories have been scripted for films; one inspired an opera. Critical studies and bibliographies have appeared in English as well as in other languages. In fall 1979, the *Irish University Review* published a special issue in which a number of scholars from different countries reexamined the corpus of Mary Lavin's published fiction and reassessed her work. Although the most recent bibliography (Ruth Krawschak, with the assistance of Regina Mahlke, *Mary Lavin: A Check List,* Berlin, 1979) supersedes the bibliography that appears in this issue of the *Irish University Review,* it is itself in need of updating, not only because additional critical studies have appeared since it was published, but because the author herself is constantly at work—writing new stories, rewriting unfinished stories, and revising stories to be republished.

3. Despite a wide interest in her work in the United States, especially in colleges and universities where there is a particular demand for fiction written by women, Mary Lavin's publishers have been unaccountably lax about issuing her stories in paperback. Only *Tales from Bective Bridge, The Becker Wives,* and a recent Penguin edition of selected titles, the latter limited in distribution to England and Ireland, are available in paperback. Viking Press recently has contracted for a new collection to be published in both hardcover and paperback, but no publication date has yet been announced.

4. For biographical and critical information concerning the life and work of Elizabeth Bowen, I am indebted principally to studies by Alan E. Austin, Victoria Glendinning, William Heath, and Edwin J. Kenny (see Bibliography); I have drawn upon these works also for my essay on Elizabeth Bowen's novels in the *Dictionary of Literary Biography.* My critical evaluation of Elizabeth Bowen's short fiction has been based on my study of her *Collected Stories.*

5. For biographical and critical information concerning the life and work of Benedict Kiely, I am indebted to the work of Daniel Casey, Grace Eckley, John Wilson Foster, Thomas Flanagan, and Mervyn Wall (see Bibliography). My critical evaluation of Benedict Kiely's short fiction has been based on my study of his two volumes of short fiction and *Proxopera,* plus evidence of his own concept of the short story in his *Modern Irish Fiction* (see Bibliography).

6. *The Irish Comic Tradition* (Oxford: Clarendon Press, 1962).

7. For biographical and critical information concerning the life and work of Michael McLaverty, I am indebted to Seamus Heaney's introduction to his *Collected Short Stories* and to the work of John Wilson Foster (see Bibliography). My critical evaluation of his short fiction has been based on my study of his *Collected Short Stories.*

8. Biographical information concerning the life and work of Bryan MacMahon has been drawn from standard references (there being no other sources for such

material). My critical evaluation of his short fiction has been based on my study of his three published collections (see Bibliography).

9. Collectively, the tales, histories, poetry, and so on, contained in Irish manuscripts of the eleventh through seventeenth centuries, the basis of information concerning Old Irish and Middle Irish cultural traditions.

Bibliography

PRIMARY SOURCES

Banim, John and Michael. *The Bit O' Writin' and Other Tales by the O'Hara Family.* 3 vols. London: Saunders & Otley, 1838.

———. *Tales by the O'Hara Family.* 3 vols. London: W. Simpkin & R. Marshall, 1825.

———. *Tales by the O'Hara Family: Second Series.* 3 vols. London: Colburn, 1826.

Beckett, Samuel. *First Love.* London: John Calder, 1973.

———. *Four Novellas.* London: John Calder, 1977.

———. *More Pricks Than Kicks.* London: Chatto & Windus, 1934.

———. *No's Knife.* London: Calder & Boyars, 1966.

Behan, Brendan. *After the Wake.* Edited by Peter Fallon. Dublin Gallery Press, 1981.

———. *Poems and Stories.* Edited by Denis Cotter. Dublin: Liffey Press, 1978.

Bermen, Robert. *The Hills: More Tales from the Blue Stacks,* London: Hamish Hamilton, 1983.

———. *Tales from the Blue Stacks.* London: Hamish Hamilton, 1978.

Blackwood, Caroline. *For All That I Found There.* London: Duckworth, 1973.

Bowen, Elizabeth. *Ann Lee's and Other Stories.* London: Sidgwick & Jackson, 1926; New York: Boni & Liveright, 1926.

———. *The Cat Jumps and Other Stories.* London: Gollancz, 1934.

———. *The Collected Stories of Elizabeth Bowen.* Introduction by Angus Wilson. New York: Knopf, 1981.

———. *A Day in the Dark and Other Stories.* London: Jonathan Cape, 1965.

———. *The Demon Lover and Other Stories.* London: Jonathan Cape, 1945; published in America as *Ivy Gripped the Steps.* New York: Knopf, 1946.

———. *Elizabeth Bowen's Irish Stories.* Introduction by Victoria Glendinning. Dublin: Poolbeg Press, 1978.

———. *Encounters.* London: Sidgwick & Jackson, 1923; New York: Boni & Liveright, 1925.

———. *Joining Charles and Other Stories.* London: Constable, 1929; New York: Dial, 1929.

———. *Look at All Those Roses.* London: Gollancz, 1941; New York: Knopf, 1941.

———. *Stories.* New York: Vintage, 1959.

Boyle, Patrick. *All Looks Yellow to the Jaundiced Eye.* London: MacGibbon & Kee, 1969.

————. *At Nights All Cats Are Grey.* London: MacGibbon & Kee, 1966.

————. *A View from Calvary.* London: Victor Gollancz, 1976.

Burke, Helen Lucy, *A Season for Mothers.* Dublin: Poolbeg Press, 1980.

Carleton, William. *Tales of Ireland.* Dublin: William Curry, 1834.

————. *Tales and Sketches.* Dublin: J. Duffy, 1845.

————. *Traits and Stories of the Irish Peasantry. First Series.* 2 vols. Dublin: William Curry, 1830.

————. *Traits and Stories of Irish Peasantry. Second Series.* 3 vols. Dublin: William Wakeman, 1833.

Carroll, Paul Vincent. *Irish Stories and Plays.* New York: Devin-Adair, 1958.

Casey, Juanita, *Hath the Rain a Father?* London: Phoenix House, 1966.

Cleeve, Brian. *The Horse Thieves of Ballysaggart.* Cork: Mercier Press, 1966.

Cooke, Emma. *Female Forms.* Dublin: Poolbeg Press, 1980.

Corkery, Daniel. *Earth out of Earth.* Dublin: Talbot Press, 1939.

————. *The Hounds of Banba.* Dublin: Talbot Press, 1920; New York: Huebsch, 1922.

————. *A Munster Twilight.* Dublin: Talbot Press, 1916; New York: Stokes, 1917.

————. *The Stormy Hills.* Dublin: Talbot Press, 1929; London: Cape, 1929.

————. *The Wager and Other Stories.* New York: Devin-Adair, 1950.

Daly, Ita. *The Lady with the Red Shoes.* Dublin: Poolbeg Press, 1980.

de Faoite, Seamus. *The More We Are Together.* Dublin: Poolbeg Press, 1980.

Edgeworth, Maria. *Castle Rackrent. An Hibernian Tale.* London: J. Johnson, 1800.

————. *Tales of Fashionable Life.* 6 vols. London: J. Johnson, 1809–12.

Feeney, John. *Mao Dies.* Dublin: Egotist Press, 1977.

Friel, Brian. *The Gold in the Sea.* London: Gollancz, 1966.

————. *The Saucer of Larks.* London: Gollancz, 1962.

Glavin, Anthony. *One for Sorrow.* Dublin: Poolbeg Press, 1980.

Griffin, Gerald. *Holland-Tide; or, Munster Popular Tales.* London: W. Simplin & R. Marshall, 1827.

————. *Tales of the Munster Festivals.* 3 vols. London: Saunders & Otley, 1827.

————. *Tales of My Neighborhood.* 3 vols. London: Saunders & Otley, 1835.

Hall, Mrs. S. C. *Sketches of Irish Character.* 2 vols. London: F. Westley & A. H. Davis, 1829.

————. *Sketches of Irish Character, Second Series.* London: F. Westley & A. H. Davis, 1831.

————. *Stories of the Irish Peasantry.* Edinburgh: W. & R. Chambers, 1850.

Healy, Dermot. *Banished Misfortune.* London: Allison & Busby; Dingle: Brandon, 1982.

Higgins, Aidan. *Asylum.* London: John Calder; Dallas: Riverrun Press, 1978. Revised edition of *Felo de Se/Killachter Meadow.*

Hogan, Desmond. *Children of Lir.* London: Hamish Hamilton, 1981.

————. *The Diamonds at the Bottom of the Sea.* London: Hamish Hamilton, 1979.

————. *Stories.* London: Pan Books, 1982. Paperback edition of the two above volumes.

Jordan, John. *Yarns.* Dublin: Poolbeg Press, 1977.

Jordan, Neil. *Night in Tunisia.* Dublin: Co-op Books, 1976.

Joyce, James. *Dubliners: Text, Criticism, and Notes.* Edited by Robert Scholes and A. Walton Litz. The Viking Critical Library. New York: Penguin Books, 1969.

Keane, John B. *Death Be Not Proud.* Cork: Mercier Press, 1976.

———. *Stories from a Kerry Fireside.* Dublin: Mercier Press, 1980.

Kelly, Maeve. *A Life of Her Own.* Dublin: Poolbeg Press, 1976.

Kiely, Benedict. *A Ball of Malt and Madame Butterfly: A Dozen Stories.* London: Gollancz, 1973.

———. *A Journey to the Seven Streams: Seventeen Stories.* London: Methuen, 1963.

———. *Modern Irish Fiction—A Critique.* Dublin: Golden Eagle Books, 1950.

———. *Proxopera.* London: Gollancz, 1977.

———. *The State of Ireland: A Novella and Seventeen Stories.* Introduction by Thomas Flanagan. Boston: D. R. Godine, 1980. Reprinted in England, the United States, Australia, Canada, and New Zealand, 1982.

Lavin, Mary. *At Sallygap and Other Stories.* Boston: Little, Brown, 1947.

———. *The Becker Wives and Other Stories.* London: Michael Joseph, 1946.

———. *Collected Stories.* Boston: Houghton Mifflin, 1971.

———. *The Great Wave and Other Stories.* London and New York: Macmillan, 1961.

———. *Happiness and Other Stories.* London: Constable, 1969; Boston: Houghton Mifflin, 1970.

———. *In the Middle of the Fields.* London: Constable, 1967; New York: Macmillan, 1969.

———. *The Long Ago and Other Stories.* London: Michael Joseph, 1944.

———. *Mary Lavin Selected Stories.* Harmondsworth: Penguin, 1981.

———. *A Memory and Other Stories.* London: Constable, 1972; Boston: Houghton Mifflin, 1973.

———. *The Patriot Son and Other Stories.* London: Michael Joseph, 1956.

———. *Selected Stories.* New York: Macmillan, 1959.

———. *The Shrine and Other Stories.* London: Constable, 1977; Boston: Houghton Mifflin, 1977.

———. *A Single Lady and Other Stories.* London: Michael Joseph, 1951.

———. *The Stories of Mary Lavin.* Vol. 1. London: Constable, 1964, 1970.

———. *The Stories of Mary Lavin.* Vol. 2. London: Constable, 1974.

———. *Tales from Bective Bridge.* Boston: Little, Brown, 1942; London: Michael Joseph, 1943; London: Readers' Union, 1945; Stuttgart: Tauchnitz, 1952: (revised) Dublin: Poolbeg Press, 1978.

Le Fanu, Joseph Sheridan. *Ghost Stories and Tales of Mystery.* Dublin: James McGlashan, 1851.

———. *In A Glass Darkly.* 3 vols. London: Bentley, 1872.

———. *The Purcell Papers.* 3 vols. London: Bentley, 1880.

Luke, Peter. *Telling Tales.* The Curragh: Goldsmith Press, 1981.

Mac Intyre, Tom. *Dance the Dance.* London: Faber & Faber, 1970.

————. *The Harper's Turn*. Dublin: Gallery Press, 1972.

Macken, Walter. *The Coll Doll*. London: Macmillan, 1969.

————. *God Made Sunday*. London: Macmillan, 1962.

————. *The Green Hills*. London: Macmillan, 1965.

MacMahon, Bryan. *The End of the World and Other Stories*. Dublin: Poolbeg Press, 1976.

————. *The Lion-Tamer and Other Stories*. Toronto: Macmillan, 1948; New York: E. P. Dutton, 1949–58; London: Dent, 1958.

————. *The Red Petticoat and Other Stories*. New York: E. P. Dutton; London: Macmillan, 1955.

Manning, Mary. *The Last Chronicles of Ballyfungus*. Boston: Houghton Mifflin, 1978.

Maturin, Charles Robert. *Melmoth the Wanderer*. 4 vols. Edinburgh: Chambers; London: Hurst & Robinson, 1820.

McArdle, John. *It's Handy When People Don't Die*. Dublin: Poolbeg Press, 1981.

McAughtry, Sam. *Belfast*. Dublin: Ward River Press, 1981.

————. *Blind Spot*. Belfast: Blackstaff Press, 1979.

McCabe, Eugene. *Heritage*. London: Gollancz, 1978.

McGahern, John. *Getting Through*. London: Faber & Faber, 1978.

————. *Nightlines*. London: Faber & Faber, 1970.

McLaverty, Bernard. *Secrets*. Belfast: Blackstaff Press, 1977.

————. *A Time to Dance*. Dublin: O'Brien Press, 1982.

McLaverty, Michael. *Collected Short Stories*. Introduction By Seamus Heaney. Dublin: Poolbeg Press, 1978.

Montague, John. *Death of a Chieftain*. London: MacGibbon & Kee, 1964.

Moore, George. *A Story Teller's Holiday*. New York: Liveright, 1928.

————. *The Untilled Field*. London: T. Fisher Urwin, 1903.

————. *The Untilled Field*. London: Heinemann, 1914.

Morrow, John. *Northern Myths*. Belfast: Blackstaff Press, 1979.

Mulkerns, Val. *Antiquities*. London: Andrew Deutsch, 1978.

————. *An Idle Woman*. Dublin: Poolbeg Press, 1980.

Noonan, Gillman. *Friends and Occasional Lovers*. Dublin: Poolbeg Press, 1982.

————. *A Sexual Relationship*. Dublin: Poolbeg Press, 1976.

O'Brien, Edna. *The Love Object*. London: Jonathan Cape, 1968.

————. *Mrs. Reinhardt*. London: Weidenfeld & Nicolson, 1978.

————. *Returning*. London: Weidenfeld & Nicolson, 1982.

————. *A Scandalous Woman*. London: Weidenfeld & Nicolson, 1974.

O'Brien, Kate Cruise. *A Gift Horse*. Dublin: Poolbeg Press, 1978.

O'Cadhain, Máirtin. *The Road to Bright City*. Translated by Eoghan O'Tuairisc. Dublin: Poolbeg Press, 1981.

O'Conaire, Padraic. *15 Short Stories Translated from the Irish* (by Con Houlihan et al.). Dublin: Poolbeg Press, 1982.

O'Connor, Frank. *The Backward Look: A Survey of Irish Literature*. London: Macmillan, 1963; New York: Putnam, 1967.

————. *Bones of Contention*. London: Macmillan, 1936; New York: Macmillan, 1936.

————. *Collected Stories.* New York: Knopf, 1981.

————. *Collection Two.* London: Macmillan, 1964.

————. *Collection Three.* London: Macmillan, 1969.

————. *The Common Chord.* London: Macmillan, 1947; New York: Knopf, 1948.

————. *The Cornet Player Who Betrayed Ireland.* Dublin: Poolbeg Press, 1981.

————. *Crab Apple Jelly.* London: Macmillan, 1944; New York: Knopf, 1944.

————. *Domestic Relations.* New York: Knopf, 1957; London: Hamish Hamilton, 1957.

————. *Guests of the Nation.* London: Macmillan, 1931; New York; Macmillan, 1931.

————. *The Lonely Voice.* Cleveland: World, 1962; London: Macmillan, 1963.

————. *The Mirror in the Roadway.* New York: Knopf, 1956; London: Hamish Hamilton, 1957.

————. *More Stories by Frank O'Connor.* New York: Knopf, 1954.

————. *My Father's Son.* London: Macmillan, 1968; New York: Knopf, 1969.

————. *An Only Child.* New York: Knopf, 1962; London: Macmillan, 1962.

————. *A Set of Variations.* New York: Knopf, 1969.

————. *The Stories of Frank O'Connor.* New York: Knopf, 1952; London: Hamish Hamilton, 1953.

————. *Towards an Appreciation of Literature.* Dublin: Metropolitan, 1945.

————. *Traveller's Samples.* London: Macmillan, 1951; New York: Knopf, 1951.

O'Faolain, Julia. *Daughters of Passion.* Harmondsworth, Middlesex: Penguin, 1982.

————. *Man in the Cellar.* London: Faber & Faber, 1974.

————. *Melancholy Baby.* Dublin: Poolbeg Press, 1978. Paperback collection of the Irish stories in *Man in the Cellar* and *We Might See Sights.*

————. *We Might See Sights.* London: Faber & Faber, 1968.

O'Faolain, Sean. *Collected Stories.* 3 vols. London: Constable, 1980–82.

————. *The Finest Stories of Sean O'Faolain.* Boston: Little, Brown, 1957; London: Robert Hart-Davis, 1958.

————. *Foreign Affairs and Other Stories.* London: Constable, 1976.

————. *The Heat of the Sun.* Boston: Little, Brown, 1966; London: Hart-Davis, 1966.

————. *The Man Who Invented Sin and Other Stories.* New York: Devin-Adair, 1948.

————. *Midsummer Night Madness and Other Stories.* London: Jonathan Cape, 1932; New York: Viking, 1932.

————. *A Purse of Coppers.* London: Jonathan Cape, 1937; New York: Viking, 1938.

————. *The Short Story.* London: Collins, 1948; New York: Devin-Adair, 1951.

————. *The Talking Trees and Other Stories.* London: Jonathan Cape, 1971.

————. *Teresa and Other Stories.* London: Jonathan Cape, 1947.

————. *Vive Moi!* Boston: Little, Brown, 1965.

O'Flaherty, Liam. *Duil (Desire).* Baile Átha Cliath (Dublin): Sáirséal agus Dill, 1953.

————. *The Mountain Tavern and Other Stories.* London: Jonathan Cape, 1929; New York: Harcourt Brace, 1929.

————. *The Short Stories of Liam O'Flaherty.* London: Jonathan Cape, 1937.

————. *Spring Sowing.* London: Jonathan Cape, 1924; New York: Knopf, 1926.

————. *The Stories of Liam O'Flaherty.* New York: Devin-Adair, 1956.

————. *The Tent.* London: Jonathan Cape, 1926.

————. *Two Lovely Beasts and Other Stories.* London: Victor Gollancz, 1948; New York: Devin-Adair, 1950.

O'Flynn, Criostoir. *Sanctuary Island.* Dublin: Gill & Macmillan, 1971.

O'Kelly, Seumas. *By the Stream of Killmeen.* Dublin: Sealy, Bryers & Walker, 1906.

————. *The Golden Barque and the Weaver's Grave.* Dublin: Talbot Press, 1919.

————. *Hillsiders.* Dublin: Talbot Press, 1921.

————. *A Land of Loneliness & Other Stories.* Dublin: Gill & Macmillan, 1969.

————. *The Leprechaun of Killmeen.* Dublin: Martin Lester, 1918.

————. *Waysiders.* Dublin: Talbot Press, 1917.

Power, Brian. *A Land Not Sown.* Dublin: Egotist Press, 1977.

————. *The Wild and Daring Sixties.* Dublin: Egotist Press, 1980.

Plunkett, James. *Collected Short Stories.* Dublin: Poolbeg Press, 1977.

————. *The Eagle and the Trumpets.* Dublin: The Bell, 1954.

————. *The Trusting and the Maimed.* New York: Devin-Adair, 1955.

Redmond, Lucile. *Who Breaks Up the Old Moons to Make New Stars.* Enniskerry: Egotist Press, 1978.

Sheridan, F. D. *Captives.* Dublin: Co-op Books, 1980.

Somerville, Edith, and Ross, Martin. *Further Experiences of an Irish R. M.* London: Longman, 1908.

————. *In Mr. Knox's Country.* London: Longman, 1915.

————. *Some Experiences of an Irish R. M.* London: Longman, 1899.

Strong, Eithne. *Patterns.* Dublin: Poolbeg Press, 1981.

Treacy, Maura. *Sixpence in Her Shoe.* Dublin: Poolbeg Press, 1977.

Trevor, William. *Angels at the Ritz.* London: Bodley Head, 1975.

————. *The Ballroom of Romance.* London: Bodley Head, 1972.

————. *Beyond the Pale.* London: Bodley Head, 1982.

————. *The Day We Got Drunk on Cake.* London: Bodley Head, 1966.

————. *The Distant Past.* Dublin: Poolbeg Press, 1975. Paperback selection of Trevor's Irish stories.

————. *Lovers of Their Time.* London: Bodley Head, 1978.

————. *The Stories of William Trevor.* Harmondsworth, Middlesex: Penguin, 1983.

Wall, Mervyn. *A Flutter of Wings.* Dublin: Talbot Press, 1974.

West, Anthony C. *All the King's Horses.* Dublin: Poolbeg Press, 1981.

————. *River's End.* New York: McDowell, Oblonsky, 1958.

White, Terence de Vere. *Big Fleas and Little Fleas.* London: Gollancz, 1974.

————. *Chimes at Midnight.* London: Gollancz, 1978.

ANTHOLOGIES

Barr, Fiona; Walsh, Barbara Haycock; and Mahon, Stella. *Sisters.* Belfast: Blackstaff Press, 1980.

Casey, Kevin, ed. *Winter's Tales from Ireland,* 2. Dublin: Gill & Macmillan, 1972.

Forkner, Ben, ed. *Modern Irish Short Stories.* London: Michael Joseph, 1981.

Kiely, Benedict, ed. *The Penguin Book of Irish Short Stories.* Harmondsworth, Middlesex: Penguin, 1981.

Marcus, David, ed. *Best Irish Short Stories,* 1. London: Paul Elek, 1976.

————. *Best Irish Short Stories,* 2. London: Paul Elek, 1977.

————. *Best Irish Short Stories,* 3. London: Paul Elek, 1978.

————. *Body and Soul.* Dublin: Poolbeg Press, 1979.

————. *The Bodley Head Book of Irish Short Stories.* London: Bodley Head, 1980; reissued as two-volume paperback entitled *Irish Short Stories.* London: New English Library, 1982.

————. *Modern Irish Love Stories.* London: Pan Books, 1974.

————. *New Irish Writing.* London: Quartet Books, 1976.

————. *New Irish Writing,* 1. Dublin: Dolmen Press. 1970.

————. *The Sphere Book of Modern Irish Short Stories.* London: Sphere, 1972.

Martin, Augustine, ed. *Winter's Tales from Ireland,* 1. Dublin: Gill & Macmillan, 1970.

Maxwell House Women's Writing Contest. *The Adultery.* Dublin: Arlen House, 1982.

————. *A Dream Recurring.* Dublin: Arlen House, 1980.

————. *The Wall Reader.* Dublin: Arlen House, 1979.

Vorm, William. *Paddy No More.* Mass.: Longship Press, 1977.

SECONDARY SOURCES

Allen, Walter. *The Short Story in English.* Oxford: Clarendon Press, 1981; New York: Oxford University Press, 1981.

Austin, Alan E. *Elizabeth Bowen.* New York: Twayne, 1971.

Averill, Deborah M. *The Irish Short Story from George Moore to Frank O'Connor.* Washington: University Press of America, 1982.

Baker, Ernest A. *The History of the English Novel: Edgeworth, Austen, Scott.* London: H. F. & G. Witherby, 1935.

————. *The History of the English Novel: The Age of Dickens and Thackeray.* London: H. F. & G. Witherby, 1936.

Baker, Joseph E. "The Trinity in Joyce's 'Grace.'" *James Joyce Quarterly* 2 (Summer 1965):299–303.

Bates, H. E. *The Modern Short Story: A Critical Survey.* London: Thomas Nelson, 1941.

Beachcroft, T. O. *The Modest Art: A Survey of the Short Story in English.* London and New York: Oxford University Press, 1968.

Beckett, J. C. *The Making of Modern Ireland.* New York: Knopf, 1966; London: Faber, 1966.

Beckson, Karl. "Moore's *Untilled Field* and Joyce's *Dubliners.*" *English Literature in Transition* 15 (1972):291–304.

Begnal, Michael H. *Joseph Sheridan Le Fanu.* Lewisburg, Pa.: Bucknell University Press, 1971.

Blissett, William F. "George Moore and Literary Wagnerism." *Comparative Literature* 12 (Winter 1961):52–71.

Bowen, Elizabeth. "Rx for a Story Worth the Telling." *New York Times Book Review,* 31 August 1958, pp. 1, 13.

Bowen, Zack. "Hungarian Politics in 'After the Race.'" *James Joyce Quarterly* 7 (Winter 1969):138–39.

———. *Mary Lavin.* Irish Writers Series. Lewisburg, Pa.: Bucknell University Press, 1975.

Boyd, Ernest A. *Ireland's Literary Renaissance.* New York: Knopf, 1922.

Boyle, Robert. "Swiftian Allegory and Dantean Parody in Joyce's 'Grace.'" *James Joyce Quarterly* 7 (Fall 1969):11–21.

Bramsback, Birgit. *James Stephens: A Literary and Bibliographical Study.* Uppsala: A. B. Lundequistska Bokhandeln, 1959.

Brown, Malcolm. *George Moore: A Reconsideration.* Seattle: University of Washington Press, 1955.

Brown, Terence. *Ireland: A Social and Cultural History, 1922–79.* London: Fontana, 1981.

Browne, Nelson. *Sheridan Le Fanu.* London: Arthur Barker, 1951.

Burkhart, Charles. "The Short Stories of George Moore." In *The Man of Wax: Critical Essays on George Moore.* Edited by Douglas Hughes. New York: New York University Press, 1971, pp. 217–31.

Casey, Daniel J. *Benedict Kiely.* Irish Writers Series. Lewisburg, Pa.: Bucknell University Press, 1974.

Caswell, Robert. "The Human Heart's Vagaries. " *Kilkenny Magazine* 12–13 (Spring 1965):69–89.

———. "Mary Lavin: Breaking a Pathway." *Dublin Magazine* 6, no. 2 (Summer 1967):32–44.

———. "Irish Political Reality and Mary Lavin's *Tales From Bective Bridge.*" *Éire-Ireland* 3, no. 1 (Spring 1968):48–60.

Connolly, Thomas E. "Joyce's 'The Sisters.'" In *James Joyce's Dubliners: A Critical Handbook.* Edited by James R. Baker and Thomas F. Staley. Belmont, Calif.: Wadsworth, 1969, pp. 79–86.

Costello, Peter. *The Heart Grown Brutal.* Dublin: Gill & Macmillan, 1977; Totowa, N.J.: Barnes & Noble, 1977.

Croker, Thomas Crofton. *Fairy Legends and Traditions in the South of Ireland.* 3 vols. London: Murray, 1825–28.

Cronin, John. *Gerald Griffin (1803–1840): A Critical Biography.* Cambridge: Cambridge University Press, 1978.

———. *Somerville and Ross.* Lewisburg, Pa.: Bucknell University Press, 1972.

DeBhaldraithe, Tomas. "Liam O'Flaherty—Translator(?)" *Éire-Ireland* 3 (1968):149–53.

Delargy, J. H. "The Gaelic Story-Teller." *Proceedings of the British Academy* 31 (1945). Reprinted in 1969 by the University of Chicago for the American Committee on Irish Studies.

Doyle, Paul A. *Sean O'Faolain.* New York: Twayne, 1968.

————. *Liam O'Flaherty.* New York: Twayne, 1971.

Dunleavy, Janet Egleson. "The Fiction of Mary Lavin: Universal Sensibility in a Particular Milieu." *Irish University Review* 7, no. 2 (Autumn 1977):222–36.

————. "The Making of Mary Lavin's 'Happiness.'" *Irish University Review* 9, no. 2 (Autumn 1979):225–31.

————. "The Making of Mary Lavin's 'A Memory.'" *Éire-Ireland* 12, no. 3 (Fall 1977):90–99.

Eckley, Grace. *Benedict Kiely.* New York: Twayne, 1975.

Ellmann, Richard. *James Joyce,* Rev. ed. New York: Oxford University Press, 1982.

Fallis, Richard. *The Irish Literary Renaissance.* Syracuse: Syracuse University Press, 1977.

Farrow, Anthony. *George Moore.* Twayne's English Authors Series. Boston: Twayne, 1978.

Finneran, Richard, ed. *Anglo-Irish Literature, a Review of Research.* New York: Modern Language Association of America, 1976.

————. *Recent Research on Anglo-Irish Writers.* New York: Modern Language Association of America, 1983.

Flanagan, Thomas. "Frank O'Connor: 1903–1966." *Kenyon Review* 28 (1966): 439–55.

————. *The Irish Novelists, 1800–1850.* New York: Columbia University Press, 1959.

————. Introduction to *The State of Ireland* by Benedict Kiely (q.v.).

Foster, John Wilson. *Forces and Themes in Ulster Fiction.* Dublin: Gill & Macmillan; Totowa, N.J.: Rowman & Littlefield, 1974.

Gerber, Helmut E., ed. *George Moore in Transition: Letters to T. Fisher Unwin and Lena Milman, 1894–1910.* Detroit: Wayne State University Press, 1968.

Gettmann, Royal A. *Turgenev in England and America.* Urbana: Illinois Studies in Language and Literature, 1941.

Ghiselin, Brewster. "The Unity of *Dubliners.*" In *Twentieth Century Interpretations of Dubliners.* Edited by Peter K. Garrett. Englewood Cliffs, N.J.: Prentice-Hall, 1968, pp. 57–85.

Glasheen, Adaline. "Clay." In *James Joyce's Dubliners.* Edited by Clive Hart. New York: Viking Press, 1969, pp. 100–106.

Glendinning, Victoria. *Elizabeth Bowen: Portrait of Writer.* London: Weidenfeld & Nicholson, 1977; New York: Knopf, 1978.

Gwynn, Stephen. *Irish Literature and Drama in the English Language: A Short History.* London: Thomas Nelson, 1936.

Harden, O. Elizabeth McWhorter. *Maria Edgeworth's Art of Prose Fiction.* The Hague: Mouton, 1971.

Harmon, Maurice. *Sean O'Faolain: A Critical Introduction.* South Bend, Ind.: University of Notre Dame Press, 1966.

————. ed. "Mary Lavin Special Issue." *Irish University Review* 9 (Autumn 1979).

————. ed. "Sean O'Faolain Special Issue." *Irish University Review* 6 (Spring 1976).

Harris, Wendell V. *British Short Fiction in the Nineteenth Century.* Detroit: Wayne State University Press, 1979.

Hart, John Raymond. "Moore on Joyce: The Influence of *The Untilled Field* on *Dubliners.*" *Dublin Magazine* 10 (Summer 1973):61–76.

Heath, William. *Elizabeth Bowen: An Introduction to Her Novels.* Madison: University of Wisconsin Press, 1961.

Henderson, Gordon. "An Interview with Bryan MacMahon." *Journal of Irish Literature* 3 (September 1974):3–23.

Hone, Joseph. *The Life of George Moore.* New York: Macmillan, 1936.

Howarth, Herbert. *The Irish Writers, 1880–1940.* London: Rockcliff, 1958; New York: Hill & Wang, 1959.

Hughes, Douglas A., ed. *The Man of Wax: Critical Essays on George Moore.* New York: New York University Press, 1971.

Jack, Ian. *English Literature 1815–1832.* Oxford: Clarendon Press, 1963.

Joyce, James. *The Critical Writings.* Edited by Ellsworth Mason and Richard Ellmann. New York: Viking Press, 1964.

———. *Letters.* Vol. 1. Edited by Stuart Gilbert. New York: Viking Press, 1957.

———. *Letters.* Vol. 2. Edited by Richard Ellmann. New York: Viking Press, 1966.

———. *Stephen Hero.* Edited by Theodore Spencer. New York: New Directions, 1963.

Kelley. A. A. *Mary Lavin: Quiet Rebel.* Dublin: Wolfhound, 1981.

Kennedy, Eileen. "Moore's *Untilled Field* and Joyce's *Dubliners.*" *Éire-Ireland* 5 (1970):81–89.

———. "Turgenev and George Moore's *The Untilled Field.*" *English Literature in Transition* 18 (1975):145–59.

Kenner, Hugh. *A Colder Eye.* New York: Knopf, 1983.

Kenny, Edwin J. *Elizabeth Bowen.* Irish Writers Series. Lewisburg, Pa.: Bucknell University Press, 1975.

Kiely, Benedict. *Modern Irish Fiction—A Critique.* Dublin: Golden Eagle Books, 1950.

Kilroy, James F. "Irish Short Stories, Past and Present." *Sewanee Review* 90, no. 1 (Winter 1982):89–100.

Krawschak, Ruth, with the assistance of Regina Mahlke. *Mary Lavin: A Check List.* Berlin, 1979.

Lawless, Emily. *Maria Edgeworth.* London: Macmillan, 1904.

Lee, Hermione. *Elizabeth Bowen, an Estimation.* London: Vision Press, 1981; Totowa, N.J.: Barnes & Noble, 1981.

Lougy, Robert E. *Charles Robert Maturin.* Lewisburg, Pa: Bucknell University Press, 1975.

Lyons, F. S. L. *Ireland Since the Famine.* London: Weidenfeld & Nicolson, 1971; New York: Scribner, 1971.

Martin, Augustine. "A Skeleton Key to the Stories of Mary Lavin." *Studies* 54, no. 208 (Winter 1963):393–406.

———. *James Stephens: A Critical Study.* Dublin: Gill & Macmillan, 1977.

Matthews, James H. *Frank O'Connor.* Lewisburg, Pa.: Bucknell University Press, 1976.

―――. "Women, War and Words: Frank O'Connor's First Confessions." *Irish Renaissance Annual* 1 (1980):73–112.

―――. *Voices: A Life of Frank O'Connor.* New York: Atheneum, 1983.

Meir, Colin. "Voice and Audience in the Early Carleton." *Etudes Irlandaises* 4(1979):271–86.

Mercier, Vivian. *The Irish Comic Tradition.* Oxford: Clarendon Press, 1962.

―――. "The Irish Short Story and Oral Tradition." In *The Celtic Cross: Studies in Irish Culture and Literature.* Edited by R. B. Browne, William J. Roscelli, and Richard Loftus. Lafayette, Ind.: Purdue University Studies, 1964, pp. 98–116.

Moore, George. *Celibate Lives.* London: Heinemann, 1937.

―――. *A Communication to My Friends.* London: Nonesuch Press, 1933.

―――. *Letters of George Moore* [to John Eglinton]. Edited by John Eglinton. Bournemouth: Sydenham, n.d.

―――. *Letters to Ed. Dujardin.* New York: Crosby Gaige, 1929.

Murphy, Maureen O. "The Double Vision of Liam O'Flaherty." *Éire-Ireland* 8 (1973):20–25.

O'Connor, Frank. "A Good Short Story Must Be News." *New York Times Book Review,* 10 June 1956, pp. 1, 20.

O'Donnell, Donat (pseud. of Conor Cruise O'Brien). *Maria Cross.* London and New York: Oxford University Press, 1952.

O'Faolain, Sean. "Daniel Corkery." *Dublin Magazine,* n.s. 11 (April 1936):49–61.

―――. "Don Quixote O'Flaherty," *London Mercury* 37 (December 1937):170–75.

Owens, Graham, ed. *George Moore's Mind and Art.* Edinburgh: Oliver & Boyd, 1968; New York: Barnes & Noble, 1970.

Peterson, Richard F. "Frank O'Connor and the Modern Irish Short Story." *Modern Fiction Studies* 28 (1982): 53–67.

―――. *Mary Lavin,* Twayne English Authors Series. Boston: Twayne, 1978.

Power, Arthur. *Conversations with James Joyce.* New York: Barnes & Noble, 1974.

Prosky, Murray. "The Pattern of Diminishing Certitude in the Stories of Frank O'Connor." *Colby Library Quarterly* 9 (1970):311–21.

Pyle, Hilary. *James Stephens: His Works and an Account of His Life.* London: Routledge & Kegan Paul, 1965; New York: Barnes & Noble, 1965.

Rafroidi, Patrick. *L'Irlande et le Romantisme.* Paris: Editions Universitaires, 1972.

Rafroidi, Patrick, and Brown, Terence, eds. *The Irish Short Story.* Gerrards Cross: Colin Smythe, 1979.

―――. *The Irish Short Story.* Lille, France: Université de Lille, 1979.

Reid, Ian. *The Short Story.* London: Methuen, 1977.

Renwick, W. L. *English Literature 1789–1815.* Oxford: Clarendon Press, 1963.

Rippier, Joseph Storey. *The Short Stories of Sean O'Faolain.* New York: Barnes & Noble, 1976.

Robinson, Hilary. *Somerville & Ross: A Critical Appraisal.* Dublin: Gill & Macmillan, 1980; New York: St. Martins, 1980.

Sadleir, Michael. *XIX Century Fiction: A Bibliographical Record.* 2 vols. Cambridge: Cambridge University Press, 1951.

Saul, George Brandon. *Daniel Corkery.* Lewisburg, Pa.: Bucknell University Press, 1973.

————. *Rushlight Heritage.* Philadelphia: Walton Press, 1969.

————. *Seumas O'Kelly.* Lewisburg, Pa.: Bucknell University Press, 1971.

————. "A Wild Sowing: The Short Stories of Liam O'Flaherty." *A Review of English Literature* 4 (July 1963):108–113.

Schleifer, Ronald, ed. *The Genres of the Irish Literary Revival.* Norman, Okla.: Pilgrim Books, 1980.

Scholes, Robert, and Kellogg, Robert. *The Nature of Narrative.* New York: Oxford University Press, 1966.

Sellery, J'nan M., and Harris, William C. *Elizabeth Bowen: A Descriptive Bibliography.* Austin: Texas University Press, 1977.

Shapiro, Leonard. *Turgenev, His Life and Works.* New York: Random House, 1978.

Sheehy, Maurice, ed. *Michael/Frank: Studies on Frank O'Connor.* London & Dublin: Macmillan, 1969; New York, Knopf, 1969.

Thompson, Richard J. "A Kingdom of Commoners: The Moral Art of Frank O'Connor," *Éire-Ireland* 8 (1978):65–80.

Titley, Alan. "The Disease of the Irish Short Story." *Beau,* no. 1 (1981), pp. 40-52.

Tomory, William M. *Frank O'Connor.* Boston: Twayne, 1980.

Walzl, Florence L. "A Date in Joyce's 'The Sisters.'" *Texas Studies in Literature and Language* 4 (Summer 1962):183–87.

Watson, George. Introduction to *Castle Rackrent* by Maria Edgeworth. London: Oxford University Press, 1969, pp. vii–xxv.

Whittier, Anthony. "The Art of Fiction: Frank O'Connor." *Paris Review* 5, no. 17 (1958):42–64.

Wohlgelernter, Maurice. *Frank O'Connor: An Introduction.* New York: Columbia University Press, 1977.

Wolff, Robert Lee. *William Carleton, Irish Peasant Novelist: A Preface to His Fiction.* New York: Garland Publishing, 1980.

Yarmolinsky, Avrahm. *Turgenev: The Man, His Art and His Age.* New York: Collier Books, 1961.

Yeats, William Butler. Introduction to *Representative Irish Tales* (1891). Rpt. in *Representative Irish Tales.* Atlantic Highlands, N.J.: Humanities Press, 1979, pp. 25–32.

————. Introduction to *Stories from Carleton* (1889). Rpt. in *Representative Irish Tales.* Atlantic Highlands, N.J.: Humanities Press, 1979, pp. 359–64.

Zneimer, John. *The Literary Vision of Liam O'Flaherty.* Syracuse: Syracuse University Press, 1970.

Index